I SEE YOU

I see you.

You do not see me.

Born of the ancient She Buh,
I am older than my once-living tree.

Vacant eyes watch and wait for fire
Evaporating all remnant of
The spirit through me who once spoke.

Now I am worn on white static walls.

I dwell in the shade of rooms,
Where imposters come and go staring
At the beauty queen preening
No longer of consequence.

Beware the lessons of shutting
Down all that matters, burrowing
With primeval taproots hungry to
Eat the food in rotting crypts:
Graveyards of the lost divine.

ANCESTORS

Published by Compound Press.
Printed in the United States of America.
First printing, 2022.
Cover and book design by Karen Sketch
www.jancthorpeauthor.com

ANCESTORS

JAN C. THORPE

COMPOUND PRESS

CHAPTER ONE

If you kill the ancestor you kill yourself.

TONI MORRISON, "*ROOTEDNESS: THE ANCESTOR AS FOUNDATION*," 1978

MOREMI STOOD IN THE SAND at the edge of the Pacific in the howling wind that spread fire all day through the California hills. The sultry wind tugged at her white nightgown as she stared across the rippling water, waiting. This was alien and familiar. A dream, and yet—real. She knew where she was. She'd been here before.

It was an unseasonably hot September, the Indian summer of 2008, and the quarter moon lit a dim path across the surf. Her husband and eight-year-old son slept soundly at home. She tried to be calm, but her pulse matched the relentless wind, racing with dread.

It was the spirit. When it came she would have to follow. *Why now? Why can't she just leave me alone and let me have some peace? Haven't I done everything I could to appease her? I gave her the bright pink bead necklace and a six-pack of Coca-Cola. I don't know what she wants.*

Her pleas disappeared into the wind over the lapping waves. She lowered her head, letting the tears break through. This malaise had gripped her far too long—why was it getting worse? But it was inevitable, a certainty she somehow welcomed and feared.

She heard crinkling cellophane and smelled burning candles—the beeswax mixed with a fishy smell that forewarned a visit from which she knew there was no escape. She'd tried every trick she could imagine to avoid its ancient call. *I have a life now, here in the U.S. I'm married to Professor Peter Abosanjo, whose parents knew my parents. We have our son, Ayo.*

But here she was, in her nightgown, barefoot and vulnerable. *I really must stop doing this.* As if she could. She cocked her head to listen as she began to hear the drumming, spotty at first, like jazz musicians starting to scat with each other. One hit a staccato note, the other hit two, yet another three, and before long they were conversing like young lovers touching their lips before the slow dance began.

She dropped her head, closed her eyes, and started to sway. Her long curly hair, usually so heavy when she let it loose, felt light and airy. *No!* She wanted to resist, to go back to bed. She had no time for this rumpus.

The drumming intensified and now was infused with soft harmonicas wafting over a deep and slow bass saxophone. The ocean began to ripple. The waves undulated to the music, and she leaned into the rhythmic swaying with the water. She felt helpless, wanting to back away, but caught in the dance. The push-pull inside her grew more turbulent as her body wanted to join the primal waters, blending sea and sky as the Pleiades, the seven sisters, stared down.

She was close to fainting. Sucking in her breath she almost fell back, and yet her feet were riveted in the sand. She knew this was the end. She was being punished for being dead inside for so many years. Her life in the U.S. after Nigeria, her marriage to Peter, their son Ayo all added up to what should be happiness, and yet something was wrong. It gnawed at her, wearing her out.

She lost her sense of time. How long had she been in limbo, hearing the music, yearning to run and yet unable? Then she spied it, far in the distance —a whirling on the water, a jetting fountain. With little hiccups at first it flew up and up, blocking the moon, whipping water like the huge, splayed tentacles of a monster octopus. In seconds it assembled into a tornado of seawater, a whirling dervish heading straight for her as she stood on the shore, a sentinel. The tornado stopped at the shoreline and as quickly as it began the waters calmed.

Slowly rising, Mami surfaced. The wild whips of her hair seemed like a whirling spray of water. She lay on the surface, her broad hips floating up and down like a small ship, torso ending in perky fins, breasts full and voluptuous, draped in beads. She fluttered her fins, a southern belle fanning herself, batting her eyes—shameless!

Mami was wearing the bead necklace and Moremi couldn't help feeling pleased. The spirit's bright pink suited her light brown complexion. The rippling python hugged her, flicking its tongue into Mami's neck while glaring at Moremi, wishing her away. In her deepest sexy voice, as if she'd smoked a million cigarettes, Mami commanded: "Come with me!"

In a trance, Moremi plunged into the ocean to follow, sinking down into the dark green of the water. Kelp entangled her as she spun searching for Mami who was nowhere in sight. Dark tangles taunted her to follow skulking shapes. Her panic rose again. *I'm not a fish.* Back to reality. *How can I survive? Maybe I'm not supposed to.* She sank into terror, reality impinging, drowning in a marginal world on the edge of sanity. Either she was all in or all out. As she pushed herself upward, craving the air, Mami appeared as if there all along, undulating, batting her eyes like the Great Vamp she was, summoning Moremi to follow deeper into her kingdom.

When Mami demanded, "follow me," she had no choice and none was offered, even when she only wanted to chat. But the prospect of a chat with Mami was never to be underestimated.

They passed through dark caverns where schools of neon minnows cattered, tiny lamps along their way, gliding over ruins—ships cracked asunder centuries ago, covered with barnacles, decaying back into their original elements in the great open seas where it all began. Moremi followed, wondering and fearing if she, like Eurydice, almost might, but never would, return. This was a sickness, and her own fault. *I haven't been paying attention. But to what?* No answer appeared. Mami would warn her about not paying attention, about forgetting the past that wouldn't let her go. There would be no escape and no excuses.

She won't let me forget. But why? I need to be happy.

She followed, dazed by the beauty of the underwater landscape. It was Olokun's palace before it became Poseidon's world. *No! Stop thinking like a human. Not good under water*. Besides, what did it matter which deity? *They're all alike. Demanding. Crazy. Narcissistic.* She swam on pushing this aside. This was her fate.

Finally, Mami abruptly turned, held up her hand while swimming circles around Moremi and spoke. Her voice gurgled and bubbled through the heaving water. "You are ill with unhappiness because you do not accept who you are, which is always who you were. Pay me homage and I will help, or otherwise forget your life. You will end up with nothing."

She retracted like an urchin from the sting of Mami's admonition—a threat, nothing lukewarm to be defended against or bargained with. She felt the hopelessness she had lived with for so long. In Mami's netherworlds there was no truth or lies—only the moment when the meaning of everything converged and where no argument could be made. The only sure thing in this moment was that everything was up to her.

She awakened, gasping for air. She clutched her chest and grabbed the nightstand to keep her steady. Covered in sweat, breathless, grateful she hadn't disturbed Peter, she staggered into the bathroom and peered into the mirror. Her face looked waterlogged as if all the blood had drained out. Through the mirror she saw another apparition, the spirit she recognized as her great-grandmother, now bedecked in cheap jewelry, updated with funky hippie clothes, preening, swaying back and forth like a snake. Moremi leaned into the mirror and whispered, "I love you, Mami Wata."

She had no other choice. Her attempts to distance herself from Mami in the last few years had failed. She knew the more she tried to disconnect the more Mami would close in on her. Tonight's visitation unhinged her more than ever. The tornado's arrival was a warning. Mami was up to something. Moremi knew only enough to understand that whatever she was ignoring in her life was right in front of her.

To shake herself out of Mami's world, she walked down the hall to Ayo's room and peeked in. His breathing was slow and rhythmic.

As she returned to her bedroom she thought about the next day. She would take Ayo to school, go to her part time job at the lab and then go to the therapist's office. She lay her head down on the pillow.

How did I let myself get talked into seeing a complete stranger in whom I am supposed to confide? A friend at work had suggested it, saying, "They're like spiritual counselors. It's confidential, very private. Only you will know." She closed her eyes. *I'll go once. That's all.*

CHAPTER TWO

Please take my hand. I give it to you as a gesture of friendship and love, and of faith freely given. I give you my hand and welcome you into my dream.

WONDER WOMAN #167

ON THE OTHER SIDE OF TOWN, Rebecca Calhoun lay in bed yearning for sleep. Her imagination traveled in circles, a hound that had lost its scent, lighting on whatever grabbed her attention, illuminating the most minor events and turning them into overblown moments. She couldn't help glancing at the clock's neon hours that promised her inevitable exhaustion.

For most of her fifty-five years sleep had come easily. Lately, insomnia plagued her far too often. She drifted into the next day's schedule, imagined going to her office to meet her psychotherapy clients. Like many of her colleagues who saw people long-term, she loved inhabiting the secret world of others, interacting with their deeper longings and memories as they entwined with her own. Those dialogues could be euphoric like dreams opening to the past, but also a little addictive. Nothing else really compares to the intimacy of two selves inhabiting each other.

Her mind drifted. She had always been this way. Even during middle school she frequently missed things her peers saw and knew, like what the teacher was talking about, or Rosemary Smith's new hairdo that made her look like Orphan Annie. But she noticed things they didn't, little things that told a secret story.

She could still hear the jingling of the charm bracelet of her sixty-year-old English teacher, Mrs. Durant, as she plunked her chalk across the blackboard demonstrating how to diagram a sentence, the jangling and thumping drowning out the lesson. Mrs. Durant would whirl around like a carnival barker to announce in her stentorian voice, poking her chalk at the board: "Subject, predicate, modifiers, clauses!"

Rebecca always wondered about the usefulness of learning all that. When she disappeared into books, the sound of words falling into place in sentences seemed like musical notes rather than rules. Mrs. Durant's demonstrations seemed beside the point—as did so many things she was supposed to learn.

That day she was distracted by those jingling charms on her teacher's bracelet, and what they meant to stern old Mrs. Durant. *Did the silver four-leaf clover symbolize the real one she found in a field long ago?* While the adult woman blathered on about the importance of independent and subordinate clauses, Rebecca saw a young girl lying in a bed of clover with her lover who put a dandelion in her hair.

At lunch with the other girls, she whispered the story of Mrs. Durant while they all leaned in.

She conjured the drama like a little journalist on the job. "During the war when she was young Mrs. Durant fell in love with a handsome soldier. She had long hair then and wore bright red lipstick. They danced under the stars and agreed to get married when he came home a hero. The day he left she found a four-leaf clover."

She paused to make sure her audience was all ears. "But they never got married!" She waited, holding the dramatic moment. "Because—" she paused as long as they could bear, "he was killed!"

Then she waited to make sure they were appropriately shocked. "Shot right out of the sky when he parachuted out of a plane into enemy fire!" She had them. "Well," she went for the denouement, "Mrs. Durant vowed never to marry. Well, maybe she did marry, but she bought that four-leaf clover, so she'd never forget him. That's him on her bracelet. I'm telling you . . . she wasn't always old and ridiculous!"

I was such a little ham! Where did all that stuff come from? My way of controlling how I was told to behave? But who could control what I imagined? And now?

She let her mind float.

Now I know what people imagine can be more real than what they think they know. Because it comes from a pure source. We don't edit what we imagine. Richard and I are so different, and he takes me seriously, but Jonathan? At first, he loved how I thought, but we both changed. Making money became his passion. And mine? Just like when I was thirteen making up stories about Mrs. Durant. I always thought I could go anywhere, but I couldn't go with Jonathan into that world where playing Monopoly got too real . . . and ruthless.

When she and her first husband Jonathan met, she quoted Antoine de Saint-Exupery's *The Little Prince. He was so impressed. Those words rolled off my tongue. "The most beautiful things in the world cannot be seen or touched, they are felt with the heart."* Tears ran down her cheeks as sadness sunk in.

We both lost heart with each other. He chased the money. And me? I found a way to follow the stories and stay in the dream.

She remembered the college fraternity party where they met in the early 80's—she was a junior at a small college and he a senior about to graduate from a large university. She hadn't wanted to go, but friends in her dorm pulled her along. She sat on a couch watching the crowd gyrate to Bad Girls. Without realizing, her feet moved to the grinding rhythm of Donna Summer's urgent, pounding voice. She closed her eyes and sang along to the chorus:

Turn away, turn away turn away
Walk away, walk away, walk away

When she opened her eyes, he was sitting next to her. His gaze was as intense as the lyrics. He grinned. She grinned back as she sang even louder. Jonathan appeared in that moment to be the only male in the room who wasn't holding a large Dixie cup of beer. He stood up and pulled her onto the dance floor.

He was president of his fraternity. They were opposites, but something clicked instantly between them. The ease with which he liked people and they liked him dazzled her while he gravitated to her intensity. They married after she graduated. After fifteen years, he started his own hedge fund, and began to disappear. When their daughter Margo started high school, she thought they might spend more time together, but it was the opposite.

For Jonathan, making money was the wild west. He seemed to have the Midas touch. Whenever he talked about "Diamond Lil," his sly nickname for his fund, he laughed, but she didn't find it amusing. *It's like he's dancing around the saloon with Diamond Lil in her leopard skin coat flashing her toothy grin and dazzling all those gold-fevered miners. How could I compete with that? I saw the end of that story early on! Hedge funds are the modern mines in the desert! Most wind up defunct. He was lucky—he's had a long wild ride. I didn't see the gambler when we met. I might even have been ok with the risk-taking, but not the addiction.*

After "Lil" had been on the scene for a while, Rebecca sat at her hairdresser's reading an article in Vogue, 'What Kind of Man Did you Marry?' The author spoke from experience: "You may have married for love, but if he likes making a lot of money you better get your own life, because money's his mistress." In that moment something clicked. *I need my own life. I won't have that if I'm always waiting for Jonathan.*

Within the year they agreed to part as friends and Margo supported her parents' decision. "Mom, I love Dad. But he needs people around him. He has fun, but he takes over. You're the quiet one. You need your own thing."

Jonathan went on to have two more marriages before he decided he was not cut out for restriction. Eventually he and Rebecca became friends. He often called her from wherever he was in the world to ask her advice. She enjoyed hearing about his adventures in capitalism, mainly because it was like being on another planet.

Now, except for the times when Richard stayed overnight, Rebecca lived alone in her small house in the Berkeley hills with The Queens—her two chows, Juno and Dido. Once she got used to living alone, she liked it. She often thought about the first Saturday morning she woke up in her own home and realized, *all I must please is myself.* In that moment she felt a sense of total freedom for the first time in her adult life. *If I decide to waste my time, it's on me and no one else.*

With Richard around for two years now she began to protect herself from the possibility that he might somehow take over, like the weedy flowering pigweed that showed up in the spring all over her backyard—a beautiful bully. Once in a fit of pique she attacked and pulled up a bunch. Later Richard collected some of the leaves and tossed them into his salad announcing with his big, broad smile, "These Amaranth leaves are edible when young and tender."

He's moving in on me.

Recently she'd taken to talking to herself in the mirror. Two days ago, she leaned in and touched her forehead. Pulling back, she stretched her mouth like a five-year old and stuck out her tongue, then leaned in again and licked the mirror, then pulled way back and giggled. "Whoo are youuu?"

"Richard!" she barked as if he were right there. "It's time you understood what's what! I like you. . . yesss! I might even love you. But here's the deal," she wagged her finger. "My rules. You may not take over. We never discuss money. We share everything." She stopped to consider. "Uhhh . . . and oh yes, If . . ." she shouted at herself, "if . . . at some future point we decide to marry it will be a small ceremony in an interesting place of my—" she gestured at herself with her thumb, "choosing!"

At 4:00 a.m., she dreamed she was seven years old sitting in a cornfield surrounded by open yellow fields edged by dense forest. Her name was Becky. The midday sun soaked into her bones as she played in the soil, soft and pliable to her fingers, speaking in imitation of her mother to the little corn doll she carried in her apron pocket.

"See," she said to the doll in that loving singsongy tone her mother liked to use, "It's time to pick the corn, Hitty, just the way I showed you." She set the doll on top of the small mound of dirt she'd made, nodding her head back and forth, approving the doll's compliance as she hopped her around doing her chores, pleasing the little mother.

Overhead Becky saw a bald eagle gliding in the ether hunting for mice.

Holding up the doll she hummed, "Poor little rodents, they're so soft." But something intruded. She dropped the doll on the mound and looked toward the trees west and away from the river, distracted by the muffled popping of her father's flintlock musket as he aimed the birdshot ahead of the trees and into the path of the fleeing quail. She resumed humming; this time, she needed to blot out frightening thoughts like little things being killed.

"Rock-a-bye baby, in the treetop."

The melody always soothed even though she knew by now the words did not, but she couldn't stop.

"When the wind blows, the cradle will rock."

The popping stopped, and a deep unease crept into her. She continued singing the words softly, rocking back and forth as if in prayer.

"When the bough breaks, the cradle will fall."

Smoke toward the river billowed into the blue sky, and she sang more urgently, *"Down will come baby, cradle and all."*

Her father was running through the corn he had planted in neat rows across his field, down to the river, the slow, meandering, soothing Juniata. He cut a wide swath wailing a high-pitched unearthly sound, "Noooo . . . Noooo!"

She was running in the forest of white pines and maples and yellow aspens, tall sentinels huddled and swaying in the hot wind. She cut through bushes as branches clawed at her, leaving bloody scratches she didn't feel. *Down will come baby, down will come baby!* She sang raggedly.

She crashed headlong into something that felt soft. It smelled of grease. It must be some kind of dead animal. But it wasn't. A large gold button scraped her cheek. She looked up into the massive face, bright red, with painted, shiny black stripes, its eyes like a raccoon's. She couldn't scream. No sound came out, not even the song.

A Delaware warrior looked down at her. Bald, painted, the falcon feathers spread out behind his head. He had a ring in his nose and wore a British regimental coat with shiny gold buttons. A great knife hung down his thigh in a deerskin pouch. She had seen him before, talking to her father. That was before. But not now, not lately.

He gently held the blond baby boy in his arm—an eagle carrying a limp rabbit. The baby chortled happily. He must think this is a new game. He made goo-goo sounds, leaning out to Becky, pumping his chubby little arm. The warrior raised the baby to his chest. The baby returned to playing with the buttons on his coat, pulling one, trying to put it in his mouth.

Panicked, she turned and ran. He followed, keeping a slow, steady pace. She knew the way and zigzagged like the rabbit running through the field toward the safety of the trees. She heard her father's voice, *"The rabbit knows what its chances are."* His voice was soothing like the sound of the river. She might have a chance.

She ran into a clearing and recognized the Delaware village. Teepees were towering peaks covered with skins and the air was dead calm. She smelled the cooking fires and saw a woman tended her fire, a sleeping baby strapped to her back. A birch-bark cradle hung nearby from the branches of an old, gnarled oak tree. Her father had made one just like it.

Her mother was sitting on a log reading from her Bible.

Becky's heart soared and she knew she would be safe now. She called to her mother, "Mother, Mother, I am here, over here." She tried to walk toward her, but couldn't move—as if her feet were in quicksand.

Her mother did not look up. She was lost in her Bible, mouthing the words.

She barely made out her mother's mumbling. When her mother was with her Bible she was not to be interrupted. She fought to behave, to be a good Christian, to push down what her mother called "your strong emotions that can get the better of you, Becky. You must learn patience." But her urge to lunge at her mother and smother her in kisses would not subside.

Her mother's head was wrapped in a red bandana. *Was that new?* She loved to play in her mother's deer-hide trunk searching for things she had never seen, as if there would always be one more treasure to find. Even though there was nothing more to find, her mother played the game as if she would find something unexpected.

Although her legs still dragged, she was comforted that she could see her mother. She began to hear more distinctly what her mother mumbled.

"The Lord is my shepherd; I shall not want. He maketh me to lie down in green pastures: he leadeth me beside the still waters."

She knew the words. Her mother would lead the whole family kneeling in prayer, and this was often the one. But now Becky felt disturbed. She wished her mother would just say the Lord's Prayer. That would be better. She had told her, "This is about your soul, Becky."

She had trouble with the word soul even though her mother explained it many times.

"Soul," she would say as she swept her slender arms wide open to the sky, "is the greater you, Becky, the little girl who will grow up to be big and strong and powerful one day, larger in all ways than yourself now, like the great trees and the sky and the heavens and angels."

Even though she loved to hear these words in her mother's soothing, soft tone, the word soul still agitated her.

"Yea, though I walk through the valley of the shadow of death, I will fear no evil: for thou art with me; thy rod and thy staff they comfort me."

Now she felt panicky. Her mother spoke with a different fervor.

"Thou preparest a table before me in the presence of mine enemies: thou anointest my head with oil; my cup runneth over."

She didn't like this part. *Why would you put oil on your head? Whose cup runneth over? It never made sense.*

"Surely goodness and mercy shall follow me all the days of my life: and I will dwell in the house of the Lord forever."

"Mother!" she screamed, "It's me, Becky. Please get up. Let's go home. I don't like it here. Please Mother, stand up now!" She was sobbing and gulping and knew her mother would never forgive her for getting this worked up. There was something very wrong.

The warrior appeared, strode over and softly pushed her mother over.

She slumped off the log on to the ground. Their old, dog-eared family Bible tumbled off her lap into the dirt.

At 6:00 A.M. Rebecca woke with a start. Juno and Dido had both come on the bed. The dream began to evaporate as her bedroom took shape, wiping away the vision of Becky's mother slumped over on the ground. Rebecca closed her eyes, bringing it back. She hoped it would fade as she scanned it, half-awake, unable to push it away.

Her eyes popped open. She reached for Juno's furry head and pulled her in, while on her other side Dido licked the tears on her cheek.

As Rebecca showered and dressed to take The Queens on their morning walk, she again tried to shake the dream. The chows trotted along, unruffled by other dogs in the neighborhood, sniffing bushes and looking around. The dream returned. . . *the warrior from the painting. . . so beautiful and deadly. . . he's tracking me. . . relentless. . . Why now?* A half-hour later back at her house she climbed the stairs with the Queens off their leashes bounding ahead through the gate. A blue jay squawked at her from the redwood demanding she pay attention. The Queens looked up as though they understood it. The dream blurred.

My mother—yes, my mother! Alive one second, now slumped over on the ground. . . and now in the hospital bed. . . across the centuries. . . head wrapped in gauze. . . dead eyes still open as she slipped away when I came into that room. Their faces merged, one fallen over onto the ground and the other in bed looking at her as she entered her room.

As she pulled into her parking place at work, she knew the dream was telling her something about her life now. Gertrude's words intruded.

"What's unresolved in you shows up again and again."

CHAPTER THREE

Voudoun is first, foremost, and inextricably
at its cosmological core, an ancestral tradition.
No one can honor and communicate with your direct ancestors
except for you.
The Vodou gods come in the blood of the African,
And many are even born from direct lineages of these gods.
It is they who experience the most profound disturbances in their lives
when they forget either deliberately
or through social conditioning/amnesia who they are.

INTERVIEW WITH AFRICAN AMERICAN AMENGANSIE, VOUDOUN AND MAMI WATA PRIESTESS: CHIEF HOUNON-AMENGANSIE: MAMA ZOGBE (2001), DR. AUSTIN OGUNSUYI

MOREMI WALKED THROUGH THE HOT WIND gusting through the sultry Bay Area streets. She understood these fall winds were becoming more frequent, threatening wildfires. Her friends at work still talked about the fire twenty years ago that burned hundreds of homes and killed twenty-five people.

She was reminded of the harmattan seasonal winds in Nigeria. They blew in from the northern desert and savanna, hot and furious, lasting through the middle of March and sparking fires that burned homes and sometimes took lives. Because they were dry, Africans called them "the doctor." They replaced the humid tropical air and were a health hazard every year.

Her maternal grandmother Buchi, an Igbo who married a Yoruba, would lean out her window, hands cupped behind her ears, eyes closed, swaying, and exclaim, "The ancestors are wailing to us from far away, and here's what they're saying." Then she would make up a story.

Moremi climbed into her car and sat for a few minutes enjoying the quiet, safe from the frenzied air outside as the leaves on her windshield fluttered about like tiny birds. She welcomed her own company. She had not gotten used to the rushed life in America even though she'd been here ten years.

Peter, on the other hand, now 58, here since graduate school in his twenties, prided himself on being completely Americanized. He prodded her to do the same. His rationale seemed simple. "My entire family left, and now, like your parents, they're passed. I've been here most of my life now. You are an American." She wanted to comply—this would now be her permanent home. As she sat in the stillness, the fear she was about to confide in some stranger flooded in.

How do you tell an American you can't get used to their culture? She'd tried with some friends at work, but they were so certain here was a better place. They were kind, intelligent and liberal, which meant they were keenly aware of racial issues. Respect for difference was paramount for them, yet for her, difference was tribal. She knew the consequences and horror of primeval impulses that could catapult that difference into genocide. How could she explain that Africa was its own victim and perpetrator in a way Americans really could understand? Or show them its beauty? And their fear of offending her often struck her as insincere. Why? She believed the way out of racism was not blindness to difference but acceptance of it as a source of misunderstanding and conflict.

Here honesty is so often considered offensive. How do I talk about that? She took solace in Buchi's words from her childhood, an echo from home.

We all belong to our own past and not somebody's idea of that.

We come from them who gave us life and we die into them.

Don't let anyone tell you different.

She shook her head, forcing herself into the present. Peter already would have picked up Ayo from school, headed for soccer practice and then home. She looked at her watch. Soon they would be rooting through the refrigerator in the kitchen, cooking as a team. Ayo would stand on the small stepstool so he could watch carefully what was on the stove. They would talk about the soccer game or Ayo's school and how he liked his new teacher and the other kids in the class. Ayo was popular. His moves on a skateboard were seamless.

When Ayo was a baby Peter was more distant. He had to learn how to be a parent, while she easily took to motherhood. One of her friends had given her a gift before Ayo was born, a book about developmental child-rearing. Her friend enthusiastically assured her: "Here's all you need to know!" It later found its way into the trash.

Moremi was tall and lithe, perfect for carrying a child. Sometimes she wrapped him in her old shawl, cocooning him while he slept as she went about household chores. Peter bought her a large, expensive baby backpack carrier with pouches for all the equipment she might need. She tried it once and put it away in the closet.

As Ayo grew older there were things she couldn't get used to. When he enthused about the Pokemon characters he loved so much, she couldn't relate. She tried and wondered if she should keep trying. *Which was worse, pretending or just telling the truth?* Her own parents would have told her, the truth. "Those are your spirits in your mind. They're not for adults to understand." But here in this culture parents would never say something like that.

She looked at the clock—she needed to hurry now to her appointment with the therapist. She started the car and wondered how her life had come to this.

She couldn't really talk with Peter about her underlying discontent. After all, it had been so many years since she left Nigeria. But rather than settling in, she felt more and more distant from her life in America as she yearned for her real home. And her feelings about Peter now? She didn't understand those either. He was handsome, successful, and intelligent. He paid her a lot of attention. She knew he found her attractive. But she had the distinct feeling that he withheld himself, constantly preoccupied. During their first years together, she was involved with Ayo, finding a part-time job, and then starting graduate school in African women's studies, so she didn't really notice. But now she did. It was as if he held something back, something he didn't want her to know.

In the late nineties, when she came to the U.S., she left behind everything she loved and feared. Her parents had just died because of one of the worst reigns of political corruption. His family had rescued her. Peter had convinced her she might be putting friends in danger if she tried to contact them, even now. But the safety she had found in her marriage to him seemed to be slowly unraveling, and she felt there was nothing she could do about it. She missed her family and friends more than ever. Rather than fading, the past seemed to be catching up with her. *How can I explain something like that to a stranger?*

She had not told Peter where she was going. As time went on, she had become used to holding her own secrets. He did not know that she kept an altar to Mami Wata in their basement cupboard near the washer and dryer. It had become her only connection to her family and her life in Africa. She was comforted knowing he rarely if ever went down there. And even if he did, she assumed he would not recognize what it was: her mother's and grandmother's connection to her and the matrilineal line of their family. After all, as he said, he had become an American.

REBECCA WAS IN HER LEATHER CHAIR chewing on a ballpoint pen, staring at the abstract print on the opposite wall in her office, but not really seeing it. She had one more hour to go before a new patient. She needed to focus, but her mind wanted to wander.

Last night's dream haunted her with the familiar feeling she could trace back to childhood, a feeling she had forgotten something important. It was as if something had happened that she knew about and then—poof—the memory disappeared, leaving only the feeling of loss. *How could this be?* It made no sense.

The usual explanation was that she'd forgotten what it was because whatever happened was traumatic, probably connected to her father's unpredictable temper and her mother's passivity. Either way, her memory lapse was about the long ago past. This made some sense to her, but not enough. She believed the explanation for her feeling of loss had a deeper and more mysterious source than the one her friends and traditional psychotherapy offered. That source was connected to a more distant past, long before she was born.

The light on her far wall went on, alerting her that her new client was seated in the waiting room. She was five minutes early. She checked her appointment calendar and saw the name. Moremi Abosanjo. She had spoken to her on the phone briefly and learned that she was from Nigeria. Rebecca's attention went to the African mask on her wall. She wondered if her client would notice it.

She had discovered African masks about ten years ago when on a whim she bought one on a trip to San Diego with Richard, her "Friendly-boy." Richard had come up with that to replace "boyfriend," not quite right at their age. She hadn't come up with a better term yet. Remembering the Queens jumping around as he tried it out made her laugh.

While she considered Richard the one she should have married in the first place, she often remembered what Imogene Cunningham said about her marriage after divorce: "I tried that once." He too, had divorced. Each had a grown child. Richard's son, Damian, lived in San Diego where he owned his own business making surfboards. Her own daughter Margo worked at the State Department and lived in Washington DC with her husband and one-year old daughter.

Rebecca and Richard had an ongoing agreement: he would keep asking her to marry him while she could say no as long as she felt like it. "I'm in no hurry," he would chime. But time was passing, and their memories like an old married couple, were starting to add up so that her resolve was diminishing. And both Margo and Damian had begun to hint that maybe it was time.

She could never forget buying her first mask with Richard. They had wandered into a small shop one evening to kill time before meeting his son at a restaurant for dinner. It was crammed with bric-a-brac from Africa, things tourists liked: carved wooden giraffes and rhinos, the sort of stuff they both disdained. Rebecca wandered into a back room filled with older masks hung all over the walls and on top of tables and some under them on the floor. She stood still and let her gaze wander around. She began to see what they really were. Intricate, old and glowing with patina. . . one was a female head, delicate long, small lips, eyes slanted down. A bird came up over her forehead with its bill pointing down between two large horns jutting out from either side of her head, all one piece of wood. She leaned in to see the price.

As she stooped down to look at more, a booming, melodious male voice spoke, "Hello."

She looked up into the broadly smiling face of the owner, African American, about mid-sixties, dancing eyes and she learned later, a former opera singer. He held out his hand. "I'm Bernard, who are you?"

"Rebecca."

He knelt next to her. "Aren't they beautiful?"

She agreed and asked where they were from.

"These are Mende helmet masks. Sierra Leone. Not too old, probably carved in the sixties. These masks are for the women's society, carved by the men and the only masks from Africa that are worn by the women in their ceremonial dances.

She ran her finger over the carved folds in the neck of one that held her eye.

"A husband, for example, will hire a master carver to make one for his wife. The neck ripples here are intended to represent her beauty and status.

They have the elaborate hairstyles," he explained, rubbing his hand over the pompadour of carved hair, "with a full forehead and small features. Only the best dancers can wear them. These would have long strands of raffia that fall from the base of the neck." He indicated the holes where the raffia would be tied. "Dyed black. You can only see the dancers' feet. Extraordinary to watch."

Twenty minutes later, after she had paid for the mask and arranged for shipping, they left the store.

From then on she bought more masks from that same dealer and began to learn about them. Some things were disturbing. For example, circumcision—essential to a female Mende's preparation for initiation into the sacred Sande society. Her western values careened headlong into a collision with a repugnant, misogynistic, and alien practice.

She asked Bernard about this.

He shrugged, looked at her and said, "These masks aren't supposed to make you feel better." Then he laughed.

Understanding the spirit within the masks was not going to be easy. Still, she wanted to learn.

She now owned about forty masks from different African countries, as well as others from native cultures. The one in her office was seventeen inches high, the lower half of the female face with full lips, a long aquiline nose, large downward-cast eyes and elaborate geometric patterns carved on her face. Her demeanor is in repose, serene and peaceful. In contrast and wrapped around her high forehead is an undulating python, its head ending along the left side, like a bandana. Coming up over the head and biting into the python over the forehead in perfect symmetry were a pair of painted blue crocodiles, a circle completed with the python biting the tail of one of the crocodiles. The upper tableau depicts what appeared to be a violent scene of animals locked in mortal combat. She learned that this Yoruba Gelede mask from Nigeria represents the power of the woman and the balance of power in human communities. If each animal held its grip on the other the tension held and there could be no change for the worse.

It was time to meet her new client. She rose from her chair and opened the waiting room door.

"Hello, I'm Rebecca Calhoun."

Moremi stood up and they shook hands. Moremi was tall at five-eleven. She wore black pants, a jacket with an off-white blouse and black flats, the backdrop for one striking piece of jewelry around her neck, an intricately linked silver chain with a simple silver pendant that contained a large oval aquamarine stone.

Rebecca, five-six, wore a long soft corduroy, rose-colored skirt, a jersey in a similar shade, with a light green jacket and brown, low-heeled shoes, and a string of uncultured pearls Richard had given her on their last trip to Kauai.

As Moremi entered, the atmosphere, the furniture, the books and things on her wall, the shadows of light and dark welcomed her.

Rebecca indicated the soft leather couch while she sat across from Moremi.

Moremi surveyed the black and white photographs, the few pieces of pottery, the desk, and plants on the floor in the corner. The effect was natural, unlike the many American rooms Moremi had encountered in her new life. Her own home was simpler still. The only item she insisted on was a photograph of the famous roped pot found at Igbo Ukwu, the ninth century site in southeastern Nigeria, discovered in the sixties. It reminded her of home. Her father had kept one in his office and told her, "Moremi, nowhere in the history of the world has this level of artistry in bronze casting been found." He would point to the photograph, "That archaeological dig proves to those Europeans that we Africans were way ahead of them." Every time he told her this she would swell with pride.

She sat down and spied the mask. Rebecca felt self-conscious and knew why. She still had not completely overcome the gnawing sense that as she collected, she was plundering objects sacred to another culture. Moremi's presence triggered the discomfort that usually stayed underground. But there it was, one of those nasty little things whispering, "You don't understand!" Then she heard Bernard. *"Yes, you do! Let it in."*

In her several discussions with him he would snatch a book from his cluttered shelves and flip to the pages of photographs that showed the masks worn by the dancers. Most of the photographs were hazy and old, taken before it became usual for a tribe to allow spectators from the outside.

"That's how you begin to understand them," he explained. "In their context. Don't worry that you're not African. If you understand that these masks are sacred, you become their caretaker." He waxed even more philosophical than usual. "Each of us is a melting pot for the other. I invite you into my culture. That's who we Americans are. Don't you think?" Then he laughed. His laugh was infectious, and she carried that voice within her and here it was—perched on her shoulder—although quieter than that earlier blue jay. *Pay attention.*

Now, sitting across from her was possibly someone who understood like Bernard. Or maybe better.

Usually after Rebecca and a new client were seated, she would casually start the dialogue with, "Well, tell me what brought you in," or something equally benign, as an open-ended invitation. But the dialogue had already begun as Moremi held her eye on the mask. Rebecca let the silence continue and felt a little uneasy, very curious.

After a few more moments, Rebecca asked Moremi to tell her why she had come in. Moremi shook herself out of something and turned to Rebecca and said, "I'm struggling to be American."

CHAPTER FOUR

Nigeria has proved to be by far the most confounding, frustrating, and at the same time engaging place I have ever visited. It simply overwhelms the senses, one of those rare examples in which the sum of its parts is, at least to date, immensely greater than the whole. It is a work in progress, though one is never too sure whether it is being assembled or torn apart.

THIS HOUSE HAS FALLEN, NIGERIA IN CRISIS. KARL MAIER, 2000.

THEY SAT IN SILENCE, each waiting for the other to speak, each gathering their thoughts.

Rebecca relaxed into her familiar pose and gazed down at the Kurdistan rug patterns at her feet, a comfortable old friend, worn but not worn out.

Moremi did not yield to the comfort of the couch, but sat upright, feet on the floor, hands crossed in her lap, fingers entwined, palms up. "I was born in 1964 in Nigeria in what was then a small village, Abeokuta, about fifty miles north of Lagos. And now here I am in America in 2008, forty-five years later."She spoke softly, rhythmically with diction that was careful and circumspect.

Even though it was the end of a long day and Rebecca was still under the influence of last night's dream she leaned forward—opening herself to hearing the story about a world of which she knew very little. Moremi's words sounded like soft strumming that beckoned her in. Rebecca wondered where this would go.

"My father was a minister in the Anglican Church. He was open to all religions and studied theology at the Trinity Union Theological College near Lagos. Some thought he was not pious enough. My mother's family were local merchants and she worked in their store. It was before independence. Before the oil. Before the dictators. At a time when the standard of living even before the oil boon, while the British were still there, was higher than it is now. My parents married in 1963."

Rebecca wanted to know more about Nigeria. She would ask Richard that evening at dinner at her house. Since he was her loveable know-it-all and purveyor of his encyclopedic knowledge of most subjects—plus being a professor of cultural anthropology—she guessed he would know something about Nigeria's history.

She stopped for a moment and looked out the window as if she had left the room. "He was also typically Nigerian—a storyteller and a musician. He loved both classical and jazz and played the drums with a local group." Again, she looked out the window as if she were far away. "You can hear the drums all over Nigeria. People who come to my country always comment about the drums."

She spoke as if she had never left.

Rebecca asked, "you said your father was later accused of not being pious enough. What did you mean?"

Moremi returned. "Well, he was religious up to a point. He believed religion should be a part of everyday life, not something to use as a force over others. He was open to all religions, so he honored the animistic ones as well. I remember he used to say to my mother, 'Piety is over-rated.'" She smiled, but neither pursued this.

"After marrying my father when she was twenty-three, my mother stayed in business and after a while set up her own portable stall in the marketplace. A cooperative of women worked for her, decorating cotton blouses with embroidery, and distributing the profits among them. People admired her."

Rebecca's dream surfaced. She saw the child watching her mother read from her bible in the Delaware village. Somehow, in the moment her association to her own dream set the stage for Moremi to tell her something equally important about her own mother.

"My parents were both Pentecostal Christians and were liberal in their views. On my mother's side of the family, the women come from a long line of priestesses who belong to a special sect that worships a deity whose lineage goes back some say six thousand years. And perhaps more." She shrugged. "Or less."

"The first prophetess was Mami Wata, who became part of an ancient pantheon of water deities. They are not part of the Yoruba Orishas my parents' people worship. The Wata were even older and matriarchal. Now there are men practicing, but the worship is for Mami Wata." She looked out the window wide-eyed, as if she just made an important discovery. Returning to Rebecca she explained. "Most Americans know nothing about Mami Wata, but those who do think she is a recent invention, and they call her 'Mammy Water' in pidgin English, as though she was a European-looking snake charmer like those in posters in bars and taverns as an evil spirit who destroys men."

"I suppose," Rebecca speculated, "trying to explain something this esoteric to the average American would be a rather daunting project."

Moremi slanted her head, nodding. Abruptly, she straightened as if she had just come back to her senses. "I suppose you know," she looked at Rebeccaas she gestured toward the wall, "your mask is a Yoruba Gelede mask."

Rebecca flushed. While she knew the mask was Yoruba and the basics of the Gelede spectacle, her knowledge did not go much beyond Wikipedia. Moremi's focus on the mask made her feel as if she were being 'outed' for the very thing she feared: her whiteness that precluded her from ever really understanding. And yet, whenever she focused her eye on the mask she nearly always was struck by its aliveness. As Moremi continued to look at it, Rebecca saw Moremi knew it was alive, too. *Don't intrude on her story. Let her tell it. This may be the first time she has told this story.*

"This may sound very odd to you," Moremi continued, "but to understand what happened to my family and why I am here in your office you need to know my mother's legacy. She taught me, during the later Roman Empire Wata priestesses were persecuted as witches because of their power for healing and their great influence. But we survived through oral tradition and there are still those who practice the rituals and pay homage to Mami. My mother was a practitioner. She told me the oldest form of Mami was the Egyptian 'Isis.'"

Moremi pointed to one of Rebecca's shelves at a small resin model of Isis kneeling with her wings spread in her cobra skin gown. "I remember asking her, 'You mean as old as the earth?' And my mother smiled and said, 'Almost as old as humans on earth.'"

"Do you mean that both Pentecostal Christianity and Mami Wata worship were compatible to your mother? I ask because that would not happen here in the U.S."

Moremi answered carefully. "The two religions are compatible. The older African religions are practiced anywhere, anytime. The deities are part of daily life, just like the Christian saints—like ones I have seen in homes here in America. In the nineteenth century, Yoruba slaves taken to Cuba easily wove the Spanish saints into their Orishas. Saints and Orishas were not so different. Pentecostals have a ritual of possession that is very close to the possession in the African Voudun rituals."

"I never thought about that," Rebecca acknowledged. "But I can see how some religions really can be compatible if people are open to it."

"Yes," Moremi agreed. "My mother treated her rituals and healings just like your mother might have prayed and taken care of her neighbors. The old religions were brought here to the U.S., and the slaves in the south practiced them, too. The owners were frightened when they did this, and many slaves were killed for it. In other countries such as Brazil, Cuba and Haiti the owners were more lax, so the practice grew and integrated more completely."

At the words "owners," and "slaves" a pall fell over the room as if ghosts entered. Both sat in silence, allowing the words to resonate.

Moremi began again, pulling them out. "The Orishas represent different pieces of the natural world."

Rebecca nodded, grateful for Moremi's calm with the topic of slavery. *She doesn't need to feel my white guilt. How does a country, just like an individual, shed its guilt? It's the denial that festers.*

She asked Moremi, "What are the Orishas? Who are they?"

"Ori' means a reflective spark in us. It's something in your consciousness and we all have it. Ori'—you, me," she pointed to Rebecca and then to herself, "and the 'sha,' means the ultimate potential of that consciousness. The two work in tandem, and that leads us to divine consciousness."

"You mean that whatever we feel as divine comes from within us, and not from without? That is how many Puritans, who came here originally, felt about their own religion and how they differed from the Catholic Church. A state of grace could not be earned, it came from what you call 'sha,' or a divine spark from within a person."

"Yes," Moremi agreed. "To Africans, our beliefs and behavior are connected. This reflects how we have evolved. And you are correct—this power is not bestowed but arises naturally from within each of us.

"In the American colonies," Rebecca added, "those Puritans came here to practice their religion more freely." She stopped, realizing she sounded like a schoolteacher telling her children a sugar-coated truth. "Of course, the real history," she corrected herself, "is one of predation and bloodshed."

Moremi smiled. She knew this.

Rebecca decided to bring their conversation back to the reason this very interesting woman sat opposite her. "You said something when you first came in, that you are struggling to become an American. What did you mean by that?"

"In order to explain that I must tell you what happened and what has brought me here to the U.S. in the first place."

Rebecca listened.

"One day in the spring of 1995, Sani Abacha, the military dictator of Nigeria at that time, sent men to our house and accused my father and mother of treason. My mother hid in the bushes behind our house, and they dealt just with my father. They said my father was working with political prisoners who had been part of an underground resistance group, and tore our house apart looking for evidence that didn't exist." She shrugged. For the first time her voice quavered as she reached for the Kleenex. "Please understand, it wasn't ever going to matter that they didn't find any evidence. They were always going to arrest him."

"Where were you when this happened?"

"I was living in Lagos, working in a hospital."

Rebecca urged Moremi to go on sensing that what she was about to hear would be horrifying.

"These men forced my father to get in the back of their black Mercedes, and as the car drove off my mother came out running down the driveway after them." She began to rock back and forth, soothing herself while the vivid memory returned. "The car slowed down because they must have seen her running after them, and my mother was shouting and waving her fists at them." She looked up at Rebecca. "My mother was never shy about showing her feelings."

Rebecca responded silently. *Not my mother. She never stood up for herself.*

Moremi blew her nose. "So, the car stopped and one of the men got out. He pointed his AK-47 at my mother," her voice broke and for a moment her head rolled back and forth as if she wanted to howl, then abruptly stopped. Looking directly at Rebecca she almost yelled, "So he shot her!"

"Just like that?" Rebecca asked, incredulous.

"Yes," she nodded. "Just like that. She fell where she was, and the car drove off. Later in the day, neighbors found her."

"Dear God . . ." Rebecca knew that in these kinds of moments, when someone re-experiences a traumatic event, there is nothing to say or do, but wait. At the same time, her own dream reappeared—Becky's mother slumped over, dead.

Moremi finished. "There is much more, of course. But I will go to the end, so you know why I am here. My father died soon after in prison. Our relatives were persecuted, as were our friends. I survived because before they were killed, some friends of my parents arranged for me to marry their son who had moved here in 1980. Peter Abosanjo became my husband. I came here for political asylum and to make the U.S. my home. I should be happy now. I have an eight-year-old son, Ayo."

She stopped abruptly as though she had lost control of her thoughts.

"But something is wrong with me, and what's worse I don't really know what it is."

Rebecca leaned forward. They were coming to the end of the hour. "Just say whatever comes to mind."

Moremi looked down, pensive. "It's more than my grief for my parents." She looked up. "They're gone, but they're with me. I know I was intended to follow in my mother's footsteps and become a healer like her. But here in the U.S. I've tried to let that go."

She stopped, then continued. "But what is wrong is getting worse, and it has to do with my husband. I can feel it. He is distant, and yet I know I'm still attractive to him. It's as if he feels guilty. It doesn't make sense. He and his family saved me."

She stopped.

They sat in silence for a minute.

Rebecca brought the session to a close, setting up another time the following week.

Both women stood up and shook hands.

Rebecca opened the door for Moremi, and watched her walk, tall and straight, slowly down the hall.

CHAPTER FIVE

Bismarck had stolen a march on everyone. Nothing could now stop that 'unseemly and dangerous race'. The most feverish phase of the Scramble had begun.

THE SCRAMBLE FOR AFRICA, WHITE MAN'S CONQUEST OF THE DARK CONTINENT FROM 1876 TO 1912. THOMAS PAKENHAM, 1992.

REBECCA CALLED RICHARD'S CELL PHONE. Just as she thought there was no answer, he picked up.

"Hi. Where are you?" Pause. "How are you?"

"I'm fine. . . I think."

He didn't respond right away. Then he did what he usually did to pull her out of her lost-in-thought moments and switched into his fake waiter accent that usually made her laugh. "Would madam care to join me for a dee-leecious concoction by zee great renowned chef 'Ricardo' who once again shall produce his ma-jeek?"

It didn't work. He quickly retreated to normal chat. "Hey, I'm here at your place. I'm making a mess in your kitchen and The Queens are watching me with love and affection hoping that I drop goodies on the floor. So, hurry. My mood might change."

She finally laughed. "Ok, I'm leaving now."

On the way home she was more distracted than usual, which made driving a hazard. Whatever it was, it had something to do with Moremi. It felt like a dream. She'd seen something and now it was gone. *Poof! Gone! Out of sight, out of mind.* As she turned into the hills up the winding, terraced street, she chased after the memory, a fleeting bird.

She pulled up to the curb in front of her house behind Richard's metallic blue Porsche 964 Cabriolet, his pride and joy. As she sat, musing on Richard's fancy chariot, the bird returned and she caught it, remembering what was nagging at her. *When Moremi came into my office, she put her hand in her jacket pocket and kept it there until she sat down.*

As she took it out her movement was more deliberate than someone who was just a little nervous. She closed her eyes, as if she was listening to something. If I'd paid more attention, I could have asked her, "What's in your pocket?" I've never been like Melanie Klein who might have asked her if she packed a derringer to use on me if she didn't like what I said. Those Freudians were so fearless, interpreting every small gesture, as though each movement involved the therapist and held the key to their psyche. I've always had trouble with that assumption. But this time . . . what was it? What did it mean? Anything? Or nothing at all?

As she stared at the Porsche and its beautiful design, it came to her. *She carried a talisman in her pocket, and it spoke to her.* Richard's talisman had given her the key. She laughed, ready to go inside. As she climbed up the rock stairs to her porch, she could hear the music. Richard had left the front door open for The Queens, as he did when he visited.

The yard was fenced all around, so Juno and Dido owned the property more than she did. They knew every path, tree, bush, rock and noted each passerby. They trolled all day like the ancient guards they were bred to be. When they didn't know someone, their bark was a low rumbling thunder. They were The Queens and Rebecca was the Princess.

"Nobody trains Chows," she often explained to friends. "They're more like cats. You get to live with them."

Richard was playing Eric Clapton. *Once I lived the life of a millionaire, spent all my money, didn't have any cares, took all my friends out for a mighty good time . . . .*

They both loved it. In college she had listened to Bessie Smith sing it, and now Richard had introduced her to the Clapton version. She stopped on the stairs to the open door and listened to his smoky voice, rising, and falling. She continued to climb the porch steps, bobbing her head, singing along. *Bought bootleg liquor, champagne, and wine.* She was half twirling from side to side as she entered the front room, leading into the living room through to the kitchen and the smells of sautéed onion and prosciutto.

Richard was holding court in the kitchen with Juno and Dido sitting at rapt attention, soft ears perched forward, fuzzy round heads following his spatula that he waved like a baton. He was in her flowery apron with ruffled edges tied in a bow around his now slightly more than middle-aged, rotund belly.

He sang with gusto. *"Nobody knows you when you're down and out. In your pocket, not one penny, and as for friends, you don't have any. When you get back on your feet . . .*" Lost in the music, he waved both arms in the air over the large iron skillet sizzling on the stove, turned around to face his audience and delivered the last lines, crooning to the moon, *"Nobody knows you."* He spun back to the skillet and whirled around to sing right at them, this time even louder, like an old coyote, *". . . Nobody knows you . . ."* again letting himself howl *". . . Nobody knows you. Nobody knows yooooooou!"* As he bowed to their furry heads they shifted back and forth on their haunches and leaned in to lick him, then abruptly bounded up and flew to the doorway to greet Rebecca.

They circled and snuffled while butting their heads into her to let her know they were glad to see her before they returned to the kitchen where the action was in case Richard inadvertently tossed a tidbit their way.

He beamed at her like a kid in a play who sees his parents, unselfconscious, with the world at his feet. He uncorked what he described as a "dee-leecious pinot" and offered her a glass, swirling it as he handed it to her.

She smiled and took a sip. "That's nice," she said, beaming all around, taking them in. "Wow, you guys have been busy."

After dinner, at the kitchen alcove table over candles and a fresh bouquet of marigolds and daisies, they finished the wine and talked. They both loved this time when they were full of good food sharing their day. Richard looked at her with a quizzical expression, the one that told her he saw beyond her cheer, into her deeper self.

She could not make up her mind whether she liked this ability of his. Her reluctance was unfair because that's exactly what she herself was trained to do.

"So," he began, leaning back in his chair and holding his wine up to the light to admire its hue, "what was your day like?"

She summoned forth the anthropologist in him, and out of the blue she asked, "What do you know about Nigeria?"

"Nigeria! What makes you ask about Nigeria?"

She didn't want to tell him. She decided to keep the focus on a history lesson rather than explain why she was asking.

He took the hint. He wasn't in the mood for anything that might disturb their pleasant night together. "Let's see. What comes to mind?" He rubbed his chin as if he were thinking deeply. "It's like when you set something free that's been repressed for too long. If you took one of those

Chows, those sweet, loving creatures, and locked her away for a year in a dark cage, who do you think would come out?"

"I get your point. Go on."

"I suppose you could say that's what happened with most of Africa when Europeans discovered its vast beauty and natural resources at the end of the nineteenth century and then colonized pretty much all of it. You've heard the phrase, 'the scramble for Africa?'"

"Yes, I think so."

"It happened very fast over the thirty years leading up to the First World War."

"What happened very fast?"

"Cecil Rhodes! A poster of a giant white man standing over a map of Africa, his arms and legs straddling the whole continent announcing his plans for a telegraph line from Cape Town to Cairo!"

"Yes . . ." she nodded, searching a distant memory. "I may have seen that in some book."

"We all probably did," he went on. "But he was a real person who had predacious plans to colonize what they called in those days the 'Dark Continent!' I don't know about you, but I had no idea what the significance was."

"Nor I," she agreed.

"I understand that once quinine was discovered Africa became open season for Europeans. By the First World War Africa was virtually owned by non-Africans."

She nodded, "You're talking about Africa, but tell me about Nigeria."

"Oh . . . right!" He took a sip. "I think Nigeria could be the most tragic of all. At one time Nigeria opposed colonialism more than any other African country. Nigeria was the voice of Africa." He paused.

"What happened?"

"During the Abacha years in the nineties it lost its position to South Africa and Nelson Mandela. The corruption during those years was crippling for Nigeria, while South Africa rose up and became a constitutional democracy."

"Do you know anyone who has lived there?" she asked.

"Well . . ." he thought for a moment. "I had a friend from college, Jerry, who worked in the State Department. He was sent to the American embassy in Lagos for a few years in the mid-nineties. I lost touch with him but then I ran across a mutual friend of ours around 2000 at a conference in New York. I asked him if he knew how Jerry was doing. He told me an extraordinary story. Jerry apparently had been involved with a human rights organization started by a well-known Nigerian activist, a writer and businessman who was very popular with the military regime. I think his name was Wiwa, who was executed by Sani Abacha."

He took another sip. "So were a lot of people during that time. Apparently, our friend Jerry was there and my friend in New York told me that he heard from Jerry's mother, still alive at the time, that he had disappeared. His body was never found."

"That's awful."

"Yes. And he said something else: that Nigeria is a place of Apocalypse where the worst and best, pure evil and pure good, have converged. The catalyst is oil. As you probably know, we Americans are the biggest consumer of Nigerian oil. The phrase 'blood oil' was coined under the Bush administration." He turned to her. "Tell me, why are you asking about Nigeria?"

She took a moment to respond; then, carefully, "I met a woman today whom I know I'm going to like. But I believe she's scared. Really scared but can't say why. There's a strange energy about her. She's very immediate, and yet at the same time, remote, distant. I think I'm about to become part of her life in some way, different from what I'm used to. I can't explain beyond that really, at least not yet."

He nodded and leaned down to pet Juno's head. She licked his hand with her soft black tongue.

"I'm really tired," she said.

"I'm not sure I answered your question very well."

"Actually, you did."

They washed the dishes together and went up to bed, with The Queens close behind.

CHAPTER SIX

A couple years into the Abacha administration, many Nigerians joked that his strategy to clean up corruption was to make sure that only he and his closest cronies profited from it.

DANIEL JORDAN SMITH, *A CULTURE OF CORRUPTION: EVERY DAY DECEPTION AND POPULAR DISCONTENT IN NIGERIA*. PRINCETON UNIVERSITY PRESS, PRINCETON, NEW JERSEY. 2007. P. 31.

IN HIS BOOK-LINED OFFICE Peter's long body was draped over his swivel chair, feet on the desk, hands behind his head. He stared out into redwoods and blue sky and lost his sense of time. Usually intense, his energy waned, as if he had called it quits in a battle against the baggage of his fifty-eight years. This seepage was something he could usually conquer by channeling his thoughts elsewhere. But not today, and lately, not as often.

A few students hung around outside in his office corridor, angling for attention. Their admiration could be a tonic. Not now. He reached for his intercom and called Annie, his assistant and guardian of the gates, to shoo them away. He shared her with other professors in the department, but he was her favorite.

She was short, plump, late-fifties and efficient. A no-nonsense den mother laced with acerbic humor, she commanded student affection. When they needed too much attention and swarmed in on her like hungry children she would point to the door: "Out!" and the room would clear. When they were whiney, they would hear, "You are privileged to be attending this great university and I suggest you make good use of it." She admired Professor Abosanjoand thought he was mysterious and smarter than the other professors. Nothing seemed to ruffle him, and he did not indulge in academic pettiness. He offered no opinions of others' work. He was above it all.

She shot back on the intercom, "Don't worry, I'll take care of them.

There weren't too many today. Only one a little pushy and I told her you were busy. She's a student in your philosophy of economics class. Alice Gordon. She'll be back. She's a fan. Oh, and by the way, don't you need to leave to pick up Ayo from school? Isn't today soccer practice?"

"Yes, I'm leaving soon." He still had some time, but was distracted by the mention of Alice Gordon, and thought of the final assignment he had given his graduate students in her class. *Why did I risk so much by presenting them with an actual situation in Nigeria, where my family had ties? Why did I do that?*

He tried to channel his thoughts by breathing steadily, quieting his mind, but it wasn't working.

What did I expect to gain by the portraits they might draw in their papers? Not to mention their analysis of the corruption? But deep down he knew why: *Would anyone catch it?* What had they done—what he and his family had done? The risk had felt innocent. A simple test. If he could plant the fraud right under the noses of his eager students and they missed it, would that erase it?

Maybe, he mused. *That's why I like numbers. You can make them show what you want. After all, in America if you have brains and money, pretty much anything can be expunged.* He flicked his head as if he could swat away the shifting fallacy that mocked him, because deep down, he also knew his hope added up to a bunch of hooey.

With the right research one of them could link his family's name with the bribery, common in Nigeria and other African countries where military regimes and oil profits converged. And not only so-called third world countries. The U.S. was up to its neck in Nigeria's oil and gas profits. But could these young, bright-eyed students make the right connections?

He yearned to be released from his guilt and get back to some normalcy with Moremi and Ayo, the joy they had in the beginning. When he had sifted through the student papers that morning he wondered if he would see something personal. At first, he felt relieved until he came upon one paper. It looked like one student, Alice Gordon, had come precariously close to guessing the truth.

As he stared out the window, he knew he had made an error. Precariously close was just too close.

He wanted to find someone to blame. There was his wife Moremi. *Was it because of her link to my past that I took the chance?* After ten years of marriage, rather than losing interest, he craved her more than ever. She had withdrawn from him and now responded out of duty and maybe gratitude. He had always been hounded by a sadness he did not want to understand, but it had never gotten such a grip on him as it had lately. *Was it her fault? Maybe.*

She had become more secretive lately. Her distant attention drew him into her private ways—a lone moth to the flame. Yes, that she cared less for him, his unrequited feelings, that must be why he felt compelled to take risks, as if one daring action could change everything.

But it was one thing to imagine something with high risk and unknown consequences, and it was quite another to take a real risk to create excitement—just to pull himself out of a funk.

He stared at the pile on his desk—a stack of fifteen word-perfect student documents responding to his assignment. They had worked hard, with tidy footnotes, creative expression, and solid scholarship. They tried to follow the footprints he gave them that could lead to what really happened.

Who am I and what am I doing? What made me do this?

He had assumed his students would accept that the pieces of the puzzle were anything but authentic. They would follow the clues like little hounds that live in a digital cartoon reality, unlike the average kid on the street in Lagos, who would instinctively understand that the grift was real.

And yet, it looks like one of them fell into the truth. He wasn't sure. He needed to re-read it. He pictured Alice sitting in the front of the class, her unkempt hair and granny glasses. An unlikely suspect in any line-up. But still, here he was, and there was her paper. He still felt excited by the possibility of one of them getting close to the truth. It had made him feel more alive.

His ostensibly bogus assignment was perfect—an unnamed developing country with plentiful natural resources, huge oil and gas profits, corrupt government, violent regime and, finally, ecological disaster. *So, what if they figured out it was Nigeria?* He'd been sure they would stop at the scenario and never dream of a connection between his cooked-up situation and the family of their very own economics professor.

His father had collaborated with an American-owned engineering and construction company back in the nineties, under investigation for alleged bribery in the construction of Nigeria's ten billion dollar liquefied natural gas export plant on Bonny Island. The investigation had widened so that it went back far enough to implicate his father, who was one of the

Nigerian officials involved in bribes that secured American contracts and helped set up the gimmick to siphon off millions in expenses so it would beat the company's earnings target and boost its stock value.

He couldn't stop the memory from flooding in.

When he wrote me that letter, my father assumed I would be amused by it all. It was true, even as a teenager growing up in Nigeria he had been fascinated, sitting in the front room of his house when his father was talking with his business associates about what amounted to large-scale white-collar crime. They ignored him, curled up in the wingback chair, reading, as they went into father's study and left the door open to let in the breeze in the late afternoon heat. They were discussing money—big money—as if it were a game. A lethal game.

He looked out again at the blue sky and green trees, thinking how much Americans took for granted: their clean drinking water and broad supplies of energy, all without thinking. Nigeria is different, but somehow the same. It's a kind of hopelessness both ways. Either you have too much, or too little. Both lead to indifference. With too much, you take things for granted and become complacent. With too little, you think change is impossible.

Peter had followed the Nigerian Extractive Industries Transparency Initiative's audits for many years, knowing that his father was involved with them back in the nineties. After his parents died several years ago, he became obsessed to know more for reasons unclear to him. It was like returning to the scene of a crime. Of course, it wasn't his crime. But more and more, it felt like the seat of a deadly secret that poisoned everything.

He made sure Moremi learned none of this. As that burdensome secret grew, his emotions about her grew more entangled.

He reassured himself that most of his students would feel successful if they figured out the baby company based on KBR was a subsidiary of the poppa company based on the larger, well-known American company, with tentacles worldwide. They wouldn't get the scope of the game or the right-under-your-nose power play. They had been distracted by the economics, and their hunt for answers would end before the reality of the environmental disaster falling like a dark cloud over Nigeria reached their consciousness. They had stayed with the numbers and avoided immersing themselves in the calamity or the responsibility for it.

But—Alice. She had exceeded his expectations. That could be a problem.

Annie's voice came through his intercom. "Professor, it's getting late," she chimed.

He whipped his feet off the desk and swiveled around, glancing at the Rolex his father had given him when he graduated with his MBA.

He backed out of the parking space a bit too fast and headed down the campus drive to the main street that would take him east toward Ayo's school. Now that he was late, he was angry with himself. He'd had difficulty all day paying attention to business. His class presentation had felt off and he knew he was not up to his usual performance. He counted on his acerbic wit and his precise pronunciation in a booming, baritone voice describing global markets in the developing countries all over the world, providing expanding opportunities for the young and savvy. But the day had been lackluster and now he felt flat, tired, and irritable.

He pulled up in front of the school. Ayo was in front jumping around with his friends, mocking it up with fancy footwork as if he were playing a guitar, lively and quick with his mother's agility.

Ayo spotted Peter and ran over to his backpack, hoisted it up over his shoulder and skipped to the car, waving goodbye to his friends. He opened the back door with a "Hi Daddio!" as he hopped in with his pack and fumbled with the seatbelt.

"Hi yourself!" Peter responded trying to sound upbeat and cheerful.

As they pulled into the driveway Ayo asked, "So, where's Mom?"

This innocent question was a swat to his ego. He answered, "Well, I think she had some work to do at the lab tonight. Or maybe she said she had a class. I'm not sure. But she won't be home until late so it's just you and me buddy. That okay with you?"

"Sure, Dad."

He loved his son's positive nature and pushed away the idea that it did not come through his own family's genes, but Moremi's. This effort added to the day's escalating irritation. He felt the need to be alone with his dark thoughts. As he got out of the car he yearned for release.

They ate leftover pizza at the kitchen table and talked about soccer. Peter loved soccer and never understood why Americans did not love it as much as the rest of the world. He was a fan of Nigeria's Super Eagles and was disgusted by the infighting and bad blood between the coaches. The Nigerians were the most talented soccer players in the world but were bogged down by graft and corruption that had rotted the country. He and Ayo followed World Cup soccer and always rooted for the Super Eagles.

With a half-eaten piece left on his plate Ayo announced he was finished and asked if he could watch TV.

Did he have any homework? Peter was relieved to hear Ayo had done it after school. He did not have the energy to help with the homework tonight nor to continue chatting with his son. He nodded with approval, picked up their plates and put them in the sink. He did not feel like washing them. He didn't feel like doing anything. She wouldn't be home until late, maybe 10:00, and would not call. She hadn't gotten used to her cell phone after so many years, and still didn't like to use it. She once explained: "Nothing can replace real talk. I never needed a phone before and I don't need one now," even though almost all Nigerians carried them.

He walked over to the cellar door off the kitchen. He could hear the SpongeBob SquarePants theme from the living room where Ayo lay on the rug watching. *She lets him watch that.* He didn't understand their attraction to that silly cartoon. *Imaginative nonsense. Not serious like soccer.*

He descended the stairs into the cool darkness of the cellar where they stored their leftover clutter, all the odds and ends from the past years, plus the washer and dryer. This was her domain. He couldn't even remember the last time he came down. But here he was, invading her territory, which is what he intended.

The Captain was shouting: *Are you ready kids?* followed by their yelling, "Captain!" and singing *Blow the Man Down*, followed by *Ohhhhh! Who lives in a pineapple under the sea?* Ayo was shouting along with the chorus, "SpongeBob SquarePants!"

He opened the plywood cupboard door and peered in at the makeshift shelves stuffed with the clutter of old jars of nails, half-used paint cans, some tools, a small hammer. She thought he didn't know she used these shelves to camouflage her altar—but of course he did. He knew all about her and that Voudou witch. It was better not to let her know he knew. This had become his little cat and mouse game.

As he studied the shelves he felt as if he were coming alive. His gaze began to organize the scene and make sense of it. He peered down at a pile of old combs and saw their antiquated beauty. Some had little rhinestones, one was carved wood, another was bright pink plastic, and one was a hair comb with tiny twinkly stones. It looked cheap but maybe it wasn't.

Where did she find all this? He knew she liked to wander into second-hand stores. If she bought little things, she rarely showed him. He picked up one of Ayo's shirts tossed on the shelf, revealing an exquisite little hand-held mirror, decorated with a sweet drawing of a rosebud. He held the mirror and looked into it. Seeing himself in the moment was a jolt. Even he could tell that his face, without the effort to animate himself, looked sad and sunken. He put it back, muttering, "Stop it. Just stop it!"

He took a deep breath, closed his eyes, and then opened his eyes, now grim, like a predator's. He assessed the altar more systematically, putting them back more or less as he found them. He focused on a little wooden dish of shells and weathered beach glass. He wondered if she collected some of these when they went to the oceanfront resort on their honeymoon, when he was sure it was all going to work out.

Piles of beads, some strung, some just loose, small jars of herbs and potions of God knew what, and then back in the corner he saw it—a snake stuffed into a mason jar. It was very realistic, but he checked. It was rubber, an Egyptian cobra with yellow background and brown speckles. Peter knew snakes. Its face was jammed up against the side of the jar, rubber fangs wedged into its mouth. One little round eye stared out of the jar. It gave him the creeps and he couldn't stop the shiver running up his spine ending in his head swarming with pinpricks.

He shivered again. Secret knick-knacks! A cheap ruby-studded watch, a real glass bottle of Coca-Cola, unopened. Some rock candies. Dishes of sand. Votive candles. He reached over and chose one and carefully placed it in the center of the shelf. He picked up a little white dish of black sand and placed it in front of the candle.

He searched over the shelves and the entire basement looking for matches. He wondered where they could be. He reached absentmindedly into his pockets thinking that magically they would be there even though he never carried them. He was irritated as he shuffled through the clutter searching for matches. He didn't want to have to go back upstairs where Ayo was. That would ruin the moment, dispel the ritual feeling he was conjuring. Then he remembered she kept an old jacket down there that she only wore in the winter. She kept it in a little closet next to the small basement bathroom. He grabbed the door, swung it open and there it was hanging with some other old stuff. He plunged his hand into the pocket and couldn't believe his good fortune as his hand cupped around a little box of wooden matches. He returned to the shelf, rattling the matches in his ear.

He struck a match and lit the votive. The small flame struggled to grow. He reached over for the jar with the snake and held it up to gaze into its essence. He set it down by the candle. The flickering flame bounced off the glass and the snake's eyes blinked.

Satisfied with the effect, he rolled up his left shirtsleeve with his right hand. He reached into his pants pocket and pulled out a small gold penknife, another gift from his father. He flicked the blade open and across his left palm he made five little cuts like a star. He winced as the sting grew into a throbbing pain and the blood seeped up and started to drip across his hand. He held his hand over the sand in front of the candle. It dripped slowly drop by drop. He stood still, mesmerized, closing his eyes as he leaned into the pain that could heal. The more it hurt, the calmer he felt. He imagined the thorns digging into Jesus' scalp and the blood dripping. The release was total, and he felt calmer than he had in many days. Even better, he had desecrated her altar. He rolled his head back, satisfied, and closed his eyes.

Finally, he reached into his right pocket and withdrew the white handkerchief, stuffing it into his hand to staunch the bleeding. He blew out the candle and put everything back as he remembered it had been. As he mounted the stairs, he heard SpongeBob upstairs. But another sound drew him back. It sounded like hissing. He halted, twisted around, and scanned the basement, cluttered and dismal as before. He laughed and bounded up the rest of the stairs back to the kitchen and into the family room.

Ayo looked up. "Hey, Dad! When's Mom coming?"

Peter smiled. "Soon. I'm sure. It's time for bed, Ayo. Let's read the next chapter of Harry Potter tonight."

They lay in bed reading the story, father and son, two peas in a pod.

CHAPTER SEVEN

Young girls who are impatient, lack self-control, and exhibit anger are not thought generally to possess this supernatural power, for their temperamental or fickle natures would expose and dissipate a power that must remain a mystery.

DREWAL AND DREWAL, GELEDE, *ART AND FEMALE POWER AMONG THE YORUBA* (INDIANA UNIVERSITY PRESS, 1990, P. 75)

MOREMI PARKED HER CAR AT THE BEACH, and walked along the sand, close to the water. The sky turned orange as an engorged sun bled toward the horizon drawing the water closer as it glistened through the dusk, forcing her to shade her eyes.

Peter would not expect her until later, so she had plenty of time to think about her session with Rebecca. She was exhausted.

The smell of sea air, a vaporous mixture of rotting fish and seaweed, reminded her of her dream and Nigeria. The waves spilled over and rolled in, trickling through her feet. A flock of Canada geese in V-formation called out to each other.

Last night's dream was an important message, but she was not ready to absorb its deeper meaning. Her sadness was a safe cocoon where she could retreat into herself, free to grieve. Mami was pressuring her but moving on did not feel right.

She carried her shoes and let the sand caress her. *I want to lie down and let the softness enfold me. I want to be like the little hermit crab burrowing into safety from predators. Mami does not understand that my sadness is my mother holding me. I never understood that being a mother meant I would need my own mother more.* She let the tears spill down her cheeks.

Rebecca Calhoun came to mind. She seemed to care in a way Moremi had missed. Like her own mother, Rebecca listened without interruption. *Of course, she'll never really understand. How could she? She's not African.* But there was the mask in her office. *Did she know it was more than a beautiful object?* Moremi suspected she did. What were the chances of that mask showing up eight and a half thousand miles away across continents in that moment when the two of them met? In Moremi's heritage such an opportune appearance was possible, even usual, and could portend either good or evil.

Moremi looked out as if her eyes could carry her across the ocean. The mask embodied what they would mean to each other. She wondered, *who will we become to each other?*

Then she turned and headed for her car.

She pulled into her driveway at 9:30 P.M. eager to see Ayo but dreading the cold between her and Peter. Ayo was the glue between them. But lately more than ever the guilt ate away at her—she could not warm up to her husband. He was handsome, intelligent, hardworking, from a good family. She knew how pleased her parents would have been about their marriage, about Ayo and how like her own father Ayo was. But there was something about him she could not trust.

She remembered a strange call soon after she arrived in the U. S. from Nigeria. One night she heard Peter talking on his phone in a low, fervent voice. He often got phone calls at all different times, but his tone was unusual—more urgent. She got out of bed and crept down the stairs to listen. He was in the entryway cupping both hands over the phone. She thought she heard him say. "Don't worry about it. I'll take care of it. Moremi will never know. Trust me. She'll never know."

Is he protecting me? She had retreated to bed and the next day decided it meant nothing. Her husband was an important man. She wanted to respect his privacy. Over the years that moment set the stage for all the little ambiguities other couples need to let go. But for her, they grew and became a startling image: Bluebeard's pile of skulls. She'd seen it in her mother's collection of folktales. When she was a child, it was just a story, but the haunting image came back with every doubt.

Now, she wondered about everything. Her rescue into Peter's family, into his arms, his ready-made world, as if all it needed was her . . . Despite her attempts to overcome her growing aversion toward him—more emotion than physical—she could not. She knew it hurt him but suspected he had given up hope she would change. Still, neither would rock the boat. Divorce was not an option.

She entered the front door and shut it quietly, soothed by the glow of indirect light. The entryway with its tiled floor, coat rack and framed photograph was her favorite part of the house. She brought the photograph from home as a wedding present for Peter. It was one of the few items she managed to keep after her parents' home was sold, the bronze roped pot that was excavated in the sixties at the Igbo Ukwu burial site in southeastern Nigeria, dating back to the ninth century. Her father had always kept it hung in his study.

She was relieved when Peter was pleased with the gift. It was one of his few concessions to anything African in their home. Peter said he had bought the large house to be their special family home, which was more than generous, but she never fully believed him. That was the trouble. Peter always said the right thing.

She heard Peter's voice reading Harry Potter to Ayo. She tiptoed into the kitchen to avoid interrupting. If Ayo heard her come in, he would jump out of bed and run down to greet her, hurting Peter's feelings. Ayo's preference for her was obvious to them both, but she tried to balance the scales. For her, family ties took priority over petty competitions, and she wanted her son to be close to his father just as she was close to hers.

She was hungry and opened the refrigerator to pull out a carton of cottage cheese. She found a spoon and carried it into the living room, eating slowly, letting the cool blandness slide down her throat. She cupped the spoon upside down in her mouth and stared absentmindedly at the silver-framed black and white photograph on the bookshelf of her and Peter. He was holding Ayo, whowas about six months old. They were standing in front of this home, and they looked like a happy family. She cocked her head and wondered if they really were happy. *Is all this my imagination? My own pain? What happened to us?*

In that moment in the living room, as she stood still something struck her. She had noticed the door to the cellar was slightly open. She went back into the kitchen. She was the only one who knew that the latch would not engage unless it was pulled shut. *Who had gone down there?* Certainly not Ayo. *Peter?* But he didn't like the cellar. It was her territory. She always did the laundry. She told him, "I always did it in my own family. I helped my mother. It was our women's work. It wasn't drudgery. It was our time to talk." Peter would grunt his assent, preserving her sanctuary.

She heard Peter say "goodnight" to Ayo and then cross the hall to their bedroom and into the bathroom. She slowly climbed the stairs, listening for any sounds that might alert her to a deviation in Peter's usual nightly pattern.

He would often read for about two hours in bed before he fell asleep. It was not his usual habit to come back down after he had gone to bed. He was not one of those men who got hungry in the middle of the night. His ate simply, and he was thin because he watched his diet. He told her that when he was young, he was a 'fat kid.' She had trouble believing that, but hoped it was true because it made his usual formality more human.

His father had been tall and thin too, but his mother was a large woman. Some would have said she was too large. Peter never criticized his mother, and now he rarely mentioned her. He would say, "My mother was an interesting woman. She always supported my father. She wanted me to have the best opportunities. She was so happy when Ayo was born." But Peter never mentioned any personal memories. She wondered if he had any.

When Peter's mother first laid eyes on Ayo, she smiled but she did not immediately hold out her arms. All she said to Peter was, "He looks like your father."

Moremi had tried in the beginning of their marriage to share her own family memories, but Peter would look pained whenever she did. She thought was because he didn't like thinking about what had happened to them, or he didn't want her to cry or be sad.

She reached the top of the stairs and walked down to Ayo's door, which was ajar, lit by the glow of his Star Wars nightlight. By his bed, Hans Solo's face was smiling. She stood outside to make sure he was asleep, then started to walk away when she heard, "Mom?"

She turned and went in. "Hi, I didn't want to waken you."

"You didn't." Sleepy, starting to sit up, rubbing his eyes, he said, "Dad and I were reading."

"I know. When I came home, I heard. I decided not to interrupt." Ayo yawned, and she helped him snuggle back down pulling the comforter up. "Go back to sleep. I'll see you in the morning." He closed his eyes and smiled. She sat for a moment and watched him fall asleep again.

She stood and left the room and headed for their bedroom to make sure Peter was in bed reading. She poked her head in and smiled. He looked up and smiled back.

Her throat constricted. The smile wasn't real. "Hey, I'm just going to go down and do a little work on a paper that's due. I want to finish it tonight."

He understood.

She glided down the stairs and went back into the kitchen. She needed to get Ayo's clothes out of the dryer. And to check if someone else had been there. Who else but Peter?

At the top of the stairs, she turned on the light, a bare bulb hanging down from the ceiling that shed a dim glow all around. She crept down the stairs and went over to the cabinet, lowering her head onto her chest and closing her eyes. She began to sway in a circular motion. She was cautious and did not want to be possessed by the spirit she knew occupied the room, but she needed it to tell her what had happened.

A hissing sound. Her eyes popped open, and she moved to the cabinet, opened the wooden doors and peered in. At first it looked the way she'd left it, her shirt rumpled and tossed about, hiding the offerings.

But there was a slight rearrangement. She pushed some rags aside to see the snake jar in the corner. It wasn't right—the head was facing out at her. She always put it away with its head facing toward the back of the shelf, hiding its gaze.

She began to shake and started to feel weak. She took a deep breath to calm herself but knew she could not escape what was coming. She focused on what she could see and learn by looking beyond the mere things and into the spirits that animated the objects. "He's been down here," she whispered. "What has he done?"

She spotted the sand in the saucer, reached out, and pulled it closer. In the dim light she squinted. She reached up high to a shelf and felt for the small metal flashlight she kept there. Flicking it on she held it over the sand. She poked at it. Something stuck to her finger. She rubbed the greasy clump between her thumb and finger and examined it with the flashlight. It looked reddish purple. She smelled it.

Again, the hissing.

She put everything else back in its place, grabbed the saucer, and went back up the stairs, snapped off the light, and pulled the door tight. She went into the kitchen and over the sink under the recessed bulb where the light was brightest, she examined the sand more closely. She set the saucer down on the counter and stirred the sand. It was still wet. She picked up more, rubbing it between her thumb and finger. She turned on the hot water, rinsing her fingers, and watched the red stuff and black sand go toward the drain. Her heart was pounding, and she felt dizzy. She dried the saucer and put it far back on a kitchen shelf.

In the family room, lit only from the kitchen, she slumped down into a chair, staring into the gloom. Her head bent forward and without passing out she fell into a trance.

This time it was her mother, with a serious and sad expression, dressed in white, her head wrapped in white cloth, and carrying a basket of flowers. At first, her mother was silent. She began to sway back and forth as if also in a trance. The drums played and her mother closed her eyes.

With a thud from the drum, everything stopped.

Her mother spoke softly, carefully.

"His family has blood on their hands. Our blood."

CHAPTER EIGHT

It is hard to cure the madness that originates in the family.

AFRICAN PROVERB

MOREMI WOKE SUDDENLY in the family room chair.

Peter was standing in the doorway in his pajamas watching her.

She froze.

"Oh," she stammered. "I guess I didn't hear you."

He said nothing, just stood like an apparition, only slightly diminished by his pajamas and bare feet.

"Did I awaken you?" she asked clearing her throat, trying to sound normal, still in shock from her mother's message. She had no idea how long he'd been standing there watching her.

"I don't know. Something woke me. What are you doing sitting here in the dark? It's 1:00 A.M. Why aren't you writing?"

She felt defensive, then angry. *Why should I have to answer to him?* Her mother's words, "our blood" returned. She'd better be careful.

"I went down to the basement."

He stiffened and pushed himself to stand taller and straighter.

His discomfort satisfied her. She might have the upper hand.

"I remembered that Ayo needed his blue jeans for school tomorrow because they're going on a field trip, so I made sure they were in the dryer for the morning."

His eyes narrowed, sizing her up. Was she telling the truth?

She didn't care. Whether he believed her or not, she just wanted him to go back to bed. She needed to be alone.

In the past months they had become used to these minor prevarications that kept the peace.

After a long pause, she looked down at her hands tightly clasped as if she was holding on.

His stare bore down on her.

She raised her head to meet his gaze.

He didn't blink. Instead, he shot back, "There's no field trip tomorrow."

He was right—how could she convince him she believed there was?

"Are you sure? I thought I saw the notice last week and I think it's tomorrow."

A tinge of doubt crossed his glare.

"No. It's next week."

She could see he wouldn't press it because he wasn't entirely certain. He was used to being right and if there were the slightest doubt, he would back down.

"Well," she said, feigning a yawn, "I guess I'm pretty tired. I just thought it was tomorrow."

He nodded the way he did sometimes to let her know that he was simply placating her, but he knew better. He turned away and headed back up to bed without their ritual goodnight.

She sat in the dim light. She thought about her mother's words.

Peter's parents had somehow remained unscathed by the Sani Abacha reprisals of the nineties. His father Kolade was one of the lower generals for the regime. Her father Moses had known his in school. They were never friends, just acquaintances who had gone in different directions and wound up on opposite sides during the civil war. Twenty-seven years later, in 1994, Moses asked Kolade to help find a friend who was a political prisoner and help him get released. The friend was released. After that the two men developed a bond. Moses was grateful because he believed Kolade had taken a risk to help him; Kolade often reminded her father he owed him a debt. Peter's mother later consulted Moremi's mother as a healer when she was ill with stomach cramps that wouldn't go away.

After Moremi's parents were killed in 1997, she had believed his family had come to her aid and rescue because of their friendship. She had been grateful when Peter's parents protected her and offered their son and a safe life in America. He needed a young, beautiful, Nigerian wife, they said. She needed to escape her parents' fate. What could be better? She had no choice. It was only a matter of time before they arrested her along with any of her father's close associates. Moremi knew that her parents would have blessed this union. She had no reason to believe otherwise.

Peter's parents offered Moremi sanctuary in their own home while they arranged her marriage and escape to America. They made her promise—all ties with Nigeria must be severed. Any contact at all with distant relatives or friends would be putting them in danger. Leaving meant forever.

She had met Peter when she was sixteen, at an outdoor festival. He was handsome, intelligent, and aloof. He didn't want to stay and looked annoyed and embarrassed when his mother made a joke that upset her father. She had clasped her hands together, pushing her whole body toward Moses for emphasis and said, "I think the oil should unite us. There really will be enough to make us all rich."

Her father had frowned, and Peter's mother shook her head, "Really, Moses, you must have realized by now your old idealistic sentiments only caused more harm during that ridiculous civil war of ours." Moses looked pained but said nothing.

Both of Moremi's parents had been on the side of the Biafrans during the 1967 civil war when the southeastern part of Nigeria fought to become its own republic. It failed in 1970. She grew up hearing her parents talk about that difficult and tragic time. So many hopes and dreams dashed by the military regime and the greed for Nigeria's oil.

She remembered Peter's reaction to his mother's remark. There was something amiss between mother and son.

In 1997, a rushed ceremony was arranged in Nigeria. One of Peter's cousins stood in for him. This seemed right and proper to Moremi, what her parents wanted. In Nigeria traditional marriage is more of an arrangement between two families than between two individuals. She remembered feeling grateful and eager to see Peter again.

Two weeks later she boarded a plane at the Lagos Airport and watched her homeland disappear. Once they were at 30,000 feet, she could only see small patches of green over brownish hazed landscape and then it was gone. Fourteen hours later her plane came in low over the water and her heart skipped a beat when she thought there was no runway, only water. The wheels bounced and they were on the ground at the San Francisco International Airport.

Peter greeted her as she emerged from the customs gate. He looked much older than the recent photograph his mother had shown her, but she reminded herself that she too had aged. He was her husband now. There was no time to grieve her family. She was convinced of one thing—she must leave the past behind. Her life narrowed down to survival and her link to home would have to exist in memory alone, an internal lifeline that stretched back to her ancestors. It was up to her to create a link to the future, to those who were not yet born.

As the years went by, the dreams and the connections started to come. Her ancestors no longer wanted to stay in memory. Mami began to visit whether she liked it or not. And now she had found Rebecca. The mask in Rebecca's office told her she was meant to do this. She understood that it was confidential, which made it feel safe.

She must find out what her mother meant by "our blood" on their family's hands. Before she finally went up to bed, she asked herself, *"Whose hands?"*

CHAPTER NINE

The Yoruba word aje, has no exact equivalent in
The English language, its closest synonym being
The "witch."

THE GELEDE SPECTACLE: ART, GENDER, AND SOCIAL HARMONY IN AN AFRICAN CULTURE. UNIVERSITY OF WASHINGTON PRESS, 1996.

PETER HAD KNOWN SOMETHING WAS WRONG when she peeked in to say goodnight. Had she discovered what he had done at the altar? He couldn't imagine how, but he lay in bed unable to sleep. It was dark except for the streetlamps that cast a dim glow over the night, matching his gloomy thoughts. He assumed she would stay downstairs for a long while, a new habit of hers. He was shaken, perhaps more than she. She knew. How, did not matter. She knew.

A sound pulled him out of his light sleep like a door shutting hard. Was it the front door? He looked at the clock. It was 1:00 A.M. He got out of bed and went down to investigate.

She was sitting in the family room lit only by the kitchen light. *Had she fallen asleep?* She was agitated, rolling her head with her eyes closed. *Was she dreaming? What was she seeing?*

She did not look like his wife. *Who is she?*

She's a witch.

He could not escape what he had done and what had drawn him down into her cellar. The release of cutting himself would not help him here. He saw in her the demon he lived with. Confronting the evil spirit in the cellar was all he knew to do, and that's what he had done. He thought it would keep the demon at bay. Watching her, he had his answer.

It was no surprise that she still practiced her magic. He had always known about her mother and that crazy grandmother. But when they married, he thought he could make her happy. She would leave the past behind. They would unite in a new world, full of hope with Ayo their innocent, glorious child. The throbbing in his hand was a signal, a beacon of truth. He had done the right thing. The cutting had calmed him.

But there was more, much more beyond his understanding. She not only believed in personal spirits—those meddlesome ancestors—she talked to them. *Her spirits were restless.* It made him sick that he believed in them at all. And here it was, even in the United States of America—that cavern of horror right under their home—he could not rid himself of the knowledge that they knew his secret, and that he believed in their punishment. He had hoped that here, where Voudou is considered cartoony zombie hippie stuff, he could shake it once and for all, and if he could make her forget—he too could forget. By confronting them in her basement he would excise her beliefs. *How perfect to marry a Voudou princess and convert her to American pragmatism! After all, her altar was just a bunch of silly little girl stuff. And that snake in the jar! It was a joke.* He hated himself for taking it seriously.

He felt sick and weak as his thoughts raced like frightened horses. His parents had pushed him into this. Not marrying had been his only true rebellion. He could have had his pick of any Nigerian girl. Living in mostly white America gave him an excuse to be single, but when he opened the envelope, they had sent containing Moremi's picture, everything changed.

He had met her in Africa on one of his visits home before his parents moved to London. He was in his twenties, and she must have been about sixteen. Even though she was still a little gawky, he could see the woman in the girl. She had poise. Her mother was beautiful, curvaceous, buxom, one of those women who looked better with more weight, graceful, flowing, and strong. Moremi would grow up to be like her mother in some ways, but perhaps thinner, like her father.

Yet, until he saw the photograph of her as a mature adult who also had not married, she had slipped from his mind. She had become everything he imagined when she was sixteen and had a vision of the woman she would become. A woman he wanted even then.

When his mother told him long ago that Moremi's mother was a priestess it meant nothing to him. Now he knew better.

When he left Moremi in the dark, his mind would not stop. The more he wished it away, the more vivid his memory became.

It was a Sunday afternoon, even hotter than usual, humid after the rain. He was about twelve and he had been playing football with some friends until it began to rain. The grass field tended to be squishy with mud but when it rained little pockets of slick mud formed, making it impossible to run over the ground without slipping and falling. They had been lazily kicking the ball around near their school because it had been too humid to play hard, even for them. At about 4:00 in the afternoon they disbanded. Most of the boys headed for home leaving just he and Eze, who stayed behind to kick the ball around some more.

Eze was gifted. He maneuvered the ball with deadly accuracy. He was swift and could run and zigzag at the same high speed, his upper torso seemed to glide while his legs and feet moved with the precision of a tap dancer. Nicknamed 'Cheetah,' the boys liked to argue over which was faster: Gazelle or Cheetah? Eze picked Cheetah, claiming that he read it could run up to 75 mph in short bursts. "Plus," he would add holding up his leg, "I'm built like one." This would make them all laugh. Eze was light-hearted and popular while Peter was more withdrawn and serious.

Eze's family was Igbo. Peter understood little about how the Igbo people were different from his. However, he had an early memory of his father grumbling, "Those Igbos think they're better than we are. But they're responsible for Biafra." But in that moment, alone after the others had gone, they were just two boys standing in the heat of a Sunday afternoon looking for something to do. Eze said, "Hey, come with me. I want to show you something." His tone promised adventure and Peter followed.

After almost an hour's dusty walk on a road through littered debris and years of neglect, lined with stately coconut palms, fronds swaying in the occasional breeze warning of something to come. They reached the greater outskirts of town near the river with large rock outcroppings and dense areas with low rainforest undergrowth.

Eze led them off the main road and they headed through rainforest thicket, following a narrow, snaking path made by tramping feet. After a while Peter could hear drums and a low chanting murmur. In the distance he saw a clearing with a straw roof over a five-foot high mud wall.

Eze grabbed an old wooden crate and set it next to the wall, joined by a few others, so Peter did the same.

They watched what was going on inside. Along the inner wall witnesses stood or sat on splintered benches and chairs. The drums were constant. The ground was packed, tamped down hard. Many closed their eyes, swaying back and forth. In the center a square pole nearly reached the ceiling, anchored in cement in a wooden platform, chest-high, a shelf painted with blue and white stripes and lined with rattles, bells, drums, and books, including jars filled with various substances he couldn't really see.

Gesturing overhead at the model of a wooden ship with sails hanging from the rafters, Peter whispered, "Look, it's a flying ship."

Eze paid no attention, transported. He pointed to a large woman sitting in a chair. "There she is! She's the Mambo. Very important person." Eze knew more about this than he had let on.

Peter watched and wondered. The Mambo sat near a small room that could only be entered from the inner courtyard and waved her arms over her head as if she were conducting something invisible. She bent over and investigated the entrance.

Out of the darkness, a woman burst forth holding her hands on the side of her head like horns. She ran around in circles tossing her upper torso up and down as if she were trying to buck off an invisible rider. At one point a man got up and went over and grabbed her arms as if to steady her. Slowly she seemed to calm down, but the strange, wild look in her eyes did not, and periodically she would leer and rush at the crowd like a charging bull.

People sitting on the sidelines jumped out of their chairs to get out of her way, both frightened and spellbound. The Mambo never took her eyes off her, as if controlling her with a steadily, connected gaze like a rein you would use to train an animal in the ring.

The wild woman stopped, immobile in the middle of the courtyard and craned her head around scanning the crowd. She squinted at the sun low on the horizon and sniffed the air. She pawed the ground with her foot. The crowd was dead silent. Then, without warning, she shot out her right arm and swiveled around and swept it over their heads as they ducked to avoid her eyes.

She stopped and let her arm fall limp for just a moment, as if she were suddenly sapped of her energy, before it jutted out like a rifle pointing directly at Peter, who was caught in her eye.

All heads turned toward Peter's face just over the wall, while Eze ducked out of sight.

Peter stared back, horrified.

The Mambo stood up, concerned, and Peter dropped down below the wall to join Eze who had missed what happened.

Peter immediately jumped down from his perch and tore out of the woods as if a wild boar were chasing him. He ran until he had to stop and catch his breath, and then ran again until he reached the outskirts of town. He stopped, bent over, and threw up in the dirt. All that came out was spittle followed by dry heaves. He managed to calm down, remembering how his football coach had taught him to breathe slowly, in and out, in and out.

Peter never knew why that crazy woman had pointed at him, but he knew it meant something. There had been other times in his life when he had been scared but never like that. At least in the past he could recognize what the danger was. But this had been different, more frightening than even his father, the Black Mamba, could be, when his dark temper flared.

He made up the nickname after he had seen one when he was thirteen at boarding school. A gamekeeper was called to the school to kill it and all the boys had collected in the yard to watch as the headmaster kept ordering them to stand back. They were eager to see the deadly snake and with no idea how lethal it could be.

Peter thought the snake was beautiful. It was yellow with a green hue, long and sleek, at least eight feet long and raised its head a foot and a half in the air. The Mamba moved back and forth as if in a hunting dance poised to strike while the gamekeeper backed away mimicking its movements. When the snake struck, missing him by an inch, he jammed the stick just below its head and held it there, grinding it into the ground. Peter saw inside its black mouth and shuddered. The gamekeeper did not let up until his assistant came and threw a net over the dead snake. They hauled it away very carefully as though it was still alive.

His father, like the Mamba, was quick and unpredictable, but Peter had learned how to get out of his way.

But nothing had prepared him for the shock of that crazy woman pointing at him. He thought she was bewitched and had sent poison arrows into his eyes. As he ran home that day, stopping to catch his breath and then running again, he tried to push the image of her wild eyes zooming in on him out of his mind.

When he reached home, his mother asked where he had been. Peter lied and said he went with another friend to his house and forgot about the time. He did not mention Eze. His mother had no real interest in Peter's wanderings after school or on the weekends and did not have the energy that evening to reprimand him. She just told him to wash up because dinner was ready. Peter never spoke of the incident and avoided Eze after that.

He hadn't thought of it except in bits and pieces since then. But now, as he lay in bed at the end of this strange and disconcerting day, there it was, together with the memory of the dancing snake, alive and close to him. As he lay still looking out into the night he thought, *who am I? The Mamba or the Gamekeeper? Which one is my father?*

His whole life he had tried to please his father while avoiding his sudden mood changes that could seem deadly. It was tricky. He wondered if he had never known the truth about what happened to Moremi's parents—if the guilt he lived with as a foundation of their marriage might not exist. But his father did not keep it a secret.

He couldn't imagine why, but before now he had never analyzed this closely. As he lay there an explanation began to grow at the edge of his understanding. His father was bragging. *He wanted me to think that he had engineered the whole thing. Got rid of her parents so that they could control Moremi's destiny.*

The thought spread inside him like a virus, and he could feel his body's immune system trying to expel it, shoving it out with denial. *No, that can't be true. I needed to know so that I could protect her.* It was critical that she believe she could have no contact with Nigeria where she had friends who knew her parents.

"People talk," his father warned. "She mustn't know. What happened to her parents was an accident, that's all."

But he knew better. He knew that his father did not try to help Moses. He had influence with Abacha and his thugs, and he could have stopped it. After some exertion, Peter shoved those thoughts aside, at least for now.

Now, as sleep settled into him like a slow death in quicksand, the thought came. *She will find out.* Because of her dead mother and that dead mother's mother and so on back into the never-ending past, she would find out the truth.

Well, he couldn't have that. If she found out, everything would be for nothing. The legacy of his parents he helped to preserve, the humiliation, possible recriminations, but most of all . . . Ayo would know. And that he couldn't allow.

Maybe I'm like my father after all. He hired people to do his dirty work, and so do I. I've had her watched for the entire year. It's not enough. Now I have to do more than just keep an eye on her. There's no way out. Moremi must be gone. Does that mean dead and gone? Well, if she's the snake and I'm the gamekeeper, then yes. Dead and gone. To save the rest of us.

The clarity of this horror finally knocked him out and he fell into a troubled sleep.

CHAPTER TEN

Instead of transcending ourselves, we must move into ourselves.

MARION WOODMAN

CLOUDS SHIFTED ACROSS THE SUN, between light and dark, between what was said and what was not.

The day after she met Moremi, Rebecca parked on a shady street in the hills amid arts and crafts bungalows while pieces of their conversation hovered.

Some things seem clear. Her parents died in the political maelstrom of Sani Abacha's regime. Why, is not clear. Who set up the father? She's not really asking—why not? She's either feeling something she doesn't know, or she suspects something she doesn't want to know and isn't telling.

Voices from her own dream of her ancestor echoed disconnected pieces, a white noise she couldn't shake: "*The mothers . . . Mother . . . dead . . . listen . . . to the silence.*"

I need to speak to Gertrude.

She climbed the rock stairs of Gertrude Lerner's house onto a wide, expansive porch. She paused, breathing in the fragrance of the wisteria that climbed across the low hanging roof, dripping with its last blooms of an unusually warm autumn. She let herself in through the heavy oak door into the cool darkness of the foyer that smelled of lemon-oiled wood, stepping into a long wide hallway lined with bookcases, tribal carpets, pottery, paintings and photographs—collections and memorabilia of a long and eventful life.

Gertrude had been a psychoanalyst since her early forties. Now 80, she lived alone since the death of her husband ten years ago. Her daughter, a successful analyst in her own right, was married and lived in New York City. Gertrude had reached the pinnacle of her profession and fully enjoyed it. A solitary queen, engaged in an analytic practice in her home, while also providing consultation services to members of the profession, occasionally addressing them in attentive groups when she decided she had something enduring to say to the community. She even remained active as a past president of the psychoanalytic institute where she had been a prominent voice for years.

They met when Gertrude became Rebecca's training analyst at the institute. She loved working with Gertrude but quickly rankled at the demands of a program that wanted to mold her in its own image. She walked in her own footsteps, not someone else's, no matter how many followed. Her final complaint was simply: "I'm not a psychoanalyst."

Gertrude was at first frustrated by Rebecca's resistance, and tried to rein her in many times with: "My dear, you are made for this life. You're an explorer of the psyche. You have the depth of character to do this." Rebecca would not be persuaded.

After a year, Rebecca was trapped between her love for Gertrude and her need to escape a training she could not believe in. "I've got to leave—now!" she nearly screamed. As she always did, Gertrude saved the day by declaring, "Then you shall be my consultee in private practice."

And that was that.

Now twelve years later their mutual respect had deepened, and they continued to meet once a week. Their synergy was a wave in the ocean—calm on the surface, a seething universe below. As Gertrude liked to say, "Rebecca, it's all one gigantic wave of cosmic surprise, above and below!"

Rebecca agreed.

Standing in the entry, Rebecca heard Gertrude on the phone, her office door a crack open. Her urgency increased. Rebecca had passed the point of telling herself to calm down and stop the anxious chatter pounding in her head.

Something's about to happen. Moremi would not have come in to see me if she didn't suspect danger. How can Gertrude be just gabbing on the phone when I need her—now!?

Controlling her urge to shove the door open, she gently nudged it a few more inches and peeked in.

Gertrude looked up and smiled, waving her in.

Rebecca didn't hesitate as she pushed her way through. Once inside, she shut her eyes, holding her finger over her lips, forcing herself to project calm and peace—a mother willing the baby to sleep while churning with impatience. As she tiptoed to the couch, she checked her watch. A few minutes early.

Gertrude ran a tight ship with no sloppy latitude for time around the appointed hour, unless necessary. She did have an irreverent side, but it was carefully measured by the rules.

As Rebecca sank into the couch, she felt a twinge of guilt. She rooted around in her bag for her notebook, which she didn't need. *I've intruded, and she knows it, no matter how pleasantly she smiles.*

"Listen, my dear," Gertrude clucked into the phone with one eye on Rebecca. "I must go but do call and let me know when you can break away from that busy schedule and let's have lunch." A pause. "Ah yes," she nodded, "somewhere quiet and sinfully good. Bye-bye."

She rose from her desk and sat down in her well-worn chair across from Rebecca. She was tall, draped in silky periwinkle blues and grays with a long strand of jade beads. Gertrude always started with the same gesture. Leaning forward with her hands on her knees she got right to the point. "What should we discuss on this lovely day?"

Rebecca looked down at the intricate design in the Turkish carpet, her automatic pose in response to Gertrude's opening. Usually this was a moment of self- reflection, but today she realized she'd looked at those geometric shapes hundreds of times without really seeing them. Her head tilted as if this might have meaning. *I feel silly. How odd. I have so much to tell her and now I don't know where to start.*

Her words fell far beneath the pent-up feelings she'd been carrying around for eighteen hours. "I'm not sure how to describe this new client." With that, she lurched to a halt.

Gertrude encouraged her to go on.

"Have you ever met anyone who is sooo different from you that you don't know where to begin?"

Gertrude looked away. "Why yes. I think so." Then back at Rebecca, "But tell me more before I assume anything."

"She's from Nigeria. Been here ten years. Married to a successful professor of economics. Also, Nigerian. They have a son eight years old. Their marriage was arranged. He's been here many years. She's having trouble adjusting to being an American. Maybe because her husband pressures her not to talk about the past."

Gertrude cocked her head.

"I know. What's the big deal? But it is." Rebecca summarized Moremi's story about her father's abduction and her mother's murder.

"She died instantly. Moremi's father later died in prison."

She was stunned how calm her own voice sounded, so matter of fact, as she let words like AK-47 roll off her tongue, as if she knew all about such weapons. Her words failed to impart the drama. She finished by telling Gertrude about Moremi's response to the mask in her office and her maternal heritage as a Voudou Mami Wata priestess.

As Gertrude listened, she bowed her head and closed her eyes.

When Rebecca stopped, they sat in silence. These moments had many permutations. Quiet, calming, anxious, wondering . . . Rebecca fixated on the gun. *How strange.* She had no idea what it would be like to hold a heavy, loaded automatic weapon. *How can something so incomprehensible sound so mundane?*

Finally, Gertrude spoke. "Some things are never fully understood, yet we just go on. But you're right. Something brought her in now. It sounds like something is brewing that even Moremi does not understand. Something that is surfacing."

"She speaks with her ancestors. Her mother. Her grandmother. A spirit called Mami Wata—and others."

Gertrude nodded as if this were the most normal thing in the world, as if it made sense. "What are they telling her?"

"I'm not quite sure yet. I assume that's why she came to see me. Someone told her a therapist like me wouldn't laugh at her. And, of course, I didn't. But still . . ." Rebecca looked around the room as if an explanation might show up. She came back to Gertrude. "I believe her, but part of me wonders if I can take this in fully enough to help her. It's not just the cultural divide. It's bigger than that."

"OK," Gertrude leaned forward as she always did when ready to challenge, "let's find the common ground between you. It's there. You just don't quite see it. Tell me, what comes to mind?"

Rebecca went to her own dream she'd had the night before she met Moremi, in as much detail as she could remember. How the little girl was playing with her home-made doll in the cornfield, how the father ran to the burning house, and she ran through the forest lunging into the Delaware warrior holding the baby. "She ran into the village and saw her mother sitting up against a log on the ground reading her bible." Tears came as the dream appeared again, feelings deeper than she'd had before. "I almost forgot the dream, but it was so intense. Meeting Moremi took over."

As Rebecca paused, Gertrude knew there was more.

Rebecca went on. "Gently, like she was a feather, he flicked her over on the ground. She was dead. As if she just evaporated, only something spilled out of her head that looked like bright red cherries."

Gertrude leaned back tapping the tips of her fingers, concentrating. In a voice low and calm, "In the dream, what did you feel when you saw your mother spilled out?"

"Horror. Pure horror. It was like the dream wanted to knock me out. And it did. More than any others because you know, I've had dreams about my mother's death. This was the worst. My ancestor seeing her mother's!"

Gertrude's fingers still tapping—thinking, wondering, inviting the meaning to come in. "Do you think it was a coincidence you had that dream the night before you met Moremi?"

They rode the wave of silence. The dream was no coincidence. The question was a punctuation point that demanded speculation. But also, a truthful answer.

"My dream prepared me for the intensity of her story about her own mother. I think the one blended into the other. My dream prepared me to hear her story where the deaths of the mothers equally horrified."

"Yes," Gertrude agreed. "The intensity of your dream helped you understand her loss. Both your mothers died prematurely. That alone brings you together."

"The little girl in the dream is my ancestor. I'm not sure what the dream was telling me—perhaps we also have that in common. But Moremi seems to be dealing with something building inside her. Something she's afraid of. I don't have that feeling about myself, but I do for her."

Gertrude looked intently at Rebecca. "Something brought the two of you together. Totally different cultures, but not so different the closer you look. Right now, you are her guide. We shall see where this goes."

"When you say 'guide', I think about familiar territory. You're asking me to guide her into her own territory that's a foreign land to me. What I know about Africa, much less Voudou, couldn't fit into my little finger."

"Think about it this way," Gertrude suggested. "A bridge exists between you that you can work with. If you're on one side and she's on the other, how do you move toward her?"

Rebecca knew not to answer this directly. *Let something—anything—help me here.* "She was holding something back, I feel sure. Maybe she didn't realize because after all I'm a stranger. But I think it's something I need to know."

"Ah . . . not a complete stranger I think, but how can you find out?"

"I don't want to push her because I might lose her, but I know she would not have come in to see me unless there were some kind of urgency."

"You probably took in more than you think. Look inward and see what you see."

Rebecca closed her eyes searching through her encounter with Moremi. She met her in the waiting room, invited her into her office and as Moremi came through the door, she saw something. "She kept her left hand in her jacket pocket. Not the whole time, but long enough for me to notice. She took it out as we talked, but I noticed she had it back in her pocket when she left." Rebecca moved her search to later as she came up the front stairs to her own house. "I could hear the music. Richard was there, holding court in the kitchen, cooking up a storm, singing and pretending to be Bessie Smith for the Queens." She opened her eyes. "You know how they love him to sing for them."

Gertrude did.

"Well, at that moment it popped into my mind that she had a talisman in her pocket. Something that reassured her. Something she could touch and feel safe. In that moment I dismissed that idea, thinking it was silly. How could I know that? There goes my over-active imagination again. You know how I can be."

"I do. But I also know your imagination can get it right a lot of the time."

They agreed.

"Let's assume this time you got it right. What could that mean? In the moment when you saw her hand in her pocket for a little longer than usual did you have any compulsion to ask her about that?"

"No. I was unaware at the time what I noticed. But I confess even if I knew at the time in retrospect I would not have asked. How could I casually ask, 'Hey, what's in your pocket?' That would be rude."

"Yes, it would be," Gertrude agreed, "but it's also one of the things you've complained about your mother and grandmother. Snoopy mothers?"

"Of course, they were. And you know how I have carefully weeded out that tendency in myself. I would never do that to my own daughter. Never!"

"I think we've found our first obstacle for you in this case," Gertrude concluded.

"What do you mean?" Rebecca replied a little too hastily.

"I mean," Gertrude continued in her calm, wise-old-owl voice, "that barrier is in you. Not necessarily in her."

"You mean I should have asked her? Is that what you're suggesting?" Rebecca's annoyance erupted before she could catch it. She knew where this was going. She and Gertrude had reached this pitch many times. Gertrude would tap into her hot spots and Rebecca would forget to take herself in hand to remain calm.

Gertrude reminded her, "This is not all about you."

"Then who is it about?" Rebecca spiked.

"Let me switch gears. Remember about an hour ago when you came into my office?"

"Sure . . ."

"My door was ajar slightly, an inch or so wouldn't you say?"

"Yes . . ." Rebecca replied tentatively—wary, suspicious.

"Well," Gertrude chirped, "in that moment you had a choice. You could have stepped back from the door realizing I was on the phone and taken a seat in the entryway, or you could have done what you did and just pushed on in. Quietly, I agree, trying not to disturb me—but then again you were a little bit early."

Rebecca's eyes narrowed, ready to pounce.

Gertrude pushed on. "I looked up and greeted you even though I was on the phone, and I beckoned you in. Then I got off the phone."

"But I knew, I mean I could hear you weren't talking to a patient or about something really important. I've done this before. Your door was open. I took that to mean the coast was clear."

"You don't need to be defensive. This isn't about criticizing. I want you to get something."

Rebecca sucked in her breath and fell back into the couch, tense. "Go on."

"You took in the whole scene from the moment you came through the front door. You were 5 minutes early. My door was slightly open. An invitation? You heard me on the phone. Nothing important. So, you came in. You were anxious to get started. I was OK with that."

Rebecca felt annoyed every time she did this. She wanted Gertrude to tell her, not lead her by the hand into a discovery like she would a child.

"I'm not getting the point."

"I think you are."

Rebecca stared at the wall. Angry. No—annoyed. She leaned back folding her arms. "Okay. Here's what you're suggesting. Maybe I was a little intrusive. You're right. I walked in knowing you were still on the phone. I wanted you to get off the phone because I did want . . . no, I needed your immediate attention. You were preoccupied. You weren't sitting there waiting for me. And if I am completely truthful, even if it ruffles a few feathers—a lesson you have taught me so well—I got what I wanted. Now let me ask you, is that what you wanted me to get?"

Gertrude leaned forward. "Yes, it is. You knew this all along."

Their eyes met.

Gertrude ended with her usual summary. "So, this is the obstacle. She has a secret. Probably many secrets locked inside that talisman. And you have a challenge, to be or not to be snoopy. If Moremi is as you describe, she will welcome directness. She's not getting enough of that right now."

A few minutes later as Rebecca descended the stairs to her car, she knew Gertrude, as always, managed to make her point as if it had been obvious all along. She settled into the driver's seat and looked up at the house declaring, "I did not know this all along, Gertrude. You knew it all along!" as she stepped on the gas.

CHAPTER ELEVEN

Bringing the gifts that my ancestors gave,
I am the dream and the hope of the slave.
I rise. I rise. I rise.

MAYA ANGELOU

ON HER WAY HOME THAT EVENING Rebecca mulled over her meeting with Gertrude. For years she had relied on her without question to validate her intuition. But she had just turned eighty. If anyone had been like a mother to her it was certainly Gertrude. More than her own mother ever could have been. She still lived with the gnawing guilt that she would never please her own mother, who made everyone else around her comfortable. In many women Rebecca saw that quality as their plus side, but she just wasn't one of them.

Nor was her own daughter, which was why they got along so well. Margo went to school in Washington DC and returned when she could to visit Rebecca. Now Margo was married with her own daughter. She worked for a congressman. As she explained to Rebecca: "Mom, it's a never-ending crazy ride here. I love being a part of it."

Transported by these memories, she didn't see the young woman come out of nowhere into the crosswalk pushing a stroller. Rebecca hit the brakes and held her foot down longer and harder than she needed. Pulled back to her senses she tried to stay focused on the road, drawn as always, into wandering thoughts.

Her mother referred to her as "my little dreamer." Her father declared, "She needs to learn how to concentrate." Rebecca felt betrayed that her mother did not stand up for her. Behind his back she was supportive, but not in front of him. Gertrude said what she meant no matter the context.

As she pulled up to her house, she remembered it was her night to cook. Richard would be coming later after a faculty meeting, in a grumpy mood, talkative and hungry. The Queens greeted her with wagging tails. Juno stretched and yawned, awakened from her nap. Both dogs headed for the kitchen.

"I know!" Rebecca laughed as she tossed her purse and briefcase on the dining room table. "I'm coming. Dinner it is."

The Queens sat politely side by side in the kitchen near the back door leading to the deck outside. Rebecca often explained, "Chows are not like hounds who live to eat. They savor their food." She filled their bowls at the sink with a cup of kibble each, telling them as usual she was mixing it with "yummy meaty stuff" and carried the bowls out to the deck, pushing open the screen door with her hip. They went to their usual spots, Juno by the geranium and Dido near the cement statue of Pan playing his pipe, peeking out from behind a hydrangea.

The deck looked out on a yard thick with trees and bushes and a variety of native plants. She referred to this end of her property as her retirement project. She kept it watered and sometimes weeded but that was about all she could accomplish. When she was seized with the gardening bug, she rushed out to buy some currently flowering plants to spruce things up, vowing after each of these episodes to maintain things. Soon she would relapse, telling herself with resignation that weeding just took all the fun out of it.

That rationale too went back to her childhood. "Rebecca loves to play," her second-grade teacher told her mother who smiled and said, "Yes, that's how she learns." But when her father grumbled, "How's she ever going to settle down?" her mother promised, "I'll talk with her." She never really settled down and the neglected plants in her yard brought home her parents' dismay.

The former owner of Rebecca's house was an elderly woman, Vera Thompson, who had raised her family there. In her later years Vera loved to garden. Now a towering English Oak provided a canopy over half the yard, grown from an acorn her father had brought from England more than seventy years ago. Out of homage to Vera, Rebecca hired a gardener who trimmed trees, blew off paths and clipped the ivy that took over the ferns that grew so well in the shade. Rebecca loved the ferns and watched over them like a protective mother even though, being in the right soil and climate, they mostly took care of themselves.

When Richard teased her about her garden the old guilt returned. He would wander about commenting on the plants, using Latin names, making annoying suggestions, reminding her how his first wife had such a green thumb. Gliding by her favorite fern bed next to the foot of the stairs he might casually point out, "That *Dryopteris arguta* could use a little pruning to let some more sunlight in so the new fronds can grow."

To which Rebecca would retaliate, "Oh, you mean my five finger ferns?"

She would harrumph at his tendency to throw these casual jabs and often snapped back, "I have more pressing things to worry about than the appearance of my yard."

Richard would reply, "Of course you do."

Rebecca knew these exchanges were a not-so-subtle hint that if he were living with her and the Queens, things around her house would get closer attention.

She kept the back door open so the Queens could float in and out. They pined for Richard. She feared they loved him best. After all, he was the glamorous visitor, a dad who came home after work to a harried mom. Richard would move in with her if she'd let him. But she feared the change—rocking the boat in relationships could upset their careful balance. She knew she was afraid to take the risk, while Richard was not. That was why he attracted her. "*It's a dilemma,*" as Gertrude liked to point out.

She put on her apron and turned on a CD of Gabby Pahinui's slack key guitar band, opened her small pantry to retrieve a bottle of pinot, and put the large pot of water on the stove for the pasta. The Queens flopped at her feet, alert for the sounds of Richard's arrival. Juno's head rested on her front paws; her back legs stretched out like a rug. Dido rolled around on her back from side to side making growly sounds. For Chows, this was as playful as it got.

She didn't even try to compete with Richard's cooking. He was a happy cook, sorting, chopping, mingling flavors, and tasting. She had never really settled into these pleasures. When she was in charge, she exhausted herself. Her mother had been fastidious in the kitchen, which intimidated rather than invited her daughter to follow her lead. But Richard just threw it all together and somehow it came out delicious every time.

"Tonight," she announced to the Queens, "the KISS principle applies." She chopped, sautéed, and stirred trying to channel his casual fun. She laughed at herself and explained to the Queens, "I need his big brain tonight."

AS HE DROVE FROM CAMPUS heading for Rebecca's, Richard's headache pressed into his eyes. He hated faculty meetings, especially the long monthly ordeals each month that started at 3:00 on a Friday and often did not end before 6:00 P.M. "When you're dealing with a roomful of egos," he once told Rebecca, "no one gives up any ground." The only reason they ended now at 6:00 was because Judith Hammond, head of the curriculum committee and a mom of young twins at forty-six, had to dash to pick up her five-year-old daughters.

He had met the twins last year when Judith brought them to the annual faculty Christmas party. They became the center of attention as one by one they dismantled various decorations that some industrious committee had put up the night before. He'd invited Rebecca so he could use her as his excuse to duck out early. He and Rebecca had joined the crowd, nodding, and smiling as Judith's monsters ran amuck.

While little Betsy hopped up and down smashing one of the cheap red glass balls, grinding it into the gray carpet with her heel, her sister wove a long tinsel ribbon from the hors d'oeuvre table around the tipsy academics. They observed her with their usual wry humor.

As she wrapped the ribbon around the legs of the round punch bowl table, she managed to snag it and tripped over Dr. Lehman's big black shoe. Though Dr. Lehman was the head of the History Department, to Betsy's twin he was just a big lummox who got in her way and made her trip. She looked around to judge whether she should let out a howl of distress when her mother swooped over like a big bird to comfort her. Betsy's twin jutted her lower lip and allowed herself to be soothed.

At that moment Richard turned to Rebecca with a smile and asked with a twinkle. "Enough?"

Rebecca nodded and they left, waving goodbye to all, explaining they had another party to attend.

They went to Rebecca's and ate scrambled eggs with sausage and toast and gobs of marmalade and a large pitcher of screwdrivers in the middle of the tray on the bed as they watched an old movie with the Queens.

On the way to Rebecca's after the faculty meeting, he thought of his first wife, Janice, who was always perfect. Of course, that was the problem. While he aspired to climb the academic ladder, Janice was right there with him. She enjoyed children, saw the best in people, looked forward to being on committees at the school where she taught first grade. Parents loved her. He did too. *What happened?* He knew.

He saw two homes. The home with Janice was graceful with just the right touch of color and texture. Art books on the coffee table, a platter of smooth stones found on the beach, a Murano vase they bought in Italy she would fill with peonies. Then Rebecca's foyer: a hodgepodge of hanging jackets, mud-splattered rain boots and a pile of garden crocs in a basket. An antique Kazak tribal rug in need of repair, a Dan tribe mask with its black face and hollow eyes, surrounded by African cowrie shells and black seeds with raffia beard. Gruesome. Rebecca explained the first time he saw it, "Oh, those cowry shells were the most popular currency in Africa. They symbolize fertility and," with a flourish of her hand, "just about anything else spiritual you can think of."

He and Janice politely divorced after twenty-five years. He gave her the house and everything in it except his books, papers, a few pieces of art and his retirement account. Their son was grown, and they thought they could remain friends. Janice remarried Fred, an investment banker. Now retired, they often traveled and used Janice's house as their infrequent home base when they were in town. Occasionally he received a postcard from her, usually from a resort in some far-off place.

I love Rebecca's quiet, introverted fierceness. With her I can be myself. With Janice I couldn't be the guy she thought she'd married. When I finally became head of the Cultural Anthropology Department and Janice wanted to celebrate—I wanted to mourn the loss of my freedom. Rebecca understands that. Janice thought my reaction was nonsense.

He pulled up in front of Rebecca's and sat in the car a moment summing up his reverie. *Only when you get old do you begin to understand how to love.* He chuckled as he leaned out of the car and stood up groaning, feeling like the Tin Man. He looked up at Rebecca's little bungalow and exclaimed to the evening breeze, "You make me happy."

Inside, the Queens were up and out of the kitchen wiggling and jostling each other, scratching at the front door. Rebecca turned down the red sauce to simmer before she followed them.

He bounded up the steps onto the porch waving a paper bag. The door burst open and flying red tails encircled him as he stooped down, letting them lick his face with their black tongues. "Hello, my little red-haired beasties," he cooed, rubbing their heads. "I brought you some treaty-treats." He held out the bag. "Hmmm, what have we here?" He pulled out two long, ropy things that looked like some sort of dried seaweed. "Yum," he smacked his lips. "I think these will be lusciously disgusting."

Both daintily, and with reverence, accepted the treats, carrying them back inside where they lay on the carpet in the dining room to lick and chew.

Rebecca crossed her arms watching with a smile. "You spoil them rotten. They expect it now."

"Yes. I know. But why else do we have them?"

"Have what?"

"Pets!" Spittle was flying. "We have them so we can lavish our love. Let's face it, we're guaranteed their undying devotion. I'm not sure we humans will ever figure out unconditional love. We like the idea. But between humans it doesn't work so well." He grinned at her. "But let's not think about that deep stuff right now." He rubbed his hands together in happy anticipation, sniffing red sauce and fresh basil wafting from the kitchen.

"Vino! Per favore!" He couldn't resist his bad Italian and headed for the kitchen to the open wine bottle waiting on the counter. "Immediamente. Otherwise, I shall faint from exhaustion." He stopped, eclipsed by an even greater thought. "No wait! Not exhaustion. Exasperation. I like that word. It comes from the Latin. Ex, meaning thoroughly, and ocerbus, meaning sharp, bitter. Acer, meaning keen. That's it. I feel keenly bitter right now. I need to pump some sweet iron back into my old brain. Did you know that as we age it's bad for our brains to be put on hold? It's a proven fact," he gestured with his left hand while pouring the wine with his right, "that faculty meetings are hazardous to an old brain's health."

He handed Rebecca her glass and they toasted to old brains staying young by avoiding meetings that lasted more than ten minutes.

"It's a fact," he continued to pontificate, wagging his left forefinger in the air while tossing a radish into his mouth with his right from the hors d'oeuvre plate and added while crunching, "most great ideas of the western world can be articulated in under ten minutes. Forget the eastern world, I'm not going to touch that."

He marched into the living room as Rebecca followed with the crackers and veggies. He sank down into the couch and Rebecca joined him, placing the snacks on the coffee table cluttered with books, an old tennis ball belonging to the dogs, some oyster shells, and an art deco bowl full of rubber bands and paper clips.

The Queens trotted in with their snacks, now slimy, smelly strings of meaty chewed globs. They dropped at their feet and gnawed as Rebecca lit the fire she had set the night before.

The cold air off the Pacific rolled in early bringing its chill to blanket their world with a spreading fog bank whipped up by the wind.

"So tell me," Richard patted the couch between them, "what was your day like? You've just heard about mine."

Well," she began, retrieving her glass, "I do want to pick your brain about something."

"Ask me anything. We'll Google my mind."

She wanted him to be serious but knew better than to push him. He moved at his own pace. He had just come from a meeting where meandering egos dragged issues down long, winding streets. Richard had a creative mind that was bound to a system he had learned to navigate.

She empathized. They had both learned to tolerate the necessity of compromise. Each understood that change came from within a community of restraints. That meant committees, meetings, conflict resolutions, publishing and paying dues. Freedom came from taking advantage of chance moments, serendipitous opportunities that popped up like bright shells on a sandy beach. Luck played a part, but without readiness and experience, not a very big one.

Talking relaxed him. She listened. He enjoyed the challenge of mental puzzles and she learned through intuition where mind and feeling intersected. Each came to conclusions along a different path. He followed the data, she, her instincts. Their enjoyment of each other blended their differences, and sometimes out of the mixture, when their differing points of view met, each was enhanced.

"Tell me, what comes to mind when I say the word 'Voudou?' "

He stared at her, savoring his Stilton on its cracker, and popped it into his mouth. Chomping, he reached for his glass, reclined on the couch, cradled the stem on his belly, twirling and sniffing. "First of all," he said, smacking his lips and swallowing, "most people don't have a clue about what that religious cosmology really is."

She nodded, waiting, knowing he might take a while to get to the point.

"I believe it has some serious underpinnings. The music that came out of the blending of the Catholic church and the Voudou ritual drumming became the roots for modern jazz, the music you and I take for granted.

It was easier for the slaves to practice their religion in Cuba than here, so they absorbed Spanish colonial Catholicism. Here on plantations in the south, if slaves were caught practicing any religion other than protestant Christianity they were severely punished, or worse. Nevertheless, Voudou survived."

Rebecca remembered that Moremi told her that Voudou survived through adaptation. She waited.

"But I digress," his usual admission before he got to the point. "People have studied Voudou their entire lives without grasping the depth and breadth of it." He paused and looked out a window at the fog blowing by. "It's based on possession. We westerners don't really understand that. To most of us, Voudou is just another Halloween myth about zombies roaming the landscape."

"How do you mean, possession? Possession of what?"

"Possession . . ." He waited for the right words. "Possession by the ancestors or their gods, or spirits." He looked at her and shrugged. "Weird but not weird. All I'm trying to say is . . ." he looked around as if he couldn't connect the words to the thought and then turned to her. "Do you ever talk to your dead relatives?"

"Richard, be serious."

"I am. At that meeting, something my grandfather used to say to me . . . I heard it loud and clear."

She went along. "What did you hear?"

"His voice leaning down and whispering in my ear, 'Now Richard my boy, if you somehow manage to learn patience in this life . . . consider that a great achievement.'"

She looked at him and slowly smiled, wondering if he had learned that lesson. "I see what you mean. I had a grandmother who told me that I needed to learn humility. I can still hear her voice. Chiding, but she meant well."

Rebecca looked out at the fog. "Yes, you're right. I carry that voice inside me."

He went on. "So, you see, our ancestors do speak to us. We just don't think of them as alive within us. But when you hear that voice of the grandparent, they're right there with us, aren't they? We don't ritualize them, but they're there."

She knew the subject was enticing him. In the silence the Queens chewed contentedly, pulling on their stringy snacks, now quite disgusting by any human standards.

"Voudou is a very old and practiced form of dissociation. Now we're getting close to your territory. It's a form of massive suspension of frontal lobe activity."

He pointed to his forehead while leaning forward for cheese on another cracker. Without waiting to finish, he spoke through his mouthful, dusting cracker crumbs from his hands.

"It's a form of mind possession fueled by beliefs that go back through a tribe's ancestry farther back than anyone can remember. That kind of belief mocks scientific certainty because look what it can do. Think of Darwin's agony toward his wife's Christianity. He knew what publishing the Origin of Species would do to her belief in her God, her certainty of a hereafter. He feared taking that away from her. If I told you that when you die you turn to dust and no one's waiting for you, and your tribe tells you that your mother and grandmother and great grandmother, all the way back to the beginning and everyone else awaits you, who would you believe?"

"That's a rhetorical question." She could see he was revved up now. She knew the dangers of asking an academic to speak on a subject they knew more than a little about, but not enough to be bored.

"And," holding up his finger as if preaching from the pulpit, "not only are they waiting for you, but they've been watching over you and speaking to you in the here and now from another dimension. Let's face it, that's powerful stuff. And let's say you've experienced this possession or watched it happen—you'd believe. I think science has given belief a bad rap for about a hundred years, and we need to think about that. Because," he was enjoying his thought, "something really does happen to these people when they're possessed. Remember when we talk about mind, we mean the brain, especially the limbic brain. We don't really understand the mind's power. We don't know what happens when people dissociate like that. You psychologists believe we leave our minds because we must. Something is too overwhelming to fully experience. But that explanation does not account for religious possession. As a species we have a great need for this kind of ecstasy."

He looked down at the Queens. "They don't, but we humans do. And you ask about Voudou . . . well it's all about that. Connection to the ancestors. Belief not only that there is an afterlife, but it's being part of an active world with your dead loved ones speaking to you in this dimension—here and now." He was finally ready to let her speak and allowed a portal of silence between them.

"So," she began, "if someone believed this, that it's all one big continuum between my life now and the life of my ancestors say in the seventeenth century, then I'm a blink in the universe. And if that universe is a personal pulsating consciousness, I guess I would be constantly alert for messages from my ancestors. But what gets me is . . . well, we just don't believe in that stuff, so if we do receive messages, our brain today is conditioned to delete them, wouldn't you agree?"

"Not necessarily. When someone close to you dies, they don't leave you. You maintain a dialogue with them the rest of your life. The very idea of annihilation of yourself is an impulse to move into dissociative states in which you believe those voices are out there. There are many examples of cult thinking in our society. I suppose it's everywhere. And we often see this in a negative light, especially in our western world. You and I value independent thinking. But what if we lived in a small community of people we'd known all our lives, whose parents and ancestors had known one another? We would trust more in the group mind."

"So, we've lost touch with our ancestors. But do you believe, Richard—now tell me the truth—that they're out there, hovering over us?"

"We live our lives thinking that our logic is sufficient to make sense of the orchestra of selves we imagine. What if logic is only a small part of the apparatus? Do I think ancestors are hovering? No, but that's not the point. If I had been born a few hundred years ago into a tribe who practiced the ancient ways, I would. And then it would be true. And that would not have been very long ago."

"So, are you saying truth is relative? That's not like you."

"Here's what I believe. Our brains are susceptible to an enormous range and permutations of what we call reality. And out there in that open space of mind I don't know what anyone will find. I believe we don't know. I also believe that if you were to study the practice of Voudou coupled with a basic understanding of quantum physics you could learn a lot about the function of mind and the nature of reality."

"You're telling me Voudou is a serious religion."

"Very serious."

"Thanks. That helps."

"To be continued?"

"Yes, to be continued."

"Let's eat." He rubbed his hands together. "I'm starving."

They went into the kitchen and Richard sat down, happy and satisfied. Rebecca served her pasta with red sauce and French bread. He poured the last of the wine.

The Queens followed underfoot.

CHAPTER TWELVE

Few things are as bad as a guilty conscience.

BUCHI EMECHETA

AFTER THEIR ENCOUNTER IN THE DARK Peter and Moremi retreated even more from each other.

He pretended nothing had happened.

She took some time to absorb what he had done. Somehow, she now understood too much, although he didn't know how. Her mother's message hit hard, a wake-up call.

Both now suspected there was a reckoning on the horizon. Their mutual involvement with Ayo contained them for the moment.

Moremi used her time with Rebecca to remember her life before the abrupt loss of her parents, before she lost a sense of security, knowing family and friends would always be with her. When she was told she had to leave everything behind for a new life in America, it had sounded silly, like a story that had no meaning, even though it was to save her life.

She told Rebecca, "My days after my father had been killed in prison were a blur. Nothing was real. Peter's parents rushed in and convinced me I was in danger and that anyone who knew me was also in danger. All I did was sit in their garden and listen to the birds. Then there was a marriage ceremony with Peter's stand-in relative. My body was there, but my spirit was elsewhere. His family hovered over me every moment. Even when I sat in the garden his mother would watch me. I went through the motions. I smiled when they wanted me to. Then I flew away like the swallows. Only they come back, and I never could."

Peter's mantra was, "We're American now." He said this as if it was self-evident. She didn't argue. Except for his talk about Nigeria's soccer team and his admiration of the roped pot from her father's office, he seemed to have no ties to the country of his birth.

She explained that in the early years with Peter her gratitude held her like a blanket. He fostered this by focusing on platitudes: "America is the land of freedom and opportunity." *I knew he didn't believe it. He was too smart for that.*

They came from a country that had been raped and plundered after colonialism for its mineral and petroleum resources. Both knew America's imperialism played a heavy part. She once dared to say, "Come on Peter, I'm a realist too. But 'land of the free?' You mean we won't get arrested and disappear while living here. I give you that."

He shook his head sadly as if she were a naïve child and looked at her. "If they knew where you were, you would be dead." He meant Abacha and his equally predatory successors. His threat scared her not only because of its content, but his tone.

She explained to Rebecca that she blamed herself because she didn't feel community in America. But his expectations for her to fit in even when she felt welcomed had not been easy. "People miss where they were born no matter what it was like," she told Rebecca. "Peter expects me to get over that and maybe I should because here, Americans are free to make of themselves what they want. . . supposedly."

After her encounter with Peter in the dark, as she brought her past more to life in Rebecca's office, the foreboding she sought to expunge only grew. The more she remembered, the worse she felt. The mood between her and Peter darkened like a fog she couldn't shake. All she wanted was to be alone with her thoughts, and the more she did this the more the thoughts chattered in her head like squawking, quarrelsome birds. Her mother's image morphed. She turned into an old gruesome crone whispering in her ear, "His family has our family's blood on their hands." The voice was no longer her mother's. It came from the bowels of the earth.

She wrestled with telling Rebecca. When she looked at Rebecca sitting in her chair, so properly, listening intently, something stopped her. *Is it because she's white?* No, it was simpler. How could she expect anyone to understand such a vision? Far-fetched didn't begin to describe it. Moremi was used to navigating between two worlds, the one most humans agreed upon and the other one that she knew through the mirror into the other dimension, where the ancestors lived.

But if she had to tell anyone it might as well be Rebecca.

THEIR NEXT SESSION BEGAN with a long silence and then Moremi leaned forward and said, "I want to tell you a dream I had last night."

Ahh, at last, she's letting me in. Rebecca picked up her pen and yellow pad to record the dream. Here we go.

"It's daytime and I'm walking down a dirt road. The landscape is familiar. I'm near my home in Nigeria and yet, somehow I feel like I'm lost. A strange feeling, to know where you are and feel lost at the same time. I start to panic a little as the landscape around me begins to shift. A cloud blocks the sun, and everything is in shadow. The more I sense I know my way home, the more things become unfamiliar. I realize I am lost. The warmth of the sun is gone, and a chill wind begins to blow. A flock of birds in a V-shape fly overhead. I look up and recognize they are ospreys. Their long bodies glide seamlessly, occasionally waving their great wings. I'm thrilled to see them, but as they fly north and fade out of sight I crumple down in the road, crying uncontrollably—the birds are gone. They know exactly where they are going as they migrate to their winter habitat. I'm lost, but I don't know why.

Then I see something approaching me very far away. It's not human. It's flapping gigantic wings. As it comes into view, I see it's an ostrich. A female. She's preening her neck back and forth at me. She must be eight feet tall. Her big eyes and long lashes are comical. I laugh. She comes right up to me and pokes her beak in my pocket. She must expect I have food for her. But I don't. I become angry and start shouting at her."

Moremi stopped and said nothing. Thoughtful.

"Was that it?" Rebecca looked up from her writing.

"Yes. I woke up."

They stared at each other.

Rebecca looked down at her notes, letting the dream seep in. "Sooo, she began tentatively, "what do you make of this dream?"

Moremi looked away, considering. "My grandmother Buchi loved ospreys. On the rare occasions she saw them migrating overhead she would announce: 'They're at home on every continent!' She loved the idea that ospreys are world citizens. When I was a little girl, she told me that probably ospreys had a nest nearby. We never found one, but she never stopped looking."

Rebecca nodded, imagining Buchi looking for nests. "The dream is in a landscape both familiar and unfamiliar."

"Yes. I've had several dreams like that. I think I know my way and then I don't. When the birds are gone, I'm on that isolated dirt road alone."

"Until that ostrich shows up!"

They both laugh. "Yes," Moremi nods, "with those bright eyes and long lashes they always look so flirtatious. They're amazing. They may not fly, but they can run up to 40 miles an hour. And she must have weighed 300 pounds!"

Rebecca shook her head wondering if she had ever actually seen a live ostrich anywhere, let alone in the wild. She asked, "Have you been around ostriches?"

"They're all over Nigeria. People raise them, hunt them, ride them, eat them, use their skin," and then she added, "wear their feathers in their hats."

"So, this ostrich in your dream comes up to you and tries to find food in your pocket?"

"Yes. Ostriches are quite bold. You must be careful around them. They are very curious and if you anger them, they can kill you. Stupid tourists get hurt all the time. They think they're friendly, which they are, but you do have to be careful and not make them angry."

"What do you think she was doing in your dream?"

"Well," Moremi wondered, "that's just it. I've never had an ostrich in my dream. Other kinds of birds, yes. But never an ostrich. And a big female one. They are the most powerful birds in the world."

With this observation they both sat in silence.

Rebecca knew the rest would unfold after a few questions. "Were you afraid of her?"

"No, not really. I probably should have been because I didn't have any food for her. I did scream at her in anger. But she seemed more indignant than ready to kick me to death, which she easily could have."

She's beginning to see it. Rebecca took in a deep breath.

Moremi weighed the question more deeply. "I think perhaps," she considered carefully, "the ospreys are connected all over the world. They comforted me. When they disappeared and I was so upset, they were going where they needed to go. Their flight paths are becoming more dangerous. They're amazing hunters and they eat fish. If the waterways on the flight paths are polluted, they die."

"Yes," Rebecca nodded.

Moremi sat still. "I guess," she began, "I miss my own flock. I miss where I come from. I'm living where I am not at home."

She's making the connection.

"When the birds disappear, I yearn for my home, but I can't go back. My home is in Nigeria. And I can't go back. It is not safe."

They both sat in silence.

The denouement is next. "Who," Rebecca began, "is the source of that information? Who has told you it would be dangerous for you?" Rebecca waited, then pushed on. "Your home is here now. Who tells you that?"

Moremi stared at Rebecca, then answered. "Peter."

"Yes." Rebecca let that sink in while moving to the pivotal question: "What if that were not true?"

Moremi sank back and blinked, as if to block its meaning. She looked away, then back to Rebecca. "Are you suggesting that Peter has mislead me?"

Rebecca took in a deep breath. "I don't know," she shrugged. But she did know.

"Ok," Moremi gave in. "Then what's that ostrich doing in my dream?"

We're there. She sees it. Rebecca waited as Gertrude sometimes did with her. Then she said, "I think you know."

Tears trickled down Moremi's cheeks. "She's Mami, isn't she? That's what you think."

Rebecca cocked her head, nudging, "Yes, I think so."

"What does she want?" Moremi asked.

She knows. "You tell me."

"The ostrich is an ancient bird, and its feather was the symbol of the Egyptian Goddess Maat who wore it on her head. Mami is a shapeshifter. She's known all over the world like the ospreys. And like her, the ostrich is ancient. In my dream she wants me to feed her and I don't. Instead, I get angry with her." She stopped and stared out the window. "She knows I have cut myself off from my African roots. And for Mami . . . well, that's not ok."

And there we are.

IN THE MIDDLE OF JANUARY, as Moremi headed home after seeing Rebecca, she was buoyant—for the first time in many weeks, Peter was out of town. He was in Washington, DC, for the week serving on an international panel of economists at Georgetown University.

Ayo was spending Friday and Saturday night at his friend's house. He and Jeremy had been friends since the first grade. She liked Jeremy's family, who lived nearby in an old, rambling house, full of music and life, like Nigeria. She was glad her son could feel at home there, too.

She walked through her front door and inhaled the peacefulness that prevailed when Peter was not there. Her memories began to wash over her. She looked at the photo of the Roped Pot and missed the clucking chickens, the women calling out to one another, her grandmother's nagging when her grandfather Baba slept in his hammock out in back.

Buchi would shake her head and waggle her crooked finger and sigh, "That old man. He doesn't use the sense God gave him, but my oh my, he can sure play that guitar." Baba was in his eighties then and Moremi only heard him play on special occasions. Sometimes a few of Baba's friends would come by, all ancient and worn out, but then they would start to play. Baba on guitar, another on drums, one with an accordion and someone on bass. She could imagine what her grandfather must have been like back in the forties. They called their music "juju." Buchi used to say, "No one could sit still when that old man played!"

Her mother explained, "When everyone danced in the evenings out under the stars, the whole world was in love." Once when Moremi was very young, she saw Buchi swaying her hips while she listened to an old 78 record of the Tunde Nightingale ensemble, and it was then she got her first glimpse of her grandparents' generation.

Their home bustled with chatter, music, dishes clanging, meals that fed anyone who came by. Her parents' home was less chaotic, but she grew up used to the comings and goings of family and friends. Her home with Peter and Ayo was lonely compared to that. But now, she craved the aloneness. *Inside the house I can fall apart if I want. He won't know.*

She dropped her purse and jacket on the chair and went into the kitchen to make tea. As she sat at the kitchen table, she remembered Rebecca had asked her, "Why don't you call your friend Jemimah in Nigeria and talk with her?"

They had been discussing her friends and Moremi mentioned how much she missed Jemimah. She explained the possible danger of contacting anyone she knew back home.

"Yes," Rebecca reasoned, "but Abacha has been dead for a long time.

Shouldn't the political situation have changed?"

She was beginning to realize how much Peter's prohibitions controlled her, and as she looked around, she felt the freedom of his absence even more. She knew things had changed after Abacha's mysterious death in 1998 and that political prisoners had been released, but Peter would warn, "It's still dangerous." It wasn't that she believed him, but this played into her worst fear—that Nigeria's political balance was always precarious. She knew what could happen.

Rebecca said something else that forced her to think. "Do any of your friends from Nigeria know where you are?"

Considering this, *No, how could they? Who would have told them? Certainly not Peter's family, and certainly not Peter.* She had left without saying goodbye, no tearful farewells. Her departure was cloaked in secrecy conducted by her father-in-law.

She got up and went into the den and retrieved her cell phone from her purse. As she approached the kitchen she stopped, returned, and reached into her jacket and folded the cowrie shell into her palm. Back at the kitchen table she laid the shell next to her phone. Her chin resting on her hands she stared at the two objects, not sure what to do. She imagined lying on her stomach on top of a great rock looking down into a deep gorge. The image was vivid enough to make her slightly dizzy.

She cherished the shell. It was about an inch and a half long with a graceful, bell-curved spine. Its background was creamy like caramel overlaid with browns. The design had intricate striated lines with splotches that looked like the night sky. She thought the back design depicted dancers in a line. Whenever Moremi looked at it, she heard the rhythms of home. She heard the music and saw the women in the market.

She remembered when her mother gave it to her. She was fifteen and she and Abeni were walking into town. It was midday with the sun high and the air, cooler than usual. They had been gossiping and laughing. Abeni saw the humor in everything, unlike her more serious daughter. Moremi told Rebecca, "My mother used to throw her head back and laugh as if the whole world had joined the moment."

On this walk Abeni became serious and asked to stop for a moment. They went off by the side of the road into a small grove of palms and found some rocks to sit on where they had often stopped to rest. Her mother withdrew something from her skirt pocket that was wrapped in a small piece of brightly colored cloth. She handed it to Moremi explaining,

"It's time for you to have this." She unwrapped the cloth and found the cowrie.

"This shell was passed down from my mother who got it from her mother who got it from her mother. I suppose it goes back as far as anyone can remember. It holds power. Consider it the symbol of the soul of our line. Like any power it can be destructive. Where there is the potential of good, there is the same for destruction. I have carried it with me since your grandmother Buchi gave it to me when I was your age. Now it's yours to carry because you are ready to have it. You have the emotional strength and demeanor to know how to use it. As my name Abeni means, 'we ask for her and we got her,' you were the same to me. I named you Moremi because you will be a strong leader someday. I asked for you and you came."

She sat with her mother a long time. They resumed their walk and Moremi put the shell in her pocket. Since then, the shell was always with her. As far as she knew Peter had never seen it. Even if he had, he wouldn't understand its significance.

She stared at her phone thinking it, too, was a symbol. *A spiritual symbol?* She wondered. She could open it and within seconds be in touch with someone from Nigeria. She could call Jemimah. *Does she have a cell phone now? Everyone has a cell phone now.* Peter had given it to her for emergencies and that's what she used it for. She never used it the way everyone else did. For her, talking in person was the only way to truly communicate. But there it was, a small silver object she barely remembered to charge. She cocked her head. Then realized that little utilitarian object set down next to her cowrie had the capacity to change her world.

It would be 8:00 in the morning in Nigeria. Where would Jemimah be? *She would be married now with her own children.* As she thought of her young, happy, carefree friend being a mother she picked up the phone and called Nigerian information.

At first, she encountered dead ends using Jemimah's maiden name. *She must be married.* She scribbled down numbers and followed leads until her phone announced low battery. She scrambled to find the charger that she'd thrown in a drawer by her bed. The more she phoned the more excited she got like a hound after the scent. Finally, she picked up the shell and it occurred to her that Jemimah had always talked about wanting to be a nurse. *What if she did? What if I could track her down that way?*

An hour and six nursing schools later she talked to a woman in the registration office of the Abeakuta General Nursing School. "Jemimah Ngoddy," the woman on the other end spoke slowly, "Hmmmm, now let's see. Ok, here's a name. Jemimah Onuoha it says, not Ngoddy, but she might have used her husband's family name. Let's see . . . ok . . . yes, here's her record."

Moremi fidgeted with the shell, impatient.

"OK," the woman finally said as if she were casually studying a map, not realizing the urgency, "her maiden name is Ngoddy."

She wanted to reach through the line and snatch the record from this woman who did not grasp the gravity of the moment.

"She graduated . . ." she droned on as if the information were difficult to read, "she graduated," she repeated, "in 2002. And according to the most recent information we have, she is living here in Abeokuta."

Moremi hung up. She held the phone away as if it had been alive but now dead. It reminded her of the tortoise in Buchi's backyard that would retreat into its shell and play dead. She heard her grandmother saying in a serious voice, "A tortoise at the back of your house in its pond brings many blessings and good fortune," and, she added, laughing, "He's a trickster too!"

She got up and made another cup of tea. She picked up the phone and held it up in front of her face like a mirror. "Ok, show me your magic." She called the information operator using Jemimah's married name. She made a list of ten numbers for Onuoha. She sipped her tea and picked up the shell feeling its hard cool smoothness warming in her left hand. She set it down and picked up the phone for the seventh call. As it continued to ring, she accepted this was not going to work.

Finally, an older woman's gravelly voice in the familiar southern Nigerian dialect answered, "Hello?" She sounded out of breath and slightly annoyed.

She asked for Jemimah.

After a pause she responded, "Just a minute," and Moremi heard a long, shrill shout that sounded as if she had gone outside—"Jemimahhh!" She heard household sounds, children playing, chickens clucking, and a screen door slammed. Someone fumbled with the phone, dropping it.

She leaned forward. "Hello?"

Things went silent. Then a softer, tentative voice responded, "Hello?"

It was Jemimah's voice. "Jemimah, is that you?"

"Yes!" During the silence that followed neither could speak.

"Oh my God! It's me . . . Moremi."

"Where are you? We didn't know what happened to you. No one did." Jemimah spewed questions trying to catch her breath.

"I know . . . I know." Moremi kept repeating, unable to explain.

Moremi blurted, "I married Peter Abosanjo. I mean . . . it was arranged . . . and then I left. They said I had to leave, or I might be arrested." She waited for Jemimah's response.

"I don't understand. Why were you in danger?"

"You know about my parents, about my father."

"Yes."

"Well, Peter's parents took me in. They said their son, an economics professor who was here in the U. S. for many years, needed a wife." Her words sounded hollow, as if she were reciting someone else's life story. She looked back into the family room at the photograph of her and Ayo and Peter in London. She ended by saying, "We have a son. Ayo. He's eight."

"That's wonderful! I'm happy for you. But how did it happen so fast? You left and never said goodbye."

Jemimah's question confronted her with all the oddities in her relationship with Peter. "I know . . . I know." She forced herself to explain more. "They . . . I mean his parents, told me that I could be arrested because of my association with my parents' political activism. If I married Peter I could start over here in the U.S. as his wife."

She heard Jemimah's sigh.

"They knew my parents. So here I am. Peter said even after Abacha's death it wasn't safe."

"Well . . . yes, it probably was unsafe back then. But not so much now. Have you stayed in touch with the news about Nigeria?"

"Not really. My son was born here. He's an American—very American," she laughed. "It was ok for a while just not to think about the past and to start over. I thought I could do that."

Then came the real question they both wanted to ask the other. "Are you happy?"

Moremi wanted to blurt out "No!" But that would mean a lot of explaining for which she wasn't ready even though Jemimah would be the only person in the world she trusted to fully understand. Instead of the truth she explained the only thing she could. "I've tried to be, but I miss home. I miss my family. And I've missed you. Happiness has been really about my son. Peter is a good man, I think, but we are not alike. I have tried to please him by adopting this culture and for Peter that means forgetting about home. Only I find I can't do that."

Jemimah snorted, an old and familiar form of agreement that pulled them back over the years into the same room. Old friendships can rekindle with gestures like sounds that propel the faraway near as if nothing had ever changed.

"Then come visit. You can stay with me. I'm married now and have three children. I work at the hospital and privately sometimes as a midwife. My husband is a good man. Not so important like yours, but he is kind. And my mother-in-law? You just spoke with her." Moremi learned that Jemimah's mother had died a few years ago and now her father was gone too. She had two girls and a boy. They were healthy and so was she.

Jemimah laughed. "Remember when we used to speak in code when we were teenagers?"

They believed their tone communicated the opposite of their words. It was a way of telling each other secrets that created their own special world.

She asked Moremi, "So, tell me again. Are you happy?"

Moremi's "yes" was long and drawn out like a foghorn.

"Well then," Jemimah mimicked the foghorn, "you need to visit."

They vowed to stay in touch.

Moremi sat for a long time at the table after saying goodbye. She munched on some almonds and grapes. The idea of returning to Nigeria for a visit started with a seed that bloomed, and now her longing began to hurt.

Even so, practical thoughts set in. *How?* First there was Peter to get around. And Ayo's passport. *When? For how long? Would it really be safe?*

Four years ago, when they went to London to visit his parents with Ayo, they all had passports. She pushed the kitchen chair back and slowly got up, wondering where Ayo's passport could be. She had her own, but not his.

She went upstairs and down the hall to the far end where Peter had turned the spare room into his private study. Out of respect, she never went there. But she needed the passport.

As she opened the door and flicked on the overhead light, she felt a twinge of guilt. Tiptoeing in she laughed at herself saying out loud to the emptiness, "No one's home!" She reached inside her pocket for the shell, then went behind the large mahogany desk and turned on the desk lamp, pulling it forward. She opened some drawers and saw all the usual stuff—pens, papers, stapler, stamps, and a few small boxes. He was neat and organized. She rifled through the rest of the drawers. *Where would he keep his most important papers, like Ayo's passport?*

She sat in the silence and peered about. A private room tells a lot about a person. This room revealed nothing that wasn't obvious. On the wall he kept photographs of his parents in front of their London flat, several of Ayo playing soccer, his degrees from Stanford and Berkeley.

There was one photograph of her. She couldn't remember his taking it or even if he had. She was holding Ayo when he was a baby, standing outside on a sunny day on someone's lawn. She smiled at the camera. Ayo looked happy.

This can't be all he's got here. I know he doesn't like clutter, but this room is too neat. Her vow to Jemimah resonated in the silence. *Nothing is this bland. There's something here. What are you hiding Peter?*

She heard her friend's voice. "Keep looking."

She surveyed the room: the beige rug on the floor, a couch with throw pillows, a chair, a few lamps. She spied the closet. *Of course. What's in there?* She got up and glided across the carpet to open the door. Nothing. Just a dark, empty closet. Not even hangars for the extra odd jacket. She looked up for a secret opening perhaps into an attic she'd never known about. But no.

As her eyes adjusted to the dark she looked down and there it was—a small black metal file cabinet with three drawers tucked in the back corner. She knelt and tried to open the top drawer. Locked.

She went back to his desk and sat down and pulled out his center drawer as far open over her lap as she could. She felt the impulse to wrench it out but resisted. Despite her new courage, her fear that he would find out stopped her from shredding his neatness. Her fingers moved like little mice scrambling over each small object until she felt a small, flat leather box. She clutched it, shut the drawer, and placed the box on the desk pad. It was the kind a man would use for his small things like cuff links. She opened it. A man's ring with a large diamond in the center, some military medals. Probably his father's. A small cameo picture of his mother. She stirred her finger through some odds and ends until she found it. A small black key. *I thought so!*

Back to the closet, she dragged the cabinet out, wobbling it back and forth out on the carpet where there was more light. The key worked. She squatted down taking everything out, arranging things in neat piles so she could return it all the way she found it, then sat in the middle intending to take her time. After reading papers Peter had written, some published, some not, letters to colleagues, she came upon a brown folder marked "Ayo." She adjusted her position sitting cross-legged and opened the folder. Among other papers she found his blue and gold passport still current. She set it aside and looked through the rest of the papers. His birth certificate, report from teachers, a math quiz with a bright red A+ on it. A photograph of Ayo with his soccer team after winning a game.

She smiled as she sorted through the papers. She held up a photograph she had taken of Peter and Ayo at the beach. He rode on Peter's shoulders, and they looked like a happy father and son team. The guilt ambushed her.

Here I am, sitting in the middle of his private papers—a spy hunting for secret documents. Maybe I'm wrong about all of this. Maybe my mind is playing tricks on me. Are my ancestors crying wolf? Is my mother telling me the truth?

She was caught in the middle. *Which of my families do I trust? My own mother and grandmother, or Peter and his parents?*

She heard her mother's voice. She was young, happy and wise. When Moremi would ask her mother to help her decide something important her mother would say, "Wait. Do nothing. The answer will come to you." The voice was supposed to soothe, but as she tried to give in to it and relax, she felt agitated by the pictures—why would he lock them away? *Keep going—then put all this back and go watch something silly on TV.*

She set aside the Ayo folder and continued to snoop through the rest of his files. Most of it was uninteresting, but when she pulled out a file marked "SAVE" she twitched. It appeared to be one of his student's recent papers, about thirty pages, marked "midterm" on the front. It had something to do with the oil industry in Nigeria in the '90's with lots of careful graphs and charts. Peter had scribbled personal comments in the margins. *Too close for comfort* on one page, and on another, *How the hell did she figure that out?* She frowned, puzzled. He was not one of those professors who brought his students home, so she had no way to evaluate what this meant. She saw the name of the student: Alice Gordon. She shrugged and returned the paper to its folder and put it down.

Finally, she started to clean up and return everything back in the cabinet the way she had found it, except for the passport, tucked into her pocket next to the shell. As she put the last folder in the back of the bottom drawer, she spotted an envelope scrunched in the back. Retrieving it she held it out. It was addressed in Peter's handwriting to his father. It was sealed and even had a stamp. Apparently, he never sent it. Why? She shrugged and put it back, and as she did, her stomach felt queasy. Her hands shook. She felt impatient and annoyed—this was her body crying wolf again. She sat very still with eyes closed breathing deeply.

After thirty seconds she opened her eyes and declared out loud, "Oh just read it and be done with it. It's a letter he never got around to sending so he saved it. It's nothing."

Because it was sealed, she had to decide. She got up and returned to the desk. She set the letter down and stared at it, imagining how to get an x-ray picture of the contents. *How do you unseal and seal a letter? Steam it open?* She waited, hoping something would come to her and suddenly she felt very silly. Jemimah always said, "You over-think things." She decided to open it, then burn it. *He'll just think he misplaced it, even if he knows it's there. But why would he? He probably forgot to send it and somehow it got thrown in the cabinet. He knows I never come in here. That's the key. He will never suspect.*

She grabbed his silver letter opener, slit open the envelope and pulled out the letter written in Peter's hand. His penmanship had always surprised her with its strangely neat flourishes, as if he were containing something wild within himself. The letter was dated right after their last visit to see his parents, who were both gone within the year.

Dear Father,

We have returned safely from our trip. Moremi and I enjoyed ourselves and are glad you both spent some time with Ayo. He is a good boy. As you know he is lively and athletic. She is a good mother and our life here in Berkeley will remain uneventful.

I know how difficult it must be for you during this time of your chemotherapy treatment. You seem to have the best care in London, and I felt reassured by your team of doctors and their optimism.

I know you commented that Moremi seemed withdrawn a good deal of the time. I believe she has bouts of homesickness and I have made every effort to steer her away from thoughts or memories of Nigeria, but she does seem to be slipping away from my control over her.

Of course, it continues to be extremely important we protect her from learning what happened to her parents. I believe she still has no real idea about the final days when Abacha was coming down hard on all the 419 corruptions, nor does she understand how involved Moses was in the underground resistance while she was away working in Lagos.

I know there was a time you admired Moses and it must be difficult for you to carry the burden of her father's execution, as it was a necessary evil. I understand the mother was a tragic casualty, an accident that was nobody's fault.

I will watch her carefully. Our family's legacy will live on, protected in your grandson.

Peter

She was frozen to the chair and started to shiver in the hot room. She gripped the letter with both hands and stared at those neatly written, politely hypocritical words.

Pulling herself up she stumbled out of the room down the hall into the bathroom and collapsed in a heap, throwing up into the toilet. Her bile tasted like Peter's words. Her head pounded and she lay on the cool tile floor in a fetal position, shaking.

IT WAS 3:00 A.M. IN WASHINGTON D.C. Peter had been asleep in his hotel room for several hours when something awakened him. His eyes opened, he sat up in bed and looked out over the lights of the city. He was on the eleventh floor. His cell phone on the bed-stand played its tune, the Waltz of the Valkyries. He looked over at the clock, picked up the phone while turning on the bedside light, frowning. "What's up?" he snapped.

"Sorry to wake you," the low male voice responded. "But you told me to call you if she did anything unusual."

Peter said nothing.

The voice continued, "She called Nigeria. Made quite a few calls, short ones, looking for someone. Well, she found the person. She talked with her friend, Jemimah Ngoddy, for about an hour. She ended by telling her she might come for a visit next spring. Anything you want me to do?"

Peter hesitated, clearing his throat. "No! Nothing for now. Just send it to my office email, with a transcript of the call."

He pressed end call, put the phone down and went into the bathroom to rinse his face with cold water. He tried to sleep—without much success.

CHAPTER THIRTEEN

One who loves you, warns you.

AFRICAN PROVERB

LYING ON THE COLD TILE, Moremi lost all sense of time, but had to get herself into the bedroom for warmth. She managed to stand up, make her way down the hall to Ayo's room, crawl under his blanket and lay shivering until she slept.

She dreamed. Abeni and Buchi were with her. Both were sitting on Buchi's front porch that looked out across a small vegetable patch with her prized cassava bush in the center, its long leaves, splayed fingers reaching out. Buchi would say, "It reaches out to bless this dry earth." She loved her cassava bush because no matter what the weather did, no matter how the soil was, it grew, it survived. Her grandmother would also say, "That bush is Africa."

They were sitting on her rickety porch while Buchi rocked in her old, rusted iron chair, head back, cackling about something while her mother shelled peas for the soup. Moremi sat on the steps drawing with a stick in the red ground. The sun was setting in an orange sky and the atmosphere was humid. It had just rained, a few clouds hovered with no breeze. The day wound down into slow motion. In the silence Moremi heard the hissing of snakes.

She woke the next morning at dawn feeling as if she had the flu. It took a while to orient herself and to remember the letter. More than ever, she was grateful for privacy. She needed to think and plan.

Forcing herself out of bed she went into the bathroom to start the shower. She pulled off the sweaty clothes that she'd slept in. She took the cowrie shell out of her skirt pocket and put it on the counter and wadded up her skirt and top and threw them into the clothes hamper. In the shower she held her face into the soothing hot water wishing it would wash her away. The dream atmosphere was still in her. She thought of Buchi and her large laugh.

In the shower, she saw herself and Buchi sitting under her grandmother's cassava bush, pulling out tubers the size of small potatoes. Buchi was preparing Baton de Manioc served with the goat stew that was her specialty. After church, friends and neighbors came over and she made enough for everyone.

Moremi had helped Buchi wash the tubers in a large tub before they pounded them into pulp. Buchi handed her one to put into the tub as she pronounced in her conspiratorial voice, "Never eat before you boil. It's poisonous. Cyanide gas in this," she instructed, holding out the cassava tuber with an exaggerated roll of her head and big eyes. "Yes, cyanide gas." She added one of her bawdy jokes that made everyone laugh: "Too much gas in this country." She threw back her head cackling wildly like a hyena, as if the thought came to her from nowhere. That was the way Buchi would tell something funny, most of all to keep herself amused. Sometimes Moremi thought her grandmother was either crazy or wise. That day she thought she was both.

When Buchi died people came from all over. Moremi only then realized her grandmother was known everywhere. Some thought she was a witch. The first time Moremi heard this she realized this made her grandmother special and so she felt proud and to her friends she would declare, "My grandmother is a witch."

She stepped out of the shower and dried herself, shaken by this combination of dream and memory. She dressed in an old cotton smock she had brought from Africa. She never wore it around Peter. But now she put it on and went downstairs to make some tea and toast. She sat down in the kitchen and forced down the toast as she stared out the window. Her loneliness dug into her more than ever. She needed her mother. Not a spirit or phantom. Not a figment of her own imagination. Not a memory. "God dammit!" she wailed. "I need you!" she cried, looking up at the blank white ceiling. "Here. Now."

She retrieved her phone and stared into it: *Speak to me!* She dialed Rebecca's office number and left a message: "I need to see you as soon as possible." It was Saturday. Rebecca probably would not return her call until Sunday night. *Perhaps that's best. I need time to think.*

She decided to call Jemimah as if she were down the street. Yesterday's connection brought her back into the friendship as if ten years had collapsed and they were just two young chatterboxes telling their secrets. It would be six hours later, about 3:00 in the afternoon—the hottest time of day.

Holding the phone, she stared out her kitchen window at the morning fog still lingering. She had never gotten used to it. There was no cooling fog in Nigeria. She remembered a few years back reading an article about a mystery fog that enveloped the whole city of Lagos. It contained higher than normal levels of sulfuric acid and no one knew where it came from. People panicked, running out of buildings, and there were worse traffic jams than usual in the most gridlocked city in the world—an anthill. The mystery fog had come from a broken petroleum pipe.

She dialed Jemimah's cell phone number. She needed to hear her friend's voice.

"Hello?" It was a whisper.

She whispered back, "It's me."

"Are you ok?" Jemimah asked, as if she knew something was wrong.

"Yes," meaning 'no.' She cradled herself holding the phone over her mouth. Her throat constricted. She rocked and breathed. "I'll be coming with Ayo. Just the two of us."

Frozen, neither wanted to let go, but Moremi realized there would be a phone bill and it would go to Peter. "I have to go. Expect me in the late spring."

"I will."

Later, she went down to the cellar and opened the cabinet and surveyed the clutter to make sure Peter had not been down there again. After a few minutes she pushed things aside to clear away the center. She peered into the back of a lower shelf for a mason jar filled with pieces of old bones. She spilled the contents onto the shelf and stared into the configuration until she began to see eyes, a nose, ears—a face. It was an old man. A warrior. She'd seen it before. She waited. She didn't know if it would speak and, if it did, whether she wanted to hear what it might say. There was only silence.

Fatigue closed in as she felt her feet ache and her head throb. She wanted to give up but stayed upright. She closed her eyes. Just as she stumbled in her tracks, almost falling asleep, she saw him coming at her.

He was on an old horse. He stopped and leaned down. She saw he was about to speak. His voice was an echo out of a deep cavern. "Lay low." The voice repeated, "Lay low." The horse spun around and disappeared.

She jerked awake, trembling, and swaying on her feet. She gathered the bones back into the jar, put things back as they were and returned upstairs.

She fell asleep early and woke up late the next day.

She made herself a full breakfast of oatmeal and toast with marmalade and coffee. She put the letter and Ayo's passport in a box of things from long ago that she kept on the shelf in a corner of her closet. Later she went out and bought groceries before she picked up Ayo. That evening they played a card game and she read to him the last chapter of Harry Potter.

CHAPTER FOURTEEN

Fluid in form, volatile in temperament, foreign in origin,
Mami Wata is feared and reviled as a spiritual loose cannon.

ART REVIEW, NY TIMES, APRIL 2, 2009, BY HOLLAND COTTER

IN LATE FEBRUARY, UNSEASONABLY COLD and almost dark outside, the hour approached 6:00 P.M. Rebecca fixed on the Gelede mask as she rocked back and forth in her swivel chair. *Did the carver love the woman he made it for?* She often tried to imagine a ritual with the men dancing in honor of the powerful women they worshipped for their balanced creative and destructive energies, supported by souls enlarged through death in an afterworld only a breath away.

Her mother came to mind. Had she had been possessed by powers that produced harmony over conflict? *You couldn't or wouldn't stand up to Dad who was such a control freak. Your faith made you good and kind, but I didn't think you were strong. Could I have been wrong? I wanted you to be proud of me and maybe you were. But you knew I would never have put up with what you did. You told me not to divorce Jonathan and I told you I couldn't stay married to someone who had to control our relationship. Ironically, Jonathan loved me for my brain, not my sweetness. He and I did have a kind of balance and at least I was there, and we had Margo, who is kinder than I am. More like you. That marriage just wasn't enough for me. But you with Dad? Where were you in that equation? I always thought you made yourself invisible to avoid making waves. You were the peacemaker—not me!*

Rebecca was in college when her mother died suddenly of a brain aneurism. Her father floundered for months, as though unable to go on. After he finally snapped out of his malaise he met and married a younger woman and started a new family. Rebecca could never reconcile his ability to start over. How could he forget her so easily? Maybe he didn't. Now eighty-six, he lived in Connecticut, a widower for the second time. Margo visited him. Rebecca made excuses until the distance was so great, they only made the effort over the phone on holidays. Margo told her recently, "Mom, he's old now. Even his two other kids don't visit. At least call him." She did and it lasted ten minutes. With him, she'd felt justified not making the effort, but looking back—not with her mother.

Whenever she thought of her mother, she felt guilty. Years of psychoanalysis had dulled it, but it was still there like cosmic super glue that sticks no matter what. She could still see the disappointment in her mother's eyes when she fought with a playmate yelling at her, "Good then. Go home you wimp. You're such a crybaby!" She saw her mother's eyes looking aghast, an expression she encountered frequently in her teen years. She thought it meant, "You are not my daughter!" *That wasn't it.* Her mother told her, "Someday you'll understand. And by the way, patience is a virtue. And so is kindness." But she never really did. As she sat in her chair surveying her office seeing her mother she sighed, thinking, *no, Mom, I could never be like you. Forgive me because I find it hard to forgive myself.*

Her thoughts turned to Moremi, what she knew and felt about her. *To understand I need to get out of my own way. Gertrude's bridge analogy was right. Moremi and I have more in common than I realized. Why should that surprise me? And yet it does. She's secretive, as I am. She is more intuitive than she realizes. And so am I. She lost both her parents suddenly and too early. I lost one early. And the other has always been lost to me. Where we differ is her closeness to her parents, never questioning her identity through their eyes. Not me. I had to struggle to find out who I was, and it's taken years. But here she is, stuck in a country not of her choosing where she feels foreign to herself. Rebecca searched further. Her ancestors are with her all the time. I wonder if that's real. Are mine there too?*

As this question hovered, she stared at the mask. The eyes gazed down, and its face remained composed and serene, while on top of its head the python's grip tightened as the twin alligators wriggled. She blinked and gasped. Instant rationalization came to her rescue: *the fading light must have created the dancing shadows—the illusion.* Even so, she was shaken. As she held her gaze, it returned to what it appeared to be—a carved fetish, a dead wooden object. Yet the moment before it was alive. Her mother? *Impossible.* Yet when she saw it come alive, it felt like her mother was here. *It really did move. Fading light and dancing shadows weren't enough—I saw it.*

The tiny red light lodged in the wall that alerted her to her next client popped on—a beady bright eye.

Moremi came in, quietly leaned back into the couch, nodding her greeting, and looked down at the rug, taking her time. "There's something I have come to realize that has to do with Peter. For a long time, I thought it was what was wrong with me." She stopped. *How to say it?* "I assumed Peter and his family rescued me and that was why I am here. But it's all a lie. Now I know they were not who they seemed. They were traitors and murderers!" she spat with venom.

Rebecca stiffened.

Moremi handed her an envelope that contained the un-mailed letter. "Read this." She settled back in the couch and closed her eyes while Rebecca read it.

As she did, she wanted to understand Moremi's Africa. *What could it have been like forced to leave everything you knew and flee to another country that seemed to offer refuge?* She felt helpless in her ignorance but pushed to find images that might help. She saw a father and mother with their daughter whom they loved. The country was warm and beautiful with people dancing and talking, going about their daily lives in harmony. Then the father is dragged away by hooded men with automatic weapons, a mother is running after them, shouting, and quickly dropped in her tracks, dead in seconds after falling into the dirt. First there is harmony, then sudden death. *The letter not only suggests, it proves that this would never have happened if Peter's father had stepped in. But apparently, he didn't, and Moremi's parents were swept up in one of Abacha's brutal purges. Peter all along had known this.*

Her own dream came into view. She was struck by the cruelty of some people, especially her own. *They took what they wanted without respecting the native peoples who were there before time began and when only the stones could speak.* She longed for the idea of an afterlife full of mothers who might speak with her through those centuries and keep alive the undiluted reality of the past. *Is this the bridge where Moremi and I meet? What was the girl Becky in my dream telling me?*

She waited for an answer. They both sat in silence knowing whatever conclusion there was, the letter presaged the collapse of Moremi's world.

Rebecca heard a voice from her own past. An ancestral voice: *Revenge begets revenge.*

She looked up at Moremi who opened her eyes. They held a steady gaze for a long minute.

"This seems pretty clear," Rebecca said, as she handed the letter back. "Do you have any reason to doubt it?"

"No. It explains everything. What I don't understand is why he never sent this letter and why he kept it. I wondered for a moment if perhaps he wanted me—or someone—to know. To find it and know. Peter was not born a bad man. An emotionally weak man, yes. He could not stand up for what was right, so he went along. He couldn't tolerate being their son, so he accepted it by trying to justify what they did. And he used me to do it, knowing if I discovered it he would be destroyed.

Rebecca considered this. They were traversing two different territories: the agreed reality of circumstances, and then an afterlife world that could never be known for sure with all its possibilities, under which danger always lurked. Were the words Rebecca heard in the child's voice triggered by memory of the dream really the words of her ancestor across the ages? *What would Gertrude say?* She saw Gertrude smiling with her head back looking heavenward, holding her arms out, her shoulders hunched conveying a gigantic shrug. She heard the echo again: Revenge begets revenge. *Is that the human condition? Is that what I feel? Or how Moremi feels?*

"What do you want to do?"

"I don't plan to do anything right now except say nothing to him. I have no intention of telling Peter what I know. I'm not prepared for what he might do. There are forces at play that I have no control over. All I can do is try to protect my son and myself until we can return to Africa. I need to return." She gestured toward the mask. "If one of those animals bites down for no reason, that would be an evil act. If one of those alligators bites down, he expects to be bitten back by the snake, and so it goes."

"I see. At least I think I do."

"Well, you bought the mask. It's what happens when harmony is disrupted in a society, and in a family. I now know my family and I have been bitten. If Peter knew that I now know, he will expect to be bitten back."

Rebecca shivered. Her logical mind wanted to undo what Moremi was telling her, but no undoing rationale came. Instead, she felt a surge of anger, the kind that fuels revenge. Perhaps the kind that fueled her turning on her father for how he dominated her kind, generous mother.

That moment she felt intense kinship with Moremi. *Two women from very different cultures connecting within what seemed an older primordial universe. How can that be? And yet, here it is, certainly more real than anything else.*

"Do you plan retaliation?"

"No. I have no plan. I don't need one. If nothing else his guilt will pursue him to the end sooner or later. I wouldn't have to lift a finger against him for that to happen."

"You say forces beyond your control. What forces?"

Moremi sighed as if there were no explanation, but she needed to try. "My ancestral mothers believe that the dead are not dead, and they play a part in what happens to the living. They will use Peter's guilt and it will push him to the brink. That's how it will work. It will destroy him in the end. But, in the meantime I must protect my son and myself." She smiled wanly at Rebecca. "I'm not naïve. There is danger all around me."

Another long silence.

The hour ended.

Rebecca agreed, "Yes, guilt can be a powerful poison."

On her way home Moremi once again stopped at the beach. As she walked along, she tore up the letter into tiny fragments and threw them into the surf. She looked out across the water. *What will be will be.*

CHAPTER FIFTEEN

A couple years into the Abacha administration, many Nigerians joked that his strategy to clean up corruption was to make sure that only he and his closest cronies profited from it.

A CULTURE OF CORRUPTION: EVERYDAY DECEPTION AND POPULAR DISCONTENT IN NIGERIA, DANIEL JORDAN SMITH, PRINCETON UNIVERSITY PRESS, PRINCETON, NEW JERSEY, 2007.

THE MOMENT HE WALKED IN HIS FRONT DOOR he saw something had changed. She acted pleased to see him. Even when they were newlyweds, she never ran up to kiss him. "Dinner will be ready in an hour," she announced in a musical tone—not her style at all. He smelled the roasting lamb and rosemary. Very different. She turned and went back to the kitchen tightening her apron. Ayo sat at the kitchen table doing his homework. He tossed his coat and suitcase in a chair and headed tentatively for the kitchen. As she stirred a pot on the stove she looked up and smiled. The scene was completely out of character, especially given their recent wariness. She hadn't cooked in months. Not like this. What happened? He returned her smile and sat down next to Ayo, wondering.

He played along hoping to discover what this was about. At the same time, he couldn't resist thinking, *Could this be real? Maybe she's had a change of heart?* Her behavior unhinged him, as if somehow behind his back she had gained control. Her elusiveness made her different from other women, more attractive.

His own mother was concrete and pragmatic. She was less than generous toward others and had taught him that money and power demanded bloodshed and sacrifice. He watched Moremi lean down and open the oven to test the roast. Yes, she had changed. The tables had turned, and as he watched her, he felt exquisitely vulnerable.

Hugo had informed him that she called Africa. *Was that it? Did that make her suddenly so happy? Should I find a way to ask? No, she's not being herself. It's not good—she's hiding something.*

He jiggled Ayo to make him giggle and invited him to follow upstairs while he changed into casual clothes. He raised his eyebrows asking for approval.

"Great! Go with your dad, Ayo. Dinner in thirty minutes."

She heard them on the stairs, jostling each other, playing phantom soccer on the way up. She sat down at the kitchen table and held her hands out with palms down to check if they were shaking. Just a little. She took a deep breath. His favorite wine was on the table. She poured a little into her glass and swallowed. *He knows something's up, but he doesn't know why.* She heard Ayo laughing. The wine felt soothing, and she wanted more. *I must be careful and not overplay things. Keep him guessing. I need time to figure things out—I need a plan. My mother told me men feel what they want to feel and it's our job to make sure what they feel about us is happiness. Your father is a happy man. But trust me, I have the power to make him unhappy if I want. We women always have the power if we choose to use it.*

Later, they played their roles as two parents enjoying dinner with their son. Ayo was talkative. They all laughed. Peter and Ayo helped her clear the table and offered to wash the dishes, but she shooed them away to go spend time together. Acting like the happy wife had taken its toll.

They went upstairs and started the next Harry Potter book.

She sat down at the table. *What am I doing?* She thought about the passport and felt the urge to pick up Ayo from school and disappear. But not without a plan. Returning to Africa with nothing did not seem possible. One step at a time. She would not act impulsively. *Besides, he'll find me no matter where I might go—I'm certain about that!*

At 9:30 she went up to the bedroom and found them both asleep. She helped Ayo get up and walked him into his own room, poured him into his pajamas, then slipped into their bedroom and changed into her nightgown. A wave of fatigue carried her off into scattered dreams. In one she tried to find her way home, although in the dream she no longer knew where home was.

As the weeks passed, she kept it up, playing the good wife, but he felt her distance. Whenever he tested the waters and attempted intimacy she backed away with polite excuses. She was busy with her own graduate school, working part time, taking care of Ayo. He knew she was avoiding him, but he still didn't know why.

AT MIDDAY ON A FRIDAY Peter sat in his car deep in the bowels of the underground university garage. He told his assistant Annie he was having lunch with a colleague, and not to expect him back at the office.

He stared at the image Hugo had sent to his I-phone that morning. His prescient student, Alice Gordon, was in one of the college joints off campus, sitting outside at a picnic table where students drank beer and ate junk food. She had a large hamburger in both hands, poised for a big bite, laughing with her friends.

He read the message again: "Do you want me to do anything?"

Peter had responded "Not yet."

He abhorred impulsivity. When he was young, he often lost his temper and the consequences had never been good. In his twenties he began to develop the practice of self-control as a form of internal martial arts.

He had to think. He knew he was probably over-reacting, but her paper in response to his Nigerian oil embezzlement puzzle read as if she managed to get her hands on actual transactions with names and dates. All the others had done what he wanted and treated his problem as hypothetical. But not her. She managed to go right to actual sources. None of that would have mattered really except his father's name was publicized frequently. There weren't that many Kolade Abosanjos, and how many with a son, an economics professor at UC Berkeley, married to a Moremi Abosanjo with a son named Ayo? She had proven herself to be quite the little snoop.

Still, none of that justified sitting in the dark of his car in an underground garage with a pair of binoculars on the passenger seat. He knew that his compulsion to spy on her was completely irrational, but here he was.

He'd received a message from Hugo detailing her schedule on campus. On Wednesdays she had morning classes and parked in the garage so later she could drive into San Francisco where she volunteered at the Greenpeace Office. She had to be there at 2:30 so he expected her to come out to her car in about fifteen minutes.

He stared at her car about twenty feet away, a fire engine red Mini Cooper. He understood she was from Seattle. Her parents work in the tech industry.

"They're a couple of Asperger types!" Hugo reported. Alice was their only child, a bit of a prodigy, clueless socially, but popular among the smart kids who find her amusing because she talks like a little professor. He thought of her in class, talking too much to others as she wriggled in her seat while at the same time scrawling notes on paper, unlike the other students who used their laptops. He also noticed she made lots of squiggles and circled and underlined things she obviously thought were important. He thought it was obnoxious how active her brain was, like an over-stuffed computer inside that round, curly head. He understood her all too well and twitched in response to uninvited empathy. He'd been like her as a kid. The smartest one in class. But all his parents had cared about was that he was fat and clumsy. Well, he showed them.

Hugo reported that Alice's maternal grandmother, now in her nineties, was wealthy. That explained why the girl was not anxious like most of the other students, about whether she would have a job. She could afford to work for non-profits like Greenpeace, an organization to which her grandmother and parents were connected. According to Hugo, "The old lady gave Greenpeace 100K."

He pulled out the report as he waited. Both her parents worked in a Microsoft department dedicated to boosting the energy efficiency of PCs, reducing the company's environmental impact, and improving its low environmental ranking.

"And oh," Hugo added, "they're vegans."

Peter didn't particularly like environmentalist types—they were narrow-minded and idealistic to a fault. He wondered if her parents approved of her eating hamburgers.

He began to feel like a predator waiting to trap a strange and dangerous little creature. Not unlike his mongoose Tavi, alert and on the prowl, his favorite pet when he was ten. He loved that mongoose and it followed him everywhere. But one day it bit him for no reason so he grabbed it by its long, wiry tail and threw it as far as he could. He heard the thud when it landed in the bushes. He never saw Tavi again. He hated that memory.

He glanced at the clock dial on his dashboard. One forty-five. Where was she? He wasn't feeling very well and the nausea he'd felt that morning wasn't going away. He knew he needed to see a doctor because it was getting worse. He had learned from his father how to suck it up when he was in pain. But this was different. He vowed to call his doctor soon. He remembered how Moremi treated Ayo when he was hurt or ill. She didn't exactly pamper him but when he was hurt, she became protective and took care of him so that he barely noticed. She never made Ayo feel ashamed when he was in pain or scared.

He pulled a large envelope out of his glove compartment and opened the two pages that he had received from Alice Gordon the day before. He didn't want to read it again, but he sighed knowing it would distract him from his stomach. It was hand-written in child-like script on cheap lined paper.

Dear Professor Abosanjo,

I cannot tell you what a thrill it was for me to write that midterm you assigned for us. Wow! You must have quite a brain to come up with such a tricky assignment.

His stomach twitched.

But I want you to know that what I had to think about when I wrote my paper is the area of Green Economics I want to write my dissertation on. What I mean is Nigeria is the perfect example of how human beings can plunder and destroy each other and the earth for just pure greed. And it was a team effort between the Nigerians and Halliburton for sure. I'm guessing that's what you had in mind for us to realize. You are such a great example of someone who is willing to look at what the world economics needs to be now to save the planet. I am going into the field of Green Economics, which is a new field that positions economics within a long-term, earth-wide, holistic context of reality as part of nature. Which also, I might add, and again thanks to you, incorporates and celebrates 'difference,' diversity, equity, and an inclusiveness within its concepts of society and community. Wow! What a mouthful!

He shook his head. 'Little Professor' indeed.

As a result, I wish to ask you if you will consider heading my dissertation committee—when I'm ready of course. I'm thinking about using Nigeria as my example country—a microcosm of everything that's gone wrong within the historical conventions of the inherent normative concepts found in the dominant neoclassical economics in the context of the last two centuries. I think by studying an example country that not only is completely corrupt morally and economically, but that exists as an iconic example for all of us how we not only poison the land but poison each other and ourselves. I just hope the CIA doesn't want to open a file on me! (Just kidding!!)

He almost choked. *The perfect cocktail of genius and clueless.*

Well, I think you probably get my point. I could go on and on. Please consider my request to be head of my committee.

Your Admirer, Alice Gordon

Reaching the end, he winced from a sharp pain in his lower abdomen and leaned forward over the steering wheel and closed his eyes.

It was then the garage exit door burst open and three chattering co-eds emerged. None was Alice and he felt relieved. He decided to leave. This had been a very stupid idea.

As the heavy gray door was about to clang shut, someone burst through, kicking it back open. It was Alice.

He snapped alert.

She was carrying a heavily laden backpack with an armful of books, her sweatshirt tied around her waist starting to unravel. "Hey you guys," she wailed. "Wait up!"

The other girls laughed and waved goodbye as if they were used to this.

She yelled goodbye as she struggled to find her keys. He heard the car's little bark as it responded. She dropped some books and as she stooped down to pick one up, he thought she might fall over because of the weight of her backpack.

He couldn't help chuckling. She seemed so harmless.

After tossing everything into her back seat she slipped behind the wheel and sped off.

As he drove away, he realized he had no idea what he was going to do with her. He had given her an "A" on the paper. He had to. But he was not effusive with his praise and wherever he could he tried to steer her focus in another direction. She didn't seem to notice.

He'd responded to her request tersely even though he knew he should thank her and sign it, but he couldn't. He was supposed to be flattered. *Dear Ms. Gordon, I will take your request under consideration and will let you know after the end of the spring semester.* He hoped she would lose interest.

But it was probably too late. Before he got her letter and told Hugo to investigate, he rationalized that he was over-reacting. He had no idea his assignment would inspire her to focus on Nigeria as a dissertation topic. And of course, since he was Nigerian, it made sense for him to head her committee. He decided she was a lot like Tavi—cute, nosey. And too smart for her own good. Amusing. Bites at random without knowing her strength.

As he pulled into his driveway his mind was made up. "She's a mongoose and I may have to get rid of her—somehow."

CHAPTER SIXTEEN

She has seduced and charmed many, who have given visible form to this spiritual entity as an integral part of the process of self-definition, self-realization, and empowerment in countless cultural worlds over time and space.

MAMI WATA, ARTS FOR WATER SPIRITS IN AFRICA AND ITS DIASPORA. FOWLER MUSEUM OF UCLA, LOS ANGELES, ED. HENRY JOHN DREWAL, 2008.

MOREMI SAT IN THE STARBUCKS across the street from Rebecca's office. It was a Friday in March and the beginning of Spring Break. Ayo had just left for a ski trip with his friends at Lake Tahoe. Peter was also gone on business. He rarely told her where he went. She had learned not to ask. All he would tell her is he would return in a week.

She liked to arrive early enough before her appointments so she could think about what she wanted to talk about. Today it was Peter. He was having bouts of illness off and on. His doctors urged him to take some time off. They explained his symptoms as too much stress. She suspected otherwise. The symptoms might be phantom at first, but she was certain real illness would follow.

Peter had grown more and more short-tempered, not so much with her, but around his work. Their truce after he came home from Washington in early February held, but they continued to avoid each other.

A few days previously she heard him slam the phone down on his assistant Annie, something she had never heard him do before. It seemed to have something to do with a student named Alice Gordon and that rang a bell, but she couldn't remember why. He'd barked at Annie, "Well just tell her I'm too damn busy and tell her to set up another appointment, preferably a month from now!"

She woke up from her reverie and looked at her watch. Now she was late.

In Rebecca's office she felt the comfort of being able to talk with another woman.

"Peter is unwell, and his doctors have found nothing."

"What do you think is going on?"

Their eyes met. Moremi looked away, to the mask, and in what seemed to be a non-sequitur she spoke. "That mask on your wall was danced in Yoruba ceremonies to ward off witches."

Rebecca nodded. "Go on."

"The dance is a masquerade called Gelede. The men dance to honor the elder women, the ancestors. Yoruba women are independent both spiritually and economically from the men. An elderly woman is respected as a witch. In your culture a witch is mostly bad and the butt of jokes. Your mask embodies the principles of both good and evil. The snake and the two crocodiles are locked together. The crocodiles hold the snake in their jaws while the snake keeps its jaw clamped down on the crocodile's tail. This is the way of the natural world and an expression of divine justice. The mask's face is of a woman gazing downward, calmly representing the peacefulness achieved in the tension of the animals above her."

Rebecca looked at the mask. "Ok, I think I can follow that."

"Try to imagine. When someone in the community betrays another the rule of order is broken. Let's say the crocodile bites the snake out of impulse or fear. The snake will react. This is the same with humans. If there is a betrayal in the community the witches serve as the snake that must react to the betrayal. And this produces justice."

"Let me ask you, do you now believe Peter's illness is a punishment visited upon him by your ancestors? He is now ill. Has the snake bitten him?"

Moremi frowned and took her time. "I believe in divine justice. For me it is a living, breathing thing. I believe that your western culture sees justice as an abstract, logical system of laws that make sense at a given time. But there are forces that come from the ancient mothers that cannot be stopped. Yes, I do believe Peter is being punished by them. He's ill. Mysteriously. And what is more, he knows that no matter how hard he tries to deny this, he cannot escape his heritage."

Rebecca couldn't resist being logical. "How do you know for sure that he knows?"

"Whether Africans are Christian or Muslim it doesn't matter. They still believe deeply in the spirit world. And heaven knows this belief has been exploited by Africans—most of all against each other. The belief is here." Her hand held over her heart. "Peter is no different. He has denied his heritage, but he knows."

Rebecca could see that Moremi's comfort in a spirit world was beyond ideas and stories. She yearned to be able to understand this more deeply but knew she couldn't quickly step across into another dimension into a world so foreign to her own. But here in the room with Moremi she heard Gertrude: "*Try.*"

"You said something I would like to understand more. You said the men dance with the masks in the ceremony to ward off the witches. I'm trying to fathom that."

Moremi searched. *How to explain?* "The witch represents both good and evil. I think to the Western psyche these two sides—good and evil—are separate. Your Devil is separate from your God. I speak of good and evil as if they were locked together in mortal combat." She searched for the words. "I know you don't think it's that simple and I don't either. We talk about justice coming from a living, breathing awareness that is instinctual. That practice started with earliest humans coming together in communities for survival and thousands of years of actions and reactions."

"You are saying that when there is an act against an individual it is against the whole community and there is an automatic retaliation. The crocodile bites the snake. The snake bites the crocodile. There is no good or evil about that. In the natural world, Darwin's universe, this is how it is. But we humans have developed advanced brains. We have written laws based on a code of ethics that works and this is also who we are."

"Yes, so have Africans. But in the old religions," she pointed to the mask, "we teach harmony through ritual masquerade. It's a ceremony to teach obedience to the rules of the communal society. These rules are living entities—they have sinew and teeth. Retribution is simply a law of nature. When laws are codified, they become capricious, not automatic, or instinctual. Instinctive retribution circumvents logic. I'm not sure how far we have come from our origins."

Rebecca needed to bring their point into the here and now. "So . . . here's what I understand you are telling me. Your connection to your mother-line, your ancestral women, is happening now. They hint to you of retribution because of the great harm Peter and his now-deceased parents have brought down on you and your family. They are also the witches who can use their power to create harmony or destruction. Do they intend to destroy Peter?"

Moremi stared at Rebecca. "This is how it works. I have no control over the forces now at play."

Rebecca stared back, pursuing a deeper connection. She pushed. "My ancestors came to this country from a place in Ireland called Ulster. Here they are called Scots Irish. They couldn't believe the vastness and richness of the land they came to in Pennsylvania, Delaware, and the southern states. They took the land from the original inhabitants, the Indians called Lenni Lenape. There were many tribes here for thousands of years before any white man. This clash of cultures set off what I think you would call a natural cycle of actions and reactions—or more to the point—a power struggle that could only end badly. And it did. Nothing could stop it."

She needed to finish her thought: "Peter's family were like some of my ancestors, who fed their own greed and forgot about what would be good for all the inhabitants who settled here. But in the end, the Indians lost and were pushed into smaller and smaller areas to live, when the whites just took everything—the land, the game, the natural resources. It's hard to find the right and wrong of the past because it would seem the forces of retribution hurt everyone."

"Well, you are right," Moremi nodded. "Peter's family joined the people in power, and they won. But if you take a closer look at people on a smaller, individual scale you will see plenty of justice. And that's what I'm doing. On a smaller scale, Peter may lose. As I said, Peter believes in this spirit world where there is a true reckoning."

"You mean like in heaven?"

"My father said we create our own individual heaven and hell."

"What did he mean?"

"Simple: Whatever we do here in this life has consequences. Your western thinking does not take into consideration the power of the ancestors who play an active part here—now. Where no one escapes."

"Do you think you should protect yourself?"

"Yes. I will do what I must."

Rebecca nodded. "I'm uneasy."

Moremi agreed. "So am I."

CHAPTER SEVENTEEN

What the Yoruba people say about their culture is also applicable to the histories and significance of Mami Wata: she is like a 'river that never rests'."

MAMI WATA: ARTS FOR WATER SPIRITS IN AFRICA AND ITS DIASPORA. FOWLER MUSEUM AT UCLA, ED. HENRY JOHN DREWAL, 2008.

THAT EVENING, Rebecca met Richard for dinner at their favorite Italian restaurant where they had their first date.

They had met in a chance encounter two years ago at the symphony in San Francisco for an evening of Bach, Beethoven, and Brahms. A famous European guest conductor was performing a benefit concert as a fundraiser.

Rebecca had gotten two tickets months in advance and was planning to attend with Margo who was visiting after the Thanksgiving holiday. It would be just the two of them, a girls' night out for dinner and a concert. She had been looking forward to the evening, but the night before Margo learned that her boss urgently needed her to return to work in Washington the next day. When Rebecca saw her daughter's suffering at this news, Rebecca accepted it and offered to drive her to the airport before the concert. As a final touch on what could have been a tense moment, Rebecca added, "That will give me plenty of room to stretch and enjoy myself. You know how I hate those cramped seats."

Margo knew her mom would always sweep in to protect her.

The following rainy, windy evening Rebecca walked briskly to the entrance of the symphony hall. She was late and hurried to join the line of stragglers when out of the corner of her eye she caught sight of what looked like Batman in a billowing raincoat streaking across the wide boulevard dodging traffic against the light and bounding up the front steps. He swept past her as he attempted to fling himself through the front door managing to spray everyone standing in line.

The staid little man about to take Rebecca's ticket rose to the occasion as if he had been waiting a long time to show what he could do. He accepted her ticket with his right hand, smiling while his left arm flew back with alarming speed and caught the man's arm. "Whoa! Hold on a minute, sir. I need your ticket and I might add the line forms outside behind this young lady here."

Normally she would have been affronted by this stranger's audacity, but there was something about him that bemused her. She wondered how this would play out. She thought of a kid in the principal's office who might outsmart the principal.

"Yes, I understand sir," the man responded, looking down at the hand gripping his elbow, "but you see I must get inside to buy a ticket because I must attend this concert."

The words sounded ridiculous given that the concert had been sold out for months, but his urgent tone put a spin on his meaning that was hard to deny, like when you are tempted to root for the bad guy who has just stolen from the bank.

"I'm sorry sir," the ticket man replied, maintaining his equanimity.

Rebecca could see he was enjoying his own authority as a school principal might.

"But it so happens that tonight's special performance is sold out. There are no tickets to be had. So, you will have to step aside and allow others who managed to secure their tickets in advance to move in since the performance starts," he checked his watch and smiled, "in exactly seven and a half minutes."

The man stared agog at this annoying creature. She saw that he was used to getting his way against all odds and rather than feeling indignant she felt impressed by his unadulterated chutzpah. She giggled.

He shot her an annoyed look.

She couldn't help herself. What popped out of her mouth in the next moment remained the most out of character and surprising moment of her life. "Wait a minute. I think I can do something here," and with great aplomb she produced Margo's unused ticket and handed it to the surprised ticket man. After that she did something even more startling—she threw her arm under his and announced, beaming up at him, "Let's go darling or we'll be late!"

Richard was hooked from that moment.

Now two years later he waited for her in their restaurant. As she entered, the waiter greeted her and pointed to the back corner table where Richard sat scribbling in a small notebook.

He carried a little spiral notebook like a reporter to write down the variety of constant, rapid thoughts on a broad range of unpredictable topics. He didn't notice her until she pulled out her chair and he leapt to his feet bumping the table, almost toppling his water glass as he apologized for being distracted.

Amused, she waved him to sit down letting him know she appreciated his attempt at gallantry.

"Good to see you," he enthused. "I hope you're hungry."

"Starving."

He'd already ordered a bottle of Barolo and began to pour when their usual waiter Gino strode over.

"Buona Serra," Richard bellowed, even though Gino had already brought the wine. But Gino knew he entertained the notion that one day they would converse in Italian. Richard studied the familiar menu through his glasses perched on the bridge of his nose and announced in his fake, debonair tone, "La dama will have il rigatoni al forno con salsa di finocchi e prosciutto cotto." With greater aplomb, pointing at himself he added, "y sono will have Tagliolini Verdi gratinati al prosciutto." He gave Gino a satisfied grin.

"OK," Gino replied in his flat American accent. "Baked rigatoni with fennel, cream and prosciutto and baked green tagliolini with prosciutto. You got it Professor."

Richard's satisfied grin disappeared.

Rebecca came to the rescue, holding her glass up to distract him from further forays into fake conversation with Gino, who spoke no Italian.

Richard had always found this hard to grasp. He responded, raising his glass to hers while Gino as usual escaped into the kitchen with their order.

They ate over small talk. After their plates were cleared, they leaned into one another across the table, finishing the last of their wine, and began a more intimate discussion. He noticed for the first time that she was more preoccupied than usual.

"So, tell me, what's going on?"

"Well, it's work-related, that case from Nigeria I mentioned. I've dealt with all the permutations of depression and anxiety, heard just about any kind of scenario you can think of, but I've never been caught up in something so different."

He suggested they go back to her place, make a fire, join the Queens and talk. She smiled, grateful for the suggestion.

Later, after she'd changed into her jeans and sweatshirt, they sat in front of the fire as he poured two small glasses of limoncello. She sank into the couch, tucked her bare feet under pillows and petted Juno's soft ginger head as they continued their conversation.

"So, what can you tell me?"

"Well, remember when I asked you about Nigeria, Vodou and all that?"

He nodded, admiring the yellow clarity of the limoncello, which was homemade by a friend.

"Imagine someone who has lost everything. Violently. Suddenly. Her parents and friends—either dead or lost to her. She fled her own country. She now faces spending the rest of her life in a strange culture, one that can't fully understand how this could really happen. And I don't mean intellectually understand because we can do that, but emotionally, deeply get it on its most profoundly traumatic level."

He wanted to say it was like this in most of the world. Terrible things happen daily. Everywhere. But those of us who live in our opulent American bubbles—we just don't see it. But he didn't want to come off as a know-it-all. *I can see she's trying to understand something not understandable by our cultural standards. Not emotionally at any rate.* He searched for something helpful. "You probably know more than you think. That's what you do—you grasp things that are hard to imagine."

She decided to tell him more. "All of what I have told you is understandable and bearable. But what is not is that she has just found out the man she married may have lied to her about what happened to her parents. His family rescued her from political danger and arranged for her to marry their successful son who is a university professor." She paused, "It seems he must have colluded with the parents, who could have prevented the tragedy."

He looked at her with his quizzical expression. "You mean she married into a nest of vipers and had no inkling of this before she married him?"

"Yes. She just found out by chance through an un-mailed letter that admits this must have been a plan, to make the marriage look like a rescue, when in fact it seems they were connected to the political arrest and death of her father. The mother's death was collateral damage. They took her like a prize heifer for their son who needed a wife to produce a grandchild—an heir for their family name."

Richard put his glass down and paid attention. "Why doesn't she leave him and take the son?"

"She's afraid. His parents were wealthy and lived their last years in London. They were involved in a corrupt regime that embezzled oil and gas profits out of Nigeria. Their name still has influence."

"How does she know this?"

"She's been putting it together slowly, piece by piece. The letter he wrote to his parents, but oddly never sent, admits the truth. And now she has concluded that her husband will do anything to keep her from knowing."

"Have you seen the letter?"

"Yes."

"Do you think she's in danger?"

"She could be."

"Should you inform the police?"

"And tell them what?"

He nodded. "I suppose you've suggested that?"

"Yes. She says no."

"Why?"

"This guy is a prominent U.S. citizen. Dual citizenship. He's a professor. He's published. He's got tenure. He travels and lectures. There's no real evidence of anything. It's just that she's scared and so am I."

"What does she want to do?"

"Well, here's the real enigma. She tells me that forces are already in motion. Vodou forces. Through her ancestors—'the Mothers' she calls them. They have spoken to her from the other side. She completely trusts in these spirits and their form of justice. She tried to ignore them. But then she read the letter. She told me, 'Now I know.'"

"Knows what, exactly?"

"That what her Mothers have told her is true. His family has her family's blood on their hands."

He whistled softly. "Where's the letter?"

Rebecca looked down and petted Juno. "She told me she ripped it into small pieces and threw it into the ocean."

"Hmmm . . ." he murmured, "well that sort of takes care of that. I assume you have consulted with Gertrude?"

"Yes."

"Well? What did the Wise Old Owl have to say?"

Rebecca sighed and smiled. "She told the story about the Emperor Claudius Germanicus when he was on his death bed. He realized that he had been poisoned by his fourth wife Agrippina, whose son Nero would therefore succeed him as emperor. In that moment of his death when he knew he had been surrounded by treachery all his life, Claudius said: 'Then let it all hatch out.'" She waited. "That's what the Wise Old Owl said."

"Yes. She would say that." He looked at Rebecca. "But I'm concerned. What if he finds out she knows what happened? What do you think he'll do?"

"She doesn't know that either, but she's afraid of him."

"So, she tore up the letter and threw it into the ocean? Was that some kind of symbolic gesture?"

"Maybe. She actually said she tossed it into the spiritual mire."

He wondered aloud. "She's feeding the mother spirits, giving them the letter as an offering so that the solution or reckoning is in their hands, not the local police who probably would conclude she's talking nonsense and say the letter proves nothing. Not to mention the fact that it seems he never sent it."

Again, he looked at her, letting her see how worried he really was. "What will she do now?"

"She says what happens from now on is out of her hands and even if she wanted to stop it, she couldn't."

"What do you think about that?"

"Ok…," sighing. "I'll tell you. I know she believes that what's happening is connected to her own ancestors—her mother and grandmother and the whole matrilineal line. She told me that in Africa when someone breaks with the ancestors, they become ill. She believes that the old religions are in the African soul." Rebecca stopped for a moment and looked into the fire. "She thinks Africans are closer to the source of existence than any other race, so they have a deeper connection to their ancestors."

He thought about that.

She waited for his response.

"Are we talking Lucy and Lucy's Baby territory? The Baby has been established to be about 4.2 million years old. Does your client believe that there is an uninterrupted continuum?"

"Well . . . maybe. She says her beliefs are so ancient and so embedded in the African psyche that there is great power inherent in their collective soul. I get that. So does Gertrude."

He knew she was much more willing than he to venture into altered realms of reality and take it seriously. He felt a hint of his former wife Janice poking at him. She was adept at disenchantment. Rebecca on the other hand was all about enchantment. This case was an exquisite collision of cultures and very possibly a deeper dimension of justice. Gertrude might be right: Let it all hatch out. But he was worried about the here and now. "You know, this could get dangerous for you."

"Yes, possibly. But maybe not quite in the way you're imagining. When our world as we know it—based on scientific principles—is questioned by something different, I believe we feel threatened. We base our sanity on assumptions about what reality is. We label people as mentally ill when they don't see things our way."

He watched her follow her own reasoning through a different prism and envied her ability to navigate the unknown. His own work was about presumptions and suppositions, the never-ending cycle of knocking down ideas just so more could crop up, like a shooting gallery at the county fair.

She added, watching him think through what she said, "I think it's important to suspend our assumptions about where the threat is really coming from."

He decided to accept her assessment and think about it. He smiled at her and took her hand. "Ready for bed?"

"Yes, I'm tired and tomorrow is another day."

She fell asleep while he lay awake. His thoughts searched for something lodged long ago in his memory. Then he found it, the Osogbo festival in the town of Osogbo in Western Nigeria, not far from Lagos, on the Osun River. There the people worshipped a powerful female deity they called Osun, who carried a brass fan and a grass cutlass. He had been impressed that it had become an international tourist attraction that drew thousands to witness the festival's grandeur. But more than that there was something he couldn't bring into view. Just when sleep took over, it appeared. Not only was this Osun worshipped for her goodness, but she was also the leader of the Aje—the elderly women called "The Mothers," shape-shifting witches. His eyes fluttered open. The Aje play a dual role of helping and hindering human events. They cause all kinds of misfortune to befall those who cross them. They cause illness and accidents. They devour human livers without vomiting and they terrify with dreams. *I'll tell Rebecca in the morning.*

He listened to Rebecca's even breathing and softly patted her arm without waking her. As he eased into sleep, he found comfort—*they can only hurt you if you believe in them. And I don't.*

CHAPTER EIGHTEEN

It could be said that General Sani Abacha, Nigeria's current supreme ruler, is like an elephant: it is easier to recognize him than to describe him. His trademark dark aviator sunglasses glued to his unsmiling tribal-marked face is a picture that has become recognizable around the world over the past three years.

'NIGERIA'S TROUBLED YEARS', CONTEMPORARY REVIEW, VOL. 267, NO. 1558, NOVEMBER 1995, P. 230 BY ABINDUN ONADIPE

MOREMI WAS ANXIOUS TO GET HOME after her session with Rebecca, inside and protected so she was free to imagine and plan. Spring was not far off, but the winter rains were not over. She welcomed the rainy season when it came to Africa. *Even here, on the west coast of northern California, surrounded by ocean, mountains, valleys and rolling hills where everything was plentiful, there had been drought. Americans took for granted their abundance of natural resources, like water and clean air. The difference between America and Africa was that Nigerians were used to the plundering and corruption of their own natural resources. And air? They knew all about polluted air.*

Today, she and Rebecca had tried to reach each other's outer limits of understanding and they came close. But the divide between them was an invisible wall. It's what you grow up with that becomes what you know. As a small child Moremi saw the spirits. She was among people who lived with them as she did. What choice did Rebecca have but to believe that spirits are like fairy tales? Rebecca could try; she could suspend disbelief. Yet Rebecca was scared. The unknown was coming out of the shadows.

Her grandmother's voice, when she was a child troubled about something, came to her: *"Listen to the wind. The atmosphere will tell you all you need to know. If there is danger, the animals smell it. So can humans—if they want."* Buchi would take in the air through her nostrils—flared open like a giant bellows—and blow it out through puckered lips, moving her head in a huge, exaggerated circle. *"Like that,"* she would say. And she would spread her arms as if she were the wind-maker herself.

The house would be hers for a week. Life with Peter was stifling. It was nothing overt. His way of controlling was invisible. She felt eyes on herself no matter where she went or what she did. How or why she felt this constant surveillance she couldn't say, but she could feel tense, or even panicked, when nothing was there. She wanted her freedom, but not without Ayo. Fear of losing Ayo felt like the thick walls of her cage. Peter would never allow her to take him. She dreamed of bringing him to Nigeria for a visit in June or July. But so far, she couldn't figure out how to convince Peter.

After pulling into the driveway, she sat for a moment in the dark, listening to the wind and rain and drops pelting the car through the trees. She thought about her friend at school making everyone laugh with her rendition of Janis Joplin singing *Freedom's Just Another Word for Nothing Left to Lose.* She had laughed too but felt no affinity for the '60's music. She identified with her grandparents' generation and the blues from the '40's. Besides, she had a lot to lose. She remembered the first time she heard Aretha Franklin singing *Don't Play That Song for Me.* It was a 1971 recording.

Don't play that song for me. 'Cuz it brings back memories, old days that I once knew, the days that I spent with you.

Those lyrics stung her heart and were more to the point.

She climbed out of the car and headed for the front porch, collecting the mail, and fumbling with the keys. She was grateful for the calm and warmth inside and went to the kitchen to make some tea. She wandered back to the living room to turn on a few more lights. The warm glow of the lamps reminded her of her mother. She sat down on the couch and closed her eyes, letting the fatigue of the last weeks take her in.

She woke with a start when the teakettle whistle shot through her. In such a mood there was no such thing as a singing teakettle—only a shrill startling alarm.

She made the tea and returned to the couch, anxious to call Ayo, but it would be too soon. She would call in the morning, imagining him playing with the other children, laughing, and having fun. It gave her solace to think of her happy child.

As she sipped the tea and again let the fatigue infuse her, she heard it.

The floor creaked over her head. Her glance shot across the room to the entryway at the bottom of the stairs. Adrenaline paralyzed her for a few seconds as she stared at the ceiling.

She sprang up from the couch spilling hot tea on her hand. She winced, set down the cup and listened for more, searching in her pocket for the shell. Silence, only the rain pinging on the gutter outside the window and the wind in the redwood tree. Seconds turned into a minute. After five minutes without further creaking, she calmed down.

The sweat on her shirt turned cold. She wiped her forehead with the back of her hand and tiptoed into the entryway to listen at the foot of the stairs. Nothing. She remembered Buchi's words. *Smell the atmosphere*, and she did. Nothing. It smelled like old, polished wood as it always did.

She felt silly and tried to take herself in hand. *I'm just jumpy, that's all.* Back to the couch and her tea, holding it close for comfort. Buchi would say, *"That wind and that old house need to talk."* She looked around. This house likes to creak. That's its language.

An hour later, after she had eaten some dinner, she went to bed, falling into a deep sleep.

AT 2:00 A.M. HE CREPT INTO THE ROOM, quietly set a chair down by the bed and watched her sleep.

The first time he met her she had been sixteen, like her mother full of life. She spoke her mind without any of the insecure gestures or equivocal fillers that most of the girls her age used. She was already sure of herself and had an athletic body, moving with assurance no matter what she did. That attracted him most even now. She could stoop down to pick up something from the floor with no effort. Sometimes he wondered how she did it. Even now in her forties he never heard her grunt or wheeze from the exertion. She carried Ayo as if he were part of her own body.

He loved their son as much as she did, but they didn't have the same connection no matter how hard he tried. He remembered his own mother, going with her to the school for the first time when he was six, shy and terrified. She sat in a straight-backed chair in the headmaster's office reciting what a good son he was. He sat next to her and watched the face of the headmaster as he smiled and nodded. *They all say that.* Peter wanted to tell the headmaster that he liked animals and especially astronomy. He wished she would say something that made him feel special, not just that he was a good boy—he didn't feel like a good boy. Dogs are good boys. He wished the headmaster would look at him and ask him something, anything, so he could show him that he was special.

When it was time for him to join his class, the headmaster followed him to the door. He looked back at his mother, hoping she would do something, but she was rummaging through her large black purse. He held back a moment. Their eyes met and she said, "Run along then, Peter!"

He had learned to dismiss these memories but sitting here now in the dim light listening to the wind he was too tired to shake them. He forced himself to concentrate. He had no plan, but things were coming to a head. He knew she was hiding something and guessed that somehow, perhaps through her friend in Nigeria—Jemimah—she had learned the truth. Her ability to stay calm and play a role with him disturbed him the most. He wanted her anger, so he could react. But she carried herself as if she were in another world, listening to voices from another dimension.

He couldn't shake his fear of her, convinced she was planning something, and that she would take his son. He couldn't have that. He had crossed a line, beginning with spying on Alice Gordon in that dark garage. The pain in his stomach intensified his fears of being cornered. His choices were gone. Their normal, all-American life was crumbling. She could legally divorce him. She could expose him and the legacy of his family name. He would lose his prestige, everything he had built up around him to shield them from the past. He never wondered why he'd permanently cast his lot with his parents, taken the easy way out. By fulfilling their ambitions he'd bought himself freedom from them. There was no turning back now—no undoing what was set in motion years ago.

He sat there without moving until 6:00 in the morning as dawn crept into the room. She continued to sleep soundly. Exhausted, his terror and uncertainty intensified. He had to somehow extinguish her from his life. *She answered to those Crazy Mother Ancestors of hers. That's why she kept that altar. She pretended to have left that kind of thing behind her.* But now he knew differently.

The final decision hit him. *If she's gone, I'm free of them. When that Houdon stabbed me with her look so many years ago, it was real, and still is. If I get rid of Moremi, I can kill that Houdon who has haunted me from the time I was twelve.* It had all come to this and now he had to act. He had to protect what he could salvage. His family name depended on Ayo.

Now he saw it. She would die accidentally. *I will pick up Ayo and we both will grieve. Our loss will bring us closer together. After Moremi is buried, Ayo and I will take a trip to London and visit friends of my parents. I will not re-marry. Ayo will be my life. My son is pure and good.*

As his resolve solidified, her eyes popped open. She sprung up and stared blazing into him. In one split second she took in the scene.

He lunged and forced himself over her, trapping her under him. His arm held her neck and he leaned his whole weight into her ear. "You will not escape from me."

She squirmed under him. He was amazed at her strength, but he was bigger and heavier and had the advantage. He couldn't kill her. He didn't have it in him, but he decided for sure in that moment he would have her killed. No more hesitation. Hugo was nearby. But first, he wanted her to be as tortured as he was. He wanted to kill her equanimity, her entitlement—her family's arrogance.

He held her down until she slowly stopped struggling. *She sees the chair by the bed. She's figuring out I must have been here all night watching her. She knows she is the prey and I've got her. No more secret worlds to hide in now.*

He wanted her to struggle. He expected she would fight him, and this might incite him enough to do it himself. When Tavi bit him, he had been infuriated for a second, just enough to grab him by the tail and toss him hard. He just needed a push, and he could do it. Although he regretted what he had done and even what he knew he had to do, he soothed his regret by telling himself it was a weakness to care for something. In the end love betrays you. In the end love bites you. If his parents taught him anything, it was that.

But she stopped struggling.

"Let me up and I won't try to run. You don't know what you're doing."

"I'll let you up if you stay calm. But if you do try to run, I will kill you."

She nodded and he slowly got off her. He stood up and backed toward the doorway.

She sat up in the bed. "Tell me. I want to know."

He stared back at her. "Want to know what?" Her commanding tone was jarring. She was all hauteur now. He wanted to feel her fear, but her rage at him made her dangerous.

"Tell me what your father did to my family. What you knew all along.

Tell me. What difference does it make? In the end one or both of us is going to die. I will never tell Ayo. On that we can agree."

He knew what she wanted, but he wanted her to beg. His father used to do this to him. Make him beg. His father was sweet and generous one minute, cruel the next. When he was five, he'd found a litter of abandoned, feral kittens—four of them. He'd gotten a box and carried them home.

His father had smiled and kneeled down to see them, which thrilled him. His father even petted them and then, without a word, picked up the box and carried them outside.

Peter followed begging him to let him keep them.

He gave the box to the gardener and told him to get rid of them.

Later his mother found him crying. "Stop that," she commanded. "They would only be a nuisance!"

And that was the end of that.

"I want to know exactly what happened," Moremi demanded. "Every detail."

"Well," he said, savoring her need, "there isn't much to tell really. It was simple. Your father had a big mouth. And he'd become too full of himself. Grandiose really. Full of his own righteousness. Preaching his message of love and forgiveness, trying to be another Mandela." He ignored the hollow echo from his past—he sounded like his own father now.

She stared at him, unflinching.

He wanted to torture her, but it wasn't working. His father petted the kittens before he took them outside. Peter thought maybe he could keep them.

"My parents really respected your father. And your mother. In fact, they often spoke well of them. Even after they were gone." He surveyed his fingernails. "My mother said that your family were good people." He took pleasure in her puzzled expression.

"Oh yes, as I said, there was no animosity between my family and yours. But your father was beginning to attract a bit of a following. It probably would have blown over as these things do but he was becoming a loose cannon. He was beginning to show his disrespect for Abacha and, if you remember—I'm not sure you do because you probably weren't aware of much—Sani was not a forgiving man. There were the reprisals." His reference to Abacha by his first name would sting her, make her realize she knew nothing of what went on. Her parents were the outsiders.

She still didn't flinch. Her only vulnerability was her parents, especially when he spoke of her father. Her family lived in their own private little cocoon. She and her mother exuded superiority because they were unaware of how they appeared while his mother was all about appearances. That was how she carried herself. Her grandmother of course was crazy. Moses cared what people thought. He was a conscientious man. But he was ambitious and that made him dangerous. He wanted to see her flinch.

"There was some kind of investigation into your parents' activities. Their sympathies were not aligned with Sani's regime and your father was becoming a little too outspoken on his pulpit. Some of his flock were beginning to listen. Your father made the mistake of coming to my father, who as you know was in an important position in that regime. He was one of Sani's generals and could have helped. Your father wanted to get a writer out of prison. His case was getting too much press outside of Nigeria. My father considered helping, out of respect for your father, but . . ." He paused to see if this was hurting. He saw the tears in her eyes. "Your father wouldn't let it go and he began to be too demanding."

More tears.

He went on. "My father was a man of few words. He said four words about your father."

She wiped her eyes.

"Moses became a pest."

She looked at him still through her tears, but he didn't see sadness—he saw revenge.

He tried to grin. "So," he looked at his watch, "that was it. Your father needed to be eliminated and your mother was just collateral damage. She just got in the way. Sad, really. I liked your mother." He started to back out of the doorway. "And now I'm leaving. I would not recommend you try calling anyone. Don't kid yourself that I won't know."

As he headed down the hall, he was seized with a pain in his stomach coursing through him. He buckled over, staggered, leaning against the wall.

She shot out behind him into the hall. "And don't kid yourself, Peter. The Witches are after you."

He pulled himself up and fled down the stairs shouting, "That's such bullshit!"

CHAPTER NINETEEN

We feel most alive when we are closest to death

NENIA CAMPBELL, *TERRORSCAPE*

HE CALLED HUGO FROM HIS CAR.

"Yeah. What's up?"

Peter's voice was frail and flat. "She's at the house. You need to take care of it." He cleared his throat. "And the other one. Take care of her too."

"Right away?"

"Now. Yes, her too. She's gone home to Seattle for spring break. But first, my wife. She knows everything. I'm not sure what she'll do, but she won't call the police. She may want to pick up our son. I can't have that. Get to the house immediately."

"Why won't she call the police?"

"She's afraid of them," he snapped. "Never mind why."

"OK. OK."

"Remember, she's a Witch."

"A what?"

Peter ended the call and pulled out of his driveway. 7:00 A. M. He hoped to miss traffic heading north toward Sacramento for the weekend. He kept slamming himself into the steering wheel shouting: "I had to! I had to!"

He intended to trap her, but he was the one trapped now she knew. She had all the power. *Everything I've done to protect my family is wasted—unless I get rid of her.* He knew he would be at her mercy now that she knew the truth. She held the key to a Pandora's box of his family's layers of corruption —a box he had kept shut for years and now it was open. *That's it! It's over!*

The last time he saw his parents was in London. As they began to board the plane home at Heathrow, his father grabbed his arm pulling him aside and hissed, "She can never know."

As the traffic thinned out, he sped up. He spotted a cop in his rearview mirror accelerating and he quickly slowed down. The pain stabbed his stomach as the cop whizzed past, obviously after someone else. He needed to get somewhere out of the way. He needed to think. He continued north.

AFTER SHE HEARD PETER swerve out of the driveway she collapsed on the floor, tucking her feet under, rocking herself as if she were her own baby. She wanted to stay crumpled there but made herself move.

She struggled to her feet, went into the bathroom, took a hot shower, and quickly pulled on her jeans and a T-shirt. Hooking her purse over her shoulder, she ran down the stairs out of the house—going anywhere, just away from there.

In the driveway, as she was about to get into her car, she turned and went back inside and climbed the stairs. Oblivious to how irrational she was being, she moved with steady deliberation down to his office.

She hadn't been in there since she found the passport and the letter. Not knowing why, she rifled through his desk drawers, throwing things on the floor. The more she scavenged the more she worked herself into a frenzy, finally pulling his middle drawer out and threw it across the room slamming into the wall. Nothing could stop her as she looked around wildly as if something she'd missed would surface. She despised his neatness that covered up all his secrets and lies. She wrenched open the small drawer on the left and saw a note pad, opened with a phone number and a name circled and underlined: "Alice Gordon." Where did she hear that name? She stared down at the number. It must be important. Still in a crazed frenzy, for no reason except the urge to do something outrageous, she picked up his landline and dialed the number.

On the third ring a voice barked, "I'm almost there. Where are you? I thought you were on the road! I'll take care of her. It'll be an accident."

She carefully hung up, grabbed the note pad, and fled through the hall and down the stairs. Just as she got to the front door, she spotted through the window a black van swerve into the driveway. She jumped back and ran to the kitchen and through the cellar door, yanking it shut. She waited in the dark at the top of the stairs for her eyes to adjust. After fifteen seconds she crept down the wooden, creaking stairs.

At the bottom she stopped, looked up and realized she should have locked the door to the kitchen. But the bolt did not fit easily and was rarely if ever used. Her panic surged as she looked around, and saw a hammer hanging on the wall with other tools. She grabbed it and bounded back up, pressing her ear to the door. Silence. With one slam she knocked the bolt into place, dropped the hammer on the step and felt a moment of relief.

She made her way in the dark, back down the stairs and stopped to listen again. Nothing. She crossed over to the locked door from the cellar into the back yard.

Before unlocking it, she looked out the high window next to the door. It was small and dusty, but high enough to see someone's legs coming along the side of the house.

She heard tromping through the weeds, then saw him as he passed by. She dropped down, crouching as close to the door as she could, praying that when he walked down the outside steps and peered through the small dirty window in the door his eye could not find her.

How does he know about this cellar door? Has he been here before?

She felt him peering in. His body was leaning into the locked door. She heard him breathing like an animal sniffing out its prey. He wiped the grime from the window and shined a flashlight inside. The gleam shot over her and up the steps where she had stood a moment earlier.

He rattled the doorknob and left. She heard him climb the outdoor steps two at a time and move back through the weeds. He might try the other high window on the side. She was a rat in a cage, certain to be seen from that window if she stayed where she was. She ran back up the stairs to the top where the beam from the high window would not reach her.

From the side window, his beam searched like a darting eye back and forth but couldn't get to where she was crouched at the top of the stairs.

I'm trapped. Why doesn't he smash the window? In her panic her wits hadn't completely left her as she realized not even a child could crawl through that narrow window, especially through splintered glass. *He doesn't really expect me to be in here. He just wants to make sure. It's the only other escape where I could get out without his seeing me. He'll come in through the front door now.* She stood frozen with her back pressed against the door, blood pounding in her neck.

She heard him leaving the window and moving around the house, presumably to the front door. She gave it ten seconds, then scrambled down the steps to the outside door, her escape route.

She pressed up against it to listen just to make sure he hadn't tricked her. Carefully, she unlocked it, turning the knob and scraped the old door ajar an inch and waited. She took a deep breath, pushed the door open and bolted out and up the outside stairs to the back yard sprinting through the weeds.

She unlatched the old gate into the neighbors' back yard and jammed it open. She wanted to pound on their back door, but instinct held her back. Too much to explain. She gave herself five minutes before he would be out stalking her.

Did he intend to kill her? *Yes. He worked for Peter. Just like in Africa, there were always thugs for hire to do your dirty work.* When he discovered the cellar door was bolted from inside he would know she'd been in there all along.

She plunged through the neighbors' back yards, zigzagging as much as possible, hoping to keep off main streets, out of sight of his van.

She found herself on the sidewalk and ducked into some trees to catch her breath. From the shadows she looked for a black van, but the street was empty. The world seemed silent. She guessed it was about 7:30 A. M., still a little early for people to be out on a Saturday morning.

She leaned forward to see if the coast was clear.

Without a sound and with an iron grip his arm pulled her back from behind by the neck. He wrenched her close and sniffed around her ear, nuzzling her. She felt his hot breath. No voice.

Had he been tracking her all along? Then he spoke softly, feigning romance. "I saw you leave. I've been right behind you."

She wriggled wildly, but his grip was amazingly strong as he dragged her back into the shadows away from the street.

She gurgled, "What do you want?"

"It's not personal," he murmured. "Not at all. I think I might like you better than him. But you know how it is. It's just business. You've become a problem."

She squirmed and sensed just the slightest loosening of his grip. *He'll let this draw out. He wants to engage. For him it's sport. That's why he took his time. I was never going to get away.*

She heard her mother's voice. *If anyone grabs you from behind—bite them! Bite them hard striking like a Cobra. Kick him in the groin. Then run as fast as you can.*

She grabbed his forearm with both hands, pulled it to her mouth and clamped her teeth into his flesh biting down hard.

He yelped and released his grip slightly. She chewed into him again even harder, going for the bone.

He yanked his arm, screamed, and jerked his arm out of her mouth.

She spun around and kicked him low and hard.

He buckled over, gasping, "You fucking bitch!"

She sprinted to the street and ran down the middle. *Stay in the streets. He won't dare chase me out in the open.*

She had no sense of time as she ran. Finally, she reached a commercial street. She walked along the sidewalk and entered a coffee shop full of early morning breakfast hounds.

She approached a friendly looking couple and asked breathlessly, "Do the buses run along here?"

They smiled and nodded, and the young man pointed at one coming down the street and pointed to half a block down. "It'll stop there."

She yelled "thanks!" over her shoulder as she ran.

The bus hissed to the curb, and she jumped on. She had no idea what the fare was, which irritated the driver, who asked, "Where ya goin'?"

"Dartmouth," the street where Rebecca's office was.

"Dollar and a quarter."

Braced against the front rail she fished it out from her purse, grateful she'd slung it over her shoulder before that call from Peter's office. As the docile passengers watched, she awkwardly struggled to both count the right change and keep her balance as the bus surged forward.

After making her way to the back of the bus, she collapsed into the lurching seat, shaking as she gripped her hands together to calm herself.

After fifteen minutes she got off and found the Starbucks across from Rebecca's office.

I bit him hard. Maybe I infected him. He'll have to bandage his arm. She had bought some time. That was all.

HE WAS MORE FURIOUS THAN HE HAD EVER BEEN in his life. Nothing like this had ever happened to him. *How did she surprise him like that? I had her. Why didn't I just drag her back to the house?* He was panting, head twisting, angry at himself. He had enjoyed tracking her, watching her. She was tall and lithe and moved quickly. He admired her agility. *I wanted to draw it out! And broke my own first rule of engagement! Never let it get personal! Hesitation breeds mistakes!*

I'll have to get stitches and a fucking tetanus shot. He couldn't remember the last time he had to get one. That meant he really did need one.

He quickly made his way back to the house, climbed in his van and pulled a metal kit out of a built-in trunk in the back. He opened it with his good arm and pulled out a plastic packet with emergency syringes already made up. He shot it into his right arm and laid his head back for a minute to let the medication do its work. He cleaned and bandaged his arm and quickly called his friend who worked in an emergency room who told him to meet him at his house.

Next, he called Peter who was still on the road.

"What?"

"She got away!"

"For God's sake! How?"

"Never mind. She won't get far. She's on foot. She won't come back for her car. I made sure of that. I'll find her. Don't worry."

"Call me immediately."

"She bit me."

"She what?"

"Goddamn bitch bit me. She doesn't have HIV, does she?"

Peter shut off his phone.

TWO HOURS LATER, Peter pulled into an out-of-the-way, nondescript motel. The desk clerk emerged from the back room where the TV blared, and a space heater magnified the odor of cat urine. He would be there just one night. Or perhaps an hour. He just needed to lie down somewhere and rest.

The no-smoking room reeked of stale smoke. He was too exhausted to complain. He wished he had his sleeping pills. He wanted to knock himself out. Then he wouldn't have to think, even if he could. He couldn't think right now.

His brain trembled with the reality of his situation and knowing there was no turning back, no un-doing what had just happened, what he had put into motion. Could he call off Hugo? Had he found her yet? He could call and tell him to forget it. But then what? He would think about what to do next after he rested, but his mind kept going.

He lay on the bed and stared at the ceiling. *What else could I do? How did she find out? Maybe she didn't but she guessed and I just told her? Could we have gone on as we were? Was it possible she really didn't know?* He quickly flushed that possibility out of his head. *No. Everything changed right after I got back from Washington. She'd been in the house by herself that weekend. She called her friend in Nigeria. Why? Why then? She'd never tried to call anyone before.*

He forced himself to think about something else. But he kept going in circles returning to the possibility that she really knew nothing. That thought stabbed at him.

And then there was that little pest Alice Gordon. *I could have made an excuse to change the assignment. Still, how could I stop her? She would cling to that stupid paper she wrote as a foundation for some kind of research. She was fixated on Nigeria now.*

He looked at his phone. *Why doesn't he call?*

A plan formed. He would go to Ayo and tell the other parents that he managed to get away for a little vacation. Ayo would be delighted, and they would go skiing together. Hugo would find Moremi and set the scene for an accident. Maria their cleaning lady would discover her Monday morning collapsed at the bottom of the stairs with her neck broken. He would be with Ayo when the news of the terrible tragedy came.

In his traumatized fatigue this scenario seemed plausible and soothing. He slid into a fitful sleep.

In the dream he was young again, about twelve. He and his mother were driving somewhere. The landscape was red earth and bright green trees. While in the back seat trying to tell her something about soccer, he wanted to tell her that he had made a goal for his team and his coach was pleased. He repeated himself over and over, but she kept laughing about something as if she were carrying on a conversation with someone else—only they were alone in the car. He knew she wasn't talking to him. He wondered if she was talking to herself.

The dream switched. He was with a group of boys. They were strangers but he thought he knew them from school. They were all crowded around something laughing and jeering and he pushed his way in to see what they were looking at. When he got to the edge of the circle, he saw it was a pile of burnt mongooses. Their bodies were all charred in a pile. Their eyes were hollow sockets.

He awakened covered in sweat, heart pounding.

HUGO STEERED WITH HIS GOOD LEFT ARM to meet his friend Henry at his house.

"What the hell?"

"Don't ask."

"It looks like someone bit you."

He watched sullenly as Henry unwound his sloppy bandage. "Just fix it. I've got to get going."

It took an hour to stitch his wound and give him a tetanus shot. Henry warned him that he needed to rest.

"Can't," Hugo shot back. "Gotta go."

He maneuvered the van back out onto the streets and headed to the house. Her car was there. Good. She's still out there on foot. He went around, down to the basement door and let himself in. He climbed the stairs and with her hammer unbolted the door. He went through the kitchen, out the living room, and back out the front door. Would she come back? He thought not. *Where will she go?* His mind wasn't tracking. Usually he was able to stay calm when the hunt was on. But she'd completely thrown him off his game.

Begrudgingly—he admired her.

CHAPTER TWENTY

When the mouse laughs at the cat, there's a hole nearby.

NIGERIAN PROVERB

REBECCA CALLED HER OFFICE as she always did on Saturday morning to make sure her calendar was clear for the weekend and heard the message from Moremi: "I've got to see you. It's an emergency. Please call my cell phone." She repeated her number twice.

It was now 8:30 A.M. Rebecca had planned her Saturday. She would clean up her back yard and plant some ferns that sat in a row on her back porch like little soldiers reporting for duty. As she listened to Moremi's message, she stared at a bedraggled, thirsty hydrangea.

She called Moremi's cell.

She answered on the first ring. "What's the matter? What's happened?"

"I can't explain over the phone. Can I meet you at your office?"

"Give me half an hour."

She dashed into the bathroom, turned on the shower, wheeled around to inspect herself in the mirror to check for dark circles under her eyes. She didn't want to look like her hydrangea when she needed to be alert. Adrenaline fed her like high octane as she showered and pulled herself together.

She drove to her office knowing Moremi would not have called unless it was serious. As she bounded up the front steps and punched in her door code, she checked her watch. *On time.*

Moremi was waiting in the hallway. Rebecca took in her frozen demeanor at a glance and knew something terrible had just happened.

A HALF-HOUR EARLIER Hugo listened to Moremi's message. He called Peter. "What do you know about somebody named Dr. Rebecca

Calhoun?"

"Nothing. I'm sure she has a few friends from work or school I don't know about."

"Well, I don't think she's a friend. She made some kind of emergency appointment with her and that's where she is now—wherever Calhoun's office is which I haven't been able to locate yet, but I will."

But it worried Peter. He thought he knew everything important there was to know about her. *But some doctor? An emergency appointment? She knew her? Paid her?*

"Find out who this Rebecca Calhoun is and call me when you find her."

He hung up and lay back down and stared at the looming popcorn ceiling. *What have you been up to?* He knew she was secretive. He thought the altar was the extent of it, an indulgent nostalgia which he'd rationalized as harmless—her dabbling in her mother's occult practices. Spilling his blood in her sand had released him from any lingering fear that her rituals touched on reality. In the past he had cut himself when he needed that soothing pain to erase those little demon fears that cropped up every now and then. Blood was the elixir that eliminated creeping, shadowy thoughts that disturbed his otherwise firm conviction that she and her mother-line were harmless.

MOREMI POURED OUT TO REBECCA the events of last night.

Rebecca focused intently, assessing Moremi's level of trauma. She was shaken, but lucid. *Given what just happened how could she think straight? I'm not sure I could. And can I now?* She took a deep breath and thought of the Queens, always so calm and unruffled—unless there was real danger. And then they could be fierce.

She leaned forward and spoke the obvious. "Moremi, this is very dangerous. I'm trying to absorb what you've just told me. I can only conclude that this man is still looking for you. Now. As we speak."

"I know."

"I think we need to call the police."

"No."

"Tell me why not. Why shouldn't I dial 911 right now? Someone just tried to kill you and I think you know this is connected to your husband. That's the only thing that makes sense."

"Please hear me out before you call anyone."

"OK." Rebecca sat back. "Please help me understand."

"I will try. First, I trust that you will understand and that's why I called you."

Rebecca nodded.

"Here is what I believe is happening. Peter has been protecting his family's secret not so much because of me, but because of Ayo. Peter wants him to grow up idolizing his grandparents—my parents and his. He will do anything to preserve his family's made-up legacy and hide their dark side. As far as the truth is concerned, I am really the only threat because now I know everything. He had to choose between Ayo and me. Of course, he chose his son. If I am dead his problem is solved. I assume that somehow that man came to the house to kill me and make it look like an accident. Exactly how, I'm not sure." She stopped and swallowed hard.

Rebecca got her a glass of water. "Go on."

"If I call the police," she sighed, sounding tired but resolved, "and tell them that my husband hired someone to kill me because I found out his family was directly involved in my parents' political murder over ten years ago in Nigeria and I went ahead and married him and have a son by him and we have lived in a peaceful upper middle class neighborhood in a prestigious university town," she drank more water, "let me ask you, how much of that would the police believe, at least in the beginning?"

Rebecca looked down, considering the question. "Maybe none of it. At least not at first. Not without evidence."

"Exactly. They would ask me for evidence, and I have none. My neck is still sore and will probably bruise where he grabbed me. I didn't get a good look at him. After I kicked him in the groin he doubled over and fell to his knees. I ran. I didn't take the time to look at him. He could be anyone. He smelled of some kind of aftershave. That was it." She massaged her neck. "I could have done this to myself. Keep in mind what just happened is entirely out of the ordinary. I would attract attention on myself more than anything else. Even I think what happened sounds crazy."

"All right," Rebecca agreed, "I get what you are saying, but I'm concerned because I do believe you. I'm concerned that this man whoever he might be is still out there."

She looked through the window at trees and sky nodding at the great unknown outside her window. Her glance shifted to the mask with the huge crocodile jaws poised to clamp down on the snake. Her dream the night before she first met Moremi flashed before her. She saw the blood spilling out of her mother's head and knew her destiny was linked to this woman's. *Moremi and I are now on that bridge that Gertrude described—meeting in the middle.*

Moremi waited. She could not see what Rebecca saw, but she knew it was important to stay quiet.

Rebecca heard Gertrude's voice. *Listen to your intuition. All events become memories that evolve into our stories creating our allegories and dreams that over time encounter crossroads in our lives based on the past. The ever-changing story moves relentlessly forward gathering into itself, becoming sometimes metaphorical and sometimes literal, like dogma. Metaphor lives while dogma dies.* Rebecca frowned. Sometimes Gertrude could only be confounding. But she trusted memory.

Both women looked at each other.

Moremi nodded encouragement to keep her looking inward.

Rebecca closed her eyes and what came next hit her like a hammer. It was her own voice: *Some of us live in the story as if it were ongoing and some fixate on the here and now as if that is all there is. Moremi stays in the story. She doesn't fixate. Where am I? I want to call the police. But she's right. If they come here everything will change. We put ourselves into their hands and where will we be? She saw that path play out: Police headquarters. Writing a statement. Looking into skeptical male eyes. Possibly being seen as delusional. Released back into danger.* She looked at Moremi and held out her hand.

Moremi took her hand in both of hers.

"Please do one thing for me," Rebecca urged. "Call Ayo."

Moremi hesitated.

"Call him to make sure nothing out of the ordinary has happened."

Moremi nodded and took out her cell phone.

"No. Use my phone. Don't ask me why. I'm not sure, but I believe that man after you is a professional and maybe I've read too many detective novels but he's tracking you somehow."

Moremi got up and went to Rebecca's desk for the landline and called the cell phone of Francine, one of the parents with Ayo's group.

Rebecca stood by her.

When Francine answered Moremi said she was just checking in to see how Ayo was doing. Francine was upbeat and cheerful. "Ayo's fine, having a great time. They're all out on the slopes and won't be back until lunch. Hey, I'll tell him you called. Any message?"

"Not really." She tried to sound casual and upbeat. "Just tell him I said 'hi' and 'love you.'"

"Absolutely! I'll make sure he knows you called." She added, reassuring Moremi, "He's such a good skier. We love having Ayo. He's so lively and friendly. Talk with you soon."

"Oh, just one quick question. Has Ayo's dad called him? Do you know?"

"Don't think so. Not yet. Don't worry. He's fine. I think we adults are having as good a time as they are. Bye."

Moremi hung up. "She just thinks I'm a nervous mother. She has no idea why I really called."

Rebecca looked out the window next to her desk into the parking lot at the back of her office building. She saw something move on the other side of the fence that was covered in ivy. She leaned into the window squinting. She thought she saw what looked like a man peering through the ivy. Her car was parked there—the only one there on a Saturday morning. Blood drained from her face and a cold, clammy feeling took over. "There's a man out there. Stand over here so he can't see you."

Moremi positioned herself so she could look out from an angle without being seen. She looked at Rebecca nodding with horror. "I think it's him."

"We leave now," Rebecca grabbed her purse and headed for the door. In the hallway she gestured away from the elevator and stairwell. "This way," she whispered. They dashed down the hall and pulled the heavy door open that lead down a back staircase and exited outside onto the commercial street. Rebecca pointed down the street. They walked briskly side by side, neither looking back. They ducked into a CVS pharmacy that Rebecca knew had an exit into a back-parking lot.

She told Moremi to wait inside the door and pretend to shop and whispered, "I'll ask the cashier if I can use her phone. I'll tell her I left mine at home and need to call my husband who might be angry if I don't."

Moremi rolled her eyes.

"Just a precaution," Rebecca added in her conspiratorial whisper. "You never know."

Moremi started to respond but thought better of it. She could see that Rebecca was possibly playing a role, but then again . . . *maybe not.*

She wanted to say, "You Americans are sooo dramatic sometimes over the slightest things." *But maybe not.*

Rebecca left Moremi to wander through the back aisles. When she asked to borrow her phone the cashier responded, "Hon, believe me I've been there. Husbands are all alike."

She returned to Moremi. "I called my partner. His name is Richard. He'll pick us up in a few minutes."

They meandered together and Moremi bought a small bottle of Advil.

Rebecca gestured for her to follow, and they both stepped out into the empty parking lot.

Rebecca closed her eyes. *Please, please Richard, don't dawdle.*

Moremi felt in her pocket and cupped the shell.

They stood together in silence, each in her own thoughts. Ten minutes passed. Rebecca looked at her watch. Moremi leaned into Rebecca as if to reassure her that ten minutes was not that long.

Another five minutes passed and just as Rebecca was about to call on her own cell he screeched into the lot in his blue Porsche. As usual, Mr. Toad's wild ride.

He lowered the window. "At your service, ladies. Hop in. Let's go have some fun."

Moremi liked him instantly. *He's light-hearted, like my father.* She got into the back as Rebecca climbed into the passenger seat.

"You better lie down," Rebecca, still in conspiratorial mode, commanded. "Just to be safe."

Richard, who had no real idea what was going on, except that he was driving the getaway car, asked, "Where to?"

"I think your place," Rebecca decided.

Richard sobered quickly taking in Rebecca's pale face. "Don't ask me why, but we're going to Daniel's house." He leaned his head back to inform Moremi. "He's an old friend and colleague who's out of town and I'm feeding his cat, so I have the key." He looked at Rebecca. "I'm guessing we need to hide somewhere safe. We can relax there. You know Daniel. He'd want us to go there." Again, including Moremi, "Daniel's one of those people who manages to involve himself in others' lives in very peculiar ways. If we didn't use his house, he'd wonder why not." With that explanation Richard peeled out into side streets.

Nobody spoke until they were inside Daniel's living room filled with books, mostly about history, especially the American Civil War, with over-stuffed furniture like old friends accustomed to accommodating visitors.

Richard added, "He's a professor of history. Semi-retired. He lost his wife a few years ago and has been at loose ends, but now he's in London teaching something. He says the British are more interested in our Civil War than we are."

Moremi understood.

Numi, Daniel's huge Maine Coon, sashayed in and preened around the furniture with his fluffy tail gliding behind like a lazy feather duster. After making his entrance, he jumped on the couch slithering onto Rebecca's lap, then propped himself on her, nuzzling her neck while he kneaded his front paws on her chest. She was trapped.

"Numi," she cautioned, pulling him off to reprimand him face to face, "I love you, too, but you do need to learn a little protocol." His ears went back but he settled for her lap without much intensity, at least for the time being, and promptly started washing himself. He licked his front paw thoroughly before he rubbed his spittle into his head producing a few wet spikes of hair.

Richard came in with a tray that included some cookies he'd found in Daniel's pantry. He set it down on the coffee table, pushing aside books and papers, including the environmental book about a pelican Daniel's wife Anna had written for children before she died. He looked back and forth from Moremi to Rebecca. "I think you better tell me what this is about. If I'm the getaway driver I better know what I'm getting away from." He grinned.

They looked worn out.

Rebecca turned to Moremi. "We are already breaking your confidentiality, but I think the crisis of endangerment has forced us out of the security of my office. But I need your permission to bring in others who can help. I also think you should summarize what has happened in the last twenty-four hours."

Moremi nodded. "I consent." She turned to Richard and in the next hour told her story with as much detail as she could.

Richard listened intently, occasionally interrupting for clarity. After Moremi had finished, he spoke.

"You have to call the police."

Moremi explained, "I do not know why this man came to my house, but I know he was supposed to kill me. He could only have done so under somebody's orders. He is a total stranger to me. There is so much I must absorb about my husband now, and what he is capable of, that I must assume he hired this man. Please understand that in Africa you can hire people to do this kind of thing. I assume you also can do this here. But in America I also assume such a practice would be more hidden." She looked at them.

They looked at each other, then at her. They agreed.

Richard was more like Moremi's father than she first thought. Fair-minded. Tough but open. She trusted him.

"I also believe," she went on, "that it is best not to alert Peter about any of this. I don't know where he is, nor what he knows at this point, but I must stay hidden for the time being. He can't know where I am. I'll keep in touch with my son and will know if Peter is in touch with him . . . but somehow, I don't think Peter will contact Ayo until I am out of his way. Of that I feel certain. Peter is trapped now. I know too much. He will not risk letting me go, knowing what I know." She concluded, "I am a great danger to him."

Richard sank back into Daniel's large brown chair whistling softly, deep in thought. "You can't do this alone. You may be right about the police, but you're not right about telling no one else."

They waited.

"I have a very good friend, an ex-Marine turned private detective. His name is Bernard, only everyone calls him 'Bear.' I'm going to call him and ask him to meet us here. He'll come because we go way back to our fraternity days. He lives up north in Washington State. In the woods."

Moremi thought about this. "What can this friend of yours do?"

"Bear has an uncanny ability to find bad guys. He's a trained intuitive. That comes from many years in Special Ops. Some people think the military is all frontal lobe." He pointed to his forehead. "Not true. These guys live in another dimension. Anyway, I'd like to call him and get him down here as soon as possible."

He looked at Rebecca. "Meanwhile, I'd like to go over to your house and pick up The Queens. That guy might be after you and I don't want him breaking into your house. He sounds dangerous enough to kill animals. So, I'll go now."

Rebecca nodded and Richard left.

He would call Bear as soon as he picked up the dogs.

HUGO CALLED PETER.

Peter was lying on his hotel bed trying to rest. He reached for his cell and looked at the number. "What?"

"They're not in the building. I got in when some old lady came out. Her office is there. Rebecca Calhoun. Your wife is seeing a shrink."

Peter groaned. *Seeing a shrink? How had I missed that?* "Where does she live?"

"I'm trying to find out. These people don't like anyone knowing that. Don't worry. I'll find her. I had to get my arm fixed. Remember your mad dog wife bit me?"

"I need to know where she is."

"Trust me. They won't get far. I assume she's with the shrink. They must have seen me. Don't know how, but they did. The shrink's car is still in her parking lot at her office."

Peter clicked off. He'd never liked Hugo. He didn't like uncouth people. But his father had said, "Never get your own hands dirty. Always hire it out. That way you maintain a proper distance from these unpleasant necessities." Peter remembered thinking at the time: *Like eliminating people who know too much?*

CHAPTER TWENTY-ONE

How do you calculate upon the unforeseen?

REBECCA SOLNIT, *A FIELD GUIDE TO GETTING LOST*

WHILE MOREMI RESTED in Daniel's spare bedroom, she studied a framed poster of Lincoln, a print of a daguerreotype taken at the end of his presidency and life, framing a quote: "Those who deny freedom to others deserve it not for themselves; and, under a just God, cannot long retain it."

Lincoln's exhausted demeanor reminded her of the face she'd seen on an African sculpture—a 19th century warrior chief from the Yoruba tribe on his horse, bald except for a long pigtail down his back. His face was a composition of triangular forms with heavy-lidded eyes and a pointed beard. She was struck by the resemblance between the two with their wise and beleaguered expressions. She wondered what a conversation would have been like between Lincoln and one of those warrior chiefs who promoted the slave trade off their shores, decimating their own people. She felt close to Daniel, safe in his house. As she closed her eyes she whispered to Lincoln: "We're all in this together."

In the living room Rebecca poured another cup of coffee and sat down on the couch to call Gertrude. She left a brief message. "Call me immediately! It's an emergency."

She leaned back into the pillows and stroked Numi who had seized the moment, working his claws in and out using her knees for a scratch pad, swishing his bushy tail across her face as if he were dusting her off. Within a minute she heard the marimba tune of her phone and tossed Numi unceremoniously onto the floor. As he padded away, he turned and telegraphed his contemptuous cat gaze, then hopped up on the chair across from her and settled in to wait for his next chance.

"Wow, that was fast."

"Yes, well you're lucky you caught me. I was on my way out. So, tell me, what could be so urgent on a lovely Saturday like this?"

Rebecca summarized the situation as best she could.

"Well . . . my goodness," Gertrude murmured.

Rebecca could almost hear Gertrude's brainwaves whirling.

"I've never been a fan of that maxim, expect the unexpected. As Bob Dylan so judiciously remarked—'Doesn't expecting the unexpected make the unexpected expected?' However, I must say," Gertrude added, "here we are in the midst of quite an unexpected turn of events."

This was so like her. She would think about what to do as she quoted something, as if solutions inevitably followed in the wake of the adages she seemed to store in an unending plethora that fit any occasion.

"Where are you staying?" she asked Rebecca. "I need to meet with both you and Moremi. I will come to you now."

Rebecca was surprised and relieved that Gertrude sized up the situation so rapidly and thought nothing about breaking the rules that bounded their professional confidentiality. She understood the need for action, not talk. "The rules are there to guide you, my dear," Gertrude had told her, "but not to dictate. Just as instincts and rules must be partners to each other." Rebecca imagined the crocodiles and snake, each depending on the other to behave—a quiet state of equipoise that could be disrupted in an instant, requiring action.

"Thank you, Gertrude. I better explain who you are to Moremi. I'm sure she will approve under the circumstances. She reached out for help and welcomes the support we bring. She is adamant about not involving the law and I have come to agree with her."

"And her code of honor," Gertrude added, "might make our brand of police involvement problematic. Her case requires sensitivity to a culture vastly different and older than our own. In her culture, my age will be accepted as wisdom and my wrinkles and crooked brown teeth are a badge of honor."

"Your teeth aren't crooked or brown."

"Yes, they are, my dear."

AS HE SAT IN HIS VAN, Rebecca Calhoun's address came through on his phone. He headed for her home about ten minutes away. Despite the Vicodin Henry had given him his arm throbbed with voltage.

"The pain will keep you awake," Henry assured.

Hugo thought of Moremi and shuddered. So beautiful and so lethal. He knew he'd hesitated, which perplexed him. When he grabbed her, she didn't struggle, but froze, remaining still like a cobra. But there had been something more in that moment as he sensed her power. It was both physical and something else. *Yes, she's a witch. A witch who doesn't know her own power.*

He drove quickly, pulling up to the curb a couple blocks from Rebecca's house. A light blue Porsche Cabriolet passed in the opposite direction. He would have taken no notice except for the two red-headed fat women he spotted from his rearview mirror as they headed down the street sitting side by side in the back seat. They had identical frizzed-out hairdos. A pair of ugly twins, he thought, being driven around by some old guy who was waving his arm around as if he were singing to them. He continued to watch as the Porsche disappeared around the corner when his perspective changed, and he realized those red heads had round furry ears. He chuckled. "And what big ears you have, Grandma!"

He moved his van closer to the curb, almost in front of her house under the cover of a draping elm. He spent a few minutes unwrapping his sandwich, still wincing at the pain in his arm as he fed himself with his left hand while looking through binoculars in his right.

After detecting no movement in or around the house he decided to risk getting out and looking around. He put on his blue windbreaker, climbed the front steps and approached the front door. He peered through the small window into the foyer. He jerked back as he spotted the Dan mask, then pushed his face close into the window, squinting, trying to see into the dark interior.

He saw clutter and decided she was the kind of academic too distracted to clean up, and too cheap to have a cleaning service. Hugo was fastidious, a reaction to growing up poor where the idea of a neat room did not exist. He did not understand wealthy people who neglected to clean. And yet, he envied people who could tolerate a little clutter. That envy could at times precipitate a destructive urge in him.

He walked around to the back and let himself through the garden gate and climbed the steps to the back deck. He surveyed the yard and was gratified to observe that it was secluded woodland, preventing any prying neighbors. He relaxed and allowed himself to take in more details.

He spotted two silver bowls on the deck and a large blue pottery bowl of water. He stared at this for a few seconds before he put two and two together. Two dog bowls. He looked off into the distance. Two red-haired dogs. He realized he had not noticed the license number. But the car stood out. He smiled at himself, sure that it would be easy to find.

And yet, he felt tricked. It bothered him. He could feel the beginning urge, fueled by the ache in his arm, to hurt someone.

He picked the lock and stepped into Rebecca's kitchen. He opened the refrigerator and surveyed its contents. Tupperware containers with leftovers, lots of mustards, a small, roast chicken partly nibbled, several beers, a bottle of Chablis. He opened a container filled with carrot and celery sticks. As he chomped on a carrot, he wandered through the dining room into the living room and stopped in front of the Dan mask that he'd seen from the front door window. He stared into its hollowed-eye sockets, challenging its mocking glare. He felt the impulse to snatch it off the wall, but he stopped himself, not wanting to leave any obvious evidence that he'd been there.

He went upstairs to the bedroom and scowled when he spotted the bed all rumpled. She'd gotten up in a hurry, he decided, as he also spotted her pajama and T-shirt thrown on the bathroom floor along with a towel. He picked up the pants, held them close to his face and then threw them back down.

He went back to his van and called Peter, who answered with a sleepy grunt.

Hugo sniffed. "I've been in the house. She's some sort of shrink, I told you. Books all over. She collects stuff, like African stuff. Not my taste but what do I know?"

He regretted admitting that last bit about his taste because he feared the distinction between good and bad taste was beyond him. His arm throbbed. It was an old habit—admitting what he didn't know.

"I think she's got a boyfriend. No husband."

"How do you know?"

"Just a hunch. I found a note written to a guy named Richard, and then the guy's response. Pretty sure he's not living there. No clothes in the closet, just an old jacket. Oh yeah, and she's got a couple of Chows. I hate Chows. If they don't like you, they can be vicious. They're not here because the guy came and got them just before I arrived."

"Did you get his license plate?"

"Ah . . . well, no." He changed the subject. "What do you want me to do?"

"Find them. Find her."

"Don't worry. It's not even noon. They're nearby. I'll find her."

He put the phone back in his pocket and took a deep breath. No matter how certain he sounded, he didn't feel it. She might have called the police. Whenever uncertainty crept in, he countered his vulnerability with rage. He slammed his fist on the steering wheel, then started his motor and moved down the street—a black cat on the prowl.

AT NOON GERTRUDE PULLED UP to Daniel's house in her pale green Prius. Rebecca met her at the door. Richard came in and they shook hands. They had met once before.

They decided to let Moremi sleep a little longer.

Gertrude accepted a cup of tea and sat down on the couch—Numi's territory. He had been distracted by the arrival of Juno and Dido and now was sitting on the built-in bench in the dining room, staring through the window onto the back deck at Juno who was sliming the glass. Numi whapped the window with his paw causing her to jump back in a huff. Dido came over to nuzzle Gertrude and then wandered outside to join her sister. They both ran down the back yard to bark at squirrels clamoring up the redwood tree, flicking their tails as they created their own little bedlam taunting the dogs. Numi got tired of watching this dog show and wandered back to his headquarters in the living room, instantly falling in love with Gertrude's plaid Burberry slacks with the soft gabardine texture, making this new lap a fine place to land.

Just as Rebecca began to fill in more detail Moremi appeared in the doorway.

Gertrude stood up, dumping Numi once again, and greeted her. "Come, my dear, sit next to me. Tell me what has been happening. I know a little, but I wish to hear it from you."

Richard offered Moremi a cup of tea, which she gratefully accepted.

She spoke slowly and carefully, filling in with as much detail as she could. Gertrude listened without interrupting. Moremi ended by thanking everyone for being so supportive. "It makes me think of my parents and how they would have been for anyone in need."

They were quiet, seeing that she needed a moment to gather herself.

Even Numi looked up and the Queens remained as if alert, but at rest.

Then Gertrude spoke. "We are now all challenged with a highly volatile situation that poses many unknowns." She addressed Moremi. "It would seem that the man you married held a terrible secret that has brought him to a crossroads in his life. We must assume this assassin who arrived on your doorstep early this morning was hired by your husband, Peter." She looked around. "What else can we assume?" Back to Moremi. "And you, my dear, now you have discovered that secret, have become a liability to him. Since your husband believes he cannot allow your son, Ayo, to know about the crime his father and mother committed that caused the death of your parents." She looked at all of them. "We must form a plan. Now."

Richard leaned forward. "We all agree. I want to call my friend Bernard Whitmore—well, 'Bear.'"

Gertrude agreed so long as Bear could be there as soon as possible. "Because" she looked around, "we must assume that man is out there now looking for Rebecca as well, now."

All agreed that Moremi, Rebecca, Richard and the Queens would remain at Daniel's house with Numi until a plan could be formulated.

Gertrude left to take care of personal business and to return later.

Richard sat on the couch in the living room planning to call Daniel who was giving a series of lectures at Oxford on his favorite subject—the American Civil War.

THE BLACK VAN CRUISED METHODICALLY up one neighborhood street and down another. His head moved from side to side, eyes darting back and forth, hoping to spot a blue Porsche and two red Chows. He knew that wherever they were, so were Moremi and Rebecca. It was a hit-or-miss approach, but he was dealing with amateurs. And one was a shrink. He had experience with shrinks.

They were stupid about reality. He had spent his adolescent years in the juvenile justice system where they make you sit in groups led by social workers. It was mostly a joke because the social workers could never understand life growing up on the back streets of any big city.

Then he met Sharon. He saw her once a week. She had blond hair and blue eyes. She gave him Coca Cola and sometimes donuts. They were friends. She saw how smart he was.

One day he showed up at her office and a much older, bleary-eyed man was there. They guy actually yawned during their little talk. When he asked where Sharon was. He said, "Oh yeah, Sharon. Well, didn't she tell you? She moved to—I think—California."

Hugo left the office and never went back. That was twenty-five years ago. Sometimes he thought about what he would do if he ever saw her again. He was sure he would recognize her.

Lost in memory, he didn't see the stop sign. The crunch of metal on metal jarred him and to his horror he realized he'd rammed into the left rear fender of an old Volvo sedan. He slammed on his brakes and pulled over.

The Volvo pulled in front of him, and a frenzied woman jumped out, screaming and waving her arms ordering him to get out of his van. She moved in, glaring at him an inch from his closed window.

He guessed she was in her mid-forties, boy thin, wearing running pants and a t-shirt that said 'Run for Your Life' across her flat chest.

She would want him to wait for the cops. He would have to show his license and registration—something he never did. But at the moment he'd been driving without insurance. He had cash, but already he knew she would milk this for all it was worth. Maybe he could talk her down. He stared at her as he slowly lowered his window.

She screamed, "Get out of your vehicle!"

He smiled down at her and said, "I'm really sorry. I know this is going to sound like a lame excuse, but you know I'm late for my son's Little League game and my ex is going to give me hell for it. She's already at the game and we're in this custody thing and there is nothing in the world more important to me than my son."

She scowled, shaking her head. "Get out of the car and show me your insurance. We'll have to wait for the police to come and I need to photograph the damage you've done to my car." She turned and pointed as if she were already in court presenting the evidence.

He tried one last-ditch play for sympathy. "I suppose it doesn't matter that my ex-wife was the one who cheated on me!"

She hissed back at him, "I-don't-give-a-shit-about-you!"

"OK, OK. I'll get it." He looked around. No one in sight. He climbed out of his van and motioned her over to the sidewalk near her car where there was some shade. He withdrew his lapsed insurance card. She extended her hand to snatch it as he sailed it around her so it would land on the trunk of the Volvo just slightly beyond her reach.

She frowned, but stepped forward and, squinting to read it, leaned over just enough for him to grab her neck and twist. She crumpled into him, dead.

He grabbed her by the waist and held her up as if she were walking beside him and maneuvered her to the rear of his van, opened the back and bundled her in.

He slammed the door shut, jumped back behind the steering wheel, and glided slowly down the block through the peaceful, empty neighborhood. As he turned the corner, he moved faster heading for the freeway north.

It took six more minutes to reach the freeway. Once he was cruising at 65 mph, he felt exhilarated. Despite the throbbing in his arm, he felt relaxed for the first time since Moremi had bitten him. He would stop and give himself a shot of morphine, after he gained some distance from the Volvo. Even though he figured it would take a while for this woman to be reported missing, and then longer for the cops to locate her car, he wanted to be away from the scene.

After thirty minutes he pulled off the freeway and into the back of a fairly deserted gas station. He gave himself the shot and leaned back closing his eyes while his mind raced. Then he jumped out and opened the back.

It took five minutes to stuff her into the body bag. She was heavier than she looked. Back in the driver's seat he pondered how he could turn this around. Then he called Peter.

"Well? Have you found them?"

"No. There's been a minor problem. I got into a little accident. Nothing major. Just a little fender bender. I took care of it. Don't worry, no one was hurt. But I think I better leave town for a few days to let this calm down. I paid the guy driving the other car and he was happy. But I'm going to drive up to Seattle and take care of that other business up there and then come back down here. That will make your wife think I'm gone, and the shrink will probably go back to her routine. They'll assume it's safe. They'll be easy to find then. I'll be in Seattle tomorrow afternoon. I'll be in touch."

He was relieved that Peter sounded tired and didn't argue.

He would dump the woman in the reservoir. *And maybe do a little fishing?* There would be plenty of time. Whenever he felt pressure, he shifted his perspective and was amazed how that could change everything.

Maybe he had Sharon to thank for something. She used to encourage him to see things from the bright side.

He began to feel better. It was a gift. He was smarter than all the other kids he knew. Now they were either in prison or dead.

As he drove along, he reached into his cooler and pulled out a chicken sandwich and then flicked on a Celia Cruz CD.

CHAPTER TWENTY-TWO

People from different parts of the world can respond to the same story if it says something to them about their own history and their own experience.

CHINUA ACHEBE

RICHARD CALLED DANIEL'S CELL PHONE.

"Richard, old boy, what have I done to deserve a personal call from you across the pond?"

"It's a long story," Richard alerted Daniel that they needed to use his house for their secret headquarters. "What's with the 'old boy' affectation? You haven't been there that long."

"True," Daniel said. "I'm having fun here at Oxford. The Brits know more American history than we do. Or maybe they're just more interested. It sounds like you've gotten yourself mixed up in some real intrigue. Mi casa, su casa! My one request is that when I do get back you tell me every detail. Besides, I miss our on-going arguments dissecting our Constitution. How's my big guard cat?"

Richard laughed. "I'm looking at him as we speak. He's considering his next step—one of the Chows is resting at my feet and I think she's obstructing his plans to land on my lap."

"That's my boy! Always strategic. When he was a kitten Anna called him her little polecat because he moved like a ferret." Anna died of cancer several years ago. Richard knew how hard it had been for his friend to lose her and that only recently Daniel seemed to pull out of his malaise with a willingness to join the human race again. Richard felt a pang in the moment because he missed Anna's quick wit too. He knew Daniel felt the same stab to the heart as the brief silence between them could have no words.

"Let me know," Daniel quickly added as cheerfully as he could, "if I can help. Not sure how, but you never know. So, the house is yours. Tell Rebecca I look forward to a night of pasta and wine when I get back. I want to hear the whole saga. And tell Numi he's the man of the house and not to give those Chows too hard a time."

While Richard had been talking to Daniel, he had flipped through a few pages of one of Daniel's Civil War books on the top of one of his piles. He stared at the open page of an 1861 photograph of Mary Todd Lincoln posing at the White House in a white ball gown with layers of ruffles and embroidered flowers spreading out from her cinched waist. She wore a flowered crown around her forehead and a garland of what looked to be fresh flowers flowing across her gown. She held a fan in her gloved right hand while allowing her left to drape over the bodice lightly touching the garland. It was a famous photograph and he'd seen it before, but never really looked. He reached over and put his finger over Mary's face and saw a perfect Southern belle. When he removed his finger, he saw that her eyes gazed out into something far beyond her immediate surroundings. *Where were you really when you posed for that photograph?* He closed the book. He'd heard about Mary's obsession with the spirit world. That's it, he decided. *You were with your spirits. . . your own secret witches!*

His cell phone rang, ending his reverie. It was Leonard.

"Hey, man," Leonard exploded into Richard's ear with a deep baritone that sounded as if it came out of a long tunnel, "What's up? I got your message. I was out fishing when you called. I'm going to have trout tonight. Rainbow trout. I keep inviting you to come and fish, but I guess you've forgotten how. Just kidding! What's up?"

Leonard and Richard met as undergraduates in the same fraternity at the University of Chicago in 1966. Richard already knew he would study cultural anthropology and Leonard wanted a degree in political science. They each thought they had made a mistake joining a fraternity. Roommates from the first day, although they were both popular, they were dubbed 'The Outliers,' which was fine with them. Richard was average height and build while Leonard was huge with a black mane of hair tied in a ponytail. Within a few weeks he was named 'Ursa Major', or just plain 'Big Bear' that later became just 'Bear.' They tried to saddle Richard with 'Little Bear,' but it didn't stick. Leonard's nickname tagged him for life.

Richard summarized the situation as best he could. Bear had one of those quicksilver minds that instantly grasped the gestalt of any situation. Richard was the idealist while Bear was the rationalist. With Bear's CIA experience, Richard knew he was talking to a trained mind used to operating in a crisis.

Bear joined the CIA out of graduate school in 1969 under Richard Helms and was one of the few who picked up languages easily, which made him a prime candidate for counterintelligence work. He learned Vietnamese quickly when he was in Vietnam and later spoke fluent Farsi and Pashto. One of his three wives had been Middle Eastern, but Richard couldn't keep up with which one. Bear's marriages had lasted a total of six years, spread over thirty-five. When he and Richard managed to reconnect over the years it was usually between Bear's wives.

Bear had been in Afghanistan during the late 80s and Richard knew he had worked closely with the Mujahedeen. During the 1990s they kept in touch sporadically and then ten years ago Bear contacted him to let him know he had left the CIA and had become a private detective. He lived in Washington State with Bessie his basset hound. Richard and Rebecca had visited Bear once at his genuine log cabin near a cold, clear trout lake in the woods. He had a companion, Susan, a grade schoolteacher, who had her own place like Rebecca. She and Bear seemed to have an arrangement that worked fine.

Bear liked Rebecca. When she and Richard were leaving from their visit in the woods with Bear and Susan, he took Richard aside and stared deeply into his eyes. "Marry that one!" he commanded.

Richard thought coming from Bear he would have to hear that with a grain of salt. But he nodded and assured his friend, "I'm trying."

Bear leaned in grabbing Richard's arm intending to offer some tips on how to go about that when Susan rescued Richard with sandwiches for their trip back.

As Richard went to his car he turned around and saw Bear looking a little perplexed by his friend's quick exit from his advice on romance and marriage. Richard waved thinking, "Some things, Bear, are best left to my instincts." But now he needed Bear's instincts.

"OK," Bear said, "I get the picture. I'll start looking into this guy Peter's background and see if I can find some links to the shadow who's after Rebecca and her client. Are you available by cell?"

"At all times. I'm cancelling all my obligations for the next week. So did Rebecca."

"OK, that's good. I'll be in touch. Try not to worry. Oh, one last thing. You said the client actually knows his number?"

"Yes."

"All right. That's going to be useful somehow. Don't want to alert him now but it'll be useful. I'll be in touch soon and then I'll get down there as soon as I can."

HUGO TURNED OFF THE FREEWAY when the sun was still high enough on the horizon to leave plenty of daylight. He would rent a small outboard motorboat and take himself and the package into the middle of the lake just as the light started to dim and the trout were surfacing to a mayfly hatch. Perfect timing. There were enough shadows moving around that would skew anyone's perception so if they thought they saw something suspicious, it could have been just about anything.

He needed to find something to weigh her down. Rocks inside the bag would do. He saw plenty of granite on the ground, but even in the afternoon jumping shadow light he couldn't collect them without attracting attention. And as he thought things through, he realized he couldn't weigh her down inside the van because then he might not be able to lug her into one of the little rented fiberglass outboards. He relaxed a little—he liked this kind of challenge.

Killing people was easy but getting rid of them was another matter. She had to be one of those cases that disappeared for twenty years. Her body would not be found until long after her file had reached the dead cases deep in the bowels of some storage dungeon. *Maybe the lake would dry up or be bulldozed to create a skating rink and her bones would be given to some bright detective. Who knows, maybe that bright young person hasn't even been born yet.* Imagining this laid to rest any fear that his plan was not fool proof.

He swung the van into a lone parking spot behind a bait and boat rental shack. He went around to the front and up the stairs onto the rustic porch and opened the screen door, which slammed shut as he adjusted his eyes to the darkness within.

The grizzled old man behind the counter looked familiar. He was probably in his late seventies and smelled like a combination of beer and a jar of salmon eggs. He was bent over his newspaper chuckling at the comics. He looked up and studied the newcomer as if he were wondering why someone would even bother to wander in.

Hugo instantly engaged, explaining that he needed to get away for a little bit from the wife and kids he left back at the campsite.

The old man commiserated. "Yeah, I know what you mean. Why do you think I keep this place open 'til eight?" His teeth shown a brownish yellow in a conspiratorial grin. "So's my old lady has less time to nag me about all the other stuff she thinks I should be doing while she folds the laundry and watches those shows about unhappy housewives like herself."

Hugo laughed to seal their bond as beleaguered husbands hiding out and then paid twenty-five bucks for ice, a six-pack of Heinekens and use of the boat for two hours.

He backed the van down close to the water near the boat and took out his cooler and put it in into the stern near the motor. He closed the back of his van and went around to open the side door that faced away from the bait shop. Just in case the old man decided to look out his window, unlikely but it paid to be overly cautious. He lifted her out, slung her over his shoulder and deposited her in the middle of the boat for balance. He returned for his Winston rod and treasured Hardy reel and small metal case with his hand-tied flies. He pushed the boat into the water and stepped in, started the motor, and cruised along the shore until he was out of sight.

He found a spot that had a small beach and pulled in. He grabbed rocks, tossing them one by one into the boat aiming for the body bag to cushion the sound. A few hit the fiberglass clanging too loudly and he winced, warning himself to slow down—five to six seconds a throw left plenty of time. He gave himself one minute to accomplish this. A lot can happen in one minute, but not much if you wanted to avoid the curiosity seekers. People might notice something on a first glance, but it was the second or third that counted. He calculated that it took 'lookie-loos' about one minute to come back for a second glance. If by then there was nothing to see they would lose interest and dismiss their first impression.

Then he steered out into the middle of the lake. Unless someone had binoculars on shore whatever he did would be invisible. He was the only late fisherman out. He stopped the motor and listened to the lapping ripples. The little boat bobbed up and down for a minute as the water calmed. He watched a family of mallards glide toward shore. The babies calmly flitted around the mother as they snagged insects hovering low over the water.

He straddled her, filling the bag with rocks, then crouched down and rolled her up over the side. The pain in his arm stabbed as he heard her plop on the surface—a glistening bulk bobbing up and down. For a few seconds it looked like she wouldn't go under, as if she were resisting the inevitable—her last brush with life. The bag ballooned out and then he watched it slowly sink into the darkness below.

"Bye bye, 'Ms. Run for Your Life.' And oh yeah, by the way, I don't give a shit about you either."

He took the rod, removed a tiny parachute fly from the small aluminum box in his shirt pocket and tied it onto the fine tippet of his fishing line, nipping off the excess neatly with his front teeth. He cast three times, back and forth, measuring out the line between casts and set the fly down gently on the water about twenty yards from the boat. He stripped in a few feet of line to straighten it and then sat back for a while, calm, relaxed, and focused on the tiny white hackled speck floating on the darkening water in the early evening, lying in wait.

He reached into the cooler for a beer and twisted off the cap, tossed it into the cooler and leaned back in the seat and narrowed his eyes. *What a day. I deserve this.* Even though his arm throbbed the pain had settled into a dull ache that he was getting used to.

An hour later he reeled in and headed for shore. He didn't care that he got no bites. His casts were quiet, smooth, even perfect. Often just the thought of the slight tug on the line, that tiny white parachute blinking out when a fish, invisible under the surface, sips it down into its mouth and then the split-second flick of the rod to set the hook is satisfaction enough. Had a fish seen his fly, there was nothing it could have done to avoid being caught. It felt good to just float in that quiet hunt and watch the last of the sun go down.

He pulled the boat onto the sand and went into the bait shop to tell the old man he'd returned it.

The old guy was still hunched over the same newspaper as if he hadn't moved a muscle in two hours. He looked up and waved at Hugo. "Any time young man. You better run along to that wife and family of yours or you'll catch hell." He chuckled to himself. "Women!"

"Yeah, you're right. Can't push my luck too far."

"Take care." He returned to his newspaper.

Back in the van Hugo was flushed with a sense of well-being. He was on his game again, a job well done. He put the rod back into its green metal tube, the fly into its box, and the reel in its vinyl case and put them back into his tackle box. As he hopped into the front seat, he reminded himself as if it were on his grocery list, *I'll need to get a new body bag.*

He would drive all night. Henry was right. The pain in his arm would keep him awake. And so would the exhilaration of thinking of that woman settling on the bottom of a reservoir.

CHAPTER TWENTY-THREE

Greenpeace's goal is to ensure the ability of Earth to nurture life in all its diversity.

GREENPEACE MISSION STATEMENT

ALICE SAT IN A BOOTH ACROSS FROM HER PARENTS in their favorite Seattle bistro. Martha and Oliver Gordon were in their mid-sixties. He was short, stocky, and solid with bushy eyebrows while Martha was taller, built like a pear. Alice was short like her father and shaped like her mother. All three had curly, unruly hair. All three were considered eccentric, super-smart and beloved by their many friends.

They volunteered for a smorgasbord of community action programs and put their money where their mouths were. The family had early roots in Greenpeace and saving the environment was their religion. Their friends called them the Three Little Bears who lamented the killing of the forests, the drinking of their rivers and polluting of their air and soil. As a family they were a united front, so cheerfully informed that not everyone could tolerate them. At meetings they were like a tornado dropping in for a visit.

Alice had come along late like a miracle after Oliver and Martha had given up hope of having a child. They watched her now as she waved her fork in the air expressing her affection for her favorite teacher, Professor Abosanjo. "He's sooo . . . oh gosh . . . well, he's just so smart! I mean like really intelligent!"

Oliver's bushy eyebrows rose as Martha's veered into a frown, both un-noticed by Alice who was used to her parents' worried but indulgent expressions. As involved parents, they were both amused and bemused by their precocious child, whom they viewed as intellectually advanced and emotionally immature. They had always assumed she needed their protective parental wing. Alice's extended family indulged and reinforced her every interest. As a result, she knew the world as a safe, supportive place. And now? The world was her oyster.

She had to finish the next semester of class work before she could finalize her dissertation topic. As Oliver and Martha listened their worry increased with Alice's rising excitement about her feelings for this Abosanjo professor they had never heard of before.

Alice had a history of impetuous attachments. When thirteen, while attending a summer camp in Maine, she attached herself to an older girl who went to boarding school. When Alice returned home, she wanted to go away to school too and was inconsolable for weeks because her parents tactfully said no.

Two months later, she developed a crush on a teacher at school.

Now, at twenty-three, doing well in graduate school, here was a new crush. It was clear to Oliver and Martha that this Abosanjo—innocently or not—had captured their daughter's immature heart and they instinctively moved in to protect her.

As they dug into their salads, Alice told them about fraudulent machinations in the Nigerian oil industry in the mid-nineties during Abaca's regime. "It was so great," she enthused as she popped half a deviled egg into her mouth, "because," she swallowed, "you know, I think I'm getting pretty good at the research. I mean you can't just rely on the internet." she whirled her fork over their heads, "I mean, I dug deep to find out stuff." She popped a radish into her mouth and crunched while looking pensively out the window, "I mean, I spent hours in the library. My bibliography was like way longer than anyone else's."

Martha put her own fork down and patted her napkin into her lap. "Sweetheart," she began, "you know all we care about is your happiness. You know that. But I'm wondering . . . you know just trying to take the long view here . . . if perhaps you should take a little more time to decide?"

Alice flipped her curls back and forth like an impatient pony. "Mom!" she declared in her "I'm a grown-up-now" tone of voice. "I know what I'm doing. I want to work on something that might really make a difference. I want to target environmental issues motivated by profit and greed that undermine our natural world. I mean we've almost forgotten about that BP oil spill thing in the Gulf. But you know we were all up in arms about that, remember? Well Nigeria has been putting up with oil spills and a toxic environment like forever . . . fifty years! Professor Abosanjo says Nigeria's a microcosm for what's going to happen everywhere. And I believe him. I think he's right."

Martha sank back as Oliver came forward. "What your mother is trying to say is that Nigeria's a long way off for you to go and do your research. It's also a very dangerous place. We just want you to take your time. We'll support you no matter what you decide, but well . . . we just think it's a little premature."

They knew nothing they said would change Alice's mind except time, when the likelihood that her focus would follow wherever her attachments led. But Oliver seemed to possess the right touch. It was his voice. Alice responded to her father's voice as a caressed child might. She might disagree, but she would calm down. He looked over at his wife giving her the look that meant, "Don't push this. You can't protect her from learning from her mistakes. Don't rob her of her own experience."

But Martha couldn't help herself. Growing up she had never been popular and had experienced cruelty from her peers. Her own parents, now dead, had sold her sanctuary, their own island in Maine where they spent their holidays and summers in the '90s. Martha never recovered from the loss, and leaned too close to protect her daughter from loneliness and disappointment, in spite of the fact that Alice tended to land on her feet.

They finished their lunch, and all tentatively agreed that when Alice returned to school after the spring break, she would do some further research into the Nigerian oil history and explore her thesis comparing Nigeria as a microcosm to the rest of the world. Alice understood that in the end they would follow her lead. Oliver added that Nigeria had never really recovered from its own civil war back in the sixties, not long after independence from British colonialism. He speculated, "When you take people's hope away and you break their spirit, recovery is all the more difficult."

Normally when her father became too philosophical about human behavior Alice would tease him with, "Come on Dad, don't be such a pessimist!" But this time she didn't. Maybe for the first time. Instead, she looked at them both as if she understood something for the first time, then she asked, "What civil war?"

Out on the sidewalk Oliver turned on his professorial tone and explained. "Between July 6, 1967, to January 1970 the southeastern provinces of Nigeria declared themselves the Republic of Biafra. They wanted an independent state. The government of Nigeria wanted to rule through power and control of the booming oil and gas industry. The Biafrans were idealists. The federal military surrounded the Biafrans creating a blockade to starve them out. Formally, we, the US, remained neutral, but informally we supported the government of Nigeria. The whole thing ended in a tragic loss and since then things have only gotten worse," he looked at Alice, "and as you say . . . the destruction of the environment was motivated by greed, not preservation of their land or culture."

Alice skipped ahead to the car. Martha looked at Oliver. "You've just supported her cause."

He grabbed his wife's hand as they followed her. "Maybe," he said. "But she's grown up now. We have to support her by not holding her back. But," he added, "I think we should meet this Abosanjo guy just to be safe."

They returned to their secluded home after driving the three-mile steep and winding climb in their sturdy Volvo and turned into their tree-lined street.

THE NEXT MORNING Hugo parked a few houses down from the Gordons. He watched Alice's red mini in the driveway. It had been easy. She left it unlocked, but he didn't need to get inside to deflate both front tires enough and then to hammer a three-inch nail in the front left tire. Just one whap with his hammer and it went through. He pulled it out and the leak began to seep like sand in a timer. He calculated the swerve coming down that hill around those hairpin turns, imagining a simple accident as she sailed over the edge. By noon he would be back on the road heading south.

He was tired. That episode with 'Ms. Run for Your Life' had drained him more than he liked to admit. And then there was the bite—throbbing again. *I need a break.*

The next moment his wish came true. The door opened and out she came. He grabbed his binoculars. "OK," he purred, "let's just move along here . . . slowly . . . that's right, open the door, hop in. 'Shhh,' the witch says . . . 'into the oven you go.'" He liked the fairy tales his mother told him when he was very young. It was only later he decided there were no happy endings.

She tossed in her over-loaded backpack and slid behind the wheel just as the front door opened and an older, taller version of Alice burst out with a bouncy Golden Retriever.

What now? He rocked back and forth, rubbing his arm to soothe the pain.

The mom went to the passenger window chattering about something as the dog jumped up plunking his front paws on Alice's window, which she lowered, giggling. He hopped down and then lifted his leg on the deflating tire.

Hugo gritted his teeth.

Mom handed a small paper bag through the window. Probably lunch.

Alice seemed impatient as she started the engine.

Mom backed off waving and retreated into the house with the bouncy dog.

The car disappeared around the corner.

He started his own engine and followed at a leisurely pace. He knew where she was going. Six minutes later he watched his plan unfold.

She swerved over the shoulder and down the embankment.

He cruised past and reached the intersection at the foot of the grade and then headed for the shopping mall a few miles away. He parked in front of a Starbuck's and ordered a non-fat latte, stirred in two packets of sugar, and returned to his van to call Peter.

"Where have you been?" Peter demanded.

Hugo checked his watch. It was 9:00 A.M. "Calm down. All is well. The Seattle job is done. I should be heading back in about an hour or so. Just need to run a few errands. I'll be back late tonight."

No response.

"Are you ok?"

"Yeah, I'm fine. Just a little colitis acting up. Nothing to worry about."

"Hey, dude, that can get serious. You should have it checked out."

"My physical condition is not your concern."

"OK. I was just trying to be helpful."

"Yeah . . . well, I'm fine. Just keep in touch."

"Sure. No problem."

He pressed end call and fumed. It wasn't what Peter said. It was always his tone. He was used to the kind of people who hired out their dirty work, and yet Peter rubbed him the wrong way. He couldn't quite put his finger on why. It had something to do with the impression that Peter didn't really understand what he was doing was wrong, that somehow, he was forced to do what he had to—as if he had no choice. Hugo mused, *even I have a choice.*

He started his engine, sipped his latte, and headed to the scene. It had been about forty minutes. By now someone might have seen her car. He needed to verify the results. But that last curve was the best and that was the one where she lost control. As he rounded the bend just before the climb began, he saw flashing lights. He pulled over and climbed out, sauntering over to the cop directing traffic. Two cop cars were on the side of the road and already traffic was being re-routed.

He waved. "Officer . . . ah . . . sir . . ."

The young cop was annoyed, looking overwhelmed.

"Sir," Hugo asked in his concerned citizen tone, "has there been an accident? Is there anything I can do?"

The cop frowned.

Hugo persisted. "My goodness, I was just wondering because I've always felt there should be some kind of railing, you know some kind of warning on those curves."

"Sir, you need to stay out of the way. A car has gone over the edge. That curve back there," he explained, nodding over his shoulder, "has been responsible for too many accidents."

"Well, that's what I mean. Maybe this will convince them so some good might come of this accident. Was anyone hurt?"

"What does it look like to you? A young woman is back there in that car. An ambulance is on the way. Now, please step aside, sir. We need to keep this area clear."

"You mean she's alive?"

The cop glared. "I really don't know sir, but I doubt it."

Hugo raised both hands up as he bowed away. "Just trying to offer some help but I can see you guys are doing a great job." He went back to the line of annoyed motorists waiting to pass.

Back in his van he made a U-turn and returned to the Starbucks to pick up another cup of coffee and a chicken salad sandwich. He unwrapped it with care, holding it up to inspect the contents. Munching, he stared out the window. A couple of tan young blond girls were sitting at the outside table with their foamy drinks and croissants. A large crow landed on their table strutting back and forth preening. One of the girls tossed it a piece of bread. The crow picked it up and, in a flash, turned and flew back to its tree thirty feet up. He thought of the signs he had seen somewhere that said: "A fed animal is a dead animal."

He waited long enough to decide she was dead. No flashing ambulance speeding by. In ten minutes, he was heading south on the freeway. The clock on his dash registered 10:30 A.M. He decided that in a few hours he would stop for a nice lunch. He deserved it.

CHAPTER TWENTY-FOUR

Synchronicity is an ever-present reality
for those who have eyes to see.
CARL JUNG

PETER STARED AT HIS PHONE. He hated being forced to rely on Hugo with no real control over the man. He knew from experience over the last few years that Hugo never told him all the details of how he accomplished a job, no matter what it was.

Peter first hired Hugo when he needed some information about an acquaintance of his father's, who had shown up one day in his office and asked to borrow money not long after his father died. *This man's request sounded like a bribe.*

"I'm sure we can come to some sort of arrangement," he smirked. Peter understood it was code for "you owe me." Only Peter didn't know what reason he might owe this man who said he knew his father.

A friend recommended Hugo: "This guy will do anything."

Two weeks later, Hugo's final report was terse: "Not a good guy. Dangerous. He will not bother you again."

When Peter asked for more details, Hugo responded, "Best you don't ask."

Peter didn't, and paid the bill for "Research Services Rendered."

A few years later, Peter asked him to watch Moremi when he found the altar in the basement and noted her increasing remoteness. They met at the back of a coffee shop, Peter had slid into the booth across from Hugo who complained, "This coffee tastes like oil slick." He put the mug down next to the plate of half-eaten chicken salad and folded his napkin.

Peter decided he was finicky about his food, a conclusion that seemed at odds with the description of "a guy who will do anything."

Nor did Hugo look like he could do anything. He was short, agile, and wiry, his hands flitted when he talked and that made him seem prissy. However, a small scar over his upper lip made him look a little sinister. Peter remembered his friend said Hugo held a black belt in karate and decided he must be stronger than he appeared.

When the slightly plump server with curls came to the table to take Peter's order, Hugo switched to a bantering, glib style as if they were old chums. After she left, he flipped a switch, riveting his eyes back on Peter, radiating chill. He spoke without a hint of that personality he'd just put on.

Peter lay on the bed, weak from his stomach pain and wishing he could sleep to gain back his energy. He thought about Alice and couldn't help wondering what Hugo had done to her. He turned on the TV to distract himself and watched Oprah. *Now, she was a fine woman.* He idly wondered what part of Africa her ancestors were from.

MARTHA AND OLIVER GORDON WAITED at the hospital to hear from the doctor. They held hands and were silent. Martha's curls gave her a wild look as she stared at the wall in contrast to Oliver's slicked-down hair as he studied his feet.

The doctor came in with raised hands, which he lowered like a minister taming his flock and spoke quickly. "She's going to be ok." Martha choked back her tears while Oliver sagged in relief. "She's a very lucky young lady. The seatbelt and airbags did their job. She's got a couple broken ribs and a concussion. She's pretty banged up but she's going to be fine. You can see her as soon as we move her into a room. She'll need to stay here for a few days for observation."

Oliver spoke first. "How long do you think she'll need? She's supposed to return to school next week."

"I recommend she not return next week and preferably next month either. She'll heal ok physically, but she has been traumatized. When patients try to recover too quickly from this type of accident there can be a residual reaction."

Oliver asked, "Like a PTSD type of thing?"

"Exactly. She could develop a fear of driving, for example. It's usually wise for patients who have suffered from a traumatic car accident to return to their normal functioning slowly."

Oliver pressed, "Should she see a counselor?"

"Let's hold off on that and see how she's doing. For most people recovery just takes time and rest."

They agreed to talk with Alice about taking time off, but both were anxious about broaching the subject. "Let's just see how she's doing," Oliver suggested, "and play it by ear."

When they entered Alice's room two nurses and a doctor surrounded the bed. Martha and Oliver stopped in their tracks fearing the worst that their daughter was not out of the woods as they had been assured. As they approached the bed both realized how mistaken they were. Alice's neck brace and bandaged head seemed to enlarge her stature. Most accident victims would have shrunk into their bandages, but not Alice who commanded the attention of everyone as she spoke. "Ursus Arctos Horribilis is not nearly as bad as people think. And . . . since they're almost extinct because there are less than two thousand left I think people need to educate themselves better."

The nurse held the straw under her chin and Alice sipped her juice.

Oliver whispered under his breath to Martha, "She's lecturing them about grizzlies!"

Martha, wide-eyed, nodded.

They sat with their daughter for several hours. Oliver broached the topic of taking time off. Alice stared at her parents while they fidgeted. "Here's what I think," she announced. "I know my car and what happened wasn't an accident."

"What do you mean?" Oliver asked.

"That's what I mean," Alice said. "Someone did this to me."

Both assumed their daughter was under the influence of the pain meds. But still they were worried. Why would she think that? How could she know? They suddenly realized Alice had become an adult somewhere along the way.

She did agree to take a few weeks before returning to school and they agreed to support her research on Nigeria. They also agreed to call the university and leave a message for Professor Abosanjo about the accident and to inform him that Alice would be doing some research from home while recuperating. "Maybe I'll just have a little chat with this popular professor," Oliver told Martha.

"Yes," Martha agreed, "and perhaps we should try to meet with him in person considering how much she admires him."

BEAR TURNED HIS EXPLORER onto the freeway south at 9:00 A.M. hoping to arrive at Daniel's house around 11:00 that night, giving him time to stop for gas and lunch at a diner. Cruising at 85 he popped in his long drive music, an old CD of Creedence Clearwater Survival singing Bad Moon Rising.

An hour and a half later he slowed to 70 navigating the traffic through the Seattle area. As he passed an on ramp in the right lane a 2010 black Dodge van forced him to swerve to the left. "What the!?" he barked as it swept past and changed into his lane without signaling.

Bear sped up behind it feeling impotent rage take over. He couldn't calculate the number of times his temper had gotten the best of him despite his training and despite the recriminations of ex-wives. Only Susan knew how to calm him. But still, she wouldn't marry him, and he knew why. They called it his temper. He called it his passion. And no one agreed. Susan called it his passionate temperament. Somehow, he knew that was better, but still . . . it was a problem.

He tried to calm himself down but couldn't help noticing the plates on the black van. *Illinois plates. Chicago*. Although he knew there was nothing out of the ordinary about out of state plates, but his military training kicked in automatically. "Any detail that attracts your attention, no matter how small," his commanding officer would bellow at his recruits, "is worthy of your notice. You are a special breed of obsessives, you are hounds on a mission, you will carry that load and . . ." here's where he delivered his punch-line, "no detail is beneath your radar!" That caveat was emblazoned in Bear's psyche. It had become instinctual. Illinois plates. Chicago. Sent to the back burner of his mind as he followed the black van, a hound after the scent.

Three hours later Bear was ten cars behind. He watched it pull over to the right lane and exit. He followed and pulled into the parking lot of Millie's Diner, a truck stop. He had stopped there before and now he was hungry. He waited and watched the driver of the black van walk in from his rearview mirror. Nothing particularly struck Bear about him except that he wore a plain black t-shirt, and his left arm was bandaged. He closed his eyes and tried to calm his thoughts reiterating to himself "nothing out of the ordinary" and then climbed out and walked into Millie's where Charlene in her white apron waved him into a booth and arrived with a menu. He ordered coffee, which arrived quickly.

As he sipped from the thick white mug, he listened to the sounds around him—clanking dishes, shouting from the kitchen, revolving doors on noisy hinges, trucks passing by outside.

Charlene returned snapping her gum.

"What's the favorite these days?" he asked.

Her bright red fingernail with the chipped paint landed on the pulled barbecue pork sandwich on rye.

He automatically summed her up—*she's not particular and probably a lot of fun and tolerant.* "Looks good. Thanks. I'll have that."

"Home fries or coleslaw?"

"Ummm . . ." he wanted the fries, but Susan's voice crowded out his desire for greasy salted crispy potatoes reprimanding, *"Leonard! Those days are over!"* She called him Leonard when she role-played his mother. He looked up at Charlene who seemed to get his internal debate as she waited with sympathy. "The coleslaw." She smiled and whirled away.

He sipped his coffee and gazed out the window at the black van parked outside with the Chicago plates. A big rig pulled in and belched to a stop and he realized that the chatter and sounds of the diner had risen. It was lunch time. Bear was trained to distinguish sounds and over his coffee he let everything recede into an orchestrated white noise that for him was like silence.

Within seconds his reverie was interrupted as the theme from Jaws began to play. That rumbling, intrepid "Deeum! Deeum! Deum deum dumdumdumdum" was out of place. Where was it coming from? He cocked his head like a hawk spying for prey and right behind the wall of the booth where he leaned the menacing melody stopped with, "Yeah? What's up?" Pause. "I told you I'm on my way. I'll be there in ten hours, maybe less depending on traffic and so far, it isn't bad."

"Look," the man continued with exasperation, "I know you're worried. She's not going anywhere. She won't leave your son. She's scared and holed up somewhere. Trust me. I'll find them when I get back." Another pause. "I'll call you. Try to relax. Get some rest. You still don't sound good." There was a long pause and Bear couldn't tell if the conversation had ended.

His sandwich arrived. He stared at his plate as he waited to hear more. And then he heard it.

"OK, OK. I know. The shrink's name is . . ." he paused as if he were looking it up—"Rebecca Calhoun, PhD."

He gulped down the sandwich. Charlene was right, it was delicious but the pleasure barely registered. His mind raced. *I've had coincidences, but nothing like this. What would he be doing up here? But I heard what I heard. He said Rebecca Calhoun! He's headed back to do a job, which means find Moremi, the wife. He said, "I'll find them." That could mean both Moremi and Rebecca. "She's hiding out, not going anywhere. And there's a son, her reason for sticking around."* Everything fell into place as Bear froze in his seat.

Bear's military training taught him to discount nothing, no matter how far-fetched. Most civilians simply did not recognize coincidental moments even though they happened all the time. As in quantum physics, every action, no matter how small, begins a chain of events that appear to have no connection. But they do. Bear decided this might be one of those moments. He had no idea why this guy would be on the freeway at the same time heading south and no idea what events may have preceded this coincidence. He just knew that behind this serendipitous moment in Millie's Café there was a perfectly logical chain of other events that would explain why here, now, in this moment in time.

He waited for the mystery suspect to pay and leave. Bear soaked up as much detail as he could. About five foot six, wiry and probably much stronger than he looked, quick on his feet, maybe Latin, hair slicked back, swaggers like a cat, and maybe trained in some kind of martial arts. Just a guess. Bear smelled a whiff of something. Like cologne. A minor detail but it stuck. Bear's conclusion? *This guy is unpredictable. Dangerous.* It was something about the way he scanned the room—like a predator.

He left Charlene a big tip and ambled out to his car just as the van peeled out onto the highway and disappeared into traffic. Only one freeway south so he knew he could follow at a safe distance and wouldn't lose him.

Back in his own van he called Richard on his speakerphone.

"Hey man, where are you?"

"On my way, buddy, on my way. Listen, I need you to do something for me. You said Moremi didn't get a good look at this guy. And yet she bit the hell out of his arm when he grabbed her from behind. She must have seen more than she told us because people always do. Ask her again, or better yet let me talk to her."

"I think she's resting right now. She had a hard night and looked pretty exhausted."

"OK, but when she wakes up could you have her call me on my cell?"

"Has anything happened?"

"Oh, probably not but you know me. Strange things happen when I'm around. It'll pass the time driving and I can think about it on my way down. If she's up for it, have her call." He didn't want to report to Richard yet what he'd heard. There was a time and a place to sound the alarm and Bear wanted everyone to remain calm if possible. Besides, there was always the chance he heard wrong. He didn't think so, but along with his training came caution when dealing with civilians. And his old friend Richard was, after all, just a civilian.

"OK," Richard responded. "I'll have her call."

Forty-five minutes later Bear's phone rang. It was Moremi.

"Hello Mr. Whitmore. I'm Moremi Abosanjo."

"Hi, it's nice to meet you. Call me Bear."

"OK."

He liked her voice. It was smooth and velvety and straightforward. He recognized her Nigerian British English accent with its tendency to stress more syllables with a musical rhythm. She used words precisely, as if she were sculpting her sentences.

"Listen," Bear urged, knowing his American accent must sound as if his words just fell out of a sack, "I know you didn't really get a good look at your attacker, but I'd like you to do something for me because you probably took in more than you realize about him."

"All right."

She seemed to understand what he wanted. This was good. He could tell she was introspective.

"OK. I want you to close your eyes and let your memory go back to Saturday morning and describe what you see, hear or smell—anything at all. Let me be the judge of whether anything is important. And if it's all right with you I'd like to tape you."

"Right now?"

"Yes, now. If you're up to it."

"I will do my best."

He heard her take in her breath and let it out as he imagined her closing her eyes. After a moment of silence, she began.

"After Peter runs down the stairs, I hear the front door slam. My legs wobble. I make myself get into the shower and I dress quickly and start down the stairs to leave. But something pulls me back up the stairs and I go to his office where I never go . . . I see a telephone number on a pad of paper in his desk drawer. I pick up his desk phone and dial the number. A man answers. He's impatient and yells, "I'm almost there. Where the hell are you? I thought you were on the road."

"I know instantly he's coming for me."

"I run to the cellar thinking I will leave by that door out into the back of the house. Getting out of there is all I can think about. But I hear him coming along the side of the house where there is a high window in the cellar, and I see his silhouette moving fast. I run back up the stairs and crouch on the landing. I'm his prey. He peers through the locked cellar door window rubbing away the dirt. He rattles the doorknob. As soon as he disappears, I dash back down the stairs and out that door and I run through yards trying to stay out of sight. Then I'm standing under some elm trees catching my breath about to make a dash down the street when he grabs me from behind. I heard nothing. No warning. His left arm clamps around my neck and he puts his lips over my ear breathing into me. I think I'm dead. But for some reason I feel him hesitate and I grab his arm and shove it into my mouth, and I clamp down hard. He screams. I let go. He releases me. I kick him in the groin and then I run. I didn't really see his face, but he has black hair. He smelled. Not body odor, but aftershave, which seemed strange to me, at odds I guess with who he is. He didn't try to run after me. I assumed he went back to his van and would track me that way. He's short but strong. And quick." She paused. "Is that enough?"

"For now. You did great. I'll see you tonight."

Bear pressed end call, his heart racing. The man in the black van with the Chicago plates was the one. The chance it was a coincidence was insignificant. That's the guy! He sped up until he saw the black van up ahead. He slowed down and knew he would follow it for the next ten hours.

CHAPTER TWENTY- FIVE

That's too coincidental to be a coincidence.

YOGI BERRA

HUGO LEFT THE FREEWAY AT 11:30 P.M. and headed toward the hills where homes still twinkled in the night, retracing his steps to the neighborhood where he had been thirty-six hours earlier. He wanted to be done with all this.

After he left Millie's Diner, he sensed that a forest green Explorer was following him along the freeway south. He had seen it parked at the diner when he left and occasionally noticed through his rearview mirror that it shifted lanes through traffic to catch up with him, never passing. Usually when a driver navigated that fast, he intended to pass all the slow cars and keep going. Hugo decided to slow down on purpose; there it would be catching up, but never passing.

To confirm his suspicion, he got off on an exit that appeared to go nowhere and pulled into a gas station a mile down the road. Sure enough, along cruised the green Explorer pulling into that same station.

"Now what are the odds?" he muttered. It was then he knew it was following him. *Why?* He didn't bother to wonder. He just kept going, keeping an eye on the Explorer.

He was tired after his long drive. Impatience undermined his skill, and his best skill was his ability to create a new persona as the moment required. He learned to do it in juvie, once he realized he looked like a dumb kid from the barrios, a patsy. Only Sharon figured out otherwise. After she left, he perfected an innocent guy act that protected him from prying adults who might take too great an interest in him. Behind his chirpy-friendly act he was a predator on the prowl. Just another lonely hunter. Killing 'Ms. Run for Your Life' was a loose end collateral damage that should never have happened. She did not buy his sad-sack-divorced-

Dad routine one little bit and that concerned him. He was slipping. *I need a break.*

He pulled over to the curb on a quiet tree-lined street that shielded him from the three-quarter moon. He liked moonlight—the persisting light held the night in shadows. He loved shadows, convinced they distorted vision and produced an ambiguous terrain where he felt at home.

He laid his head back. He couldn't remember when he had felt so completely drained. He knew he couldn't sleep so he teased himself, allowing his eyes to close, inviting the relief of sleep but forcing himself to stay awake—another trick he had developed over the years.

He expected the green Explorer to pass by soon. He had no idea why it followed him, but he'd already started finding out, researching the owner's license plate, contacting an old girlfriend at the Department of Motor Vehicles that led to his contact at the FBI and from there put together a scenario that made sense.

After five minutes he sat up and took a sip of lukewarm coffee from the thermos on the passenger seat. He moved his jaw muscles from side to side, twisting his head around to wake himself up. Fatigue made his arm throb more. He rubbed it and winced.

I'll go to Brazil for vacation. Rio has good coffee, good music, and samba. Real samba. It was too late this year for the carnival but that didn't matter. Samba is all year round in Rio. On the rare occasions he allowed himself to go to dance clubs, all the women wanted to dance with him. He had never found dance partners even in Chicago or LA as good as the ones in Rio. Here in the U.S., it was mostly salsa, not samba, which was his specialty. *Rio it is.*

About ten minutes into his reverie the green Explorer passed, cruising about 15 mph. Hugo now knew who he was. He ran his plates through his Chicago friend and knew all he needed to know. He recited the points to himself. Leonard Whitmore, BA and PhD, University of Chicago, Political Science, 1970. Army. Made colonel. Special Ops Afghanistan, 1980s. Popular with his men. Respected for his high moral standards, but no Boy Scout. Too much of an outsider. Married three times. Current girlfriend: schoolteacher, third grade, avid environmentalist. A think tank type. Maybe sympathetic to the neo-cons back in the 60's and 70's but stayed more of a liberal as they went conservative. Left the military in 1995. Lives in the woods north of Seattle. Private detective now. Reasonably respected by the police force. Probably confused and upset by where the country is headed. Nickname Bear. And oh . . . one last detail: published a paper in 1979 with his best friend, Richard Wilson entitled Our American Democracy Now.

And where had he seen the name Richard Wilson? In Rebecca Calhoun's house. His business card stuck right on her refrigerator like a neon sign where no one could miss it! *Soooo* . . . he put it together. *Richard has called his friend Bear to the rescue. Okay, Mr. Bear, let's see where you lead me.*

Hugo now became the tracker, letting the Explorer turn left out of sight before he started his van. With no traffic in the neighborhoods this time of night he could easily be spotted. He didn't follow beyond a certain point assuming that Bear might spot him. He would wait until morning. He would be somewhere nearby. "I'll find him at daylight. Where he goes, they will be."

BEAR CALLED RICHARD.

"Hey, I'm here. I'm gonna drive around a bit and see if I can find something." He hadn't yet told Richard about the black van.

"We're all here waiting for you. Moremi, Rebecca, me, Gertrude and oh yeah . . . one cat and two dogs. I told you about Gertrude. She's unlike any 80- year-old you've ever met. It's late. Maybe you should come straight here," Richard urged. "Gertrude says she has a plan."

"All right," he acquiesced. In the old days Bear would not have given in so easily, but once again he heard Susan's voice call him "old man" as a reminder of his mortality. He drove around a few minutes before he pulled over and waited in the silent shadows. He got out, grabbed his small duffel bag, and headed for Daniel's house that was not far, listening for the sound of a cruising van. All was quiet except for a slight breeze and the sound of a barking dog far off and the faint on-going roar of a freeway in the distance.

They were all gathered in Daniel's living room. Numi had settled contentedly in Moremi's lap vigorously washing his head while she stroked his back. Dido gnawed on a rawhide bone while Juno sprawled with her back legs splayed out, paws up sleeping with her head touching Gertrude's foot.

Bear who stood 6' 2", dressed like a lumberjack in his red plaid shirt, baggy khaki pants and steel toe logger boots. His ample, out of control hair was now salt and pepper, which gave him a Bigfoot wildness. And yet Bear's manners were impeccable.

When Richard escorted Bear into the room, everyone stood except Gertrude. Moremi bounced Numi unceremoniously off her lap. The Queens were up in a flash sniffing to decide if this intruder was friend or foe.

Only Gertrude stayed put in her chair. Bear grinned as he bounded over to Gertrude first. Holding her upheld hand cupped in his he announced with d'Artagnan aplomb, "My dear lady, what a delight to meet you."

Gertrude blushed.

He moved to Moremi taking her hand and stared into her large brown eyes. "What a pleasure to now meet you in person."

After he hugged Rebecca, Richard escorted Bear to the bathroom where he was invited to take a shower and refresh himself. As they walked down the hall Bear planted his big hand on Richard's shoulder and asked, "How are you all doing—really?"

"We're all OK, but it's been difficult to know what we're dealing with here. We know the assassin is out there somewhere, Moremi's husband has disappeared, and their eight-year-old son is skiing with friends, presumably safe. But who knows? All very worrisome and hardly predictable at this point. So, my friend," Richard put his hand on Bear's arm, "we're counting on you to help us make sense of all this. I believe Moremi understands better than any of us, of course, so we will need to understand what she does. If we can."

Bear's eyebrows raised inviting Richard to explain.

"She's African. A Voudou priestess from her mother-line. What she knows and understands confounds our western-thinking." Richard leaned into Bear whispering conspiratorially, "Prepare yourself to enter the unknown."

"Hmmm . . ." Bear looked skeptical. "Richard, you've always been a little melodramatic."

Richard looked serious.

"OK, OK . . . I get it," Bear said. "I'm interested." He threw his small duffel bag into the bathroom and disappeared.

After he took a shower and changed his shirt and tried to tame his unruly hair, he entered the living room. They'd set a coffee pot on the table and a plate of sandwiches.

Bear checked his watch. "OK, let's go for an hour, then get some sleep. We will all need our rest." He explained the coincidence of this man in his van on the same freeway south from Seattle, that he'd contacted a friend from the Chicago police force to run a check and that he expected to hear the next morning. "I have no idea what he was doing up north, nor why he was heading back south just as I was . . . but I'm sure all of you in this room understand there are really few coincidences in life. And for this coincidence, based on the call I overheard, I believe there is an explanation. Right now, we just don't know what it is."

Moremi spoke first. "Peter had a graduate student from Seattle."

All eyes turned to her.

"When I found that letter Peter wrote to his father . . ." her voice cracked and she cleared her throat, "I saw a paper he had kept from one of his students. Her name was Alice Gordon. Peter scribbled notes in red pencil all over that paper, which I did not read. But it piqued my curiosity. At the top he wrote in bold "From Seattle." I also remember Peter talking with his assistant in his office at the university on the phone. I believe they may have been talking about this student because Peter seemed to feel pestered. I believe he referred to her as 'that pesky one named Alice.'"

Rebecca asked, "Do you remember what her paper was about?"

"The oil industry in Nigeria during the Abacha regime, a time of extreme corruption when so much of the oil and gas profits were siphoned off into offshore accounts leaving my country an ecological nightmare, which it still is and getting worse."

Richard leaned forward. "Didn't you explain earlier that your husband's father was connected to Abacha? One of his lesser generals?"

"Yes," Moremi agreed. She looked around at all of them. "Peter's parents were very wealthy. They lived their last years in London, which was not unusual for many who profited during Abacha's regime."

Gertrude entered the discussion. "Mr. Whitmore . . . I mean Bear . . . what is your guess about this man on the freeway? And I take it he is out there now prowling around, or parked somewhere nearby?"

Bear smiled at Gertrude for cutting to the chase. "He's out there. I followed him off the freeway, but I didn't see him after that. I also didn't want to alert him that I know of his existence, but he may know I'm here. If I spotted him on the freeway and heard him in the diner, it's quite probable he did the same with me. I would not be surprised if he knows who I am and has also put two and two together." He could see from Gertrude's expression that she understood the imminent danger. He turned the question around and asked Gertrude, "What is your intuition?"

She smiled and turned to Moremi. "My dear, do you think it is possible that this man whom Bear has identified as the man in a black van is the same man who attacked you?"

Moremi was emphatic. "Yes, I do."

"But why," Rebecca jumped in, "would he have gone to Seattle? He was tracking you, Moremi, why would he suddenly have changed his plan and gone up to Seattle? It doesn't make sense."

"No," Richard agreed, "this doesn't make sense right here, right now in the moment. But I bet that when we know more of the pieces to this puzzle a logic will reveal itself."

"Remember my dears," Gertrude added, "you know what Albert Einstein supposedly said: 'Coincidence is God's way of remaining anonymous.'" She watched their puzzled expressions, then explained. "We are skeptical of coincidences unless it's divine intervention."

Moremi agreed, adding, "In my culture it is different but perhaps the same. The Yoruba believe it is our ancestors who determine what happens and there is no escape when the ancestors want retribution. It is like karma, and one cannot escape it." She looked at Gertrude. "In my culture coincidences are accepted as ordinary circumstances."

"And that," Gertrude announced, "is what we must accept as driving what is going on." She leaned over and petted Juno who had arisen from her nap. "So," she addressed Moremi along with the others, "let us combine our instincts and good old American know-how and see what we can figure out."

"OK," Bear said, "so let's start with you, Gertrude. What can we assume about this assassin out there, about his motives and temperament?"

"Well," she speculated, "he may be from Chicago. If he is what I think he is, he kills for money. And that means what he does is not personal. It's just a job. However," she raised her finger to let them know there was more, "not just anyone can do that kind of work. There is a personal side to it."

"Let me guess," Bear added, "Killing for hire is not who he thinks he really is."

Gertrude smiled. "That's right. He may even consider himself very sensitive quite apart from what he does for a living. He hesitated with Moremi just enough so that she could retaliate quickly. Something stopped him and now he will feel weakened and perhaps vulnerable to making mistakes. If this is the same man who went to Seattle, he may have had a reason and that reason would have somehow repaired his equilibrium that was shaken when he failed with Moremi."

"You mean," Richard said, "that maybe he's getting tired, I don't know . . . getting sloppy?"

"Yes," Gertrude agreed.

Moremi looked around. "I agree he hesitated and did not expect my reaction, which crippled him for the moment. But I can tell all of you that without a doubt my mother, my grandmother and my great-grandmother were right there with me giving me the strength of a lioness. He could not have escaped my jaws, nor my kick that temporarily disabled him. My strength was not all my own. In that sense I was temporarily possessed."

"No doubt," Bear agreed. He turned back to Gertrude. "What do you make of his cologne? Moremi smelled it and so did I."

"Your and Moremi's physical description is of a small, but wiry man. Nimble on his feet. He is a little vain. And perhaps," she looked around at all of them, "a bit of a lady's man."

"What do you mean?" Rebecca asked.

"I mean he may split off inside himself two very different characters. One worships beauty and intelligence in women, and the other has contempt if he is aroused by a woman's negative power, and he might kill her out of impulsivity if he feels betrayed. And that could be his Achilles' heel."

Bear added, "You think he's losing it? Psychologically?"

"Yes. I think he may well be unraveling. And that would be because he is conflicted. He is dealing with two forces in opposition. On the one hand, he was amazed by Moremi. On the other hand, she out-played him. That may never have happened to him before. He will both admire and hate her."

Moremi added: "I must re-emphasize that I was not alone when I did that. My mother especially was there with me who told me how to behave if I were ever attacked. She was the one who told me to bite down hard if I was ever attacked. And that is what I mean about how the ancestors wield their power. They know this man's weakness and that is how they will track him to his death. How he will end I do not know. But end he will. And soon."

Bear looked at Moremi. "I get that. But let's help his ending along. In my military culture background, it is never a good idea to under-estimate one's enemy. He's out there and if what Gertrude says is true—and I think it is—he is very motivated to redeem himself, which makes him even more lethal than usual. And I assume Moremi's bite wound on his arm is a constant reminder that a beautiful woman whom he could have admired in fact betrayed him."

Moremi added, "I agree with what each of you has said, but I think we have forgotten to speak of the more important person than that man out there in the van and that is my husband. I do not know where he is nor what he is doing. I spoke with my son earlier this evening and he is having a very good time in the snow with his friends. And he has not heard from his father. Wherever Peter is I am certain he will not be far away from his son."

Bear picked up on her description 'his son.' "Moremi," he asked, "why do you refer to your son as his son?"

"I said that deliberately. To Peter and his family, Ayo is their lineage. He is a first and only son for Peter and an only grandson for Peter's parents. The oldest son even in your American culture holds a high position. If Peter had to choose between me or our son, he would choose Ayo, who will carry on his family name. And on top of that, it is of primary importance that Peter ensure that Ayo knows nothing about what really happened to my parents, his grandparents, whom he was never able to meet."

Bear turned to Gertrude. "Can you speculate and give us a psychological portrait of Peter? What drives him now? How desperate is he? And can we all assume that assassin works for Peter?"

"I will try," Gertrude assented. "Of course, he is much more complicated than our assassin. He is undoubtedly riddled with internal conflicts and carries secrets which must be like time bombs in his psyche."

"Let me just add," Rebecca offered looking at Moremi for agreement, "that although he covered up for his family, I believe Peter genuinely loved Moremi and of course Ayo, but as time went on living here in America he came to realize that his wife did not grow into their new life, but rather grew away from it. He began to realize that she suspected something was wrong, only she didn't know what."

"Yes," Moremi agreed. "And I tried to break off with my mother line and from Mami Wata, the spirit of my mother's lineage, but I could not. I kept an altar to her in our basement, which I assumed Peter was not aware of. But recently I realized that he knew of it." She bowed her head remembering the blood in the sand.

"This is very important information," Gertrude said. "Let me try. Moremi you will tell me where I may be off, if I am." She looked around.

Numi had been sound asleep on her lap and decided to wake up by stretching his back into a shivering hump before re-positioned himself and settled back down, ears twitching.

"Imagine," Gertrude continued stroking his back, "that you grew up with parents who only admired your achievements that reflected well on them, and that anything you cared about that differed from that was frowned upon. Or worse, you are made to feel ashamed for caring about something because that showed weakness. There is no in-between, no allowance for being different from your parents or—God forbid—making mistakes. With very self-centered parents, there is no room for failure. From such parents there are no encouraging words. No supportive reassurance." She looked around. "Who might that person become?"

Moremi leaned forward. "I believe Gertrude's description fits. But I must emphasize, not as an excuse for Peter, but I believe he was born with a good heart. He came to the U.S. early. He remained here. He lived distant from his parents. He tried to make them proud by going along. He thought he could escape what his parents did. He thought he could live a lie. He thought he was not culpable." She looked down, then out the window. "But of course, he was wrong. He lacked the courage that my father had to stand up for what was right. He thought he could remain on the margins of life and escape responsibility. Wherever he is in this moment I am sure he is suffering."

Gertrude agreed.

Richard looked at his watch. "I think we need to talk about our plan for tomorrow."

Gertrude announced, "I have a plan."

HUGO PARKED HIS VAN ON A STREET near some trees in front of what appeared to be a vacant house. It seemed isolated enough that no one would notice him parked there for the night. He opened his sleeping bag in the back over his foam pad and slept.

He had the recurring dream. He was about eight years old and with a bunch of other kids, both boys and girls. He knew in the dream they were all orphans living in an abandoned house. Some of them were scared and crying. Another boy was like Hugo—not crying but acting tough and contemptuous of the others. It was getting dark in the house, and they had no light. The boy produced some matches and started flicking lit matches everywhere. He was laughing and acting like a crazy arsonist. The floor quickly caught fire and the flames licked along the floor and up the walls. Kids were screaming. Hugo scrambled out a small window and ran into the woods as far as he could, holding his hands over his ears to drown out the screams.

He woke up covered in sweat. The dream was always more or less the same. He was with the orphans and there was some sort of catastrophe. He was the only one who escaped. He opened his pack and pulled out a small bottle of brandy and took a few swigs. He lay back down and listened to the trees in the wind. He couldn't shake his unease. The irrational thought played over and over in his head like a mocking voice. *"It's the fire . . . the fire that will purify you!"*

He forced himself to concentrate on the next morning. *I'll find them and when I do, I will unleash my wrath. They will all be dead. And then I will take myself on a vacation to Rio.* He finally fell asleep flying around the dance floor with the Queen of Samba.

CHAPTER TWENTY-SIX

If you are not setting a trap,
then you are probably walking into one.
It is the mark of the master to do both at once.

JEDEDIAH BERRY

AT 1:30 A.M. GERTRUDE LEFT FOR HOME over everyone's protests, assuring them all that at this point in her life, nothing really frightened her.

Using his macho know-how Bear tried his best to dissuade her. "Gertrude, we need you. That man is out there, and we all know he could be lethal. If he spots you that could not only put you in danger, but all of us as well."

"Mr. Whitmore," she addressed him using her age and authority, "he could follow me home and murder me on the spot of course, if he felt so inclined. But I ask you, where would that leave him?"

"No, he won't murder you, he'll force you to tell him where we are."

At that point Gertrude, with a twinkle in her eye, reached into her large shoulder purse and produced her pepper spray.

"That might not do it," Bear argued. "Remember, this guy's a professional."

Gertrude tossed the pepper spray back in her purse, rooted around a little further and produced an antiquated derringer. "My late husband gave me this. It's not loaded, but I assure you it is real."

With that, Bear gave up, and Gertrude disappeared out the door.

The next morning at 7:00 A.M., she returned with bagels and cream cheese. They gathered in Daniel's living room once again quietly looking at each other, waited for Gertrude to reveal her plan when Moremi's cell phone erupted with the familiar marimba tune.

They all froze as she picked it up and stared at the phone she was not used to, but kept in her pocket in case she heard from Ayo.

She looked at all of them. "It's Peter's office. They never call me. And certainly not this early."

"Better pick it up," Bear instructed. "It might be important."

She spoke with someone for several minutes. The others could not fathom what the call was about, but her tone and expression changed from puzzlement to alarm.

They heard Moremi respond to the caller. "He hasn't called in since yesterday," she lied, "but I will let him know the news about Alice Gordon as soon as possible."

She hung up and laid the phone down on the coffee table. She looked up and they all knew at once that she had heard news that not only explained something, but also frightened her.

Numi jumped on her lap as if to provide something for her to hug. The Queens also rose from their floor postures and sniffed the air as if something foreign just entered the room.

"Take your time," Gertrude encouraged.

Moremi nodded. Then she explained. "The parents of a graduate student of Peter's, the Alice Gordon we mentioned last night, left a voice mail message for him yesterday evening. They called from their home in Seattle where Alice was home for Spring break. Peter's assistant Annie picked up the message early this morning on her way into the office and had not been able to reach Peter. She assumed I might have been in touch with him, so she called me."

"Reasonable assumption," Bear concluded.

"Yes, I suppose it is. I have only spoken to Annie a few times over the years because Peter always has his phone on him and keeps his teaching business quite separate and private." Moremi went silent for a moment.

"What are you thinking about that?" Gertrude asked.

"Just that I really would have liked to know more about his work and his students. I always felt it was odd how he kept his work so separate from us. I knew that many professors were different about that. Their students even visited them in their homes." She waited a moment, then explained, "I would have enjoyed having young people around. In my parents' home we had many young visitors."

Rebecca added, "It would seem that although Peter expected you to become more Americanized, he also kept you isolated."

"I must tell you more about this call. Alice Gordon's parents explained in their message that their daughter had been in a serious car accident and that she survived—miraculously—but they wanted her to take a semester off so she could recover while she was doing research on her thesis topic about the Nigerian oil and gas industry under Peter's advisement."

They were all stunned as the room went quiet except for Juno's meticulous gnawing on a rawhide bone.

"Soooo . . ." Gertrude broke the silence, "this may well explain Bear's coincidental meeting on the freeway south from Seattle. Our assassin for some reason left here to go there on business that was even more urgent?"

Richard was lost in thought the whole time as he listened. "I've got it," he announced, commanding all eyes on him. "Peter's student Alice Gordon wrote a paper on the corruption about the oil and gas industry in Nigeria during Abacha regime. That's the paper Moremi found in his file cabinet at home."

They all acted as if this was not exactly earth-shaking news.

"Follow the scent," he commanded. "Who assigned that topic? Her professor, Peter Abosanjo, whom she admires. He keeps her paper and scribbles all over it. What does that tell you?"

Bear picked up the scent. "That whatever Alice Gordon found out through her research may have come too close to home for the professor because it was during that time, I understand from Moremi, that her in-laws benefitted from the profits that were being siphoned out of the country."

Moremi looked troubled. "It is difficult for me to imagine Peter would have taken such a risk to allow one of his students to learn so much that might jeopardize his family name."

Rebecca leaned into Moremi. "I don't know if this helps, Moremi, but think about this for a moment. You married a man who lived with many secrets, the biggest one being what his family did to yours. Sometimes people who feel very guilty have an unconscious desire to be caught."

"Or," Moremi explained, "in the context of my culture and my mother-line, my ancestors are after Peter as we speak." She looked around to make it clear what she was about to tell them reached more deeply into Peter's motivation.

"The mothers have made sure that Peter's end will be of his own undoing. By marrying me Peter was to be reminded each day of what he and his parents had done. There is a popular proverb in my country that says, 'Guilt is like the footprint of a hippopotamus.' As you can imagine, a hippo's footprint is very large and obvious. Peter's guilt will ultimately consume him because he cannot escape its footprint on his memory." She looked at Rebecca. "And you are correct. He wants to be caught. I believe he is very tired and scared. He denies his belief in the power of the ancestors, but the more he denies it the greater his deeply ingrained belief swallows his soul."

Gertrude smiled. "And we thought psychologists had all the answers. I think what we understand about human desires and motivation has been known for so long in our human history that what Freud and others who discovered psychoanalysis offered less than we believed."

"OK," Bear's voice boomed into the room. "I get it. Forces are at work. But my job is to help them along. I'm texting my Seattle friend to see what he's got on this guy who's probably driving around now looking for us."

Just as they settled in to listen to Gertrude's plan, Bear's cellphone rang. He nodded, then hung up. "Ok, here's the scoop. Alice Gordon is a graduate student in economics. Her parents are well-known environmentalists. Serious people with deep roots in Greenpeace. Yesterday morning as Alice was driving down a steep mountain grade from her parents' home her car went over a cliff near the bottom. She should be dead. But she's not. She's banged up and still in the hospital, but she'll be out in a few days. Her parents want her to stay out the next semester and do research from home on her dissertation, which, surprise-surprise," he looked around at all of them, "is on the Nigerian oil and gas industry. Alice's parents contacted the university to ask permission for her to take the semester off. Alice's doctors think she will be physically fine, but they're worried about her emotional recovery. There's some thought that Alice has a bit of Aspergers and her parents are very protective of her. She's also extremely bright."

"Any suspicion of sabotage to her car?" Richard asked.

"Maybe. They're looking at the tire that seemed to be the cause of the accident. When Alice got into her car in the morning, she must not have noticed a leak in her front tire, which was punctured. Looks like a nail did it. But curiously there was no nail. When a tire runs over a nail usually the nail stays in and acts as a plug so that the leak is fairly slow. Well, this leak was done they think by a nail—but there was no nail."

"You mean," Richard offered, "someone could have used a nail to make the puncture, then extracted it to make sure the tire deflated more quickly, but not too quickly. They wanted it to look like a nail but didn't want the nail to act like a cork because it might have deflated too slowly. In short, there was a timing issue. And . . . it's also possible someone knew exactly what they were doing."

Bear nodded. "Something like that."

Gertrude added, "This seems to confirm our suspicions that this man for some reason abruptly stopped tracking Moremi and left for Seattle to kill Ms. Gordon. If he is working for Professor Abosanjo then," she turned to Moremi, "he is following orders from your husband. Does that make any sense to you?"

"What makes sense," Moremi explained, "is that Peter is now running away from himself. He is a man who prides himself with how much he is in control. But he ran out of our home and now I believe he knows that forces out of his control are tracking him. So yes," she turned to Gertrude, "he is doing things quite out of character. Let us just say the hippopotami tracks have caught up with him and he is on the run from himself, which makes him dangerous." She took a moment and then added, "Peter is a good man who made a wrong turn long ago, hoping to escape without paying a price, and now he has found himself in his own trap."

Gertrude indicated she understood, and then began to explain what she had in mind.

Just as they all stood up Bear's phone went off again. They all jumped and then laughed. Juno barked. He took the call and listened. They were all ears.

"Well," he explained, "this gets more and more interesting. That was my Chicago contact who told me that the license plate on the black van is registered to Hugo Jankovic. No current address, but he did grow up in Chicago. Went through the juvenile justice system. Father disappeared when he was three and the mother died mysteriously when he was seven. Hugo was in and out of foster homes until eighteen, when he disappeared. Nothing on him after that."

"So," Gertrude surmised, "I think we are about to learn more of what he's been up to." And to Moremi, "Thanks to you my dear we have his cell phone number, which makes him a phone call away."

They all gathered at the door and prepared to follow Gertrude to her home. They decided that Bear would leave his Explorer parked on the street and ride with Gertrude, assuming that Hugo would find it and wait for him to return. Hopefully, Hugo would wait for quite a while, buying them time.

Only just as they were all walking out Daniel's front door Moremi's cell phone went off again. This time the caller was a stranger.

AN HOUR AFTER WAKING UP AT 7:00 A.M. and driving to find coffee, Hugo returned and spotted the green Explorer tucked under a row of big leaf maples. Last night's dream had jangled his nerves and left him feeling vulnerable. Finding Whitmore's van buoyed his spirits. Although he rejected anything superstitious, he did not reject the impact of dreams. He understood that dreams could control his mood like a hangover, especially the ones with orphans in them. And the ones with fire? They haunted him longer and he didn't know why.

He sipped his coffee and nibbled on a piece of banana nut bread while he watched the Explorer. It was 9:00 A.M. He expected Whitmore to show up soon because it was morning and he assumed by now Whitmore was in contact with the women.

His cell went off. He didn't bother to check the incoming number because it could only be one person—Peter.

"Yeah?" he asked, keeping his eye on the target.

"Hello, Mr. Jankovic, you don't know me," a deep, mature female voice filled his ear like a cloying web, "but I have something of great urgency to discuss with you."

It took him a few long seconds to orient himself. He held the phone away and stared at the number he didn't recognize. He wanted to disconnect, treating it like a sales call, but he knew it wasn't. She knew him and wanted to talk.

"Who are you!?" he shouted, a little louder than he intended. He held the phone out as if it were a dirty object.

On the other end, Gertrude was unruffled. "As I explained, Mr. Jankovic, you don't know me, but I am getting to know you. Let me just say that I have reason to believe that in the last thirty-six hours, you have attempted to take the life of a lovely Nigerian woman, and I think you may have caused a fatal accident involving a young woman in Seattle."

He breathed into the phone imagining his hot breath on her.

"Shall I go on?" she asked.

He stared at the tiny screen as if the words coming out could not possibly be saying what he heard. Like anyone who hears shocking news, his mind ran around, attempting to explain away what he heard, only his mind was blank.

"I shall take your silence to be assent," Gertrude continued, knowing that her calm tone would increase his anxiety. "I also have strong reason to believe you are scheming to kill several more people. And I suspect this may just be the tip of the iceberg regarding your past accomplishments. For example, Ms. Alice Gordon? A young student of Professor Peter Abosanjo. Am I correct in this assumption?"

Stupefied, he held the phone out drilling his stare into it as if he could obliterate her with his blistering gaze. In all the years and through all the vicissitudes in his line of work he had never encountered anything so completely out of nowhere. Her voice embodied a righteous calm that cut through him. The sound resonated all the authority he was forced to tolerate while growing up and as an adult all the authority he wanted to kill over and over to expunge it from his memory.

It was his dreams that brought back his memories. Irrationally, he hoped if he could kill the voices of authority, the dreams would stop.

"Who are you?" he asked.

"Actually," she responded cheerfully, as if this were just a friendly getting to know you moment, "I am someone who would like to help you."

"Help meee!?" he shrieked. If he hadn't lost his equilibrium before, he did now.

"Yes," Gertrude confirmed. "I would like to help you. I believe you are in a situation that may have gone out of control. Now if you think you can calm yourself down, I will be happy to explain. Do you think you can do that, Mr. Jankovic?"

He was even more outraged by her condescending tone, but he needed to know who the hell she was and how she had gotten his number and what deadly little game she was playing. Usually, his mind assembled the picture quickly. He could organize the cast of characters he was dealing with, but this high and mighty old woman did not fit. He looked at the number. No name. His mind was still blank and that never happened.

Gertrude took his silence to mean that he was still listening. She knew he would be trying to figure out who she was and whether he had to take her seriously. She went on. "First of all, I believe you are unaware of how precarious your current situation is. Attempted murder, murder, and intention to commit murder are serious crimes." She waited to let that settle in.

"I don't know what you're talking about." The moment he voiced his denial he regretted it. He had developed rules for himself, and Rule Number One was: *Deny nothing. Say nothing. Proof was like a bad smell. Hard to recognize exactly where it came from and once it started to evaporate . . . well everyone asks, what was that? And then they forget because it's gone.* But paying too much attention might cause it to linger and that wasn't good.

When he felt trapped, he liked to imagine he could make himself invisible—*I can disappear right now into a shadow world and vanish forever out of sight, out of mind.* But then again in this moment another, more immediate and pragmatic thought occurred—*I need the money.*

Peter didn't pay until a job was done. Hugo had money stashed away, but not enough to last. He had in mind moving to Brazil. He fit in there. He needed more money for that.

Her voice made him want to kill something, but her cavalier tone felt like tentacles on his brain, constraining him. When he finally responded, he heard his own voice whining, which he detested.

"Lady," he screeched, "I don't know who you are or who you think you are, but you are messing around with things you know nothing about!" He scrambled for words that would cut and slice her, but all it did was set her up for more.

"Perhaps you are correct, Mr. Jankovic, that I don't know what I'm talking about. However, your irritation tells me otherwise."

"Lady, shut your mouth!" Now he'd lost it but he hadn't slept well and this job had pushed him to the edge. And here he knew that he had just broken Rule Number Two, which was *Never (under any circumstances) Lose Your Temper because then you screw up and start doing damage control, which was what this case had become. And then there was Rule Number Three: Never blame.*

But here he now was –falling into an abyss, his rules tumbling down after him.

He shouted, "I don't know who the fuck you fucking think you are, but clearly you are a psychopathic nut job because to speak to me this way tells me you have no idea what you are dealing with!" His words thudded after her as he twisted around in his seat squeezing the phone, and accidentally disconnecting her. "Do you hear me?" he shook it as if he had both hands on her neck. But there was only silence.

He stared at the dead screen, frozen. How could he have done this? It had all gone disastrously wrong. He wasn't finished with her. He shook the phone, blaming it. He wanted to wring someone's neck and almost tossed it but managed to control himself. He saw into his own rage like wildfire—red, orange, and black. His eyes started blinking like shutters to pull him back from the flames.

He had no idea what to do. He tried to calm himself and reached for his latte. As he drank his mind raced. *What kind of fucking old crow thinks she can push me around? Lady, you have no idea what I'm capable of. I could teach you a thing or two.* As he wondered what that could be he headed straight into blankness. No more fire fueling him. Just blank nothing. A dead end with nowhere to go.

He yanked open the van door and spilled out onto the weedy patch of ground next to a crumbling sidewalk. He lunged over to one of the maples and slammed his foot into it. The pain shot up his leg into his groin, which calmed him. He leaned over to catch his breath, then limped back to the van and climbed back into the driver's seat. He leaned his head back and wallowed in the pain.

After a minute he picked up the phone.

GERTRUDE LOOKED AT THE DEAD PHONE on her desk. "The trap has been set," she announced to Bear and Richard who stood next to her. "When he calls, we'll put him on the speakerphone."

"Ok," Bear agreed. "I think the longer the better. You got to him, Gertrude. So now, hopefully he will calm down enough to fully understand how trapped he really is. Maybe he'll be ready to deal."

"Where are the Queens?" Gertrude asked.

Richard responded. "They're out on your back deck. They're fine. They may not know their role yet, but don't worry, they'll do what you want," he assured her.

"Of course," Gertrude agreed, "I wanted to make sure they are familiar with my house. They haven't been here before."

"They know you and it's you they will guard," Richard assured her.

They sat in Gertrude's office. She was behind her desk while Richard and Bear retired to her couch to wait, each grappling with their own thoughts. At first their silence was welcome and calm, a time out from yesterday's fast pace, but as the minutes ticked by, they all became anxious. What if he didn't call back? What then? And now with the latest news just before they left Daniel's house, they all knew the outcome for all of this was anything but predictable.

Bear leaned back with his arms spread out along the couch while Richard leaned forward to study the book titles along Gertrude's shelf.

Then her landline rang.

Richard bounced up and over to stand behind Gertrude.

She smiled and nodded. On the third ring she picked up and Richard hit the conference button as if turning the page for a pianist.

"Well, hello again, Mr. Jankovic," she chimed. "Have you calmed down?"

"Shut up! Just shut the fuck up!"

"Well, okay." Her tone was calm and patient. "However, if I shut the fuck up as you suggest we will hardly be able to have a conversation and it is unlikely you will learn what it is you want to know. Wouldn't you agree?"

He was still beside himself. There are times when one person can control all the levers that play with another, so they become the cat hunting the triggered psyche's mice. Gertrude did not have the advantage of face to face, but she did know how to use her voice to play all the sensitive notes. She assumed not only that he had an aversion to her disdainful tone but also that it forced him into a defensive posture from which he could not escape. If Hugo could have let go of his fear of losing power he might have gained ground.

But now she no longer wanted to irritate him. She wanted to draw him in.

He imagined being in the room with her. He would hold the blade up to her neck while he fondled her cheek, watching her terrified eyes. He wouldn't kill her. He would humiliate her. He imagined she had led a rich, spoiled life. Her voice was full of entitlement. He knew it well. She would plead with her eyes. He could make her crawl on the floor. He would rip that voice right out of her.

"I'll come straight to the point, Mr. Jankovic. I have a proposal that I hope you will consider. However, to discuss this with you I would like to meet with you in person. I suggest we meet at my home. Would that be amenable to you?"

While he was thrown off balance once before and thought he had regained a foothold, she threw this in. He couldn't imagine what she had up her sleeve. Once again, his mind went blank, and he was free-falling.

What saved him was *Rule Number One. Deny Nothing, Say Nothing.* He let the silence settle on her.

After ten seconds he spoke. "I'll get back to you." And this time he hung up on purpose. *Then it all seemed to tumble into place. They were all together now. Moremi, her shrink, the shrink's boyfriend, Whitmore, the boyfriend's friend, those silly red dogs and last but not least,* he looked at his phone, *that old lady who thinks she's running the show now. So, where are you all? Nearby, I'm sure. At the old lady's house? Well, they think they'll trap me there, but maybe I'll just consider it the other way around—I've got them trapped.*

He decided to call Peter and check in. He wouldn't tell him about this latest call, or about anything else. But he thought perhaps Peter by now knew something that he didn't. He pressed the blue circle and heard it ring. No answer. He left a short to-the-point message: "Call me." He waited. He looked at the clock. It was 9:30 A.M. *What's he doing?* He assumed Peter would call right back so he waited. He called again at 9:45, then again at 10:00 A.M..

At 10:10 he called Gertrude. She answered on the first ring. "Yes?"

"Give me your address."

CHAPTER TWENTY-SEVEN

There are so many traps.
There are so many opportunities.
Life is a river and we take our boat and we go down it.

FREDERICK LENZ

HE CRUISED SLOWLY past 27 Juniper Way without stopping. He circled around the block, not caring if they saw him. In fact, he hoped they did. He hoped they would wonder what he was doing driving around peering out, sniffing the air like a hunter.

He assumed they would all be there at her house. Killing Moremi was no longer a simple deal. *She'll be with others and whoever that old lady is somehow she thinks she knows all about me. All I can do is play along.* He wanted to see it clear. He knew it wasn't.

Sometimes he wished he had a gun, but he didn't like them. They weren't really sporting. Just as he preferred fly-fishing to hunting with guns, he preferred the art and dance of kung fu karate to stupid brute force. What he had done to Ms. Run for Your Life was not brute force. In fact, it was art. Not many could kill with just a quick twist of the neck.

He remembered his teacher Bruce in LA. Bruce taught actors and told him he had the gift. "You're graceful, not like those buffed-out muscle guys." It was then he started to feel proud of his smaller size, because it made him quick and agile.

He would not worry about Whitmore either. He'd seen him at the gas station. He would be slow because he was hulky and lumbering. *I am a cat. It's never good to look me in the eye like Ms. Run for Your Life had done. If you'd played the helpless, distraught female you'd still be jogging around town with cash in your pocket to cover that little fender bender instead of providing food for the fishies.* The thought consoled him.

Finally, he pulled over a block away and parked. Out of habit he grabbed his binoculars and peered at her house. It was an older home built into the hillside several stories high surrounded by well-kept hedges, plants, and trees. A large bay window faced out and down, which he assumed had a view of the San Francisco Bay. She had lived there for many years. *She has money. Maybe enough to pay me to go away?* He wondered how he might manage that. *How much cash could make me go away?*

This idea lifted his spirits even more. He didn't recognize that he had just entered the arena of wishing rather than controlling.

He climbed out of the van. As he walked up Juniper Way toward her house he stopped under an elm and listened, looked around to get his bearings. Like most high-end neighborhoods it was quiet except for the sound of a leaf blower a few blocks away. He stopped on the sidewalk in front of her house, facing up, legs apart with his hands on his hips. He was a big cat, a panther, about to move into view.

He hopped up the cement steps, then along the stone path across the lawn and then to Gertrude's wide verandah. He rang the doorbell—a melodious chime. Dead silence. It took a full minute before he heard soft footsteps approach. The door opened and he peered through the screen at an older woman he could tell had once been beautiful and still was, even in old age.

Gertrude was dressed for the occasion. She wore a flowing brown skirt with a muted periwinkle blue silk blouse and a soft paisley scarf around her neck tossed over her shoulder.

"Good morning, Mr. Jankovic. Won't you please come in?"

She slowly nudged the screen door toward him. He grabbed it, swung it open wider than he needed and planted himself inside her long hallway. The Tibetan carpet was soft under his sneakers and the interior smelled like wood. The lemon polish mixed with the scent of fresh flowers calmed him despite his need to remain hyped up and scary.

Unhinged by the serenity of her interior he managed to growl, "I'm here. What do you want?"

"Follow me, please." Gertrude turned her back on him and glided down the hall, presuming he would follow.

For a fleeting second, he considered taking her out right then and there with no thought of the consequences. But the urge failed. He followed her as she led him through the large, airy living room. He looked up into the peaked ceiling held with a muscular cedar beam that might have taken a whole tree. At the front end of the room, he looked out the window he had just seen from the other side and saw redwoods and other evergreens that framed the bay in the distance. The furniture was over-stuffed and pillowy, inviting comfort and friendship. A huge oil painting over the mantel depicted a large female figure that seemed like something out of a fairy tale draped in red hues crossing into a green-gray mist. He had never been in such a beautiful room. He felt out of place, and his anger quickly returned.

She paused at the arched doorway leading from the living room into a darker interior and beckoned him to follow. This was the dining area with a large table that opened into an expansive, bright kitchen. She led him to a back door overlooking more manicured private gardens. A four-foot stone Quan Yin stood in repose on the deck near the steps down to a grassy area. Now he felt conflicted. He wanted to sit down and look up into her while at the same time he wanted to smash her head off.

Gertrude waved him toward one of her green rattan chairs set around a low, glass-topped iron table.

He obeyed and sat down hoping she would get to the point as soon as possible. He was curious what she had to offer, but was fully prepared to pounce if she made the slightest move to cross him. But were the others close? He had walked into ambushes in the past. This just didn't strike him as being one of those times.

A large glass pitcher and glasses were on the table. More than two glasses. "May I offer you some lemonade Mr. Jankovic? It's made from those lemons over there." She pointed out toward the back of the garden toward her large lemon tree.

He sensed a slight disdain back in her tone, which put him on higher alert than before. He began to feel manipulated.

He shrugged, and she poured two tall, thin glasses. She sipped hers and set it down on the table. He started drinking his, intending to set it down as well but found himself very thirsty. It was the most delicious lemonade he had ever had. He put his glass down half drained.

"OK," he said, hoping to communicate that he was fed up with the feigned tea party atmosphere. He looked around and locked his eyes on her. "I get that you live in a big, fancy house and your husband probably cheated a lot of people to make his money, so you're rich." Wrong path and he knew it.

She wore a bemused expression that he wanted to swipe off her face.

He pulled himself back invoking *Rule Number Two—Never (under any circumstances) Lose Your Temper.* He recognized that she conducted herself as if she knew exactly how to play him. *Well, two can play at this game. She expects me to react to throw me off my game. But I am the game!*

"Get to the point!" he demanded.

"All right. I will get to the point."

He watched her, wondering if now that she supposedly was getting to the point, she had any real point to make.

"You have been hired by Professor Peter Abosango to kill several people. One, his wife, Moremi Abosanjo. And two, Ms. Alice Gordon, one of his graduate students."

He stared back at her. Does she know about the collateral damage, '*Ms. Run-For-Your-Life?*'

"You did not succeed," she went on using an even, neutral tone that just stated the facts, "in either of these enterprises. Both are alive and well. Very soon knowledge of what almost happened to them will be known by many people, not the least of which are the authorities."

"Both are alive and well." Before, she had referred to Alice Gordon's murder. What could she be talking about? Rule Number One: Deny Nothing, Say Nothing. But his mind raced. *Alice sailed over that cliff in that little red tin box. No one could have survived.*

He hunched forward and started to stand up to leave. He wanted her to know what he thought of her information.

She ignored him and went on. "I assume you and I could have a lengthy discussion about why you failed to accomplish what you were paid to do. I'm referring to the possibility that you are suffering from enough depression that you are no longer able to kill on demand. I suspect you might kill out of rage, but no longer just for business."

He sank back down. Her calm, condescending authority enraged him while also rendering him momentarily impotent. Then his impulse to flee subsided. Strangely, her words soothed him because they happened to be true. *I am tired. It's not the same. I did kill 'Ms. Run for Your Life' out of rage. If she hadn't said, "I don't give a shit about you." I would never—*

He shrugged. "You may think you know what you're talking about, but you don't know anything about me."

"Perhaps," she agreed, "but I know about being an assassin for hire."

This annoyed him but didn't make him furious because really, what could she possibly know?

"Let me explain a little further," she went on. "You of course remember Mr. Bernie Madoff and his securities fraud that went on for so long without being discovered?" She didn't wait for him to agree. "He managed to cheat a large group of very intelligent people out of billions of dollars with no one the wiser . . . well, until he was finally caught."

I have no idea where she's going with this. What's she talking about? I've never cheated anyone out of their money. There were times when he wondered about that himself. That he had chosen a very dangerous, but not so lucrative business. *I do believe I've earned every cent of my measly pay.* And he thought as he stared back at her, *your friend Mr. Abosanjo is a cheap bastard!*

"What's your point? How does this make you an expert on me or anything else?"

"Just this. I think in the end Mr. Madoff got very tired and yearned to be caught. He knew he should have been caught long before he was. I believe he simply wore out, and if someone had offered him a way out before he was caught, he would have taken it."

Suddenly, he felt very tired. Her words were drugging him into a state of perplexity, forcing him to wonder about everything. *I should kill you. I can't think.*

"Go on."

"I'm going to offer you a way out."

"Get to the point."

"If you leave here immediately you will be escorted to the airport. You will be given a one-way ticket to Costa Rica, or somewhere else if you choose. This ticket will be purchased for you, and you will board a plane to that country. When you arrive, you will have an account set up for you in your name, or some other name of your choosing, with some cash in it. Once it is established that you are safely there, Mr. Whitmore will put cash in that account for the amount Mr. Abosanjo would have paid you for your work."

Hugo's mouth fell open and he gaped at her while his eyes narrowed into slits sizing up this insane old woman who took him for a fool. A rattlesnake coiling, he got ready to strike as his gaze jerked back and forth taking in the landscape. Again, it wasn't what she said but her dismissive tone. *Treating me like a child, as if I don't understand shit. As if I should just trust her. Rather than get rid of her, which I could do. But not yet.*

As his body tensed with adrenaline, he heard a strange commotion off to the side. He swiveled to investigate as Juno and Dido burst out of nowhere onto the deck. Both lunged and crouched near Hugo's chair, baring their fangs, revealing black gums and blue tongues in a chorus of menacing growls.

"What the . . . !" He yelled.

Juno jutted her lioness head, snarling, punctuated with vicious, staccato barks as if ordering him to shut up.

"Jesus . . . for Christ's sake, call off your dogs!"

"If you remain there and don't make any sudden movements the dogs will be fine," she assured him. "As you can see, they are well trained. However, if they think you are in any way a danger to me, they will surely rip you to pieces. Best to just sit still and listen. Chows are very loving and loyal. The breed is originally a native of Mongolia and Tibet."

He stared at her dumbfounded as she spoke calmly, as if she were giving a lecture on the breed rather than using the dogs as lethal weapons.

She finished with her final documentary. "They were much adored creatures and, according to some historians of the breed, Genghis Khan kept a kennel housing five thousand Chow Chows which he took with him into battle."

At that moment Bear and Richard appeared out of nowhere. He recognized Bear and figured that Richard was the guy who had transported the dogs instead of a couple of old ladies. Recalling that little blundered episode agitated him. He squirmed in his seat while eyeing the dogs.

"So," he concluded at Gertrude, "you had this planned all along."

"Of course. I'm sure you knew I would not be meeting with you alone."

What took him totally by surprise was the Chows. He hated dogs. Once he had been attacked by a Pitbull that left scars on his right leg. For Hugo all dogs were the same. And these two sitting at her feet were like something from another world—fuzzy and menacing. *If I had a gun, I would shoot them.*

"Let me introduce you, Mr. Jankovic."

"No need," he said petulantly under his breath.

"Shall I continue?"

He did not respond. His muscles ached. Fatigue enveloped him like a blanket. Listen and wait was all he could do.

Bear and Richard were quiet sentinels behind her. She was a queen with her knights and vicious dogs.

The whole scene was completely preposterous. He had never felt more like a fish out of water.

"You will remain out of the country for the rest of your life. Mr. Whitmore here," she waved her hand back at Bear, "will arrange it so that every immigration agency and homeland security office has your photograph on file."

"You can't do that."

"Well, if you accept this offer, which we all," she nodded at Bear and Richard, "consider to be very fair, of course we can't prevent you from trying to return incognito. I'm sure you are an accomplished imposter. However, consider the consequences if you are caught. You will be on a terrorist alert list and could end up in some no man's land like Guantanamo awaiting a trial that never happens."

"I'm no terrorist. Besides you have no proof of anything about me."

"This is true," she sighed. "However, I'm afraid Mr. Jankovic we now live in a time when proof is, shall we say . . . an ambiguous proposition. Why, I heard just the other day an old lady not unlike myself was detained by airport security for forty-eight hours because somehow, quite mistakenly, she had wound up on some agency's watch list."

He didn't know what to make of Gertrude. *She's bluffing, shooting from the hip, just making stuff up in the moment.* On the other hand, she threw out information with such self-confidence he couldn't be sure. Either way he felt begrudging respect. He decided to play along since there was not much else he could do right now.

"What happened to the old lady?" He was curious.

"Oh, she's fine now. It was all a colossal misunderstanding. However, this misunderstanding cost her about $20,000 by the time her lawyers were able to sort things out and convince the rather confused—and might I add not terribly astute—airport security that she was not a terrorist. You see, Mr. Jankovic, we live in strange times, rather hysterical really, but there we all are." She lifted her palms and shrugged. "We must all do the best we can under the circumstances that now surround us."

He couldn't stand it any longer. "You're lying. You just made that up."

"How is that Mr. Jankovic? How can you be so sure?"

"They wouldn't keep some rich old lady like you for forty-eight hours. On what charge?"

"Oh, didn't I mention? She had just returned from a safari in Kenya and in her carry-on, they found a small bag of white powder. It seems that it wasn't cocaine, but a particularly well-known poison that comes from Africa. It's made from the gall bladder of crocodiles and has a reputation all over the continent for being quite powerful. It seems that the gall bladder of the dead crocodile is removed, then the gall is dried and ground in a little mortar or on a stone. The symptoms are said to be great pain in the stomach, swelling and discoloration of the tongue, loss of speech and finally—death."

He stared in disbelief.

Gertrude went on as if she were telling a simple story. "Of course, this dear lady had no idea how it got there nor who might have put it in her luggage. But I'm sure you know how it is, Mr. Jankovic, when the truth becomes a he-said, she-said proposition, well then the truth becomes like a ball in the air. Who knows in whose court it will land?" She shrugged. "Let's be realistic, the ball usually lands where there is the most money. I'm sure you would not disagree?"

He believed every word was pure bullshit, entirely made up on the spot. And yet, he felt like she had him. He squirmed.

The dogs emitted a low growl warning him to stay still.

"You see—I repeat—these are precarious times we live in now. The truth doesn't really seem to matter very much anymore. Most things are simply a matter of perspective and, as I'm sure you know very well, perspective is an annoyingly subjective phenomenon."

"I don't know what you're talking about," he snarled.

The Queens snarled back like a Greek chorus.

Hugo felt like they were all in an altered reality play and they each knew their lines, but nothing was as it should be.

"Yes, you do," she asserted. "You see the world through a lens of grief and despair, Mr. Jankovic. You didn't ask to be born to parents who would abandon you and leave you to fend for yourself to grow up in the juvenile justice system." She watched his eyes shift back and forth, trapped in his chair by the Queens, trapped inside himself with her words clanging around him like a prison door—shutting.

"And now," she went on, "you think you are getting even with the world. Well, that's your perspective. You annihilate threat. You kill because the world is a dangerous place—and I give you that. Minimizing your pain and loss is about all you can do, isn't it?"

He glared at her. "You don't know shit about me. You're a raving psycho, lady!" He smirked. "With a twisted imagination. You think I'm whacked! You're whacked! You think you can see me, don't you? There is no way you can understand me."

"I think you've just made my point."

He was feeling more defeated than he could admit. "I'm getting tired of this. What if I don't accept your deal?"

"Oh, I'm glad you mentioned that" she chirped. "If you don't accept the offer, then Mr. Whitmore will call the police and you will be arrested on charges of attempted murder. Professor Abosanjo is ready to testify against you to save himself," she lied. "In fact, we can call him if you'd like right now, and you can speak with him directly for confirmation. I believe he is waiting for our call."

She watched him consider this. It was a calculated risk. She remained calm looking into his shifting eyes—an experienced gambler in the realm of the human psyche.

He had no intention of calling Peter. She could be bluffing, but he didn't want to take the chance. Suddenly everything became clear to him. He needed to get out of this insane hall of mirrors. *Forget the money. Get out now while you can,* he told himself. *This old woman is casting spells. I'm dealing with a witch. If Peter betrayed me, it would be easy to solve that. I'd kill him. And one thing I know for certain, I'd would return and kill this Queen Witch. But not now. I need to escape somewhere I can think and rest.*

Suddenly inspired, he looked at them and said, "I need to use your bathroom." It was a simple ruse, and the beauty was that everyone fell for it.

"Of course," Gertrude nodded. "Mr. Whitmore, would you kindly escort Mr. Jankovic to the bathroom off the kitchen."

Bear approached and stood beside Hugo.

"Keep those vicious dogs away from me," he warned, glaring down at Dido.

Bear took Hugo's arm to help him up. Hugo stood and wrenched his arm back.

"Follow me," Bear said.

The dogs also followed.

Gertrude remained seated and took another sip of lemonade.

Richard pulled up another chair and sat down next to her, composed.

Neither said a word.

He stepped into the bathroom and shut the door. It was small with a toilet and sink. The blue rug was soft under his feet. The room smelled of lavender. He looked at himself in the mirror as he calculated whether the window was big enough for him to escape. He decided it was. He flushed the toilet and turned on the faucet. The toilet was old and took time to shut off, giving him enough time to raise the window. He couldn't believe how easily it slid open. He peered out and down. The ground was about eight feet below shaded by a Japanese Maple. He moved quickly slithering like mouse bones through the portal, landing on his feet. He sprinted toward his van.

Bear waited a few minutes before he opened the door to see if Hugo was gone.

The Queens pushed in sniffing around. They too became satisfied that he had fled.

He and the Queens returned to Gertrude and Richard. "Well, Gertrude," Bear said, "you called that right."

"It wasn't so difficult to predict. We're not his worst enemy now. Let's give him time. Soon enough he'll learn about Professor Abosanjo. And then I hope he'll be back."

"Or gone," Richard added.

"Yes," Gertrude agreed. "There is no real way to predict what he will do now. He might try to just disappear. I think he wants the money, but that's not what drives him. That could still be a problem. So, we shall see." She added, "Now we better find out what's really happened to Professor Abosanjo."

CHAPTER TWENTY-EIGHT

Fear the reckoning of those you have wronged.

NORSE PROVERB

EARLIER THAT MORNING, MOREMI'S CELL RANG as they got ready to leave Daniel's house. The area code was from the north, where Ayo was skiing.

"Hello," she rasped, clearing her throat.

"Mrs. Abosanjo?" a female inquired and without waiting for Moremi's answer she went on. "I'm calling from the Placer County Hospital."

"Oh my God," Moremi choked, clutching her throat.

They all moved closer.

"Has something happened to my son? Why are you calling?" She clapped her hand over her mouth to prevent what was coming.

The voice responded by asking someone in the background, "Is her son here too?"

Moremi demanded, "Tell me . . . is my son ok?"

"Ah . . ." the voice hesitated, "No ma'am, it's not your son. It's your husband. Are you Mrs. Peter Abosanjo?"

Moremi mouthed to the others, "It's about Peter."

They pressed in.

Gathering herself she said, "Yes. What's this about?"

"Okay," the voice continued. "I'm calling to let you know that we admitted your husband to this hospital about an hour ago. He will be undergoing an emergency appendectomy. He's going into the operating room as we speak because there was no time. He waited far too long before coming in. The appendix has ruptured and it's difficult to estimate the internal damage at this point. We called his work and got your number."

She stepped backward to distance herself from this information as Bear guided her to a chair while the voice moved into caretaking mode.

"I realize this must be a terrible shock Mrs. Abosanjo. Do you have anyone there who might assist you to get here? We have no idea how the surgery will go. He must have been in a great deal of pain. By the time he called the ambulance from the motel he was barely conscious."

"Motel? Where was that?"

"Ah . . ." the voice hesitated, "I'm not sure."

Moremi quickly shot back, "Never mind," then added, "I'll be there."

They calculated the driving time about two hours and decided Rebecca would drive with Moremi to the hospital. Richard, Bear and The Queens would go to Gertrude's and stick to the plan.

Within twenty minutes Rebecca and Moremi were in Daniel's car, hoping that if Hugo were watching he would not recognize it or them. Rebecca had grabbed one of Daniel's ski caps from his hallway coat rack and put on her dark glasses. Moremi lay down in the back seat until they were on the freeway. After stopping for coffee on the way, she moved up front to the passenger seat. They drove mostly in silence, each lost in her thoughts.

Rebecca hated hospitals. No matter how much carpet, art and Muzak to cover the stench of physical trauma, they were to be avoided at all costs. She admired the nurses who could be cheerful while attending the excretions of human distress. Her mother had died in a hospital. The aneurism that came out of nowhere struck like a bullet to her brain. She and her father drove to the hospital while all he told her when he met her at the airport was, "This was very sudden." When they arrived, her mother was dead.

Moremi was locked inside herself thinking this might be it, his ending. She didn't want him dead. Not before she could get to him alive. Alive he would suffer, but dead? She wasn't sure. She believed what her parents believed, that there was an afterlife where their souls would meet. For Peter's soul she had no thought beyond his death. She needed to meet him here, now—close to death. She was certain that his emergency appendicitis was the work of her mother-line intended to punish him and she was part of it.

Nearing the hospital, she imagined herself standing over him and his knowing she would survive him with all his family secrets. She wanted him to die realizing she held the power. Rage lapped at her, swelling up like a tsunami. Only she couldn't discern whether it was coming at her—or him.

They entered the hospital lobby and looked around. The warm stale air smelled antiseptic mingled with flowers like perfume and a faint whiff of cafeteria food. The man behind the information desk, calm amid the distress around him, looked up. He sent them to a bank of elevators that would take them to surgery on the third floor where they were directed to a small waiting room and informed, "The doctor will be with you shortly."

Rebecca went out to call Richard who would call the parents taking care of Ayo and arrange for him to come to the hospital. She returned and let Moremi know she had left a message. "They're at Gertrude's and are not answering their phones, but Richard will make sure the message is delivered so that arrangements can be made for Ayo to see his father."

Moremi accepted this, and they waited.

After an hour a young doctor with raccoon circles under his eyes quietly entered and introduced himself. He was not the surgeon but the on-call assisting intern. "Dr. Johnson had to leave fifteen minutes ago in a helicopter. He was needed for another emergency surgery in another county. A ski accident."

Moremi and Rebecca both looked at him and said nothing.

Perplexed by their silence, he cocked his head and went on. "Your husband is stabilized for the moment. He's still in intensive care and should be fully conscious in an hour or so. He's being given heavy doses of antibiotics to fight the systemic infection. It's impossible to predict how well he will respond, but we're hopeful." His encouraging smile looked silly.

Moremi was deadpan. "Thank you. I'd appreciate it if someone would let me know when I can see him."

"Of course." He turned to leave, and hesitated.

Rebecca thought that maybe Moremi's immobile expression unsettled him. *He'd expected hysteria.*

He turned and started to say something that sounded like "I'm sorry," then vanished.

After forty more minutes, another messenger arrived—an older, more experienced looking doctor clad in green who did not mince words. "Mrs. Abosanjo, your husband is not responding as well to the antibiotics as we hoped. But he's awake and understands you are here. Follow me."

Moremi stood up and followed him down a long hallway through several heavy doors, then into a labyrinth of recovery rooms until they reached Peter's. She peered in and saw him on the raised bed. His eyes were closed. She stood still inside the room and watched his chest raise and lower with each breath. He was surrounded by a clutter of tubes, monitoring instruments and trays on wheels.

The doctor approached Peter and leaned into whisper "Your wife's here," as he kept his eye on Moremi.

She moved a few feet closer and stopped. His handsome face was gaunt like an old warrior's. For a few seconds she froze losing all thought or sense of time.

After the doctor left, she felt chilled even though it was hot in the room. She moved closer until she stood over him. His eyes were closed but she felt he was aware of her. She studied the drain coming out from under the white sheet, the intravenous line pumping antibiotics into his bloodstream, the nasal tube for his oxygen. She crossed her arms as if to hold herself back from ripping it all out.

Forty-eight hours ago, he'd sat by her bed all night watching her sleep. Now she watched him. *Is he afraid of me? He knows I'm here.*

After a few minutes his eyes blinked and opened. He didn't look at her, but he may have whispered, "I'm sorry." Then his eyes closed.

She waited a long time before she moved in closer and leaned her lips down to his ear and whispered, "Alice Gordon is alive."

She straightened up, letting that sink in. She didn't tell him to give him relief, but to let him know the student he feared was still living. And, pointed in the right direction, Alice could expose his parents' corrupt dealings. But that wasn't the worst of it.

She knew that he would dread death because he knew the afterlife was only available to those connected to their ancestors. His family's corruption put his soul in jeopardy. If he died disconnected from his family ancestors his soul would fade into nothing, lost to the memory of his descendants. He had failed to protect his parents. He had denied the old ways. There could be no redemption now. At least none that she could imagine.

She watched for the slightest gesture that he heard her. He lay so still she wondered if he'd stopped breathing. She moved closer again ready to repeat herself when his eyes flipped open, startling her. She stepped back.

He spoke more clearly. "I'm dying. Did you do this to me?

She continued to watch him; her brow furrowed. *He blames me*. She leaned in and hissed, "I did nothing to you. You brought all of this onto yourself!"

He rallied. "You said the Mothers were after me. Didn't you have something to do with that?"

She knew what he wanted. She weighed the words focusing on her mother and Buchi to invoke inspiration.

It took a few minutes before she heard Mami whisper in her ear. The words were garbled. As the sense of it came to her, she spoke as a mouthpiece for an echo of voices. "You could have chosen to walk the path of our ancestors. Your life could have been about bravery and the moral courage to speak the truth no matter what the consequences. But you fell into the colonial-incited greed that poisoned so many of our people and destroyed your family. I wasn't there when you started down that path long ago. Our marriage shielded you from facing the truth. You used me." Then she dug in the knife. "And you used your son."

He choked and looked at her. "Why don't you just kill me?"

"Because" she moved in closer, "that's what you want." Her eyes moved around the room, then back to him. "Physical pain is one thing, but knowing that you lived your life like a coward, turning away from your own people . . .I can't imagine that pain. And you will never know whether I tell our son." With that she turned and walked to the door.

"Wait!" his voice croaked.

She turned.

"You won't do that."

"I will not spare you, Peter. Of that you can be certain."

"Can I see my son?

"Yes, he'll be here soon."

As she walked back down the linoleum hallway pushing through the exit doors, she thought she might collapse. No single thought offered a way out as her mind raced.

An old woman shuffled toward her pushing her intravenous drip. When she reached Moremi passing her, she looked up and said something.

Moremi forced a smile and walked on trying to think what the old woman had said. She went through more doors and down another hallway, then stopped in her tracks. She was sure the woman said, "Don't worry. It will all be over soon dear."

Rebecca looked up when Moremi returned and sat down. "How is he?"

"I think not good."

"Will he live?"

Moremi thought about what to say. "He might live, but I can't imagine Peter having to face what has happened. He's spent his life denying the truth. Now that he can't do that any longer, I don't know how he could survive."

AFTER MOREMI LEFT THE ROOM Peter was infused with something he'd never felt in his whole life: complete relief. Alice was not dead. He wasn't yearning to feel redeemed or innocent. He knew all his scheming and covering for his parents had come to nothing—which was the emptiness that had grown inside him. Knowing he had not killed Alice filled him with temporary relief, but Moremi's survival still had not fully registered. He recognized she had always scared him. That false snake in the basement had power. As he lay helpless, remembering her standing over him, hearing her whispers, he knew she was a living snake. *Was that really her? Now? Whispering to me?*

She would be strong and righteous. That was her nature. He knew she would do the right thing. *Ayo would be taken care of.*

A plan began to form that gave him hope. As he fell into a deep sleep, he resolved to heal enough so he could carry it out.

In the dream his father came toward him. Peter had a knife. He held it way back and hurled his arm in an arc shooting the knife square into his father's forehead.

His mother crawled out of the shadows and crumpled down over the father wailing, "What have you done?"

Peter replied blankly. "I've ended it."

SOME HOURS LATER Moremi led Ayo into his father's hospital room. She stayed near the door as Ayo approached.

Peter's eyes were closed.

"Dad?"

His eyes opened and he saw his son.

"Dad, are you gonna' be okay?"

He struggled to speak.

She backed out of the room and returned to Rebecca, who had learned about Hugo's escape. Moremi listened, but said nothing.

Rebecca concluded, "They don't know where he went. Gertrude

thinks he will be back, but she isn't sure. What she is sure about is that now it will all hatch out quickly. I'm not so sure."

They sat down in silence.

Soon, the nurse escorted Ayo back.

Moremi put her arm around him asking, "Are you ok?"

He nodded. He looked up at his mother. "Dad wanted me to tell you that he loves you."

She hugged Ayo as she looked over at Rebecca.

As they walked out to the car Rebecca asked Moremi, "You ok?"

She answered, "Yes, I'll be ok."

CHAPTER TWENTY-NINE

When a snake misses its stroke, it never says anything or gives any sign of what it means to do next.

RUDYARD KIPLING, *RIKKI-TIKKI-TAVI*

HUGO SWERVED HIS VAN IN AND OUT OF STREETS oblivious to where he was going. After a few minutes he pulled over. His arm throbbed. He grabbed his pills and popped three into his mouth, gulping like a hungry bird. His thoughts buzzed around making no sense, exploding his head with pain. He didn't want to think. The voice in his head commanded: *Just leave. These people are crazy.*

He rarely felt at a loss about what to do. Somehow, he knew escape was not right. The question squeezed into his thoughts: *Why would they just let me go?* Gertrude's calm superiority not only infuriated him but made him feel weak. He closed his eyes as if the darkness could erase her, but it only made things worse. She had played with him as if she knew all along exactly how he would react. *What did she expect me to do?* Whatever it was she expected, he finally consoled himself by going to his greatest strength in a crisis—doing the unexpected.

He wanted to stomp on the accelerator, but he remained frozen. He couldn't generate the momentum to leave. He grabbed his phone and pressed the call button to Peter. At least he could find out if Peter had betrayed him as the old lady had said.

The familiar deep voice greeted him: "Hello, you have reached my private line. Leave me your name and number and I will call you back."

He shrieked into the phone, "Where the hell are you?" His rage was impotent, and he knew it. Without direction or a plan, his rage and fatigue needed release.

He sat for few minutes staring straight ahead as if the answer were out there somewhere, and then he saw a woman in a red sweater with mouse-colored hair walking two little trotting Pekingese, each panting and pulling on their twin rhinestone leashes. He watched one take a leak on a flowerbed and felt the urge to go over and wring its neck while the woman and other dog would witness in horror. He controlled the urge by starting his motor and revving it in neutral, forcing her to look up and take notice. He felt satisfied that she looked concerned, even a little scared. He started moving and cruised slowly by her smiling, as she stared at his van now looking stricken.

At least he was moving, which felt better than frozen. He didn't think about where he was going but within fifteen minutes he pulled into the professor's driveway and stopped under overhanging trees out of sight and turned off the motor. The engine creaked as it wound down and he waited for silence. He checked the time. Noon.

He emerged from the shadows into the sunlight as if he had arrived home—their home. 'Mi casa, su casa.' He allowed the sensation to cheer him up and realized he was hungry. Ravenous in fact.

Within seconds he was inside the entryway. He surveyed the interior and spotted Moremi's photograph of the Roped Pot. He went over for a closer look. He had no idea why it drew him in, but since it was on their wall, he assumed it held some significance. Mostly to her? Was it some kind of family heirloom? He stared at it realizing the craftsmanship was impossible as the iron rope held the pot within perfectly with carefully proportioned knots. It reminded him of her—contained, but somehow at the same time wild and free. Like Rebecca's masks, he had the urge to destroy it, but he couldn't. He had hesitated to twist Moremi's neck when he had the chance and now, he felt the same hesitation. He still respected her. For him that feeling was rare. He felt sentimental and sad about what was probably going to happen, even though he wasn't exactly sure what that would be.

His reverie was interrupted by the sound of a car door slamming, followed by footsteps crunching on the gravel driveway toward the house. He hopped to a side window and peered through the small panes. "Holy shit," he hissed under his breath. The woman was short and muscular carrying a plastic container of cleaning supplies.

He stepped back, spun around, and headed for the kitchen, to the door that opened to the basement stairs. He slipped through and pulled it shut descending into the dark.

As his eyes adjusted to the dim light, he heard her come into the kitchen. She was speaking to someone in Spanish. At first, he thought she wasn't alone but then he realized she must be on her cell because her speech was punctuated by pauses and he couldn't hear another voice. Finally, he heard the familiar "Si, si. Hasta luego."

After silence returned, she flicked on the little kitchen counter radio, flipping through the static until she landed on the crooning of Vincente Ferrandez: "Yo quiero estar contigo mi amor. Yo quiero darte todo mi Corazon."

He liked ranchero music, but he wasn't in the mood. Right now, it sounded too mournful.

The place was his now, and she was intruding. He found the switch and turned on the single bulb hanging from the basement ceiling. Cobwebs.

He opened the cupboard doors to peek in. Even when his eyes began to adjust to the shadows, he couldn't make any sense of all the silly stuff strewn around on the shelves. It looked like it was for a little girl's playhouse or something. *They had a boy, didn't they? Was this his? Not Peter's boy*. Peter had expressed his pride in his son's ability at soccer. Here were little mirrors and combs and beads and stuff. *Ridiculous. Who keeps this in their basement? Certainly not Peter. Her? What for?*

He began to see a pattern. Or was it something he remembered? He stood transfixed as the delicate combs and mirrors turned into a memory like a movie playing out in front of him. His mother was sitting at her frilly dressing table in front of her mirror. He was playing on the floor by her feet with his Matchbox cars making car-crashing sounds. "Vhroom vhroom!" Spittle flew out of his mouth as he shot them at each other. His mother ignored him, humming, and combing her long black hair. He knew she was going out and he didn't want her to go, and he knew she would go anyway. She leaned into the mirror and covered her lips in thick, bright red. Then she puckered them as if she were kissing herself. Her nails were the same bright red as her lipstick. She turned around and smoothed out her stocking, her hands caressing her calf.

"Hugo honey," she cooed, "would you hand me my shoes?"

"Sure, Mommy." He hopped up to get her the shiny spiked silver heels. Her dancing shoes.

"When will you be back?"

She smiled and pulled him over and hugged him. He smelled her lily of the valley perfume. "You know, Hugo," she purred, "you're the only little man for me. No one could replace you. Marlo is making your favorite supper right now." She would always say that before she left.

That was the last time he saw her. She was running with a tough crowd. There had been a bar fight. Somehow a stray bullet hit her, and she was gone before she reached the hospital. He entered the orphanage and then foster care.

Shuddering, his reverie ended.

The sound of accordions and guitars still came from upstairs. *Stupid ranchero waltzes.*

The mason jar with the snake struck his eye, its fangs pressed against the dirty glass. *Weird.* He cocked his head. Just as he decided it wasn't real it twitched. He jumped back. *How ridiculous.* He reached over for it and the pink mouth drew him in. The red eyes glared. Before he could take a breath and calm down, he threw it across the cellar. It crashed on the cement floor. Before it hit, he knew he'd screwed up. The music went dead. He heard her approach the cellar door. She hesitated, probably with her ear pressed against it.

His heart pounded, his neck pulsated, and he felt a pain spasm in his arm.

She opened the door and called down, "Who's there? Anybody there?"

If she came down even a few steps she could see him. He pressed himself to the sidewall as far into the shadows as he could.

She waited and listened, then closed the door and retreated inside the kitchen.

His relief was cut short when he heard her thumping footsteps return. She opened the door again, this time casting a flashlight beam. She moved down a few more steps and sent the beam around like a gyrating disco, missing him by an inch.

He calmed down a little, realizing she was too nervous to know what she saw or put two and two together—that someone was down there. *She's using a flashlight because she doesn't know how to turn on the light. She's never been down here.*

He stood still as a mime, his arms hanging loose, body slightly crouched. A silly thought crossed his mind—that he had absorbed the snake. He was the snake, ready to strike.

He eased the air out of his lungs and willed her to come down the rest of the way. He'd wanted this the moment he laid eyes on her. She would be his goodbye token before he was out of here and away from all these crazy people. *It really wasn't personal. She just happened to be there in the wrong place at the right time. Or was it the other way around?* He couldn't decide.

"Anybody there?" She descended the stairs and went over to the cabinet.

As she peered into the cabinet he lunged, springing almost five feet, landing on top of her—the greatest flying leap he'd ever made. Her scream was muffled and guttural. She crumpled instantly. In a matter of seconds, she was dead.

He stood over her, staring down at his prey. A clean kill.

He bounded up the steps into the kitchen and locked the door from the kitchen side. He stood there for a minute looking around. Suddenly he felt normal, actually euphoric, and famished. He turned the radio back on. The station was now playing Cuban music. He was pleased as if it had read his mind.

He rooted through the refrigerator, doing little samba steps as he pulled out the eggs, butter, bacon and marmalade, checking its label. Robertson's Golden Chunky Orange. He smiled at the little Paddington Bear sticker with Paddington sitting on his suitcase holding up his sandwich.

He set three places at the kitchen, even though it was really for a trilogy of one—me, myself, and I. He grinned as he fried up the bacon and eggs. Then he sat down to eat, savoring each bite.

After eating he went upstairs and took a nap in their bed for several hours. He was tired and deserved rest after all the stress of the last few days. When he awakened he saw it was early afternoon. He yawned and stretched and headed for the bathroom. He took a long, hot shower, pouring an entire bottle of their expensive soap all over himself.

Dressed in one of Peter's pima cotton shirts that fit him well enough, he ran a comb through his hair in front of the mirror. He leaned in closer, proud of his teeth, so even and white.

He whistled his way back down the stairs and headed for the front door where he stopped as if he'd forgotten something. He whirled around and went over to the photograph and removed it from the wall. He went out to his van, opened the back, and carefully placed it inside. *A memento, not just for the day, but for this whole ordeal. And mostly—a memento of her.*

From his van he retrieved a red, five-gallon can of gasoline, which was nearly full, and carried it along the side of the house to the backyard door leading into the cellar. He had to shove the door to open it.

Inside, he yanked it shut. He pushed it to make sure it wouldn't open and was pleased that it seemed stuck.

He splashed the gasoline throughout the cellar and shook the last bit all over her body. He flicked the match with a flourish and threw it into the corner on a pile of laundry. He stood back and watched the flames licking at the air like little snakes—flaring up and slowing down. He was in no hurry as he stood near the door enjoying the dancing flames.

But it took longer than he thought and for a split second he worried that he hadn't poured enough gasoline. It would be a great bother to interrupt the ritual and go buy more gas, but finally the flames coalesced in the center of the floor and exploded, forcing him to jump back. He glowed with satisfaction as they licked around and over her.

"Hasta luego, mi amor!" It was time to depart.

He pushed against the door. At first, he thought it was just stuck, but even when he used his whole body and all his strength it wouldn't budge. He didn't panic. Stepping back, he took a running leap and struck it with both feet.

It couldn't be locked from outside, but try as he might, he couldn't open it. As the fire caught hold it now spread faster than he expected. Sweaty streaks dripped down his face and his eyes started to burn with the smoke.

He leaped past the blaze, up the stairs to the kitchen, and twisted the knob. Only then he remembered that he'd bolted it from the other side.

Still, he didn't panic as he bounded back down the stairs three steps at a time and stopped. He spotted the high window on the side near the door and searched for something to break the glass. He grabbed the empty can of gasoline and flung it at the window. The glass splintered. Gasping for breath, his vision almost completely obscured by the thickening smoke he found a shelf of tools and whacked up at the window with an old wrench to clear more of the glass away.

The window was almost too small, but he was certain, right up to the end, that he could make it out. After all, he'd slithered through Gertrude's small bathroom window, and this looked about the same.

Perhaps if he had more time, a chain saw and stepladder, things would have turned out differently.

CHAPTER THIRTY

Some say the world will end in fire.
Some say in ice. I hold with those who favor fire.

ROBERT FROST

BY THE TIME THE FIRE DEPARTMENT ARRIVED the house had almost burned to the ground. How it started had not been determined, but speculation focused on faulty wiring in the basement. Charred remains of the bodies, buried beneath the rubble, had not been found three days later and so far, any investigation remained on hold until the insurance inspectors determined a cause.

Maria's family had not expected her return home for several weeks since she planned to go to Mexico to visit family that afternoon.

Hugo's van blew when sparks caught the branches overhead.

Until Peter was well enough to speak with the police the investigation was on hold.

Moremi and Ayo remained at Daniel's house, going to the hospital as often as they could for Ayo to visit Peter. She stayed out of their visits.

Peter's recovery was slow, and she wondered if he malingered. Surely, he did not want to answer questions about the fire, but that was not his kind of cowardice. She wondered what went through his mind now that she knew the truth. He could seamlessly deny reality, as their marriage had been a spiral of lies and deceit. She imagined different final reckonings between them but couldn't get past what the old woman pushing her oxygen in the hallway had said: "Don't worry. It will all be over soon dear."

Later, when she and Ayo returned to the hospital, she searched for that old woman without success and none of the staff recognized Moremi's description. It was then she remembered Mami's shape-shifting humor. The old woman wore a gaudy, bejeweled barrette peeking out through her matted gray hair. Of course! That was Mami's style. I should have known! As usual she realized the message was cryptic, but the meaning was clear.

She decided not to interfere, and yet "all over soon" could mean just about anything.

On the fourth day, they walked down the hall where she found a seat in the waiting room and Ayo headed to Peter's room. A minute later he returned to her. "Dad's not there."

They went to the nurse's station and asked where he was. The nurse looked startled. "Why, I thought you knew. He checked himself out this morning." She looked up the time. "Here it is. He checked out at 9:00 A.M. this morning. He said he was going home."

"Did someone pick him up?"

The nurse put on her kindly expression. "He was taken down that hallway in a wheelchair and I don't know who took him from there."

On the drive back to Daniel's house she tried to think what to say to Ayo who stared out the window in silence.

"You OK?" she finally asked.

He looked at her. She felt his eyes boring into her as she watched the road.

"Where did Dad go? He didn't even say goodbye."

She didn't want to lie, and yet she was not ready to tell him the truth either. In fact, she hoped he would never have to know. She longed for her mother who knew how to sooth people in a way that told enough truth for them to bear. She knew she had to say something.

"I believe Dad had very important business he had to attend to."

"What kind of business?"

"Well . . . it's really hard to understand. Even for me. But it's about your grandmother and grandfather, and their business in Nigeria." She looked over at him. Ayo was again staring out the window.

"Mom . . ." he looked at her, "I know you and Dad were mad at each other."

She hadn't expected that. Like most parents, she believed she and Peter had hidden their conflict from their child. Then she heard her mother's voice. "Children know more than you think. Ayo is very intuitive. Like you."

She imagined her answer: *you forget how taken in I was by Peter and his family. I'm not like Ayo. I didn't see what was right in front of me.* But she was relieved that she heard her mother's voice.

"You are right. Your father and I were having trouble with each other. We didn't want you to worry." She looked at him. "You were the most important person to your father above all others."

"More than you?"

"Yes, far more than me."

"Will he come back?"

She didn't want to lie. "I don't know."

THE DOCTORS HAD TOLD HIM he should remain in the hospital a few more days. "You've been very sick Mr. Abosanjo. Your immune system has been seriously, and the infection was systemic and virulent. You may be coming out of the woods, but you need rest."

Peter assured them he would get more rest at home.

They hadn't heard about the fire and knew nothing about an investigation, although Ayo had told Peter about it.

Peter had called Hugo's number multiple times after he recovered enough to make phone calls. Each time the call went dead. After these attempts he simply stared at the ceiling. The conclusions were unavoidable no matter how he analyzed it—Hugo had vanished and probably had something to do with the fire.

In one of their exchanges something Hugo had said resonated: "Don't worry. We firebugs know how to leave scorched earth!"

He wondered . . . and then made up his mind. He took a cab from the hospital to the motel, picked up his car still parked in the back and headed for the airport, parking it in the long-term lot. He bought clothes in the airport with cash and changed in the bathroom. He bought as many painkillers as he could to supplement what he had taken from the hospital. Then he bought his ticket to Zurich with the rest of the cash he had taken with him when he left to drive north to Ayo.

Within eight hours he was buckled into a first-class seat on Swiss Air washing down Vicodin with scotch. Once in the air he closed his eyes and managed to sleep for most of the flight.

He checked into a modest hotel where no one would notice him and slept for three days, waking occasionally to order room service.

By the fourth day he felt well enough to take a cab to the bank to open an account in Lagos where he transferred all the money his parents left him in Moremi's name as his beneficiary. Even he was shocked by the amount they had managed to sock away. He took plenty of cash for himself. The whole transaction took several days. During that time, he rested and woke up hungry, so he went out to dinner as if each were his last meal. He would order a bottle of expensive wine and drink only one glass, slowly, purposefully. He bought more clothes, as if he were going on a safari and a leather carry-on.

Seven days after leaving the hospital he landed at the Murtala Muhammed International Airport in Lagos. He checked into the Sheraton and rested for three more days, and then he went out to buy a laptop and small printer, which he set up in his room. Everywhere he went, people eyed his pockets, watched him buy things with his ready cash, following him until they knew he saw them. He got used to using an expression that translated to, "Don't even think about it." He felt lethal and clear.

He bought snacks, set up the laptop and printer, two bottles of his father's drink, Johnny Walker Red, and began to type.

Growing up, I believed my father was a tough, albeit sometimes mean-spirited man, but despite his meanness I believed that he was stronger and better than anyone else. I thought I could not compare myself to him. I believed it was my mother's role in life to look up to and support my father. I was their only son and a disappointment to them. I knew this at a very young age. I wasn't like either one of them. I loved my pet mongoose Tavi more than anything, but somehow, I knew this was a terrible weakness in me. When I killed Tavi I thought I had cleansed myself of that weakness. At least in their eyes. They seemed to both approve. Then I thought my father would start to love me. But nothing changed.

I realize now that when he killed the kittens my heart turned to stone.

He spent the next five days writing down every memory he had of his parents and their role in the systematic ransacking of Nigeria and their own people. He became crazed with the zeal to finally tell the truth. He didn't exaggerate what he knew and had seen, nor avoid the truth as he knew it. He wouldn't let anyone in to clean the room. Once each day he put the room service dishes on a tray outside the door, and several times ordered more scotch to wash down the Vicodin, staving off the pain that was slowly, but surely, coming back.

One time the hotel manager came to the door to make sure he was all right. Peter handed him some cash and explained he was a journalist working on a deadline.

When he was finished, he had written a hundred pages. After he read it over, he added one last paragraph: *I don't want forgiveness. That doesn't interest me. What does interest me now is the truth—for whatever good it will do. My life is over, but my son's is not. I leave these pages for his mother to use as she sees fit. I hope she will decide to spare our son from having to know all of it.*

It was three weeks after he had left the hospital. He knew that a net could soon close in around him. *Surely by now she will have guessed this is where I am.*

He printed three copies of the manuscript and sealed each in a manila envelope. He mailed one to his parents' solicitor in England with specific instructions to never open it unless Moremi Abosanjo instructed him to do so in writing. The other he sent to a lawyer in Zurich with the same instructions. The third he took to the bank in Lagos where he deposited all the money—a small fortune for Africa—and opened a safety deposit box in her name with the envelope and the Rolex watch his father had given him, with a note, "for Ayo."

He returned to the hotel and slept fourteen hours.

TWO WEEKS AFTER THE FIRE Moremi took a sublet until June when Ayo's school let out for the summer. She had quit her lab job. While she had no definite plan, she did not plan to stay in Berkeley.

She was in touch with the Gordons, and it was decided that she and Ayo would take a few weeks and drive to Seattle to visit them. They had met soon after the fire when the Gordons came down to collect Alice's things. Moremi felt comfortable letting them know what she could about what had happened. She left out the part about Peter going after her through an assassin. She told them mostly about her own family. She liked the way the Gordons spoke. What they said, they meant.

Moremi and Ayo drove north in early June. Two days later they walked into the Gordons' living room where they were greeted by Alice, Oliver, and Martha with their friendly golden retriever Daisy. Martha invited them to stay in their home rather than a motel, an invitation that pleased all.

Ayo and Alice bonded and spent most of their time together. Neither had a sibling so Alice became the big sister, while Ayo enjoyed the role of little brother. Alice took him on hikes, showing him places where he could spot bald eagles' nests, whales and maybe a bear or two. In the evenings she taught him to play chess while Moremi, Oliver and Martha talked about the plight of Nigeria's toxic environment. Moremi and Ayo decided to stay on a few more weeks.

While she was in Seattle, Moremi also intended to meet with Bear, who was back home doing what he could to find out where Peter had gone.

The police wanted to find Peter as well, but their search was half-hearted at best. They had identified Rosa's charred bones in the basement, but not Hugo's, and his van was the same—no links to anything. The best the police could figure was that an intruder had entered the basement when Rosa was there, and somehow the two had ended up in the basement trapped in the fire.

Moremi did not tell the police about Peter's relationship with Hugo, who had been identified as the intruder who, for reasons not fully understood, had set the house on fire killing Rosa and himself. Rebecca, Gertrude and Bear were bound by confidentiality, and it was Moremi's call whether they spoke about what they knew. The mystery remained: Where was Peter Abosanjo?

Moremi knew his ending was in the hands of the mother spirits. She also knew she would come to know about his ending as much as she was meant to know. But still, she wanted Bear to find out what he could. It was a strange mixture of trusting fate, and yet at the same time trusting her actions would not hinder a final outcome. The world between the real and not real was home to her. It was where her family spirits lived and where one day, she would join them. But now, she remained in the known world with her son. Whatever redemption Peter might find she left up to him. That was no longer her business. Hers was to raise Ayo and make sure his African legacy remained strong and true and known to him when he was ready.

Two weeks into her visit, Bear called Moremi and wanted to meet for lunch. He had news.

Moremi left Ayo with the Gordons and drove into town, past the scene of Alice's accident.

They ordered coffee and sandwiches to carry outside to a picnic table. It was one of those warm days that wrapped her in a sense of well-being.

Bear asked, "What's your guess about him . . . where did he go?"

She thought for a long time.

He was intrigued by Moremi and her intuition. She thought about things in a logical way, but when it was time to come to a conclusion she would leap. She was like a raptor, hunting as it hovers, gliding back and forth taking in the territory below before descending swiftly for a bullseye. He thought she would have made a good CIA operative. She's capable of being audacious while keeping her thoughts to herself.

"I'm not sure, but I think Peter might return to Nigeria. He might be able to hide there for a long time."

He smiled. "You're right. That's exactly where he went. It wasn't easy tracking him. He only used cash. I started with the hospital. They knew he had come there from a motel—a shabby one. When I went there the old guy at the desk remembered a tall, distinguished Black guy who seemed out of place in such a fleabag motel. How did he put it . . . 'You could tell he wasn't from around here. Talked with that fancy accent.' He also remembered the ambulance coming early in the morning. The hospital had to let him go since his infection was improving and what he mainly needed was rest. They didn't know about the fire, so they believed him when he assured them he was going home. He picked up his car at the motel and drove to the airport and got a flight to Zurich." He waited for her to comment.

"Well . . . that's probably where his family kept their money. He never talked about his family's money, and I never asked. He didn't flaunt it."

"Exactly. I couldn't get much information on that. I found the hotel where he stayed for seven days. I suspect the bank there transferred his parents' money back to Nigeria."

She nodded, not surprised.

"He took a flight from Zurich to the Lagos International Airport and stayed at the Sheraton for several weeks. He told the manager he was a journalist working on a deadline. He bought a second-hand Land Cruiser with cash and vanished. We lost him after that."

They sat at the picnic table and said nothing for a long time. A raven landed and strutted in small circles at the end of the table, checking their mood. Then he came near, stabbed a breadcrumb and was gone in a second.

Finally, she told him she planned to take Ayo to Africa for the rest of the summer and she had no plans after that. As they parted, Bear promised he'd visit Africa with Susan if she were still there. He told Moremi that maybe by then they'd know what happened to Peter.

CHAPTER THIRTY-ONE

There are only three possible endings—aren't there? – to any story: revenge, tragedy or forgiveness. That's it. All stories end like this.

JEANETTE WINTERSON

REBECCA PARKED IN FRONT OF GERTRUDE'S HOUSE. It was sunny and warm. She let herself in and sat in the hall on the cushioned bench and waited.

After a minute, Gertrude opened her office door and invited her cheerily to "come on in." Rebecca craned her neck peering hesitantly through the door and they both laughed. "Now you're being too careful. It was never my intention to inhibit you," Gertrude assured her. "You may have to figure out for yourself what my mood allows, whether I'm feeling expansive or irritable or something else."

Rebecca sank into the couch.

"So," Gertrude began, "how are they doing?"

Rebecca was silent for so long Gertrude thought she'd forgotten why she was there.

"Bear called Richard. He's meeting Moremi today—they lost Peter's trail, but he'll tell her what he knows." Rebecca held a long silence. "I saw Moremi before she and Ayo left for Seattle. She brought in a short but powerful dream." She reached into her satchel for her notes and read the dream she had written down as Moremi told it.

I'm with my mother and grandmother. We're at Buchi's house. We're preparing the cassava from a plant my grandmother grew in front of her house. We're making her Baton de Manioc she always made when she was planning a big gathering of people who would fill her whole house. We're sitting on the ground pounding the tubers into paste we will carefully wrap and tie in banana leaf packets to be steamed for eight hours. We're all happy and laughing because we are preparing for a big celebration.

Rebecca looked up from her reading. "You asked how they're doing. In a way, they're coping better than I am."

"You know, I think that's to be expected." Gertrude sounded so sure.

"What do you mean?" Rebecca heard the irritation in her own voice.

"I mean you are left with more doubts and loose ends than they are. What happened to Moremi as a daughter, mother and wife is clear now. But what happened to you as her psychotherapist may be less clear."

Rebecca knew where this might go, and she wasn't in the mood for grappling with her own existential guilt. She wanted Gertrude to praise her and tell her that she had done everything she possibly could and that it was the right thing to do. But she knew she wouldn't get that. She wondered how old Gertrude must have been when she finally moved beyond needing praise, when she knew she could take complete responsibility for how she acted and no one else could make the consequences either better or worse. *She wants me to be like her. And I'm not.*

Gertrude added insult to injury. "If the way to go in every situation were clear, then the work we do would be easy. But when it's good work we're doing . . . then most of the time it's not. There's no right way."

Now she was annoyed. "I feel like you're placating me."

"No, I'm telling you in this case there were too many unknowns. Moremi's comfort with her relationship to her ancestors made our work more interesting and more difficult. When you began your work with her, you had your own dream about a little girl who lived two-hundred-fifty years ago. You knew the little girl in the dream. She was you. And yet she was also a complete stranger. Your connection to her allowed you to understand Moremi's relationship to her mother-line more, but not entirely. Your connection to your mother-line was not as continuous for you."

"What are you getting at? The nine-year old in my dream is a stranger to me now?"

"Of course, she is. Only now less of a stranger. She was in your memory, wasn't she? She's been there all along. The dream came from inside you. Not out there," Gertrude said waving her arm to the window. "Dreams are our imagination made real. Moremi lives in that dimension more than you or I do."

"I suppose running into a wild Delaware warrior wearing a British coat is in my memory. I assume that dream came to me just before I met Moremi as some kind of preparation?"

"Yes, Moremi's case challenged all your assumptions, and yet you found yourself prepared."

"I agree, . . . in a way. But I'm still not sure how the dream influenced, or as you say, prepared me."

"Let me ask you something. What were your feelings throughout the dream? In other words, did the sequence of your emotions tell a story that is relevant now?"

Rebecca closed her eyes and took herself into the dream memory. "At first I'm playing with my doll. The cornhusk one my father made and my favorite. I feel safe. Then I hear the gunshots and I think my father is shooting the quail. I don't like it when he does that, so I start singing the cradlesong and the melody—not the words—soothes me and pushes my awareness away from the sound of the gunshots. But then my father is running toward the house, and I can't hold back the reality that I know something terrible has happened—the fire. I don't see it, but I know it. I run through the woods in a panic still singing the song. Going faster and faster I run headlong into the wall which turns into the Delaware warrior holding the cooing baby. Then I run again as fast as I can into the Indian camp. She's there. My mother reciting her favorite psalm. I'm elated . . . joyous . . . so relieved. She's alive. And then she isn't. The warrior pushes her over. Her brains spill out. Then it's horrible!"

Tears rolled down her cheeks.

Gertrude played her fingertips off each other like jumping beans. After a few minutes, she began. "Okay. Let me tell you a parallel story. She learns about the death of her mother. Then her father is killed in prison. She shuts it away because she doesn't have time to grieve. She needs to escape to survive. She walks into the enemy camp—the Abosanjo family. They offer rescue in the form of their son Peter. She thinks her parents would have wanted that. She doesn't know about her father's relationship with Peter's father—that her father begged him to help release a political prisoner. She believes what they tell her because it's a solution. They were friends with her parents. Their son is handsome. An American citizen. The family arranges the marriage. In America her feelings betray her. Her mother and grandmother speak to her more and more urgently. The truth begins to leak through. The horror of it. She pushes it away until she can't. She is in great danger. She survives because of her child—for her child."

Rebecca picked up the narrative. "In both stories the courage to face the truth comes through the child. In the child resides innocence."

"Yes. The child in each story is the conduit to the truth. You were courageous with Moremi. Your and Moremi's instincts interacted on the bridge, fueled by both your dreaming minds connecting to the ancestors, the tellers of truth."

A long silence passed between them.

"Give it time . . . give it time." Gertrude bobbed her head to the rhythm of her speech—the Delphic Oracle. Who knew what she really meant, but for Rebecca the words were soothing.

A WEEK LATER Rebecca and Richard sat on her deck in the early evening looking out into her backyard. The Queens sprawled on the grass ignoring the chatter of squirrels.

"How are you feeling?"

"That's what Gertrude asked."

Silence.

"I'm okay."

Silence.

"Do you think he loved her?" he asked.

She stared out then looked at him. "Yes. But sometimes for certain people who were harmed early, love is just too painful. It disturbs deeply buried memories that bleed out and can't be controlled. I think he had to kill her to stamp out his own memories. Only he couldn't make it happen. He couldn't stamp her out. Moremi was too strong a force."

Richard nodded. "He thought the boy alone would be enough? That he could somehow redeem himself through his young son?"

"Maybe," she agreed.

"Do you think Peter Abosanjo was a sensitive child?"

"He may have been. Yes, I think so."

"Really? What makes you think so?"

"His assistant Annie told Moremi something when she went to his office to clean out his desk. Annie was a single parent. She said Peter paid for her six-year-old son's heart surgery—$250,000. He was born with a near-fatal defect that had to be repaired. Annie's insurance wouldn't cover it claiming he was born with it. Peter's only condition was that Annie was never to breathe a word to anyone that he had done that. Annie agreed. Well, until she told Moremi."

Richard thought about that. "How does that make him a sensitive child?"

She glanced over at Richard thinking he was right, and yet knowing he was wrong. "I don't know for sure," she answered, "but I think that generosity toward a child suggests he sees himself in them." She sighed. "At least it's a strong maybe."

He didn't feel like arguing and moved on. "Bear told me that Peter returned to Africa. It may seem obvious to you but why do you think he returned to Africa after all these years?"

"Well Moremi left a message for me this afternoon. Bear told her that Peter stopped in Zurich to transfer money before continuing to Nigeria. He opened a bank account in Lagos making her the sole beneficiary. I believe it's a lot of money."

"Blood oil money. He wants redemption."

"Yes, I suppose. After his parents died, he could have spent the money, but apparently, he never did. Except on Annie's son. Now he's given the rest to Moremi knowing I assume that she will use the money for a good cause. She's not interested in personal wealth. I think she will put the money where it's needed. She mentioned a nonprofit with Alice Gordon's family. She and Ayo have grown close to them."

"I like that. Do you think we'll ever know what happened to Peter?"

It was Rebecca's turn to be the Oracle. "I think he didn't want anyone to know. He lived in the shadow of a dark secret and yet I think there was a part of him he preserved. That part I think was humane and worthy of redemption."

"When will Moremi leave for Africa?"

"Soon. She and Ayo will stay with her friend Jemimah and her family for a while. She'll find a place of her own. She wants to have some land. She's going to bury her family posthumously."

"How do you do that?"

"You're the anthropologist." After a moment, she added "I don't really know but she seems to have her ways."

"Do you want to visit her in Nigeria?"

"Perhaps. Yes. Perhaps next year."

They sat in silence.

He looked over at her. "I'd like to come with you."

She smiled. "I assumed we'd both go."

"You know . . . I've been thinking . . ."

She laughed, knowing what he was going to say. "You want to get married in Africa."

"Well, yeah." He grinned. "But the Queens can't be there."

"I think they'll forgive us."

CHAPTER THIRTY-TWO

It would be difficult to imagine a place more attractive to water spirits than the Niger Delta, or to design one that offered a greater variety of aquatic habitats.

SACRED WATERS, ARTS FOR MAMI WATA AND OTHER DIVINITIES IN AFRICA AND THE DIASPORA, EDITOR: HENRY JOHN DREWAL, INDIANA UNIVERSITY PRESS, 2008.

HE BOUGHT THE LAND CRUISER from an American married to a Nigerian. They had two young children born in the U.S. The American worked for Haliburton and had been stationed two years in their Lagos offices. Since he would soon be returning with his family to the U.S., it was a fortuitous exchange. The American needed to get rid of it and Peter had the cash.

He spent three days buying gear and supplies for camping in the bush. Tent, two forty-gallon water containers, high-lift jack, shovel, netting, sleeping bag and mat, dry staples, and anti-malaria pills. As a teenager he had imagined floating along the Niger in one of the pirogues fisherman navigated throughout the delta. He kept this to himself since he had learned long before to keep childish yearnings from adult view.

He drove out of Lagos in an easterly direction. His instinct was to head for the river above Lokoja and above the confluence of the Benue and Niger, but he decided to take an indirect route. He wanted to drive through some of the delta areas around Port Harcourt before heading back in a northwesterly direction where he could find an isolated spot.

He considered the Benue because it was blue and clear, but he remembered growing up and hearing in school about the Niger, originally called egerou nigereou, the River of Rivers. He had only seen the floodplains around the delta and now he wanted to see it flowing southeast from its original source in the Gulf of Guinea, one-hundred-fifty miles inland from the Atlantic. It took a boomerang-shaped route and made a sharp right turn near Timbuktu in Mali where it headed southeast into Nigeria. He asked about camping places along the river below the Kainji Dam, but no one seemed to know.

He knew about the necessity to take mosquito netting. The clerk in the outfitter's store was emphatic. "There's nothing mo' important, man, than that. Why, the mosquito probly de mos' important dangerous creature in all Africa—maybe de world, man. Malaria, yellow fever, West Nile—hey, man—you name it!"

This information didn't concern him particularly, but he was on a mission now and didn't need more complications. He took the malaria pills, mosquito netting and enough fresh water even though it was heavy to carry.

He could feel the infection working its way, nipping at the edges. He had one round of antibiotics left to keep it at bay, about three weeks' worth. Time enough for what he wanted.

He would look for a place by the river that was secluded but where it was wide and fast. More than anything he had ever wanted in all his fifty-eight years, he wanted to do this as homage to her.

I've never done anything out of love. Except kill. Well, I helped Annie's son, but I'm not counting that because I didn't know her son. I loved Tavi and I killed him. My parents killed hers. I tried to kill her. And Alice. She's Ayo's mother and she was special all along. I hated her for that. I loved her the moment I saw her with her parents when she was sixteen and later, I tried to kill her.

He understood the paradox of her. He always had.

He knew from the moment he had thrown Tavi into the trees that his end had begun. He felt Tavi's death as if it were his own. Now he would end the pain of it all. This would be a reckoning—an atonement with himself. He wasn't sure how it would play out, but he knew it would happen, not knowing what the most important part was. She and Ayo were merged in his mind—one person, one love. He would do this for them. She would know.

He drove on roads that were well enough maintained. But he'd been told how dangerous the Lakoja-Ankpa Road corridor would be, and now he saw it first-hand. Trucks barreled and swerved along carrying timber and oil and other products heading either for Lagos or Port Harcourt.

But he wasn't afraid because he knew this would not be where he ended. He wanted to be away from the poisoned delta, which reminded him of his parents' oil money. He drove defensively, pulling over to let road warriors run the high-stakes game. He wasn't interested in a confrontation with a driver on a mission of his own.

He could imagine his end as an anonymous splatter on the road and the vision terrified him, especially because he knew he deserved it. Being terrified made him feel alive in a way he hadn't felt for a long time, and it made him more careful. *This is not where I end. I know where I'm going.*

Thoughts of his parents arose as he drove. He gripped the steering wheel even tighter and felt the pain shoot through him. He forced himself to relax. As an antidote he thought of his son and wondered how he was. He imagined Ayo running down the field kicking the ball past the goalie who would fly helplessly through the air attempting to stop it.

After several days of hectic driving, dodging manic trucks, and sleeping in the Land Cruiser at night, he pulled over to the side of the road. He took out his map and decided this might be a good place to go in. There were no signs to guide him. Only the mileage in the Land Cruiser suggested he was at the part of the river he imagined.

He maneuvered it into the forest. There were a few tire tracks, which he followed as far as he could, until he came to a ridge where they disappeared. He found himself on a plateau, and he could only go down a treacherous, rutted ravine that flattened out about thirty yards below.

It took him an hour to coax the cruiser through deep ruts and jutting rocks, often forced to stop, using the jack, and placing rocks under the tires to keep moving. Once he was sure he was stuck, but with a final gunning of the engine it lurched forward and skidded to the bottom of a ravine where the Cruiser stopped for good.

He tried to start it but like a horse that had been ridden too hard, and with a few pops and sizzles and an overheated engine it refused to go on.

He got out and put as much as he could into his pack and started to walk, using his compass in the direction he thought would take him westward to the river.

He pushed his way through heavy undergrowth under a tall, thick canopy of tropical evergreens. Palms and irokos, with their goliath spreading trunks, shielded him from the harsh sun with the added thickness of climbing foliage creating webs and underbrush. He could smell the boggy atmosphere, the humidity and layered peat rising like a wallowing, pregnant creature, and it made him feel nostalgic. For what, he wasn't sure.

After an hour he heard what he thought was water in the distance moving at a low roar, and in a few more minutes he came out on a beach that was part rock, part sand. The rainforest lined the river behind him and as he looked out across the expanse of swift, brown water, he saw a horizon of more rainforest on green and gray rolling hills. He had left a few rocks piled up along his way from the Land Cruiser so he could find his way back for the rest of his supplies. He was heaving with fatigue, but he smiled as tears welled up from deep inside him.

He dropped the pack at his feet and walked to the water's edge. It seemed to flow faster as it moved around a bend, past a peninsula of low woodlands, and disappeared on its way southwest back to the Gulf.

Downstream, he spotted a flock of egrets strutting and bathing on the shore. He was somewhere south of the Kainji Reservoir and south of Jobba. He felt strange, that somehow, he had been guided to this spot. He had never entertained such things before—that were as natural to Moremi as breathing. Purely instinctual, and yet guided by spirits in a netherworld she trusted implicitly.

He sat down on a log that had washed up and unfolded his topographical map. He tried to locate the spot but gave it up. It occurred to him that he was nowhere on the map. Illogical, but the thought soothed him. He put the map down on the rocky sand and watched the water. He paid no attention to how long he sat in reverie but after a while he noticed a separate current in the river that seemed slower, as if it moved in its own way. It became a serpent flowing across the land. At last, he was sitting at the life's blood of the country he'd abandoned and tried to forget.

Later the sun moved enough to reconfigure the shadows. His mind emptied. For the first time the omnipotent memory of his parents had faded. Even after they died, he felt their constant presence, their opinions and judgments overriding his own. Now he couldn't see them in his mind. In the past he would have started to feel uncomfortable, sitting as he was, watching a river, thinking about nothing.

After a while, Moremi and Ayo came into view. They were sitting together on a rock watching a flock of birds overhead. Calm. Intelligent. Capable. He welcomed the tears.

Then he saw Tavi with his bright little black eyes twinkling playfully.

On top of that out of nowhere came Alice—that strange, little, too-smart for her own good, innocent creature. She was laughing with her mouth full of hamburger. Alice's paper had given him a jolt. *She wasn't after me. Alice wants to save the world.* When Moremi told him as he lay in the hospital that Alice Gordon was alive, he hadn't moved outwardly. But inwardly? That was the moment he changed. His relief over that news was like returning to a self he never knew, but who he could have been. He hunched over, holding himself like a baby, allowing the emotions to surge through him.

When the tears came no more, he picked himself up and found his way back to the Land Cruiser and carried as much as he could back to the river, arriving just as dusk faded into night. He heard the cawing of a flock of geese heading downriver.

He managed to put up the tent on the beach, throwing his gear inside while leaving his pack outside, filled with utensils and all the paraphernalia he would organize for his campsite in the morning. He kept the foodstuff inside the tent, hoping for the best. Closer to the water he arranged rocks in a circle to make a campfire where he could sit and watch the river and the night sky as the stars and planets came out.

He put on repellent for the mosquitoes that seemed to swarm even more at dusk and rubbed it into his hair and scalp. It stank and felt greasy, and he wished he could be doing this with Ayo. He wished he could have been that Dad he had wanted. The Dad who wasn't afraid of mosquitoes. He imagined telling Ayo that those little insects were the deadliest animals on the planet—more than rhinos, lions, mambos and scorpions—while they slathered themselves with repellent, laughing off the danger.

He sat down on a log he had managed to push closer to the fire and gazed up at the night sky. He searched for the constellation Centaurus. A voice from long ago said, "Find the two brightest stars and follow them to the right and you will find the Southern Cross, or Crux, shaped like a kite." It was Benjamin, his teacher from boarding school.

When Peter was in the fifth grade Benjamin would take him and some of the other boys outside on a moonless night to look up at the night sky. He told them, "Even though the Southern Cross is the smallest of all the constellations, you can always spot it because of its four very bright stars. But first you have to find Centaurus."

Peter was the first to spot Alpha Centauri when Benjamin pointed up. He learned to follow it across to Beta Centauri, which was the path to Crux.

Benjamin told the boys that if they moved their gaze down from the top star in Crux to the foot of the crucifix this was the way to the Southern Celestial Pole, and that was how mariners in the southern hemisphere could navigate their ships as they did in the northern hemisphere by using the North Star, also called Polaris.

As he gazed upward, he also remembered being home on vacation from school sitting at the dinner table with his parents. He mentioned that he was learning about astronomy at school and how much he liked it. His father reacted, "What a waste of time! I'll speak with the headmaster. What's that teacher's name?"

Peter lied and said he couldn't remember and tried to minimize his enthusiasm by changing the subject, but when he returned to school later in the fall Benjamin was no longer there.

He didn't know how late it was when he climbed into the tent. He lay on his sleeping bag and listened to the jackals howling. He wasn't afraid. His pain had subsided. He slept soundly, better than he had in a long time.

Early the next morning, just as dawn began to light the world, he awakened with a start to loud rustling just outside his tent. He heard grunting and heaving breath. Images raced through his mind. *Wild dogs? Monkeys? A lion?* He looked around for a weapon and grabbed the long, heavy flashlight he had put under his sleeping bag. He crawled half-way out of the tent, pushing up the flap with his head. He waved the flashlight beam around, trying to make scary, shooing sounds to chase off whatever it was.

At first, he couldn't make sense of what he saw. The man was very small, old, and wrinkled, but spry like a child as he hopped around and squatted over the fire, frying fish. Peter noticed he'd helped himself to his cooking oil and wrought iron skillet. He was wearing shorts, plastic sandals and a faded vintage Hawaiian shirt with hula dancers and surfboards. He seemed oblivious to Peter, intent on his fish, cackling and rocking from foot to foot as he squatted over the coals. Peter stared agape, blinking several times as if he could restart the scenario before him. *Oh my God! It's an African Yoda!*

The old man set the skillet down on the rocks and popped up to burrow into Peter's opened pack. He found tin plates and cups and tossed them on the ground. He babbled to himself, grunting, and generally amusing himself, chuckling frequently as he bustled about. Peter crawled out the rest of the way and stood up. He was stiff but rested. He cleared his throat, coughed loudly, and rubbed the sleep from his eyes.

"Who are you?"

The old man ignored him as he transferred the fish onto the plates with a large spoon and sprinkled some chopped tomatoes and onions on the side. As he handed a plate to Peter, forcing him to reach for it, he spoke. "Coffee?" He pointed to Peter's shiny new aluminum pot perched in the coals, then without waiting for an answer, poured a cup and handed it to Peter as if he were the guest.

Peter took the coffee and continued to stare at this uninvited host squatting by the fire, feeding himself the fish as he slurped coffee to wash it down. He ate with his hands and Peter squatted and copied him. It was delicious and they ate in silence.

Finished, Peter set the plate down on the sand. He smiled. He couldn't imagine his age. *Possibly eighty?* He was bony and wrinkled, with a head of wild curly gray-white hair. But he was agile as a child. His center of gravity looked to be about three feet off the ground. *Maybe a leprechaun? Some sort of forest sprite? A pigmy?*

"Old man, who are you?"

He was eating the last of his fish. He bit down, showing gnarled, blackened teeth, or what was left of teeth. He grinned at Peter as he chewed, nodding his head but did not answer the question.

"I see you've made yourself at home with my things. Do you mind at least telling me where you're from?"

At that question the old man giggled and pointed across the river.

"What's that?"

The old man shrugged.

After a while Peter gave up trying to find out who he was. Maybe it didn't matter who he was. Pulling himself together, Peter walked down to the river's edge and rinsed his face. He returned and sat down on the log thinking he would try a different tack with this strange little character, who showed up out of nowhere. But the old man was bustling about cleaning the plates and tidying up the campsite. He built a table with rocks and an old board and put the food he'd found in the tent into an old metal cooler he'd produced from somewhere.

Peter could see as he looked around that this old guy had brought some of his own supplies to his campsite and was settling in. He decided to watch and say nothing.

The old guy knew what he was doing, so Peter turned around and continued to watch the river. He began to hear the sounds of animal life. A large, dark hornbill, silhouetted against the bright sky, circled overhead flying like a kite, bobbing and weaving as it rode the currents over the water. He heard screeching from the trees. *Monkeys? Birds?* He couldn't distinguish this unfamiliar cacophony of sounds. This was a beautiful and dangerous place. He began to feel the old man's presence as protection and comfort so he could relax—a foreign feeling—and take in this wild place he'd felt compelled to find.

He lost track of time and was startled when the old man came up from behind and tapped him on the shoulder. He turned around as the old man headed up the beach beckoning him to follow.

He disappeared into the underbrush of thick grasses and mushy ground. Peter stopped, not sure where he had gone. Then he reappeared, grunting, and pulling something. Peter went over to help and recognized it—a well-made, flat-bottomed dugout. A canoe or pirogue, like the ones he'd seen as a child. It was about twelve feet long and had a small cabinet built in the stern, both for structure and a place for supplies. There were crossbeams for seats and a steering paddle, and a sheet of old canvas Peter assumed could be a sail. Even though the old man was huffing and puffing the boat was amazingly light and easy to maneuver into the water.

The old man hopped in and looked up at Peter, nodding and pointing to get in, which he did, wading into the water to the bow. He hoisted himself in, rocking the canoe with his weight, and settled into the seat at the bow facing his captain who was skillfully pushing them with his paddle, navigating onto the river. He may have been old and boney, but he was all sinew and muscle.

As they glided along the river Peter assumed the old man didn't speak. But he was wrong. After they had been out for an hour he began. He started talking as if there had been a conversation right from the beginning. He pointed to the shore at a flock of five yellow-billed storks strutting in the shallow water. He giggled. "Look how they sweep the water with their huge bills. The river is their fish soup. Catfish. African carp. Nile perch. We had that for breakfast. My favorite." He smacked his lips, grinning, showing his mottled teeth.

They spent the whole day on the river. Toward the end of the day as they returned and pulled closer to their campsite the old sprite hopped up and down, rocking the boat and pointing. "Look, look!" Several monkeys were climbing over their gear. One was ready to go into Peter's tent. He was pulling on the flap, with his rump in the air and his huge reddish tail swaying from side to side like an extra hand. Peter looked at the old man who was doubled over laughing.

"Sclaters monkeys." He shrugged. "My friends," he explained. As they pulled the boat ashore the monkeys scattered for the trees, screeching, and looking offended, as if Peter and the old man were the intruders.

That evening the old man made a fish stew over the campfire. He'd brought supplies from somewhere and seemed to have a store of spices that he kept in the cooler. That night they ate catfish stew. Peter thought he'd never eaten anything so delicious. Even though he was hungry, which was rare for him lately, the mixture of tomatoes, onions, peppers, palm oil and thyme and ginger, mixed in a broth, tasted better with each spoonful. Later, the old man produced a jug of palm wine from an old thermos he kept in the canoe's storage. They sat on the log together sipping the wine from tin cups.

The next morning as they set out to pull the canoe into the water, Peter wore his expensive new Ray-Ban sunglasses. The old man pointed to his own eyes that Peter had noticed were bloodshot from the sun. He put up his hand to tell the old man to wait a minute and he ran back to his tent and crawled inside to find his small duffle bag of clothes. He returned with a pair of older Ray-Bans. They had big round yellow tortoise frames. He handed them to the sprite who chuckled like a kid being given a piece of candy. He put them on and looked around. He jerked his head around like an owl pointing his gaze in an almost 360-degree arc.

"Now you really look like a Sclaters monkey."

The old man liked the similarity and off they went for another day of exploring the river.

From that moment on he only took off the Ray-Bans when the sun went down. They settled into a daily routine. They explored the river during the day, catching fish for their supper. Peter became used to seeing the herons, egrets and storks along the banks. One day they spotted a crocodile cruising nearby, ignoring their presence altogether.

Peter began to realize there were monkeys everywhere. Bright-eyed and curious. The two they had seen the first night became fixtures around their campsite. The old man said they were a male and female pair. Peter even started to feed them scraps from his dinner. Together, he and the old man named them Oba and Eshu.

One evening after a week had passed, Peter and the old man sat on their log and the old man told him a story about the forest.

"There was a spirit called Musa who lived in the forest and who came across a hunter who was looking for food for his family. He wasn't much of a hunter if he was having so much trouble and I guess you'd have to say the forest wasn't his natural habitat. So, Musa decided to help this poor old hunter. Musa told him he needed to find twelve types of trees in the forest and take some bark from each and grind it up into a powder and make a paste by mixing all the bark with water. Then he should spread the paste all over himself. That way he would become invisible to the animals of the forest."

The story prompted Peter to remember Benjamin as he looked at the sky and could find the constellations and remember the stories.

"I get it!" Peter laughed. "If the hunter learned enough to recognize twelve separate types of trees, he'd become part of the forest and not such a foreigner there."

Several days later as they launched the boat and set out on the water Peter asked the old man what the boat was made of.

The old man nodded and said, "Bat trees. It's made of a bat tree."

The old man pointed to the forest and said, "The Iroko tree. It's rot-free. Many Yoruba masks are carved from the Iroko tree. Those masks were worn by strong men who paid tribute to the forbearers of great importance. To the mothers and kings and warriors. Bats eat the fruit of the tree and disperse the seeds and make baby trees. Now you know about that tree. It's very important to Nigerian people. You can't imagine all that it provides. It's like the river."

Peter listened and wondered if the old man was Yoruba. As if he'd read Peter's mind the old man pointed to himself and said, "I'm Igbo."

Their routine went on for two more weeks. They navigated the river each day, watching the wildlife, catching fish for dinner each night.

A few times the old man dropped hints about another life. *Maybe he'd had a family long ago? Were they dead?* The old man mentioned Biafra. Peter didn't push but he wondered if the old man had lost his family back in the civil war when so many starved to death. That would have been forty years ago.

Peter told little about himself, but the old man seemed to understand that he too had come from an entirely different world.

Peter began to grow a beard, and his hair went wild. He too was turning bony and sinewy, and he began to shed all memories, living only in the moment. The river and its wildlife and the old man's presence seemed to envelop him into another world. Even his wishful thinking about what could have been different vanished out of the moment.

On the twenty-fourth day, Peter woke up in the morning and crawled out of his tent looking forward to breakfast. No fish was cooking, and no coffee was brewing over the fire. The dawn felt cool and empty. It had rained during the night. Peter looked around and saw the canoe was gone. He thought maybe the old man had gone fishing without him and assumed it must be later than he realized. The old man had decided to let him sleep.

As the day wore on and dusk fell, he realized that he might have gone. He cooked his own dinner. He still had some rice and dried soup. He went to bed and hoped that the next morning he would once again emerge to the hustle and bustle of that little sprite and those monkeys.

Oba and Eshu seemed to have disappeared as well.

For the next three days he walked along the river. He had gotten used to the old guy and missed his company. He had never had a companion where they could be themselves and allow the days to just while away.

On the fourth day he sat on the log at the shore by himself. It was sunset. He could feel the infection moving in.

He realized that he felt calm and ready. He stood up and undressed. He entered the river slowly and when it reached his chest, he stood for a long time with his eyes closed in the waning sun. When he went under, he felt as if he were becoming part of the river. He could feel himself float away.

He saw her almost immediately. Her hair flowed out like ribbons, and he was relieved because she wore a smile that radiated out like her hair. She lifted her finger to her mouth and then she winked. She turned and flipped her fins, beckoning him to follow.

ACKNOWLEDGEMENTS

Writing *Ancestors* was a long process of discovery, research, and exploration. I remember so many years ago when I wrote that opening sentence: "Moremi stood in the sand at the edge of the Pacific in the howling wind that had spread fire all day through the California hills." I had no idea this beginning was the first tiny step into what became the greatest adventure of self- discovery of my life. I owe a lot to the people in my circle who took that journey with me, especially all you intelligent, avid readers out there (to name a few but not all: Kathy Zotnowsky, Marion Weil, Kim Thoman, Marianna Goodheart, Linda Hardham, Heather Pegas, Jamieson Haverkamph, Isabelle Stierli, Lawrence Kohl, Nina deCreeft Ward, Catherine Kibira, Sara Proctor, Tania Williams, Marge McNabb, Brendan O'Malley, Patti Wiley, Jacaranda Summerfield, Gabrielle Thorpe and Diane Brown) who gave me invaluable feedback especially about my characters, plots, while also providing both developmental and line editing, catching so many of those niggling little details so necessary in the end. My husband, Larry, became an amazing editor (he learned my voice and how to improve it) and listened patiently through all my wildly fluctuating epiphanies with a steady hand. And it was Larry who finally encouraged me to persist to find the right editor, Carol Burbank, who continues to nudge me into being a better writer. When she says "I'm not feelin' it" I re-write! Finally, I am grateful for Karen Sketch Caldwell, my sister-in-law, who seems to understand exactly how to design, with both humor and style, the book covers I want and need.

Ten years before I began *Ancestors*, I wrote my PhD thesis in clinical psychology on my work of many years, that still continues, with dreams from my clients in my private psychotherapy practice in Berkeley and San Francisco, California entitled: A Labyrinth-Matrix Model of Working with Dreams in a clinical Setting. A few friends said I should publish it. I said, "Naw! I'd rather write a novel using dreams! The conclusion expressed in my PhD Dissertation as follows, has been useful in my portrait of the clinical dream work. This work is mutually collaborative, so that following the labyrinthine, Ongoing emotional meaning creates the never-ending matrix of possible connections. In short, this is what dreaming is all about. It's not about demystifying the dream. Rather, it is about following the mystification as consciously as possible to wherever it will lead.

Without the interaction of the shared experience with many clients, I could not have so naturally incorporated dreams into the development of my characters. Only the dreamer knows what the dream really means, but it helps to have a guide who knows the dreamer's life story

at the same time I wrote this dissertation, I discovered the beauty of African masks, which I began to collect. One of the sellers of these masks asked me what I saw in them. I couldn't really say. That moment began my research into discovering that to the African, the mask's beauty was not really of interest. What did interest Africans who understood the meaning of the masks, was that they all channel and represent their ancestors. This became an ongoing revelation for me into the ancient and mysterious, almost impossible to grasp energetically dynamic world of Voudun.

While *Ancestors* is a work of fiction and all the names, characters, places, events, and incidents are either the product of my imagination or are used in a fictitious manner, I have endeavored to accurately reflect Nigerian cultural norms consistent with my research as indicated in the accompanying Selected Bibliography.

– Jan C. Thorpe

My research for *Ancestors* introduced me to a vast array of amazingly creative and informed scholars and writers to whom I am eternally grateful. A few that stand out for me include with a brief passage from each, followed by the complete Selected Bibliography that has guided me through this process.

Achebe, Chinua. *No Longer At Ease*. New York: Anchor Books, 1960.
"Four years in England had filled Obi with a longing to be back in Umuofia. This feeling was sometimes so strong that he found himself ashamed of studying English for his degree." (p. 57)

Adichie, Chimamanda Ngozi. *Half of A Yellow Sun*. New York, Anchor Books, 2006.

"The real tragedy of our postcolonial world is not that the majority of people had no say in whether or not they wanted this new world; rather, it is that the majority have not been given the tools to negotiate this new world." (Chapter 5, p. 129)

Correal, Tobe Melora. *Finding Soul on the Path of Orisa. A West African Spiritual Tradition.* Berkeley, CA: The Crossing Press, 2003.
"Just as we each walk with a piece of our ancestors' pain, we also carry some of their blessings and magic." (p. 111)

Deren, Maya. *Divine Horsemen, The Living Gods of Haiti.* Foreward by Joseph Campbell. New York: McPherson & company, 2001.
"Myth is the twilight speech of an old man to a boy." (p. 21)

Drewel, Henry John and Thompson, Margaret. Gelede, *Art and Female Power Among the Yoruba.* Bloomington: Indiana University Press, 1983.
"Evidence of the otherworldliness of Yoruba spectacle, whether it is a masquerade display, a festival for the gods, or a narrative performance, is to be found in its clearly demarcated openings and closings, which bring it into the world and return it or "carry it away" again, i.e., back to the underworld (orun)." (p. 2)

Drewel, Henry John. *Mami Wata. Arts for Water Spirits in Africa and Its Diaspora.* Los Angeles: Fowler Museum at UCLA, 2008.
"The earliest images of African water deities may be paintings on rock estimated to have been created nearly twenty-eight thousand years ago." (p. 28)

Falola, Toyin and Heaton, Matthew, M., *A History of Nigeria.* Cambridge University Press, 2009.
"The boundaries of present-day Nigeria were created by the British colonial administration in the late nineteenth and early twentieth century." (Chapter 1, p. 17)

Galembo, Phillis. *Divine Inspiration, From Benin to Bahia.* Brooklyn, New York: Athelia Henrietta Press, 1993.
"We could visit many altars in the Black Atlantic world, for they are literally everywhere—beside a cash register on Thirty-sixth Street in

Manhattan; on the beach of Copacabana on New Year's Eve; on a bank of the Osun River in Nigeria; under a Ceiba tree one block from Revolution Plaza in Havana." (Divine Countenance, Art and Altars of the Black Atlantic World, p. 15)

Hunter-Hindrew, Vivian, Editor. (Mama Zogbe, Chief Hounon-Amengansie).*Mami Wata, Africa's Ancient Godddess Unveiled, Reclaiming the Ancient Mami Wata Voudoun History and Heritage of the Diaspora, Volume 1*. Martinez, GA: Mami Wata Healer Society of North America, Inc., 2007.
"In order to understand Mami Wata, it is necessary to travel to the original ancestral home where civilization for the clans of the Mami Wata Vodoun first began, that being in ancient Egypt and Mesopotamia." (Part One, Mami Wata in the Ancient World, p. 42)

Maier, Karl. *This House Has Fallen, Nigeria in Crisis*. Boulder, CO: Westview Press, 2000.
"Nearly half of Nigeria's two million barrels a day in oil production was exported to the insatiable U.S. market." (Chapter 3, p. 42)

Phillips, Ruth B. *Representing Women, Sande Masquerades of the Mende of Sierra Leone*. Los Angeles UCLA Fowler Museum of Cultural History, 1995.
"The Mende, like most African peoples, do not have a separate word for mask, for to distinguish the costume from the human being who wears it, or the headpiece from the rest of the costume, would contradict the notion that a masked figure is an ngafa (pl. ngafeisia), a spirit." (The Concept of Hale, p. 53)

Rush, Dana. *Vodun in Coastal Benin, Unfinished, Open-ended, Global.* Nashville: Vanderbilt University Press, 2013.
"The Vodun religious system is best understood as a network that is open-ended and in incorporative, and thus 'unfinished.'" (Understanding Vodun, p. 4)

Soyinka, Wole. *A Shuttle in the Crypt*. New York: Hill and Wang, 1972.
"Roots, be an anchor at my keel. Shore my limbs against the wayward gale" (O'Roots!, p.1)

Saro-Wiwa, Ken. *A Month and A Day & Letters*. Banbury, United Kingdom: Clark Publishing Ltd., 2005.

"It is sickening that a company with such resources, that is a 'win-win' situation in Nigeria—an organization that has earned billions from our land—remains unwilling to take responsibility for its actions and is trying to portray itself an innocent bystander and even victim of unscrupulous, Black Africans. Poor little rich Shell!" (A Letter to My Father, p. 219)

SELECTED BIBLIOGRAPHY

Achebe, Chinua. *No Longer at Ease*. New York: Anchor Books, 1960.

Adichie, Chimamanda Ngozi. *Half of A Yellow Sun*. New York: Anchor Books, 2006.

Anderson, Martha G. and Peek, Phillip M., Editors. *Ways of the Rivers: Arts and Environment of the Niger Delta*. Los Angeles: UCLA Fowler Museum of Cultural History, 2002.

Blier, Suzanne Preston. *African Vodun, Art, Psychology, and Power*. Chicago: University of Chicago Press, 1995.

Correal, Tobe Melora. *Finding Soul on the Path of Orisa, A West African Spiritual Tradition*. Berkeley, CA: The Crossing Press, 2003.

Cosentino, Donald J. *Vodou Things, The Art of Pierrot Barra and Marie Cassaise*. Jackson, Mississippi: University Press of Mississippi, 1998.

Deren, Maya. *Divine Horsemen, The Using Gods of Haiti*. Foreward by Joseph Campbell. New York; McPherson & Company, 2004.

Drewel, Henry John and Thompson, Margaret. *Gelede, Art and Female Power Among the Yoruba*. Bloomington: Indiana University Press, 1983.

Drewel, Henry John, Editor. *Sacred Waters: Arts for Mami Wata and Other Divinities in Africa and the Diaspora*. Bloomington: Indiana University Press, 2008.

Drewel, Henry John. *Mami Wata, Arts for Water Spirits in Africa and Its*

Diaspora. Los Angeles: Fowler Museum at UCLA, 2008.

Dunaway, Wayland F. *The Scotch-Irish of Colonial Pennsylvania*. Chapel Hill, NC: The University of North Carolina Press, 2007.

Eisenhofer, Stefan. *African Art*. Cologne: Taschen, 2010.

Faiola, Toyin and Heaton, Matthew M. *A History of Nigeria*. Cambridge: Cambridge University Press, 2009.

Fatunmbi, Awo Falokun, *Inner Peace, The Ifa Concept of Ori*. Volume 1. Brooklyn: Athelia Henrietta Press, Inc. 2005.

Fischer, David Hackett. *Albion's Seed, Four British Folkways in America*. New York: Oxford University Press, 1989.

Foundation Cartier pour 'art contemporain. *Vodun, African Vodoo*. Germany: Hirmer Publishers, 2011.

Galembo, Phyllis. *Divine Inspiration, From Benin to Bahia*. Brooklyn, New York: Athelia Henrietta Press 1993.

Grant, George. *The American Patriot's Handbook, The Writings, History and Spirit of a Free Nation*. Naperville, Illinois: Cumberland House Publishing, 2009.

Hahner-Herzog, Kecskési, Maria and Vajda, Laszlo. *African Masks from the Barbier-Mueller Collection*, Geneva. New York: Prestel Verlag, 1998.

Hamilton, Janice. *Nigeria in Pictures*. Minneapolis, MN: Lerner Publications Company, 2003.

Hunter-Hindrew, Vivian, Editor. (Mama Zogbe, Chief H'ounon-Amengansie). *Mami Wata, Africa's Ancient God/dess Unveiled, Reclaiming the Ancient Mami Wata Vodoun History and Heritage of the Diaspora, Volume I*. Martinez, GA: Mami Wata Healers Society of North America, Inc., 2007. Ibid: Volume II.

Hutson, James H. *Religion and the Founding of the American Republic.* Washington: Library of Congress. Distributed by University Press of New England, 1998.

Jones, U. J. *History of the Early Settlement of the Juniata Valley, Embracing an Account of the Early Pioneers and the Trials and Privations Incident to the Settlement of the Valley.* Westminster, Maryland: A Facsimile Reprint Published 2007 by Heritage Books Inc.

Kennedy, Billy. T*he Scots-Irish in Pennsylvania and Kentucky*: Belfast, Northern, Ireland: Causeway Press, 1998.

Kipling, Rudyard, *Rikki-Tikki-Tavi.* Illustrated by Lambert Davis. New York: Harcourt Brace & Company, 1992.

Mack, Angela D. and Hoffius, Stephen G., Editors. *Landscape of Slavery, The Plantation in American Art.* Columbia: University of South Carolina Press, 2008.

Maier, Karl. T*his House Has Fallen, Nigeria in Crisis.* Boulder, CO, Westview Press, 2000.

Martin, Stephane, President, Musee du Quai Branly. *Masks, Masterpieces from the Musee du Quoi Branly Collections.* Paris: Musee du Quai Branly, 2008.

Miller, Judith. *Tribal Art.* New York: Dorling Kindersley Limited, 2006.

Murphy, Joseph M. *Santeria, An African Religion in America.* Boston: Beacon Press, 1988.

Murphy, Joseph M. and Sanford, Mel-Mei, Editors. *Osun Across the Waters, A Yoruba Goddess in Africa and the Americas.* Bloomington: Indiana University Press, 2001.

Nelmark, Phillip John. *The Sacred Ifa Oracle.* New York: Harper Collins Publishers, 1995.

Ono, Yuji and Kerchache, Jacques. *Voudou, Vodun*. Foundation Cartier pour l'art contemporain, Paris, 2011.

Pakenham, Thomas. *The Scramble for Africa, White Man's Conquest of the Dark Continent from 1876 to 1912*. New York: Perennial, 2003.

Phillips, Ruth B. *Representing Women, Sande Masquerades of the Mende of Sierra Leone*. Los Angeles: UCLA Fowler Museum of Cultural History, 1995.

Phillips, Tom, Editor. *Africa, The Art of a Continent*. New York: Prestel Publishing, 2004.

Rigaud, Milo. *Secrets of Voodoo*. Translated from the French by Robert B. Cross. San Francisco: City Lights Books, 1969.

Rosenberg, Anne. *Nigeria the Culture, The Lands, Peoples, and Cultures Series*. New York: Crabtree Publishing Company, 2001.

Rosengarten, Theodore. *Grass Roots: African Origins of an American Art*. Seattle: University of Washington Press, 2008.

Rush, Dana. *Vodun in Coastal Benin, Unfinished, Open-ended, Global*. Nashville: Vanderbilt University Press, 2013.

Saro-Wiwa, Ken. *A Month and A Day & Letters*. Banbury, United Kingdom:
Agebla Clark Publishing Ltd., 2005.

Smith, Daniel Jordan. *A Culture of Corruption, Everyday Deception and Popular Discontent in Nigeria*. Princeton: Princeton University Press, 2008.

Soyinka, Wole. *A Shuttle in the Crypt*. New York: Hill and Wang, 1972.

Vogel, Susan M. *African Art Western Eyes*. New Haven: Yale University Press, 1997.

Washington, Teresa N. *Our Mothers, Our Powers, Our Texts. Manifestations of Aje in Africana Literature*. Bloomington, Indiana: Indiana University Press, 2005.

Weaver, Lloyd and Egbe!ade, Olukunmi. *Maternal Divinity, Yemonja, Tranquil Sea, Turbulent Tides, Eleven Tales from Africa*. New York, Athelia Henrietta Press, 1999.

Wicker, Kathleen O'Brien and Opoku, Kofi Asare, Editors. *Mami Water in the Ewe Tradition*, Legon, Accra, Ghana: Sub-Saharan Publishers, 2007.

Coming soon the new psychological thriller
by Jan C. Thorpe

CHAPTER ONE

"And while they slept the lazy, rainy breeze drifted through the East Woods and the West Wood and the cornfield and riffed over the copings of the stone bridge to the south, touching them for the last time before dead men made them famous. The flags were furled and the bugles stilled, and the hot metal of the guns on the ridges had cooled, and the army was asleep – tenting tonight on the old camp ground, with never a song to cheer because the voices that might sing were all stilled on this most crowded and most lonely of fields. And whatever it may be that nerves men to die for a flag or a phrase or a man or an irrepressible dream was drowsing with them, ready to wake with the dawn."

BRUCE CATTON, *MR. LINCOLN'S ARMY*, NEW YORK: ARCHER BOOKS, 1960, P. 260

HE FLEW IN LOW LIKE A DAZED, WEARY HAWK beneath the high canopy of oak and hickory as a steady rain fell. A dark mist shrouded the outlined branches above swaying in the breeze. He spotted the orange glow on the ground before he saw them, four in all, huddled over the dying embers. Why bring me here? He must want to talk about something important.

He landed on his feet and walked to the edge of the small clearing where the men crouched, rocking themselves for warmth. Not until he was right behind them did he hear their low murmurings and occasional chuckles.

Through the rain came a clap of thunder that seemed a long way off, but when the low-riding rumbles followed, he wasn't sure. A few Coehorn mortars sent to warn of tomorrow's impending doom?

The men looked up as if they, too, wondered—thunder or mortar?

"Shit," one hollered into the wild, "don't you Rebs ever sleep?"

Closer in, almost in his ear, he heard his grandfather Zakariah speak. "Those Johnny Rebs don't have more than half a grain of the good sense God gave 'em."

Silence.

One of the men spoke: "I used to own a mule who'd start a hee-hawin' up a storm when he was tired from a long day's work and I knew he'd kick me if'n I didn't let him head for the barn. He was the best workin' mule I ever knew, but damn if he weren't also the stubbornest. Seems like nothin' could stop him when he got a hankerin' in his blood. Just like them Rebs out there. We might out-number 'em, but God help us . . . and those damn mules they rode in on."

They all chuckled.

His grandfather rose to his feet.

"Where ya goin' Sarge?" another asked.

"Back to the barn's where I'm going – back to the barn. I'm just a stupid old mule too."

Tom waited at the edge of the clearing. His "grandfather," actually his 4-great grandfather, would be appearing to him shortly, the way he always did when he wanted to talk.

"Howdy, Tom, my boy."

"Hello, Zak. I assume you brought me out here because you wish to speak with me about something."

"That I do, my boy. That I do."

He watched his grandfather find a rock to perch on. He waited. He always had to wait. With ghosts, waiting was part of their game. Zak had explained during his first visit, "I have all the time in the world." Now eighteen, Tom had been carrying on a ghostly relationship with his grandfather since he was ten. So, this was old hat.

When they met the night before Antietam, there was always something very important to discuss. Even so, his grandfather would make him wait, and the small talk would be endless.

Finally, Zak spoke. "Your grandfather was a foolish man. But his grandson, your uncle, is not so foolish."

I wonder what this has to do with Antietam. Twenty-two thousand dead in one day. The battle that put all others to shame. What's up with the old ghost? He watched while Zak took out his pipe and slowly filled it with Virginia tobacco, he carried in a pouch in his shirt pocket. He wouldn't smoke it. He never did. He's a ghost for God's sake!

"What's going to happen here tomorrow should have been studied by everyone and anyone who wants to understand human nature. But true to human nature, those who did study it focused more on the battle details than on what it showed most about humans. Some understood, but not enough. You're my kin. You need to understand."

He hated this kind of singling out his grandfather did. Expecting him to get something so momentous about human nature based on history. Like the great ghost he was, his grandfather always made the kinship argument. I just want to be myself—Tom. An average guy. But this old Zachariah ghost of an ancestor won't let me. Why? What could he possibly think I can do about the world now? He talks as if he's grooming me for something. Maybe I'm about to hear what.

"Everybody thinks Lincoln knew—but he didn't."

Silence.

Oh, God. He's going to speak in riddles. "Didn't know what, Zak?" He'd started calling him that during one of their little chats about three years ago.

Zak went on, amused by his grandson's exasperation. "Lincoln spoke to ghosts, you know."

"I know. You told me many times. Did you ever speak to him?" They'd had this discussion before too.

As usual, Zak pretended to look startled. "Hell, no. I was alive then. I told you, I was a mere sergeant in the cavalry."

Mere sergeant, my foot! "Zak, maybe you should get to the point."

"A little testy this evening, aren't we?" He pointed his pipe toward the men still around the fire. "See those men?"

Tom knew when Zak brought him into the ghostly tableau that he would eventually get to the point. It would be roundabout, but at least he had begun.

"They'll all be dead tomorrow. Piled up on that sunken road. Why not me? Stupid luck. Meaningless, stupid luck! My life was nothing but a long, monotonous road after that day. I lived forty-five more years for only one purpose—to remember, and make sure they were remembered down through the ages. But, Jesus, Tom, your kin aren't very smart. Maybe educated, but I don't give a damn for any one of them – except you. I like you. You're a good mule. Let me tell you, boy, a good mule is the best animal alive, except maybe for a camel."

Tom knew that was supposed to be funny.

"Independent, yes. But you've got the right kind of brain." He chuckled, pointing to his temple, "We don't often grow camels in these here parts."

Ghostly humor. Tom knew Zak loved mules. Tom's father used to say, "Your four-times-great-grandfather was a master rider in the cavalry. He liked horses but he loved mules. Sure-footed. Could take you anywhere." His father still had an old McClellan saddle he kept for sentimental reasons. "It was," he said, "a cross between a Western and European saddle."

He'd never asked Zak about being a ghost. Somehow, he knew it wasn't good etiquette. When his grandfather first came to him, Tom acted as if it was just normal, and it was clear that Zak approved of him right off the bat.

"Well, I've been thinking . . ." Zak waved his pipe around as if to include the whole universe. Then he looked as if he had forgotten his train of thought, as if he were going to fall asleep and disappear. He raised his big head of hair like a horse flipping flies with its mane and began in his meandering way, "Seems to me there's a whole lot of religiosity going on now in the world." He looked out. "But there isn't any substance, my boy. No substance."

Tom waited. He'd heard this prologue before. Zak loved to talk about the South as if Southerners had some kind of superior passion for God, even if misdirected. Of course, anyone who'd read about old Robert E. Lee knew he was lit up with an aura like Jesus. Zak would say over and over, "We all loved him. Didn't matter whose side. He was a Virginian first. The land was sacred to him. Everyone understood that in those days."

Tom knew better than to interrupt, but this was always the point where he wanted to say, "I get it. You were all passionate about your beliefs. You were willing to die for them."

"You're impatient, boy. I understand. But what we fought for in this Civil War has been forgotten and I can't let go of that. Hell, why would I hang around talking to you if there weren't something important you needed to know? It's not about facts or even feelings . . . it's about what's worth fighting for. And if there isn't anything worth fighting for—well, hell—then you might as well give it all up now."

The rain had let up some and the trees dripped in the mist. Zak opened his mouth as if he was going to bellow something but what came out was soft as the rain. "Wars are no longer viable. Your generation amuses itself with them. The whole world's become a game. Nothing's serious. That's all gone. And religion's a weapon."

He knew his grandfather liked to speak in the vernacular of the Pennsylvania woods, but he'd been a self-educated man. Like Lincoln.

Zak looked down at the dusty ground and swished it with his big brown boot, leaving no mark. Then he looked straight at Tom. "You're about to be challenged, Boy. You need to be ready. There's danger lurking near you and it will force you to either reckon with yourself or be reckoned with. How you play it out will define your generation. I'm sorry to put this upon you but I want you to pay attention. You'll have help, like your Uncle Daniel ¬– he's smart – but you'll need to grapple with this yourself. And it's all about what you believe deep down inside. What's worth fighting for – really fighting for. Not with weapons. In the small fights is where you'll find the lessons."

Tom didn't know what that meant but he assumed he was about to find out.

Zak often said, "An illusion? It's all illusion."

Tom heard the familiar whoosh like a tornado sucking all the air out of the atmosphere, and the scene was gone.

He sat up in bed covered in sweat. It was 3:00 a.m.

BIO

Born in Pennsylvania and raised in California, Jan Thorpe grew up on the grounds of a hospital. Her father was medical director and she and her brother had the run of the place. People would say, "There go Doc's kids on their bikes!" On their vacations with their father, an avid fly-fisherman, they camped throughout the western Sierras, cooking trout over a campfire next to rivers and lakes. Jan's mother, while braiding her hair, told her about a flea named Skeezix that bothered everyone, an early influence that inspired her to make up her own stories.

In childhood Jan was a contradiction to most of the adults – too dreamy and a bit wild. She graduated from Vassar College with a degree in English literature, then married Larry Thorpe. Living in the San Francisco Bay area they bought a cabin at 7400 feet on a small lake where they spent summers with their two sons and many beloved dogs. After ten years of creating limited edition serigraphs, Jan found her way to earning a master's degree and later Ph.D. in clinical psychology. In her Jungian-oriented psychotherapy practice, specializing in dreams, she began to write novels that weave the strange and elusive dimension of dreams into her psychological thrillers.

CPSIA information can be obtained
at www.ICGtesting.com
Printed in the USA
BVHW080432190522
637189BV00007B/14